The Legend of Shannonderry

a Novel

OTHER BOOKS AND AUDIO BOOKS
BY CAROL WARBURTON:

Midnight Whispers

Edge of Night

Before the Dawn

Eyes of a Stranger

The Legend of Shannonderry

a Novel

Carol Warburton

Covenant Communications, Inc.

Cover image: *Beauty* © adpics, *Stud in Enclosure* © Filonmar. Courtesy of istockphoto.com.

Cover design © 2010 by Covenant Communications, Inc.

Published by Covenant Communications, Inc.
American Fork, Utah

Printed in Canada
First Printing: September 2010

16 15 14 13 12 11 10   10 9 8 7 6 5 4 3 2 1

ISBN-13 978-1-59811-902-2

To my Irish ancestors who whispered from the past to urge
me to write of Eire's thatched cottages, castles and green rolling hills.
The magic of the Emerald Isle not only molded their lives,
but touched mine as well.

Acknowledgments

My heartfelt thank you to the following people:

My husband, Roy, who over the years has shown enormous patience for delayed meals and my talk of imaginary people and places who have come to fill the pages of my books.

The Fortnightly Group—fellow writers Dorothy Keddington and Ka Hancock and connoisseur of books Lou Ann Anderson. Your friendship, listening ears, encouragement and keen insight have done much to bring this book to life.

Nancy Hopkins for welcoming hospitality and friendship to The Fortnightly Group when we've stolen away to Cape Meares for our semiannual writers retreats.

The kind people at Covenant—my editor, Kirk Shaw, for understanding and insightful editing suggestions; Mark Sorenson for the wonderful cover design.

Prologue

Yorkshire, England—1788

MAURICE BEDDOWS HURRIED ACROSS THE stable yard, his boots striking the cobblestones in an angry staccato that exactly matched his mood. He swore between clenched teeth, yet even as the words were uttered, part of him quarreled with the epithet. It couldn't be true—other men's wives perhaps . . . but not Deirdre. This reassuring thought momentarily calmed him, and when he entered the house, the only outward sign of his anger was the heightened color of his cheeks.

Even so, his thoughts remained on his wife. If only the evidence against her weren't so strong, but the tale had come from Parson Cranston, a man whose honesty couldn't be questioned. Moreover, the parson had twice seen Deirdre with the stranger. The fact that the goodly parson had waited five months before informing Maurice of the incident only served to whet his anger further. If the parson knew, how many others were aware of his wife's betrayal?

"Fool!" The word rushed from his lips as he climbed the stairs. He'd trusted Deirdre, believing her love for him was deep and true. He should have known he couldn't trust the Irish. Look at the stallion he'd purchased in Cork two years before. Hadn't it gone lame before the year was out? And the Irishman he'd hired to bring the stallion to England had proved to be just as unreliable. They were all a pack of thieves, forever plotting against the crown and anything remotely English. Crude, devious, proud—all this and more—and now it seemed that Deirdre was no better than her countrymen.

Maurice struck at the wall with his riding crop. The action did little to alleviate the pain and humiliation of being duped. He'd believed his wife when she'd told him she was happy to leave Ireland, just as he'd believed that she loved him and looked forward to a new life in England. Had it all been lies? Was her love for him but another part of the pretense? Fired with anger, Maurice flung open the sitting room door without knocking. Under other circumstances, the startled expression on his young wife's face would have caused him to smile. Today it made him scowl.

"Is . . . is something wrong?" Deirdre had stammered, astonishment and concern clearly evident on her face. It wasn't like Maurice to scowl at her or burst through the door in anger.

"You should know the answer to that." Maurice paused to gauge the effect of his words. Rather than showing alarm, Deirdre looked puzzled.

"I fear I don't."

"Then perhaps I should refresh your memory by relating the story I heard today. The tale of how my wife was seen . . . not once, but twice, with a stranger under questionable circumstances."

Deirdre's fingers stilled on her embroidery. "Who told you this?"

"Does it matter? What I want is the man's name . . . and why you were meeting him."

Deirdre gazed at him without expression, the stillness of her fingers transmitted to her face. When she spoke, her mouth hardly moved. "I can't tell you."

"Can't or won't!" Maurice exploded. "Is it Irish treachery . . . or the need of another . . . man you hide?" Maurice's voice choked. The thought of his wife in another man's arms made him feel sick.

"Don't say such things!" Her voice held a mingling of hurt and outrage.

"Then tell me the truth so I'll know whether 'tis treason or adultery I deal with."

"I can't!" she cried, struggling to get up from her chair. The awkward burden of her advanced pregnancy caused her to stumble. Before she could regain her balance, she fell heavily to the floor.

Maurice forgot his anger as a low moan escaped her lips. "Are you all right?" he asked, dropping to his knees beside her.

"I've been having strange pains all morning." She suddenly clutched her middle. "Oh, Maurice. I think . . ." The words died as her face contorted with pain.

Maurice picked up his wife and hurried toward the bedroom, calling for Kate, his wife's Irish maid, as he went. The fright on the maid's face and the quickness with which she appeared made him suspect she'd been listening at the door. Was a man never to have any privacy?

His irritation was quickly forgotten as Kate's deft hands helped him settle Deirdre onto the bed. Only then did he notice the moisture that wet his wife's skirts and dampened his coat. His frequent presence in the stable during a foaling brought jolting knowledge of the source. Fear shot through him. "The birth sack has broken."

"'Tis too early," Kate whispered, crossing herself. "The babe's not due for another six weeks."

"Don't you think I know that?" Maurice snapped, disliking his abruptness almost as much as the maid's Papist ways.

A tiny sob brought his attention back to Deirdre. "The baby," she whispered. "Can it live if it comes now?"

Maurice glanced at Kate, but before he could answer, Deirdre grabbed his hand. "Please, Maurice. Don't let our baby die."

"I shall do my best," he promised. "I'll ride for Mrs. Grady at once."

"No!" Her cry was as frantic as the clutch of her hand. Then her voice softened. "Don't leave me," she pleaded. "I'm afraid."

He looked at her small oval face and read the pleading in her lovely blue eyes. *How beautiful she is . . . even when she's frightened.* In that moment his anger melted, leaving only his love for the black-haired Irish girl who'd stolen his heart and made herself indispensable to his life. "I'll be right back," he promised, soothing her protest with a kiss. "Instead of riding, I'll send the groom to fetch Mrs. Grady."

Turning, Maurice strode to the door. Kate followed him, her face pale and her self-assurance vanished. She looked as frightened as Deirdre, and little wonder. Only sixteen, she had probably never watched a birthing.

"I'll fetch Bess, too," he said, imploring the maid with a look to remain calm. "She's helped with birthings before."

Maurice hurried down the stairs, calling for Bess as he went. The sight of the woman's round, placid face took the edge off his fear. Bess would know what to do until Mrs. Grady arrived. And she did, accepting the summons to attend her mistress as calmly as she saw to the roasting of a lamb.

"Deirdre will be all right," Maurice told himself on the way to the stable. But the memory of the difficult birth that had taken his mother's life wouldn't leave him. She'd been slender like Deirdre, and he'd never forgotten the sound of her terrible screams.

The task of finding the groom and sending him for the midwife took Maurice's mind away from his worry. But his concern returned as soon as he reentered the house. His pace slackened as he heard a low moaning—one that spoke of pain and terror. The childish horror of his mother's death gripped him. Though Maurice had never lacked courage, he felt it leave him now. He would sooner face a howling mob or a wild boar than watch his wife's suffering, but he'd promised to return.

Bess frowned when her master came through the bedroom door. Surely he knew a birthing was no place for a man. "There's naught ye can do," she said, wiping beads of perspiration from her mistress's face. "Such things take time. Why don't ye go downstairs and have Mary fix ye a cup of tea."

"No," Deirdre cried in fear as another contraction wracked her body. She reached for Maurice, her fingers cold as they clutched his hand.

"It will be all right," he said, wishing he could bear her pain.

"First you must listen. It's not what you think . . ." She licked her dry lips as another wave of pain made her wince. It was obvious she longed to explain herself to Maurice. "That man . . ." A pain-filled gasp escaped Deirdre as she tried to talk.

"Later, love. You must save your strength for the baby."

Deirdre's fingers tightened on his hand, and despite her resolve, a tiny cry escaped her clenched teeth.

"Master's right," Bess said when the pain subsided. "Ye must save yer strength. There'll be time for talkin' after the babe be here."

Deirdre nodded and sighed. "Please go. Bess and Kate will see to me until Mrs. Grady comes." She attempted a smile, though it took effort, for another contraction was building.

"Mistress'll do fine," Bess assured him, though her words were more optimistic than the expression on her face. Seeing Deirdre try to stifle another cry of pain, he took her hand and pressed it to his lips. "I'll be downstairs." Then he hurried from the room and out to the stable, where he saddled a horse and rode away.

It was dusk when Maurice returned from a grueling ride across the windswept Yorkshire moors. Expecting Deirdre's labor to be over, his steps were eager as he entered the house.

The maid's frightened eyes and the anguished moans permeating the house told him otherwise. As he approached the bedroom, a piercing scream sent him hurrying to the sanctuary of his study.

It was there he spent the long night pacing the floor and wondering if the agonizing torture would ever end. Twice he went to Deirdre's door, and twice a grim-faced Bess sent him away. Just as the sun rose over the hilltops, the moaning stopped.

Maurice stood transfixed. Was the child safely delivered, or had it and Deirdre succumbed? Fear and uncertainty held him frozen, his ears straining for a sound . . . any sound. It came in a thread-thin wail that pierced the quiet like an echo to Deirdre's screams.

"Thank God, it lives," Maurice whispered. "And Deirdre?" He ran from the room, almost colliding with Kate as she descended the stairs.

"Mrs. Grady says come quick. Mistress be—"

Maurice paid little heed to Kate's words and Bess's whispered warning. He flung open the door. Only when he saw Deirdre lying white and still on the bed did the warnings hold meaning.

"She be bleeding awful and no way to stop it," Mrs. Grady whispered.

"Deirdre . . ." Maurice bent close, willing his wife to open her eyes.

After a long moment Deirdre's eyelids fluttered open. "I . . . I meant to give you a son."

"It doesn't matter. What matters is you. You must live, Deirdre . . . for me . . . for the child."

As Deirdre looked at the small babe cradled against her shoulder, a faint smile touched her bloodless lips. The morning sun cast golden rays across the room and touched the tiny head, outlining a crown of hair shining white and fragile as thistledown. "White hair," she whispered and smiled again as if the knowledge pleased her.

"You must call her . . . Gwyneth," she went on with effort. "Gwyneth . . . the white . . . blessed one." Her eyes locked on Maurice until she'd extracted his promise. Then she turned to Kate. "Take care of her, Kate. Take care . . . of my . . . child."

1

County Cork, Ireland—1810 (Twenty-two years later)

Moira O'Brien Donahue stood by the dainty Queen Anne desk holding a heavy vellum letter in her age-spotted hand. Her fingers trembled, and she braced herself against the pain and anger that always came when she read the words on the paper. Although it had been written twenty-two years before, it still had the power to wound. The expensive paper was worn from frequent reading, its message so brief Moira had committed it to memory.

> *I regret to inform you that your daughter Deirdre died*
> *this morning in childbirth. The child, a daughter, lives.*

Moira closed her eyes against a fresh spate of pain—her daughter gone before they could be reconciled, the Irish Sea and England separating them as effectively as the grave. As her eyes fastened on Maurice Beddows's signature, her anger surged past the pain. It wouldn't have hurt the Englishman to have offered his sympathy or given the details of Deirdre's last hours. Like him, the letter was cold and impersonal. More than that, he hadn't told Moira her granddaughter's name.

Sorrow for all that might have been threatened to engulf the old woman. Taking a deep breath, she put the letter back into the drawer and closed it as a shield against pain.

Sighing, Moira walked to the window where rain fell in slanted sheets against the glass. The dismal weather only added to her depression. She hadn't slept well, and her joints ached from the dampness.

"You're getting old, Moira." The habit of talking to herself was so firmly established that she gave it no thought. How else was a woman to pass the time when she was old and lonely? Kate and Biddy looked after her well enough, but they were only servants, and much as she loved them, there were times she longed for more stimulating company.

"You've no one but yourself to blame for your loneliness," she said, recalling how she'd begun to withdraw from her friends when Deirdre had eloped with the Englishman. Her husband's death five years later made her withdraw even more, although the process hadn't been completed until the death of her only son.

"Now there's only me and Shannonderry . . . and we're both growing old." Moira looked out across the dripping parkland to the stable; its leaking roof and shabby facade were but further indication that both she and Shannonderry had seen better times. There was never enough money.

This last thought filled Moira with despair. As she had aged, she'd spent much time with her Bible and in prayer, but today even these failed to bring peace of mind. Her unrest increased each time her mind turned to the fact that no one of her flesh and blood would inherit Shannonderry after she died. If only her son had married and sired a child with the O'Brien fire and determination. Then she'd have reason to live and something for which to fight.

Shaking her head, Moira turned from the window. She didn't want to give up, but she couldn't afford a competent agent any more than she could hire a man to look after the horses.

In the past, she hadn't required the services of either. Pride had set Moira to prove that she could manage the affairs of Shannonderry herself. And she'd succeeded. Every man along the Blackwater River would attest to her success. That had been ten years ago. Now . . .

Moira sighed, not wanting to admit how her last illness had sapped her strength. Since then she'd begun to let things slide, staying home instead of riding over the estate to oversee the farms and check on her tenants.

"What shall I do, William?" She addressed the portrait of her dead husband that hung on the wall. The sight of his strong, handsome features never failed to buoy her spirits. She sought his eyes as if expecting to hear an answer. "What we need is new blood—someone young and strong to manage the affairs when I have to stay in bed. Who, William? There's no one . . . no one, unless—" She shook her head, dismissing the thought. Not Deirdre's child.

Bitterness rose in her throat. Much as she'd loved her daughter, Moira couldn't think of Deirdre's elopement without pain. She'd betrayed both her family and Ireland. No, not Deirdre's child.

The problem of what to do about Shannonderry had weighed heavily on Moira's mind for months. She'd spent much of the past week pondering and praying. She bowed her head and voiced another silent prayer. *What shall I do, God? Please, show me what to do.*

Moira stared without seeing at the rain, her mind a jumble of half-formed thoughts. Then like a beam of light from a freshly lit candle, her mind honed in on the letter. If Shannonderry was to survive, Deirdre and bitterness must be put aside. She must concentrate on the future and Deirdre's child—the two were inseparably connected—she could see that now. What she couldn't see was how to bring them together.

She looked out at the checkered fields of the demesne. "Shannonderry," she whispered, feeling a familiar surge of pride at the sight of the land that had nurtured the O'Briens for so many generations. Tales of past glory and bravery committed for Shannonderry's sake came to Moira's mind. "You must do your part," she concluded. "You must try to contact the child. Even if it means confronting the Englishman and reopening old wounds. But how?" The question hung in the air as Moira frowned in concentration. Though her body was old, her mind was still keen. She must think of a way.

The old woman was still deep in thought when Kate came with her tea. "I want to speak to Cormac D'Arcy," Moira said. "Ask Flynn to ride to Clonglas and invite Mr. D'Arcy for tea."

Kate's eyes widened as she set the tray on the table. It had been years since Moira Donahue had invited anyone to share her tea. "I'll see to it at once." Although Kate's tone was respectful, she made no effort to hide her surprise. Nor did she waste any time in telling Biddy.

"A visitor for tea?" Young Biddy's pretty mouth flew open. Then she frowned. "But why would she invite Cormac D'Arcy?"

* * *

Cormac was as surprised by the invitation as Kate and Biddy. He hadn't been inside Moira's home in Shannonderry since he was a boy of twelve, his eyes large as gold guineas as he stood with his father and gazed up at the enormous stag head in the great hall. Now, fifteen years later, his concern mingled with his surprise. Why would Moira Donahue, a woman old enough to be his grandmother and a recluse, invite him to tea?

Intrigued, Cormac donned his best frock coat and ordered the carriage. Although he knew Moira Donahue too well to think his attire would impress her, he sensed his effort would bring her pleasure. Heaven knew the old lady could use a little pleasure, what with her illness and the loss of her last stallion.

Cormac shook his head as he recalled his unsuccessful attempt to save the horse. If Moira had sent for him sooner, he might have succeeded.

Her pride had stood in the way, however, and now the last of the famous
Shannonderry stallions was gone, erasing Moira's dreams of restoring her
stable to its former reputation. What a pity.

Cormac liked the old woman and respected her fight to keep
Shannonderry prosperous, but even courage and indomitable spirit must in
time bow to age. The days when Moira Donahue rode out on a fiery stallion
to inspect the demesne were long gone. Now, on the few occasions she left
the house, she plodded along on a donkey, her small body erect and proud
as she called instructions to Flynn.

Cormac wanted to shake the pair. Couldn't Moira see that Flynn was
too old to look after the place? As for the stable—Cormac shuddered
each time he entered it. How did she expect a near-blind old man and a
ten-year-old boy to look after eight mares? She needed help. Perhaps that
was why she'd invited him to tea.

Cormac's frustration returned when the carriage swung through
Shannonderry's arched gate. Were the gates always left open? Surely Moira
knew marauding bands of peasants watched for such acts of carelessness.

Moira did, however, keep Irish wolfhounds to guard Shannonderry.
Three of them bounded down the graveled approach and intercepted the
carriage. The rearing horses brought the carriage to a jerking halt. As the
coachman cursed and cracked his whip, the dogs crouched, snarling and
ready to spring at the horses' throats if they tried to proceed.

A shrill whistle split the air, and Cormac let down the carriage window
in time to see Cluny O'Donnell, Flynn's young grandson, run from the
stable.

"Bradach! Cearnach! Come!" he shouted.

The dogs gave a last warning growl and slowly retreated.

"I'm . . . I'm sorry, Mr. D'Arcy," Cluny stammered. "Biddy told me to
keep the dogs inside, but I got busy helpin' Gran'far and forgot."

"If ye ever forget again, I'll take a whip to ye," the driver shouted.
"Don't ever set yer dogs on my horses again, hear?"

Cluny clenched his fists and looked ready to fly at the coachman.
"They're but doin' what they be trained for . . . protectin' Shannonderry."

"Let the boy be," Cormac called. "There's no harm done." He pitied
the boy, who had to do the work of two, but he admired his spirit. All were
fighters at Shannonderry, from the dogs to the lady of the castle.

Since his estate adjoined Shannonderry, he'd resolved to visit more often.
If only Moira Donahue weren't so proud. The old woman wore her pride like
a suit of armor, the once fashionable black riding habit her buttress against
pity. Cormac shook his head. Because of pride, every meeting with her had

to appear accidental. On the few occasions when she rode out to inspect her estate, Cormac made a point to intercept her. Over time he'd become adept at drawing Moira out and turning the conversation to the affairs at Shannonderry. From little things she let slip, Cormac was able to assess her needs and quietly see that the work was done. Of late, she'd hardly left the house, and Cormac's visits to her stable on the pretext of checking on the mares had proved unsatisfactory. Old Flynn was as proud as his mistress and viewed Cormac's efforts to clean and organize the stable as an affront to his capabilities.

The sight of overgrown shrubs and leaf-matted flowerbeds jarred Cormac's senses as the carriage pulled up at the front steps of Shannonderry. Why didn't Moira ask for help?

The question stayed with him as he entered the gloomy entrance hall. Though Biddy smiled brightly, she was the only spot of color in the poorly lighted room. As she led him down another gloomy corridor, Cormac contrasted today's visit with that earlier time when he'd stood in awe with his father. Then the house had been ablaze with hundreds of candles, the happy sounds of music and laughter filling the air. Now everything was wrapped in a silence as tangible as the rolled-up rugs and sheet-shrouded furniture. He grimaced when he thought about what age and poor health had done to Moira Donahue and her home.

"This way, sir." Biddy stopped before a carved oak door. Seeing Cormac D'Arcy at such close proximity left her breathless. She stole another glance at his dark, handsome features and wished he weren't so aloof. "She be waitin' for ye in here," Biddy added, hoping he might smile at her.

Cormac's only reaction was a nod, his frustration evident as he entered the room.

"Doesn't my company agree with you?" Moira asked.

"It does. You know I always look forward to seeing you."

A smile lit Moira's gray eyes, their brilliance bringing life to her wrinkled face. "One would never know it by your expression. You look like you've swallowed one of the concoctions you give to my mares when they're sick."

Cormac smiled and took the old woman's hands. They were small and strong, like the character lines in her finely chiseled features. Her answering squeeze lifted his spirits. Although Moira had lost weight, she still looked alert and in control of her faculties. "I'm glad to see you looking so well. I heard you were ill and feared I might find you in your sickbed."

Moira shook her head. "I'm not that ill, although my health is not as good as I would like. That's one of the reasons I asked you here." She released his hands and motioned to a chair. "You'd best sit down, for what I have to say will take time. Biddy should be along presently with tea."

Seating himself, Cormac was aware that Moira was watching him closely. The intensity of her gaze made him uneasy. What did she want? He crossed his legs and waited with mounting curiosity while Moira engaged him in small talk until Biddy brought tea and left the room. As always, Moira's approach was direct.

"The last time we met, you mentioned you were going to England on a horse-buying venture. Do you still plan to go?"

Cormac nodded. "I hope to leave by the first of April."

Moira's fingers tightened on her teacup. "Do you go to Yorkshire?"

"I go to London first. Where I go after that will depend upon the news I hear of horses. Is it a stallion you wish me to find for you?"

"My granddaughter."

Cormac's dark brows lifted. Although he was acquainted with the story of Deirdre's elopement and subsequent death in England, he'd given no thought to her child. Wasn't she half English? Surely such a child would be reprehensible to the likes of Moira Donahue.

"I haven't taken leave of my senses," Moira stated, "though if you'd suggested such a thing last night, I'd have thought you mad." Her expression sobered. "I've no other recourse. You have but to look around to see how badly things are. I can no longer manage Shannonderry alone. I need help."

"Help from a child?"

"She's not a child. By my reckoning she must be almost twenty-two."

Cormac's mouth tightened. Child. Woman. What did it matter? Moira needed a man familiar with horses and the management of an estate, not an inexperienced young woman. Choosing his words with care, Cormac set his cup on the table and leaned back in his chair. "Have you thought to hire an agent?"

"On several occasions, but I've rejected the idea each time." Her chin lifted. "I prefer to oversee things myself. When I cannot, then it must be someone of the O'Brien blood."

"Your granddaughter?"

Moira nodded. "If you can find her. I haven't had word of her since Mr. Beddows sent Kate back to Ireland thirteen years ago. I've written several times but have never received an answer."

The news didn't surprise Cormac. "Being English, the girl probably doesn't want to acknowledge her Irish background."

Moira frowned and stirred her tea. "That's why I want you to find her. You must try to change her mind and persuade her to come to Shannonderry."

Cormac wanted to tell the old woman it would be a waste of time. He was well acquainted with English sentiment for the Irish.

"You will be recompensed for your efforts," Moira said, sensing his reluctance.

"Where in Yorkshire can I expect to find her?"

"Her home is called Hawarden. It's in northern Yorkshire. There's little more I can tell you except that her father's name is Maurice Beddows. Kate says that, like you, he deals in horses and that he is well known for his fine stable. That's why I thought of you."

Cormac frowned. Instead of a stallion, his quest was to find a granddaughter. "I'll see what I can do."

"Don't let Mr. Beddows know you come from Cork," Moira cautioned. "If you do, he'll become suspicious and won't let you talk to her."

Moira's plan made Cormac's frown deepen.

"Kate said Mr. Beddows's dislike of the Irish is such that he's forbidden the child to speak of her mother."

"Then what makes you think he'll let her talk to me?"

Amusement flicked across Moira's lined face. "I don't know that he will, but if the woman has two eyes, she'll arrange it. It's not every day a young lady has the opportunity to meet such a handsome man." Sensing Cormac's embarrassment, she hurried on. "I'm confident you'll be able to arrange the matter. Don't think I'm not aware of your talent for subterfuge . . . how you contrive to meet me and of the help you give my tenants. Flynn keeps me advised of your efforts to improve my stable as well." She paused and held Cormac's gaze. "I appreciate what you've done . . . but it must end. That is why I send for my granddaughter. If you must resort to subterfuge to get her here, is it such a great price?" The old woman paused, her voice gaining in strength as she went on. "I must think of Shannonderry, Mr. D'Arcy. Shannonderry must be saved."

Cormac's face was grave as he rose from his chair and took Moira's small hands. Although he wanted to tell the old woman she dealt in dreams, her impassioned speech wouldn't let him. How could a young, untried woman help save Shannonderry . . . and an English one at that? By now the granddaughter was likely married. Couldn't Moira see she courted disappointment?

The hope in the old woman's blue eyes made him bite his tongue. "I'll do my best," he promised. In an effort to lighten the mood, he added, "And I'll try not to be so obvious."

Moira laughed. "It took me several months to see through your purpose. Fortunately, Mr. Beddows won't have that long."

"I hope not, for I plan to return by May."

Moira smiled and released his hands. "I'll have a letter ready for you to take to my granddaughter . . . one that will explain what I have to offer."

Cormac strove for optimism as he took his leave, but as soon as he quit her presence, his doubts returned. Even if he succeeded in persuading the young woman to come, there was little chance she'd stay. He could imagine her reaction to the shabby rooms and neglected dwelling. She'd turn and leave. He'd seen her kind during his years at Trinity College, watched how the English looked down their noses at anything Irish.

Cormac's mouth tightened. He didn't want to see Moira hurt, but the alternative was just as upsetting. An English woman at Shannonderry was an affront to everything the old castle stood for.

Arriving at his carriage, he looked up at Shannonderry's turreted facade. The gray, weathered stones of the structure still bore the scars of its turbulent past. Three hundred years of sun and rain couldn't erase the damage from the Desmond uprising in 1581 anymore than time had healed the grim reminder of Cromwell's cannons. But somehow, Shannonderry and the O'Briens had withstood their enemies. Until now.

Cormac shook his head, wishing he hadn't promised to carry out Moira's errand. The thought of an English woman living at Shannonderry saddened him. It signaled the end of an era, and he disliked being a part of the downfall.

Perhaps the granddaughter wouldn't come. The idea cheered him until he thought of Moira's disappointment. She'd set her heart on it. More than that, Cormac had promised to help. He'd have to see the matter through.

2

G WYNETH BEDDOWS CAUTIOUSLY APPROACHED THE deserted cottage, keeping close to the tall hedge that encroached on the dooryard. The cottage sat at the edge of the far meadow and, except for haying time, was never used. Even so, she waited before she ran across a patch of grass and stepped through the sagging door.

The buzz of flies filled the shadowy interior and mingled with the smell of dust and mold. When her eyes adjusted to the dimness, Gwyneth's gaze settled on a pile of clothes lying on the seat of a dilapidated chair. Good. John hadn't forgotten.

Fear of incurring her father's wrath didn't prevent Gwyneth from donning John's breeches and jacket. Her desire to ride free and unencumbered astride her black stallion was too strong. More than that, several days of rain had kept her confined to the house and subjected to her stepmother's tiresome opinions.

Waking to a morning of sunshine, Gwyneth had used the excuse of delivering a dinner invitation to Parson Cranston as her means of escape. John had readily agreed to leave his clothes in the cottage. By the time she finished changing, the young groom should arrive with her stallion.

John had been her friend since childhood, the two of them haunting the stable where John's father, Peter, was Hawarden's most valued trainer. Although her father didn't approve of Gwyneth spending so much time in the stable, the knowledge his daughter had gained about horses couldn't be ignored. Not only could she handle her spirited stallion, but no other woman in Yorkshire could hold a candle to the way Gwyneth rode a horse.

Humming softly, Gwyneth fastened the final button on John's jacket. Over the years, she'd managed to keep her rides astride the great stallion a secret from her family. Only John and his father knew of the gallops in the secluded meadow. Tucking her blond curls under the brim of John's cap, Gwyneth walked to the door of the cottage. As she did, she saw movement in the copse of trees bordering the meadow. A moment later John and Toryn appeared.

Seeing Toryn's tossing head and dancing hooves made Gwyneth pause in admiration. Had there ever been a more beautiful stallion or one with more speed and mettle? The fact that she owned the magnificent horse was something for which she daily thanked God.

Toryn's history was as complicated as Gwyneth's. For years, northern Yorkshire had been plagued by a wild, black stallion who raided the paddocks for mares. His cunning for ferreting out the most valuable dams was uncanny and had gained him the name of The Demon. Twice he was followed and the mares retrieved, and once he was briefly captured. Unfortunately, the stallion had lived up to his name, fighting his way free in a flurry of slashing hooves, killing a groom and seriously injuring his captor. When word spread that The Demon was also a killer, he was hunted in earnest and gunned down by a musket blast.

Before his death, the stallion had raided Hawarden's stable and made off with Maurice Beddows's best brood mare. By the time the mare was retrieved, she was with foal, her offspring labeled a killer before it was born.

Perhaps this was what attracted Gwyneth to the situation. She was well acquainted with being condemned for her ancestry, although in her case, her Irish mother was the cause. Already a frequent visitor to the stable, Gwyneth drove her father to fits of temper with her incessant pleas for his mercy. When the mare finally delivered a fine foal, Gwyneth begged to have the colt.

Oddly enough, Maurice had agreed, but the gift came with stipulations. "The colt will be shot if he shows any signs of becoming a killer. He'll also be destroyed if you can't train him to the saddle." Maurice's gaze was as challenging as his voice. "I've known horses that never outgrow their hatred for saddle and rider. The colt's background doesn't bode for success, but he's yours, daughter, if you want him." Pausing, he fixed her with his gray eyes. "Remember, you've been warned. I won't tolerate tears if you get the worst of the bargain."

The gamble had paid off, though not without setbacks. Gwyneth personally saw to the colt's grooming and talked to him as if he were her closest friend, which, if truth be told, was almost true. It wasn't long before she and the horse had established a rapport. By the time the colt was six months old, he would come when she whistled and would follow her around the pasture. Only then did Gwyneth feel confident enough to give him a name. She spent days agonizing over his title. In the end she'd settled on Toryn, an ancient Irish name meaning "chieftain."

The title proved appropriate. By the time Toryn attained his second year, he was challenging the fastest bloods of Yorkshire, and, as a three-year-old, he remained unbeaten. Despite Gwyneth's careful training, Toryn was as much a product of The Demon as he was of his gentle dam, and except for Peter and herself, he refused to allow anyone else to ride him. For a time, she feared that the stallion's strong will and spirited temperament might cause her father to declare the bargain forfeited. Toryn's speed could make a man forgive much, however. The length of his stride was phenomenal, his mettle untouched. In time Maurice Beddows became one of Toryn's most ardent admirers.

Watching Toryn approach the cottage, Gwyneth put her fingers to her mouth and whistled. Pricking his ears, the stallion jerked the reins from John's grasp and galloped to meet her. Instead of waiting for John to help her mount, she sprang onto Toryn's back and set him on a course across the meadow.

Gwyneth caught her breath at Toryn's speed, thrilling to the furious pace that showed none of the controlled suppression he exhibited when she rode him sidesaddle. Like it or not, it was Peter who rode Toryn in the races while she was forced to content herself in riding him sidesaddle when others looked on. There was scarcely a day she didn't ride the great steed, but she knew Toryn reserved his best for when she rode him astride.

The exhilarating rush of the wind on her face made Gwyneth forget her usual caution. When Toryn jumped the rushing beck without breaking stride and sailed over the fence separating Hawarden from the property of Mr. Turnbill, she didn't slow him but let him gallop on, hooves pounding as she leaned close and urged him to a faster pace. The stallion's excitement was as great as hers.

The next thing she knew, they took the hedgerow that hugged the track to the village. As Toryn's hooves touched the ground, Gwyneth caught a flash of movement from the corner of her eye and turned in time to spy a horse and rider galloping behind them. As Toryn cleared the second hedgerow, she lost the rider from view, but a second later she heard a shout. Glancing back, she watched the stranger and his horse take the hedgerow as effortlessly as she and Toryn had.

Realizing that the man's shout had challenged her to a race, Gwyneth set Toryn to an even faster pace. Her heart leaped with excitement, pleasure flooding her slender frame as she felt the stallion's response. Elated, her disguise and the fact that she didn't recognize the dark-haired man were forgotten. It was as if she and Toryn were running in the St. Leger race, the imagined shout of the crowd heard in the rushing wind and pounding hooves.

The stranger and his mare stuck to them like a burr, dogging their steps and taking each fence with a skill that matched Toryn's. Determined to win, Gwyneth leaned close. "Go, Chieftain, go!"

The speed with which the stallion responded whipped the cap from Gwyneth's head, tossing it onto the path behind them and loosing her curls so they streamed like silky white ribbons over her narrow shoulders. Realizing her disguise had been discovered, her concentration broke and Toryn faltered. *What to do?*

An excited shout from the rider cut through Gwyneth's indecision. Leaning forward to encourage Toryn, his drumming hooves and furious pace resumed. On they flew, the mare now unequal to Toryn's great stride. A quick glance showed the distance between them widening. When Gwyneth looked again, the rider lifted his hand in salute and disappeared over the brow of the hill.

Gwyneth cantered on, her eyes on the rolling landscape for any sign of the horse and rider. When they failed to reappear, she brought Toryn to a trot and then a walk. They had won! Laughing, she patted Toryn's neck and turned the stallion toward home.

As they cantered along, Gwyneth's spirits soared like a lark in flight, and she broke into song. This must be how Peter felt when he and Toryn won a race. Her exuberant singing broke off when, as she crested a hill, she saw John's cap jauntily swinging from a tree branch.

Reining in her stallion, Gwyneth stared in disbelief. "Well," she began, her voice dripping with chagrin. "What nerve." Her mouth tightened as she ran her fingers through her long, tangled hair. The rider's message was clear. He was on to her secret.

"Well," she repeated. Endowed with the chattering tongue of the Irish, it was unusual for Gwyneth to be at a loss for words. Snatching the object from the tree, she wound her hair into a coil and tucked it under the cap's brim. Suddenly struck with the incongruity of the man's gesture, laughter spilled from her lips. "What nerve," she repeated, "and had I been he, I'd have done the same."

Even so, Gwyneth rued leaving the meadow. It was fortunate her challenger hadn't been a neighbor. Not wanting to risk meeting someone she knew, Gwyneth kept close to the hedgerows and trees on her return to Hawarden. As she rode along, her mind was on the rider. What did he look like? Was he new to the area? Eligible men were few and far between, and any addition was always welcomed.

* * *

THE STEEP PATH TO HAWARDEN followed the beck that rushed down from the hills. Still elated from winning the race, Gwyneth paused to look up at the house that sat atop the hill. Hawarden had once been a hunting lodge, but today the redbrick structure was known throughout Yorkshire as a place of beauty and fine racing stock. Beautiful as the home was, its furnishings were worn, and the grounds showed signs of neglect. The truth was, Maurice Beddows cared more for his horses than his home, and Hawarden suffered at the expense of the stable.

Such didn't set well with Gwyneth's stepmother, Sylvia, who'd married with greater expectations. But since her husband controlled the purse strings, there was little she could do to change the matter. Each year the promise of new furnishings was postponed. A new brood mare was needed, new stalls must be built, and Sylvia had to be content.

Gwyneth wondered if her dead mother had fared any better. She doubted it. Even after more than twenty years, her father refused to speak of his first wife, Deirdre. Without Kate, her Irish nursemaid, Gwyneth wouldn't have known anything about her.

Dear Kate. Gwyneth's lips curved as she thought of the woman she'd loved like a mother for the first ten years of her life. At night it had been Kate's Irish lullabies that had soothed her to sleep; Kate, who'd filled her mind with wonderful tales of leprechauns and fairies. Gwyneth's favorite stories had been those of her mother and Shannonderry. Kate's colorful word pictures of the stone castle surrounded with fields had been embellished with tales of her mother and Kate searching for fairy rings, Deirdre's black curls bouncing with excitement as they ran across the meadow.

Although she'd been but ten at the time, the memory of her father's rage when he'd discovered Kate counting her rosary beads and speaking to Gwyneth in Gaelic was still etched into her mind. Kate had been packed off to Ireland, but her absence hadn't diminished Gwyneth's love for the sandy-haired woman. Over time she'd outgrown her belief in fairies and leprechauns, but she still clung to the strong belief in God that Kate had instilled in her. Gwyneth often thought of Kate and Ireland, wondering how she and Shannonderry were doing, but for the most part, her thoughts were taken up with Toryn and her life at Hawarden.

Almost twenty-two years of age, Gwyneth had fully expected to be married by now. She'd had a few admirers, but none had caught or held her attention. Even had one done so, Gwyneth doubted anything would have come of it. Not only was she without a respectable dowry, it was well known that her mother had been Irish. Although both were marks against her contracting an acceptable marriage, Gwyneth hadn't given up hope. Kate had raised her on Irish tales of adventure and love. Someone was sure to come.

Humming to herself, Gwyneth passed through the front gate at Hawarden, the excitement of winning the race putting a lilt to her voice. By the time she'd dressed for dinner that evening, some of her elation had diminished. Except for Parson Cranston and his wife, Gwyneth felt little enthusiasm for the dinner guests. Having no wish to impress anyone, she chose her least favorite gown, one of forest green muslin with a creamy kerchief arranged over the bodice.

Dinner wouldn't be such an ordeal if Mr. Steane and his son James weren't coming. The elder Mr. Steane had come for dinner on Wednesday for as long as she could remember, but James hadn't accompanied his father until six months ago. Although James's heart had been set on Sarah Morgan, Sarah had married someone else. Since then, James had begun a bumbling attempt at courting Gwyneth. She knew he acted on his father's prompting. For more than a year, Mr. Steane had attempted to purchase Toryn. When he'd failed, he commenced bringing his son to dinner.

Gwyneth frowned at the impasse her life had come to. In her daydreams of love and adventure, she'd always believed she'd find a man to catch and hold her heart, but none had appeared, and she was left with no better prospects than James.

Sylvia's voice interrupted Gwyneth's gloomy musings. "Are you ready to go down for dinner?" she asked, entering the room.

Gwyneth paused with brush in hand, the tangle of her hair but partially subdued by vigorous brushing. "Almost."

Sylvia eyed Gwyneth's pale curls. "Surely you don't plan to wear your hair like that. Here, let me help you."

Gwyneth bit back a protest. She and Sylvia were as different as night and day. Experience had taught Gwyneth to choose her battles, and since she didn't care two figs about impressing anyone at dinner, she handed the brush to her stepmother.

Sylvia immediately set to work, trying first a set of combs, then a wide green ribbon, in an attempt to control Gwyneth's unruly curls. "I wish the Steanes weren't coming for dinner," she complained between strokes of the brush. "I can tolerate Mr. Steane, but his son's company is impossible. I'd far rather have Lord Ransford as your suitor." Her voice grew petulant. "Your father remains adamant on the matter and thinks an alliance with his friend is more important than having a title in the family."

Thank heaven, Gwyneth thought with a shudder. Despite his title, Lord Ransford was a corpulent old man whose pudgy hands and foul breath disgusted her. More than that, he'd made three other offers of marriage over the past year—all to ladies young enough to be his daughters. Now it was Gwyneth's turn. Since Sylvia was obsessed with having a title in the family, she encouraged the courtship.

In the mirror, Gwyneth locked eyes with Sylvia. "I fear you and Father will both be disappointed, then, for I don't plan to marry either man."

Sylvia tugged harder than was needed on one of Gwyneth's curls. "Without a dowry, not to mention the stigma of your Irish blood, who else will marry you?"

Gwyneth shrugged. "That I don't know, but it won't be James or Lord Ransford."

Sylvia threw up her hands. "You surely can't mean to remain a spinster and live the rest of your days at Hawarden."

A quick glance at her stepmother's frustrated reflection told Gwyneth that Sylvia was already counting the days until she could be rid of her. Despite her efforts to grow a thick skin, it still hurt that Sylvia was eager to be rid of her.

"Can we discuss this another time?" As Gwyneth spoke, she glanced at her reflection. It was the wrong thing to do. No amount of imagination could turn her into the dark-haired beauty Kate said her mother had been. Not only did Gwyneth's fair oval face seem to fade to nothing in the shimmering paleness of her hair, her lips were too wide and full for the current fashion. Her eyes were good, however. Even Sylvia conceded to that. They were an unusually deep shade of blue-green, a hue Kate claimed was exactly like her mother's. Looking hard at herself, Gwyneth caught a glimpse of fear lurking in the image. She straightened her shoulders. Not for anything would she let Sylvia see that she was not as confident as she tried to appear.

Sylvia gave an exasperated sigh. "I fear there's no hope for either you or your hair. We must stop dillydallying, or we'll be late for dinner."

Gwyneth followed Sylvia from the room, fully aware that the bright yellow gown the woman wore had been designed to show off her tiny waist and ample bosom. Although her brown hair and broad features were unremarkable, no one looking at Sylvia's slim frame would guess she'd presented Maurice Beddows with a male heir the first year of her marriage and a second son two years later. Gwyneth had tried to like her. She truly had, but times like tonight made it difficult.

"Do hurry, Gwyneth." Sylvia's voice was edged with irritation. "And remember not to chatter so much. Not only does it irritate your father, it certainly won't help you find a husband."

"Yes, madam," Gwyneth retorted, making no effort to hide her sarcasm.

Sylvia threw an angry look over her shoulder, but she held her tongue lest any of the guests overhear her as they descended the stairs. Her mood grew darker when she saw Gwyneth removed the ribbon she'd painstakingly threaded through her curls.

The women paused at the drawing room door where Maurice Beddows expounded loudly on his favorite topic. Not a tall man, he had begun to put on weight around the middle. His once-handsome features, though coarsened by time, still gave him a look of distinction, his dislike for change was evident in the long, slope-away coat that hung past the knees of his dun-colored breeches. Unlike his wife's gown, it was sadly out of style. Likewise, his hair, which he continued to wear lightly powdered and pulled back. His lack of style, however, did nothing to detract from his reputation as the most knowledgeable horse breeder in the north of England. His advice on breeding was as readily sought for as were his horses, and since he never wearied in talking on the subject, he was a popular host.

Gwyneth was one of his greatest admirers and had he but paid her more attention, he might have become her greatest friend. But he seemed unaware of her admiration and clearly preferred the company of Sylvia and their two young sons.

Catching sight of Sylvia, Maurice paused. "Here is Mrs. Beddows now." His manner was jovial, and he showed pleasure as he came to greet her.

The company for dinner was larger than usual. In addition to the Steanes and Cranstons, the Turnbills were also present. When a gentleman sitting in a high wing-backed chair suddenly arose, Gwyneth's heart jumped and landed with a thud in her stomach. She stared, feeling like she was seeing a reincarnation of one of the dark Irish warriors about whom Kate had told her. As Gwyneth strove to collect her scattered thoughts, she knew with certainty that the black-haired guest was the same gentleman who'd raced her on his chestnut mare.

"My dear, this is Mr. Cormac D'Arcy," Maurice said to his wife.

Cormac bowed and took Sylvia's hand. "Your servant, Ma'am."

He hadn't yet noticed Gwyneth, whose thoughts now vacillated between admiration and unease. What was the handsome man doing in their drawing room? Maurice Beddows seldom entertained prospective buyers at dinner. Indeed, it was a rarity for them to be shown more of Hawarden than his study.

"Mr. D'Arcy has recently come from Ireland," her father went on. "I've invited him to stay with us a few days to discuss matters of business."

Sylvia smiled and seconded her husband's invitation, although Gwyneth knew her stepmother was as surprised by the hospitality as she was. Prospective horse buyers had to put up at the local inn.

Before Gwyneth could think more on their surprise guest, her father motioned for her to come forward. "My daughter, Miss Gwyneth Beddows. She owns the stallion you admire."

"I'm happy to make your acquaintance," Cormac said, trying to hide his surprise on seeing Moira's granddaughter. His eyes fastened on Gwyneth's unbound hair that gleamed in the candlelight like platinum ripples on a sun-gilt stream. It was all he could do not to stare. He hadn't expected the O'Briens, who were noted for flame or raven hair, to produce this unusual creature. Her porcelain skin was faintly flushed with unease, but he read spirit in her aqua eyes.

Aware that everyone in the room watched them, Cormac searched for a way to let Gwyneth know that her secret was safe. He took her small, gloved hand in his and gave it a tiny squeeze. "Miss Beddows."

As Gwyneth arose from a curtsy, Cormac smiled and winked. Seeing it, her mouth lifted in a grateful smile. "Mr. D'Arcy."

Before he could say more, Sylvia Beddows put her hand on his elbow. "I believe dinner is ready, Mr. D'Arcy. Would you join my husband and me in leading our guests into the dining hall?"

Politeness kept Cormac at Mrs. Beddows's side until they reached the head of the table. Only then did he have a chance for another look at Gwyneth. She held her head high and moved with a grace that reminded Cormac of a younger Moira Donahue. He watched her enter the dining room on the arm of a gawky, brown-haired man. Although Moira's granddaughter didn't have the look of the O'Briens, she certainly possessed their poise and pride.

Taking her chair, Gwyneth offered Cormac a quick smile. Like every other woman in the room, she couldn't help but notice the way his dark blue coat molded to his broad shoulders and how the folds of his immaculately tied cravat enhanced his rugged good looks. Cormac D'Arcy was clearly the most handsome gentleman to sit at their table in many a month. Seeing the sparkle in Sylvia's eyes, Gwyneth knew her stepmother had come to the same conclusion.

Gwyneth kept up a bright stream of conversation with James and the Turnbills during dinner. Instead of impatiently biting her tongue at James's bumbling replies, she bore them with tolerance, as she did the Turnbills, who weren't noted for interesting conversation. Even so, threads of unease pulled at her thoughts each time she met the Irishman's amused gaze. His blue eyes and mischievous smile smacked too much of challenge. What did he plan to do?

She found out when Mr. D'Arcy rose from his chair and met her at the door as she prepared to retire to the drawing room with the other ladies.

"Your secret is safe," he said in a low voice, "but it comes at a price." Then in a voice loud enough for everyone in the room to hear, he announced, "I mean to buy your stallion, Miss Beddows."

3

GWYNETH HAD A DIFFICULT TIME falling asleep that night. Memories of the race and the unsettling presence of the Irishman at dinner set her mind skittering in a dozen directions. Usually not one to seek release by pacing, she did so now, six steps to the right, then back to her dressing table. Although her first impression of Cormac D'Arcy had been favorable, his bold pronouncement as she left the dining room filled her with disquiet. Was his promise to keep her secret contingent upon her agreement to sell Toryn to him?

"I won't!" she declared to the wainscot border on the bedroom wall. "If Mr. D'Arcy thinks to blackmail me into selling Toryn, he's sadly mistaken. I've weathered Father's rage before, and I can weather it again if he's told that I've worn breeches. Toryn is mine! Father gave me his word and . . ." Her voice went on, its cadence rising and falling as she paced the room, bravado a bolster against her fears that Maurice Beddows would renege on the bargain he'd made three years before.

It wasn't until she knelt to say her prayers that she felt a measure of peace. "He'll not do it," she said when her prayer was finished. Maurice Beddows was known as a shrewd but honest businessman. Surely he would do as much for his daughter. Gwyneth held to the thought as she closed her eyes and drifted off to sleep.

* * *

THE NEXT MORNING GWYNETH WAS in the stable before anyone else was astir. She felt a sense of optimism as she took Toryn from his stall to brush his sleek black coat. It was a task she and Toryn both enjoyed, and she broke into an Irish street song as the grooming progressed.

Oh, Paddy dear, and did ye hear
The news that's goin' round
The shamrock is by law forbid to grow
On Irish ground.

She crouched to brush one of Toryn's legs, so engrossed in singing that she failed to note the Irishman until a pair of expensive brown leather boots were planted squarely in front of her. Her eyes took in the lean, muscled calves molded into fawn-colored breeches then traveled up to the broad shoulders encased in a buff hued waistcoat worn under a dark brown coat.

"Do I meet with your approval?" his amused voice inquired.

Gwyneth's cheeks were warm as she straightened and encountered a pair of gleaming cobalt eyes. "You . . . you took me by surprise."

"As you did me. I didn't expect to hear an Irish street song sung in England."

"My mother was Irish. So was my nurse. She taught me many Irish songs."

"Did she now? And did she also tell you that singing such songs was grounds for arrest in Dublin just a few years ago?"

Gwyneth shook her head. "She left when I was too small to understand such things, but I can read, and I know of the terrible repression and your inhumane treatment of the Catholics."

"Our inhumane treatment!" For a moment, Cormac was speechless.

"We may have injustices in England, but I doubt any country has abused her poor in a more shameful manner than Ireland."

"Ireland!" His voice came like an explosion. "It was the blasted English that did it. First Elizabeth with her plantations . . . then the butcher Cromwell. We still haven't recovered." Cormac glowered down at her. "Don't try to blame the English abominations on the Irish," he shouted.

Toryn's ears flattened, and he tensed to rear. Before he could, the Irishman grasped his nostrils. Toryn stilled, his hooves settling into the stable floor as if they meant to take root. Cormac spoke to the motionless stallion in Gaelic, his voice so low Gwyneth only caught a word or two. Toryn seemed to understand as clearly as if they were two men conversing. A long shudder rippled the length of the stallion's great frame, and he settled his hooves more firmly into the straw-littered floor.

A chill like the touch of an icy finger ran down Gwyneth's back. She'd heard of men with this power but had thought them no more than superstition—devil talkers some people called them. Her shiver didn't go unnoticed.

"Don't let the power frighten you," Cormac said. "Some say 'tis a gift from the fairies; others aren't so kind. Whatever its source, it never fails me."

Gwyneth stared at the Irishman in amazement. "Toryn has never let anyone except me and the groom and trainer touch him, but you—"

"Toryn? Did I hear you right?"

"You did. My nurse taught me more of Ireland than its songs of protest."

"So you speak Gaelic?"

"A little."

Cormac silently assimilated the information. Moira's granddaughter was more Irish than he'd expected. And she had spirit. "Toryn," he repeated softly. "'Chieftain.' A most appropriate choice, Miss Beddows."

Feeling more comfortable, Gwyneth resumed brushing the stallion's long neck. "We plan to win the St. Leger at Doncaster in September."

Cormac studied the horse, its large build and powerful legs contributed to its tremendous stride. "He might well carry it off, but it won't be easy. Have you considered that you might be entering him in the wrong race? His ability to jump makes him a certain winner in the steeplechase."

"There's no money or prestige in winning a steeplechase," she scoffed. "One of the classics—either the St. Leger or the Derby—is his best chance."

"He'd be noticed if you took him to Ireland. The gentry there are obsessed with owning good hunters, and the steeplechase grows more popular every year. One has only . . ."

"Ireland," Gwyneth interrupted. "I can't take him to Ireland."

"Why not?"

"Father hates the Irish. Indeed, I'm surprised he's even talked to you, let alone given you access to Hawarden."

Cormac smiled. "Perhaps the one thousand pounds I offered for your stallion caused him to change his mind."

Gwyneth gasped at the astronomical figure. No wonder her father had invited Cormac D'Arcy to stay. The knot of unease she'd subdued the night before returned with vengeance. Maurice Beddows was always looking for money to build up his stable. With one thousand pounds . . . She refused to let the thought go any further. Lifting her head, she met the Irishman's gaze. "My horse isn't for sale, Mr. D'Arcy."

Cormac silently stroked Toryn's neck. He'd traveled the length and breadth of both Ireland and England looking for just such an animal. For a moment, he forgot his promise to Moira. Having Toryn at stud in his stable at Clonglas would assure his success as one of Ireland's leading horse breeders. The big stallion could also bring the steeplechase title back to County Cork, where it rightly belonged. As for Emmett Weston . . . A sardonic smile touched his lips when he pictured Emmett's face when he lost another race to Cormac. The longstanding rivalry between the two men had gone on for years. For the skip of a heartbeat, Cormac forgot about honor. If he told Moira Donahue her granddaughter had refused to come to Ireland, the old woman need never know where he'd found the stallion.

Without thinking, Cormac reached over and covered Gwyneth's hand with his. "Don't be too sure, Miss Beddows."

Shivers of fear gathered at the nape of Gwyneth's neck. Pulsing through the fear was an awareness of the warmth of Mr. D'Arcy's hand. Did the Irishman's magic extend to humans? She raised her eyes to his and felt their cobalt power as he returned her gaze. The nearness of his tall frame made her feel small and vulnerable. It was all she could do to maintain her pluck. Taking a deep breath, she willed her swimming emotions back to an even keel. "You may talk all you wish, Mr. D'Arcy, but it won't change the fact that Toryn is not for sale."

Cormac weighed the horse against his promise to Moira. As he did, he made the mistake of looking at Gwyneth's upturned face. He'd never seen such large and expressive eyes or ones filled with more spirit and determination. She was an O'Brien, all right, and O'Briens belonged at Shannonderry.

"Your stallion is safe." The words slipped out before Cormac could think. Pushing past his disappointment, he focused on his true purpose for visiting Hawarden. He must give Moira's letter to Gwyneth. Aware of a stable boy cleaning the next stall, he added. "Would you be good enough to accompany me on a ride, Miss Beddows?"

Unsure of the Irishman's motives, Gwyneth studied his blue eyes shadowed by the slash of dark brows. Did he plan to get her away from the house so he could steal Toryn? The thought melted almost as soon as it formed. How could it not when he met her gaze with such open candor? Despite herself, Gwyneth smiled and spoke in a low voice. "Do you think to challenge me to another race, Mr. D'Arcy? If you do, you should know that Toryn doesn't give his best effort when I wear my riding skirt."

"And so the breeches," he whispered.

She nodded. "I'd be happy to accompany you," she replied in a louder voice.

After she'd instructed Peter to saddle Toryn, Gwyneth hurried to the house and changed into the most attractive of her riding habits. Though she told herself it was only to show the Irishman she was someone of consequence, she didn't forget that the jacket's aqua hue enhanced the color of her eyes.

As she and Mr. D'Arcy rode out of the stable yard, Gwyneth wanted to laugh at her good fortune. Now she would have a chance to question him about Ireland. Before she could do so, Cormac spoke.

"If your father dislikes the Irish so much, why did he marry an Irishwoman?"

Gwyneth shook her head. "It's something I've often wondered, but Father refuses to speak of it."

"Perhaps they had an unhappy marriage."

"Maybe, though that doesn't explain . . ." She frowned, her eyes on the lane they followed. "I know very little. Mother died when I was born, and my Irish nurse was sent back to Ireland ten years later. Since you're Irish, I hoped you'd be able to tell me something about my mother's people. She came from County Cork, and . . ." Aware of his intense gaze, she paused.

"Does the name Shannonderry mean anything to you?"

Gwyneth's heart jumped. "Shannonderry. How . . . how did you know?"

Hearing the eagerness in her voice, Cormac relaxed. "I live near Shannonderry, and although I am in truth looking for a stallion, I have another purpose for visiting Hawarden." He looked back to ascertain that they weren't being followed before taking Moira's letter from his jacket pocket. "Your grandmother sent me here, Miss Beddows. She asked me to find you and give you this letter."

"My . . . my grandmother?"

Cormac nodded. "She's written to you several times but never received an answer. Three weeks ago she asked me to deliver this to you in person."

Gwyneth felt as if her mind were swimming. "There have been no letters. Unless Father . . ." She stopped. Was it possible he'd kept them from her? She suddenly knew he had. "He had no right," she cried indignantly. "And he's never once mentioned my grandmother . . . though Kate sometimes spoke of her."

"She's old and in failing health. That's why she sent me." He handed Gwyneth the missive. "No doubt she explains it in this."

Gwyneth rode Toryn a short distance away and, after dismounting and tethering him to a tree, turned her attention to the letter. Her hands trembled as she broke the seal, her gaze going to the spidery lines on the single sheet of paper.

My dear Gwyneth,
I have tried to communicate with you on several occasions over the past twenty-two years, but to no avail. Your silence leaves me to wonder

whether my letters failed to reach you or if 'tis your way of saying that
you have no wish to acknowledge your Irish grandmother.

"Never that, Grandmother." Shaking her head, Gwyneth's gaze returned to the opening words of the letter. Tears misted her eyes as she read the salutation. In all her years, she'd never once been called "my dear Gwyneth." *Oh, Grandmother.*

Whatever the case, I'm entrusting this letter to my neighbor, Mr. Cormac
D'Arcy, who will bring me word of your health and progress at Hawarden.

She glanced at the Irishman who'd ridden a short distance away to ensure her privacy. Like Gwyneth, he'd dismounted and stood with reins looped through his arm, looking out at the rolling countryside. Eager to return to her grandmother's letter, she quickly forgot Mr. D'Arcy.

This is not the only purpose for my letter. I also wish to invite you to
live with me at Shannonderry. I am alone now, my husband and
children all dead. You are my only grandchild. Should you decide to
make your home with me, Shannonderry will become yours. I have little else
to give you save the castle and the few acres that surround it.

Shannonderry! Gwyneth stared at the spidery lines. Did her grandmother know how many times she'd dreamed of going there? Images from Kate's stories tumbled through her mind—wee people, fairy rings, the gray turrets of the castle piercing the mist. Warmth and an overwhelming love for the old woman washed over Gwyneth as she read on.

I can give you a rich heritage, however. Generations of O'Briens have
called Shannonderry home. When I die, I would like to know that
those who live here have O'Brien blood flowing through their veins. It is my
hope and my one last dream that strangers will never possess Shannonderry.

Momentarily overcome, Gwyneth wiped a tear with her fingers. A feeling of belonging swirled through her pent-up emotions as long dead O'Briens seemed to call from across the Irish Sea. Instead of embarrassment for her Irish background, she experienced a powerful surge of pride.

I am aware that many in England bear no liking for the Irish. Should
these be your sentiments, or if you have no desire to come, you have

only to tell Mr. D'Arcy. My dearest prayer is that you will come, for I'm anxious to meet you. In the meantime, I shall await your answer.

With affection, your grandmother,

Moira O'Brien Donahue

The need to cry in earnest tightened the cords in Gwyneth's throat. Someone wanted her. More than that, she *needed* her. Gwyneth gazed at the letter, trying to picture the woman who'd penned the shaky lines. Mr. D'Arcy said she was old and failing in health. A wave of longing for this faceless person washed over her, along with the thought that Kate would be at Shannonderry too.

Carefully folding the letter, Gwyneth slipped it into the pocket of her riding jacket. Only then did she look for Mr. D'Arcy. He and his mare had moved closer, the horse cropping at grass, the Irishman's buff-colored breeches and brown coat silhouetted against the morning sky. Although the distance was too great for her to read his expression, she sensed his interest in her reaction to the letter. Untying Toryn, she gave the reins a tug and walked to Mr. D'Arcy.

"Have you an answer?" Cormac asked.

Gwyneth shook her head. "I'm in such a state I can't yet think . . . and I have a hundred questions." She paused and met Cormac's eyes. "Tell me about my grandmother. Is she really so old?"

"Old enough. Probably in her seventies."

"Do you think she and I will get on?"

The sight of Gwyneth's tear-stained cheeks touched Cormac, yet he'd also witnessed Moira's strong will and biting tongue. Not wanting to raise false hopes, he chose his words carefully. "It's hard to say. Like you, she has a way with horses. That should provide a common ground."

Cormac's evasive reply didn't escape Gwyneth's notice, but she didn't let it dampen her enthusiasm. She'd been too long without news of Shannonderry. Falling silent, they led their horses to a hill where hedgerows and stone fences divided the valley. "Is Kate still with Grandmother?" Gwyneth asked.

"Kate and her young cousin Biddy."

"I want so much to see her, but Father . . ." She shook her head, unwilling to think of her father just yet. "Is Shannonderry really so old?"

"The oldest in the district. At one time, the O'Brien lands sprawled across much of the county, but now . . ." He shrugged. "Hard times have reduced it to a fraction of its size. The harsh penal laws . . ." His expression turned grim.

Gwyneth had heard about the laws and how they penalized the Catholics. "Are my family Catholic then?"

Cormac gave a short laugh. "At first they were, but like any Irishman who wished to keep his property, they changed to the Church of Ireland. Unfortunately, professing English loyalty and changing religion didn't keep Shannonderry safe or the O'Briens wealthy." The Irishman paused, wondering how to best explain the situation. "It would be well for you to know that the O'Briens have long been famous for their stallions," he went on. "As their holdings diminished, they came to rely on the stallions for additional income. Until recently."

"What happened?"

"The last stallion died last year. When your grandmother contacted me, I thought she meant to ask me to look for a new stallion. Instead, she asked me to find you." Cormac fixed his blue eyes on Gwyneth. "Today, Moira Donahue is more interested in finding an heir than in buying a stallion."

Heir. Gwyneth savored the word. Not only did she have a family in Ireland, she was also an heir. Toryn's impatient tugging on the reins reminded her of the stallion. "Perhaps we should resume our ride."

They rode in silence until they neared Hawarden. "Tell me," Gwyneth said, "was the exorbitant price you offered for Toryn your device to gain access to Hawarden?"

Her question caught Cormac off balance. "Perhaps . . . though if you ever change your mind, I would very much like to buy him."

"I'll never sell him."

"Were he mine, I should feel the same."

She nodded, intending to turn in at the stable, when Cormac's next words stopped her.

"I hope you'll seriously consider your grandmother's offer, Miss Beddows. She is a woman of great inner strength and courage . . . one for whom you can feel great pride. But she's growing old, and she needs you."

"Thank you. I appreciate all you've told me." Gwyneth turned in the saddle to study the Irishman. She liked his assurance and the steady way he met and held her gaze. Instinct told her he was a man she could trust, and she badly needed such a person. Even so, she must think of her own well being. "Since you promised to remain silent about the breeches, I shall keep your secret, as well, Mr. D'Arcy."

Cormac blinked. "My secret?"

She winked in fair imitation of the one he'd given her the night before. "I shan't tell Father you deceived him with your offer of a thousand pounds." Smiling, she set Toryn toward the stable.

Watching her, Cormac felt the urge to laugh. In addition to pride, it seemed brains were also part of Gwyneth's heritage. The sight of her slender figure atop the great horse reminded him of Moira. When she'd been younger there wasn't a man along the Blackwater who didn't pause to watch in admiration as she and one of her stallions sailed over a hedgerow. Although Cormac had been but a boy at the time, he'd been numbered among her admirers. What a pity such a vibrant woman had grown old.

But Moira's granddaughter wasn't old, and she certainly had a way with horses. Now that he'd met her, Cormac was inclined to think that Gwyneth could help the old woman more than he'd first supposed, especially with Toryn. Cormac felt a lift to his spirits. Perhaps it wasn't the end of the Shannonderry stallions after all.

4

GWYNETH STOOD AT HER BEDROOM window, her eyes taking in the wide expanse of lawn sloping toward the trees and distant meadow. The view was one of her favorites, embodying all that was dear and familiar. She opened the window and breathed in the aroma of the lilacs that grew beneath her window. *Home,* she thought, *England.* But her grandmother wanted Gwyneth to leave it and go to Ireland.

She went to the bed to retrieve the letter. Although the shaky handwriting had been difficult to decipher, the message was clear. Shannonderry was Gwyneth's if she would go to Ireland and live there.

Shannonderry. For a moment, she was a child listening to Kate's whispered stories of wee folk and fairies. Woven through the tales was Shannonderry, stronghold of the brave.

A knock on the door startled Gwyneth. Fearing it was Sylvia, she slipped the letter under her pillow.

Rather than Sylvia, a maid stuck her head past the door. "Yer father sent me to fetch ye. He wants ye in his study."

Gwyneth eyed her pillow, wondering if she should show the letter to her father. Knowledge of his temper made her hesitate. Since Maurice Beddows had destroyed her grandmother's letters, who knew what he'd do when he learned she'd written again. There was Mr. D'Arcy to consider as well. He'd be sent packing if her father learned he'd come on Moira Donahue's behalf.

The thought of the Irishman's departure filled her with disquiet. He was her only link with Ireland and the path to her mother's past. *I'll wait. Perhaps Father won't mention Mr. D'Arcy.*

Unease followed Gwyneth when she stepped into her father's study. Usually it was one of her favorite rooms. Books and trophies crowded the shelves, and paintings of horses decorated the walls. Worn leather chairs and an oversized desk spoke of the man himself—masculinity, confidence, and success. Today there was also an element of tension.

"Has Mr. D'Arcy made an offer for Toryn?" he asked as she closed the door.

"Yes."

"What did you tell him?"

Gwyneth seated herself in one of the chairs. "I refused, of course."

Maurice scowled. "Have you considered the exceptional offer? Even Eclipse, great racehorse that he was, only sold for 1,800 guineas."

"I know. I'm also aware of what the money can buy. But think of how valuable Toryn will be when he wins the St. Leger."

"If," her father corrected. "The race is not sure."

"Toryn shows great promise. There will be other races, too . . . not to mention his stud fees."

"All dependent upon whether he wins St. Leger." Her father's gray unwavering eyes held hers. "Men don't forget that The Demon was Toryn's sire. We can't be certain of his future, but Mr. D'Arcy's offer is sure."

"Is it?" When he nodded, she wanted to laugh and tell him how he'd been duped, but caution and the need to protect the Irishman kept the words buried.

"He showed me his purse," Maurice went on. "Mr. D'Arcy is well able to pay the price. You are to accept it, daughter."

Her father's determined expression increased Gwyneth's unease. She wanted to refuse, but again caution bade her take care. Although Toryn was three years old, her father hadn't yet given her the papers that legally made the stallion hers. Until he did, she only had his word. Dared she challenge him? Gwyneth scorned women who used tears to get their way, but today she sensed they might be her only hope. "You gave him to me, Father. Please . . . don't make me sell him."

Maurice dropped his gaze from his daughter's tear-filled eyes. They were the same vivid turquoise as Deirdre's. Guilt for having largely ignored this child pummeled his heart. It wasn't that he didn't care about Gwyneth, but her temperament upset him—laughing and singing one moment, stubbornly defiant the next. He laid the blame on her Irish blood, though the nursemaid had played a part in it too.

Hoping an Englishwoman would erase Kate's influence on his daughter, Maurice had married Sylvia. Unfortunately, it hadn't taken long to see that there was little affinity between Sylvia and the child. Over the years, a demanding wife, the arrival of two sons, and the affairs of his stable had become the focus of his attention. As for Gwyneth . . . Maurice lifted his shoulders. Of late, he'd actually become proud of her. No woman, and few men, could sit a horse as well as his daughter, but he wished to heaven she didn't remind him so much of Deirdre.

Disliking his thoughts and Gwyneth's pleading eyes, Maurice pushed his chair back and went to the window. "I'm not trying to take Toryn away from you. I know how much you love him." He paused before forming his next words. "I have concern for you, Gwyneth. I'm not a wealthy man, and I have the boys to think of. There's not enough money for your dowry and their education. That's why . . ." He shrugged, deliberately keeping his gaze on the window so he didn't have to see his daughter's face. "If you were to accept Mr. D'Arcy's offer, you'd have the beginning of a dowry. I'll match it. Two thousand pounds isn't a great deal, but it's enough to get you an offer from someone better than James or Lord Ransford."

Gwyneth stared at him. "You'd do that?"

He nodded. "I know you've no wish to marry either, and I don't blame you. James is an imbecile, and Lord Ransford . . ." He swallowed an oath. "The man's older than I am."

"And twice as stout," Gwyneth ventured.

A faint smile touched his lips. "That too. I'd never consider him were it not for your Irish mother and the scandal attached to her name."

"Scandal? What scandal?"

"It's better you don't know."

"But—"

"Who your mother was will go against you. Men are particular that way . . . the same as they are about their horses."

"You didn't let it stand in the way when you married Mother."

"That was different. She was . . ." He stopped, not wanting to discuss Deirdre.

"She was what?" Gwyneth demanded. When he failed to answer, she crossed the room and clutched his arm. "Tell me, Father. I'm not a child anymore. I have the right."

Maurice brushed Gwyneth's hand from his sleeve. "She was beautiful . . . and she betrayed me! There . . . are you satisfied?"

The hurt and bewilderment on Gwyneth's face gave him a measure of satisfaction. Even after all these years, part of him wanted to hurt the child who'd precipitated Deirdre's death before he could learn the truth. "Are you satisfied?" he rasped. "Does it please you to know what kind of a woman she was? Deirdre was beautiful, and she betrayed me!"

Gwyneth stared in disbelief, hearing the words yet scarcely comprehending. This wasn't what she wanted to hear. "How?" she whispered, her mouth trembling.

"Does it matter? Isn't it enough to know that she did . . . and that I was foolish enough to trust her despite her Irish blood?" He gave a harsh laugh.

"Your mother made me look the fool . . . and there are plenty who still remember. That's why you must sell your stallion. It's the only way you'll make a suitable marriage."

"Never," Gwyneth declared. "Not Toryn!"

"I say you must! There's no other way."

His harsh voice brought life back to Gwyneth's paralyzed mind. She raised her chin. "I will not sell him."

Maurice's shock was quickly replaced by anger. Stubbornness he could deal with, but not open defiance. "Very well," he said in a voice as smooth as butter. "Then you will marry James."

"No!"

He stopped in mock surprise, his rounded figure silhouetted against the light streaming through the window. "Is it Lord Ransford you wish to wed?"

"You know I don't."

"Then you must sell Toryn."

"No."

All of Maurice's gentler feelings vanished. "You will marry James then. Mr. Steane and I leave in the morning to attend the races in Doncaster. When we return at the end of the week, I'll see that the marriage contract is drawn up."

"Please! Not James . . ."

"You no longer have any choice in the matter. My decision is made." With that, he opened the door and strode from the room.

Gwyneth's face crumpled as the door closed. While she struggled to regain composure, she remembered her grandmother's letter. "I won't do it, Father." Although she spoke to the door, her voice and eyes were filled with fire. "I'll go to Ireland before I'll marry James Steane!"

* * *

THE STORMY SCENE IN HER FATHER'S study left Gwyneth shaken and close to tears. "I won't marry him," she whispered. Saying it brought a sense of triumph. She'd done it—mustered the courage and defied her father. What's more, she'd survived it and won, though he didn't know it yet.

As she set off for the stable, she pictured Maurice Beddows's astonishment and rage when he returned from Doncaster and found her gone. It was what he deserved, but she must work quickly, and she would need Cormac D'Arcy's help.

Gwyneth purposely kept her mind from the disquieting words Maurice had spoken about her mother as she searched the stable for the

Irishman. Stuffing them in a dark place in her mind where she kept other unpleasantness, she concentrated on finding Mr. D'Arcy.

"'E rode out more'n an hour ago after askin' the way to the inn," Peter volunteered when she inquired.

When she asked him to saddle Toryn, Peter frowned, but he refrained from speaking until he helped her mount.

"Ye ain't meanin' to do somethin' foolish like racin' the man, are ye?"

Gwyneth laughed when she saw Peter eye her riding skirt. "In these clothes? And, no, I don't have John's breeches under my skirt."

"Just bein' sure. Ye seem uncommon anxious to find the man."

"I am, though you needn't worry. Just don't tell Father."

At his nod, she set Toryn in a canter toward the inn, scanning the countryside for the Irishman as she rode. She rode more than a mile before she spied him.

Cormac's surprise showed as he doffed his hat. "Good afternoon, Miss Beddows."

Gwyneth used a smile to hide her nervousness. What if he refused to help? "I . . . I must speak to you before Father sees you. I . . ." She stopped as the enormity of what she was about to ask swept over her. "I've come to ask you to take me with you when you return to Ireland."

Cormac's brows lifted. Although he'd hoped Gwyneth would accept Moira's offer, he hadn't expected her to decide so quickly. He studied her for a second, wondering about her reasons. "What did your father say when you told him?"

"Father doesn't know. That's why I must ask for your help." Mr. D'Arcy's close scrutiny made her more nervous. "You will help me, won't you?"

"Perhaps. First, I need to know why you haven't told your father."

"We . . . we quarreled." She didn't like having to share her problems with a man she scarcely knew. But his expression told her he wouldn't help until she did. "Since I have no dowry, Father ordered me to sell Toryn to you. When I refused, he said I must marry James Steane."

Cormac's mouth tightened at the memory of the bumbling, red-faced man at dinner. As he did so, he felt a momentary lift to his spirits. He hadn't misjudged the girl after all. "You choose Ireland over James Steane then?"

"That isn't the only reason. I've always wanted to find my mother's people."

"Even when we abuse our poor in such a dastardly manner?" Although Cormac spoke in jest, she took him seriously.

"I'm prepared to keep an opened mind."

"But are the Irish? There are many who bear the English no liking."

Surprise flicked through her eyes.

"I must warn you that if you go, you'll encounter hatred . . . perhaps even danger."

Her chin went up. "I'm not afraid."

"Perhaps you should be."

His words made her uncertain. "You act as if you don't want me to go to Shannonderry."

"I only want you to be aware of the difficulties you'll encounter," Cormac said, hedging. Although Moira's granddaughter might be able to help her, he still didn't like the idea of an English girl residing at Shannonderry. "Your coming will create problems for your grandmother as well. Perhaps more problems than it will solve."

"Then why did she invite me?"

"Because she badly needs your help."

"Then you must help me go to her." Anxious to have the matter settled, Gwyneth hurried on. "We must hurry . . . and you mustn't tell Father. If he finds out . . . if anyone finds out—"

Cormac edged his mare closer. "You mean you're running away?"

Not liking the expression on his face, Gwyneth lowed her eyes and nodded.

Cormac threw back his head and laughed. "And you want me to help you?"

His laughter cut to the quick and made Gwyneth feel like a child who'd said something foolish. Hot tears pricked her eyelids. She blinked them back with practiced calm. "Then I shall have to make my own arrangements." Not waiting for a reply, she urged Toryn into a gallop toward Hawarden.

Spurring his mare, Cormac galloped after her. The woman was acting like Moira, pretending she didn't need help, but she'd need it if she wanted to reach Ireland safely. A woman traveling alone! Her father would find her before she'd gone ten miles—and if not her father, then someone far worse. Recalling the disreputable men loitering near the wharf, he set his mare to a faster pace.

Since neither Gwyneth nor Toryn were in a mood to be overtaken, Cormac was unable to draw close enough to call until Toryn slowed at the gate. "Wait!" he called. "I didn't say I wouldn't help you."

Swallowing her hurt, Gwyneth reined in the stallion. "Didn't you?"

"No, and had you but waited instead of running off like an offended child—" Seeing her chin rise, he clamped his teeth down on his words. "I'm sorry, Miss Beddows. Can we begin again? I believe you said you planned to run away."

Gwyneth studied him before she nodded.

"Do you think it wise?"

"What else can I do? I told you how Father feels about the Irish, and after today . . ." She shook her head. "He'd never allow me to go to Ireland now."

"What about your stepmother?"

Gwyneth shook her head the second time. "Much as Sylvia would like to see me gone, she'd like to thwart me even more. Once she knows I wish to go, she'll do all she can to keep me here."

She threw an uneasy glance at the house. "Will you help me?"

"Yes, but it will take time to make arrangements."

"Father and Mr. Steane leave for the races in Doncaster tomorrow."

Cormac's eyes brightened with interest. "How long do they intend to be gone?"

"Until the end of the week. That's when he plans to draw up the marriage agreement with James's father."

"We'll be gone before that," he promised. "I've bespoken a room at the Falcon's Nest in case your father asks me to leave."

Gwyneth threw another anxious glance at the house. "He's probably looking for you so he can do so."

"Meet me in the morning after your father leaves. Is there someplace where we won't be seen?"

Gwyneth's mind raced. "Do you remember the copse of trees where you hung my cap?"

Cormac's lips twitched. "I'm sure I can find it. I'll watch for your father's departure and meet you there an hour later."

Realizing the risk the Irishman was taking on her behalf, Gwyneth felt a rush of gratitude. "Thank you, Mr. D'Arcy. I appreciate your help more than I can say."

"You are more than welcome, Miss Beddows."

Cormac watched in admiration as Gwyneth cantered the stallion toward the stable. Whether walking into the dining room on the arm of James Steane or sitting atop the big stallion, Moira's granddaughter was a woman to turn heads. The smile hovering on his lips split into an open grin. Not only would he have the pleasure of Miss Beddows's company on the trip to Ireland, but they would also be neighbors once she got there.

5

Two days later, excitement laced with apprehension plagued Gwyneth as she sat in the coach she shared with Cormac D'Arcy. She wanted to laugh aloud and look over her shoulder all at the same moment. She was on her way to Ireland to be reunited with Kate and to meet her grandmother!

The ease with which she and Toryn had gotten away from Hawarden filled her with satisfaction. The arranged meeting with Mr. D'Arcy at the ruins of Rosedale Abbey had gone well too. Even the rendezvous with the hired coach had been successful. Ireland was still many miles away, however. The worry that she or Toryn would be recognized or that her father might return early from Doncaster would not leave her.

Unable to repress the impulse to look through the back window, she searched the countryside for any sign of pursuit. Nothing. Only then did her gaze fasten on Toryn, which, with Mr. D'Arcy's mare, was roped to the back of the coach. Her mouth tightened. Gone was the magnificent black stallion, transformed by shadings of lime painted on his body and legs. The sight of his cropped mane and tail still caused her pain. The Irishman had trimmed them while Gwyneth had been occupied with changing into the boy's clothes he'd procured for her.

Even now she wanted to rage at the Irishman, something she'd done with great force at the Abbey. Mr. D'Arcy had borne her caustic words without speaking, though the tight lines of his mouth told her it had taken great control. Only when her anger was spent had he spoken.

"Do you desire to reach Ireland?" Before she could answer, he'd gone on in a cold voice. "As soon as it's discovered that you and your stallion are missing, men will scour Yorkshire looking for both of you."

Gwyneth hadn't needed him to point out that a horse such as Toryn would be remembered, but he'd done so anyway. "You might find the notion of being arrested and put into prison exciting, but I do not," he'd concluded.

D'Arcy had tactfully refrained from reminding her that by helping, he'd risked his own reputation and safety. Swallowing her pride, she'd apologized for her outburst, and the matter had not been spoken of again.

Such didn't make Gwyneth like what had been required, nor could she look at Toryn's changed appearance without pain. With a sigh, she settled back into the seat of the coach.

Seeming to read her thoughts, Cormac spoke. "I hate the cruel practice of cropping horses as much as you do."

"I know, just as I know you have put yourself at risk to help me. I hope you don't think me ungrateful. I couldn't have carried it off alone."

Cormac raised his brows. "Am I forgiven then?" At her nod, he smiled. "I own I was more worried at your reaction to my cutting your hair than I was with bobbing Toryn's mane and tail."

Gwyneth quickly ran her fingers through her short locks. "Did you truly see women in London with short hair, or did you just say it to reassure me?"

"'Tis the truth, and I heard that the fashion gains." Glancing at her shorn locks, Cormac recalled the softness of them as he'd cut her hair. Instead of looking more like a boy, the short curls had turned Gwyneth into an even more arresting young lady. Before, her lovely eyes and delicate features had been lost amid the mass of unruly hair; now her deep turquoise eyes and pink mouth begged to be admired. Cormac found himself hard pressed not to do so. Shaking his head, he pointed to the low-crowned hat lying on the seat between them. "We're nearing Thirsk, so it would be wise to put on your hat."

After the hat had been arranged to Cormac's satisfaction, Gwyneth gave him a shy smile. "Will I do?"

Cormac surveyed her with a critical eye. Although the brown coat was over large and the leather boots in need of polish, he was not displeased with the result. "You'll do," he said after a moment. "Though I doubt anyone will ask the name of your tailor." Worry stiffened his shoulders. "Whatever you do, remember to doff your hat when you pass a lady."

Knowing that much of the success of their escape depended upon her carrying off the masquerade as a young man, Gwyneth concentrated upon all the things she must remember. Besides doffing her hat, Mr. D'Arcy had emphasized the need to speak in a low voice or as seldom as possible. There were also the gloves. She reached in her jacket pocket and put them on. Like everything else, they were a trifle large, but not so much as to draw attention. At least, she hoped not.

So much could go wrong. If only the journey could have been undertaken with her father's approval—with calls of farewell and her trunks strapped to the top of the carriage. Instead, she'd left with nothing besides her aquamarine riding habit. After changing into breeches and coat at the Abbey, her skirt and jacket had been put in Cormac's valise. With a sigh, she forced her mind away from worry and the loss of her possessions. Ireland and Shannonderry were her future. It was there she must put her thoughts.

The movement of Mr. D'Arcy's long legs sent her mind leaping to him. That she was much aware of the Irishman was an understatement. It had punctuated everything she'd thought of and done since meeting him at the Abbey. In the close confines of the coach, it was even more pronounced. Using the wide brim of the borrowed hat to hide her scrutiny, Gwyneth glanced at his handsome profile. What were his thoughts as he gazed out the window? The line creasing his forehead made her suspect Mr. D'Arcy was also uneasy about what lay ahead.

Toryn's neigh jerked Gwyneth's mind away from Cormac. They both turned to look back. Toryn's flattened ears and tossing head showed his dislike for the jostling traffic on the outskirts of the thriving market town of Thirsk. Cormac had hoped they'd be less conspicuous if they rode inside and tethered the two horses behind the coach. Now he saw the potential for trouble.

"Toryn will break loose if I don't ride him," Gwyneth said.

Cormac nodded and called for the coachman to stop. As he did, he gave Gwyneth a measured look. "It will be better if I ride Toryn. Wait inside the coach until I come for you, and don't speak to anyone until I'm with you," he instructed.

Trying to quell her nervousness, Gwyneth nodded and reminded herself that she was a young woman, not a frippery schoolgirl. As such, she should be able to carry off her impersonation.

Cormac and Toryn were able to thread their way through the bustling traffic faster than the heavier coach. They were waiting at The Golden Fleece when Gwyneth arrived.

"Remember to keep your voice low if you have to speak," Cormac warned as she stepped out onto the paving stones.

She gave a nervous smile and looked up at the brick facade of the busy posting inn. Even though it was almost dark, she wished Cormac had chosen a less popular place.

"Swagger a little," Cormac whispered as they entered the inn.

She tried to remember how John walked when he led Toryn—his pride at having the stallion follow him and his confidence worn like a badge. Gwyneth lifted her shoulders. There, that was better.

"Don't mince," Cormac added in a growl.

A confusion of voices and bustling servants greeted them inside the inn. Several gentlemen loitered in the oak paneled main room. Was their scrutiny of her more than was warranted?

"Wait here while I speak to the innkeeper," Cormac instructed, the undercurrent in his voice telling her to look sharp and hold on to her courage.

Determined not to give them away, Gwyneth walked to the far side of the room and pretended to study the painting of a horse grazing in a meadow. Bits of memorized prayers tumbled through her mind. If she wished to carry off the masquerade, she must rely on a power greater than her own.

"Excuse me, sir."

Concentrating on the painting, Gwyneth paid no heed to the voice, but it came again accompanied by a tap on her shoulder. Gwyneth swung around, certain she'd been discovered.

"I . . . I'm sorry," a startled serving girl stammered. "Yer uncle asked me to show ye to yer room while he sees to the horses."

Gwyneth nodded and frowned, hoping her expression would do away with the need to reply, but the maid possessed a curious nature, and she glanced several times at Gwyneth as they climbed the stairs.

When they reached the landing, the maid paused and smiled. "Ye have the prettiest eyes," she whispered. "Should ye want company this evening, my name be Mary."

The maid's cheeks flushed prettily, but their color couldn't compare to the brightness of Gwyneth's blush.

"Which . . . which room is mine?" Gwyneth stammered, forgetting to keep her voice low.

The maid giggled and indicated the far door.

Hurrying past the maid, Gwyneth almost collided with a gentleman emerging from the next room. "Excuse me, sir," she murmured. Though haste was uppermost in her mind, Gwyneth remembered to keep her voice low now. It was fortunate she did, for a glance at the man's startled face showed him to be Frederick Whiting, one of her father's friends.

"I say . . ." Mr. Whiting began.

Gwyneth pretended not to hear as she slipped into her room and closed the door. Holding her breath, she listened for his reaction. She detected a faint harrumph followed by the sound of footsteps as he descended the stairs.

Imagining the scene that would have transpired had she been recognized, Gwyneth released the breath she had been holding and leaned against the door. While waiting for her heart to resume its normal rhythm, she took in her surroundings. The room was small and obviously not the inn's best. It held a sagging bed, two chairs, and a table with a basin and ewer. Her gaze returned to the bed. Surely Mr. D'Arcy didn't expect them to share the same bed.

In her eagerness to run away, Gwyneth hadn't considered sleeping arrangements. She thought of the long journey ahead—one that would entail several nights. If she expected to reach Ireland, she would have to continue to rely on Mr. D'Arcy. More than that, she needed to trust him. Surely he would be a gentleman.

The moment Cormac entered the room, her positive thoughts deserted her. His tall frame seemed to dominate the chamber, making her forget everything except that he was a man and she a woman.

"The horses are stabled," Cormac said in a matter-of-fact voice. Their sleeping arrangements didn't seem to cause him concern. "I've also ordered our dinner. As soon as I wash, we can go downstairs to dine."

His plans jerked Gwyneth's mind back to Mr. Whiting. "I think it best if I stay in here."

"Is something wrong?"

"I saw one of Father's friends in the hallway. He gave me a long look, and if he sees me again . . ." Her voice trailed away when she saw Cormac frown.

"Has he been at Hawarden often enough to recognize Toryn?"

At her nod, Cormac's frown deepened. "I knew we took risk by stopping at The Golden Fleece, but if we'd stayed at a smaller inn, there's greater chance we'd be remembered should your father follow us." He poured water into the bowl to wash his hands. "We'll have to make an early start in the morning before your father's friend awakens."

"What about dinner?"

"We can have it brought to our room."

Gwyneth swallowed a protest. The thought of sharing a meal with the Irishman in the intimacy of the tiny room was more upsetting than chancing another encounter with Mr. Whiting.

When she made no reply, Cormac noticed her furtive gaze at the bed. Thunderation! She surely didn't think he intended them to share the same bed, did she? Cormac didn't know whether to be angry or laugh. Instead of doing either, he fixed her with a look he sometimes used with his cousin Edwina. "May I speak frankly, Miss Beddows?" He didn't wait for an answer. "Since we're going to be in one another's company for several days and nights, I think we should come to an understanding of our relationship.

I have told the innkeeper you are my nephew . . . and I intend to treat you as such. Tonight you may have the bed and I shall sleep on a pallet, but tomorrow night you will take your turn on the floor. Is this agreeable?"

"Yes." Gwyneth's voice was a mortified whisper. She'd never had anyone read her thoughts so clearly before.

"As for dinner," he went on, deliberately ignoring her flaming cheeks. "I'll dine downstairs and give you the privacy of eating here." When she made no reply, he dried his hands on the towel and walked over to her. "I'm sorry if my frankness embarrasses you, but perhaps now we can get on more comfortably."

She shot him a quick look, looked again, then bit back a surprised gasp. Despite Mr. D'Arcy's show of nonchalance, his high color told her that he was as uncomfortable as she. The knowledge put her on a more even keel. "No, I'm glad you spoke thus. Now we can both be more ourselves."

Something in her expression made Cormac think it wise to change the subject. "Will you be all right while I'm gone?"

"I'll be fine. I often took dinner in my room at home."

Hearing this made Cormac dislike Maurice Beddows all the more. "See that you bolt the door after I leave." He frowned when he saw the flimsy bolt. A narrow object inserted between latch and frame would render it useless. "I won't be gone long," he promised.

Pleased at how easily Mr. D'Arcy had dealt with her concern about their sleeping arrangements, Gwyneth attacked her dinner with a hearty appetite when it was brought to her. Fortunately, it wasn't Mary who brought the meal. While Gwyneth ate, she turned her mind to playing the role of Mr. D'Arcy's nephew. If she could carry it off, the act could prove entertaining.

After she finished eating, Gwyneth strode around the room in what she hoped was a fair imitation of a young man, taking special effort not to mince. When she was satisfied that her swagger had become more confident, her thoughts turned to other matters. Since she must play the part of Mr. D'Arcy's nephew, she would need a new name. Several came to mind. In the end, she settled upon Cedric.

"I say, Cedric," she mimicked in her deepest voice, "if you're a good lad, I'll let you have the bed tonight, but tomorrow night you must sleep on the floor."

Gwyneth giggled, and she was still smiling when a quiet knock came at the door. After letting Cormac in, Gwyneth showed him her practiced walk. "See," she said, swaggering a little. "Take note that I do not mince . . . and I've thought of my new name."

Her impish smile made Cormac lose his train of thought. She was too fetching by half, and he would have to take care. "Name?" he asked, smiling.

"Since I'm your nephew, you can't very well call me Miss Beddows. I've always liked the name Cedric. Did you know he led a band of the wee people against the Norse and conquered them with his great cunning?"

Cormac's smile broadened. "I fear that particular tale escaped my notice, but if you have a fondness for Cedric, then Cedric it will be." Relieved to note that her embarrassment was gone, he slipped into an Irish brogue. "Well then, Cedric, since 'tis yer night for the bed, I'll be suggestin' that ye make good use of yer time there. As for me, I've a hankerin' for a quick stroll afore I settle me old bones on the wee pallet."

Gwyneth's laughter came quick and easy, just as he'd hoped it would. He gave a wink as he quit the room. *Miss Beddows can now get herself into bed without embarrassment.*

While he made the circuit of the passageway, he wondered what Moira Donahue would think if she saw Cormac D'Arcy cooling his heels in the The Golden Fleece while her granddaughter passed herself off as his nephew.

6

A SHOUT AND THE SUDDEN braking of the carriage awakened Gwyneth from a nap. A day of travel had brought them to the Awbeg River valley, inland from where they'd debarked from the ship on reaching Ireland. She sat up and looked out the window. Why had Mr. D'Arcy ordered the driver to stop? A quick glance gave her the answer. The leaden Irish sky, which had threatened to spill its contents through much of the morning, was doing so in earnest. She watched while Cormac, sodden with rain, fastened Toryn onto the leading rein with his mare behind the carriage. A moment later he joined her inside, bringing with him droplets of water and the smell of damp wool.

Gwyneth drew herself into the corner of the seat to prevent her crumpled riding skirt from becoming more wrinkled. She gave a rueful smile as she took in Cormac's dripping clothes and rain-plastered hair. "If this keeps up, Grandmother will mistake us for a pair of vagabonds."

Cormac grinned and mopped his face and hair with a handkerchief, his white, even teeth contrasting with the black of his well-shaped brows and glistening hair. "Then it's fortunate I sent a man ahead to alert her of our coming." His expression sobered when he looked at Gwyneth's crumpled clothes. The pressing they'd received the night before hadn't succeeded in putting them to rights. "I'm sorry about your clothes," he added, knowing of her wish to look her best for her grandmother.

"By rights I should demand new ones," Gwyneth teased. "But I'm too excited and grateful to be in Ireland for that." She glanced out at the misty countryside. "Even in the rain, it's lovely. Have we far to go?"

"Another hour should see us there unless the storm worsens."

Hearing this, Gwyneth watched the scenery more closely. The valley they passed through was open and lush, with farms set deep and sheltered amongst borders of trees. A lonely stone bridge arched over the river at an angle to the track they followed, and ahead the weathered ruins of an old keep guarded the gorge where the river rushed on below.

A tingle ran along Gwyneth's spine. Some of her O'Brien ancestors had probably passed along this very track, looked out at the same scenery, and felt pride and a sense of homecoming just as she did. Perhaps some had even lived in the crumbling keep above the gorge. Something familiar seemed to pulse through her veins. *Ireland. Home.* "How beautiful," she whispered, unable to find more adequate words.

"Aye, 'tis that, all right. Each time I return, I count myself fortunate." Cormac's gaze fastened on Gwyneth's animated face surrounded by its froth of light curls. His intent to deliver her to Moira Donahue with no more thought than if she'd been a package from England had been altered by five days of the young woman's company. His design to think of her as his nephew Cedric had been equally unsuccessful. How could he not respond to her sparkling eyes and the smile that seemed always to hover about her full lips? Breeches and coat had not diminished her charm, nor had her crumpled riding habit.

Cormac's attraction to Gwyneth was woven through his concern for her. Her high spirits might well be dashed by the reality of what lay ahead. Wanting to prepare her, he spoke in a more somber tone. "Don't forget that Ireland's beauty masks a land seething with anger and repression. Times are troubled. Your life at Shannonderry won't be easy."

"My life at Hawarden was not easy."

"True . . . but I doubt it held any actual danger."

Gwyneth turned her head to meet his steady gaze. "This is the second time you've mentioned danger. Of what are you trying to warn me?"

Cormac chose his words with care. "The age-old friction between Catholics and Protestants is always a factor. The hatred goes deep, as deep as their hatred of anything English."

"I see." Gwyneth felt a stab of irritation. In England she'd experienced prejudice because of her Irish blood. Was it to be the same now because she was part English? Gwyneth couldn't understand people's inclination to hate because of one's blood instead of their character. When would it end?

For a time, they rode in silence, the jolt of the wheels and the crack of the whip the only sounds. Through it all was Gwyneth's awareness of the Irishman. His presence dominated the close confines of the carriage, the breadth of his shoulders and the length of his legs seeming to take up the whole of it. She couldn't seem to get enough of him, darting quick looks when she thought Mr. D'Arcy wasn't looking, noting his well-shaped nose and the strength of his long-fingered hands. She told herself that her limited exposure to attractive men was the reason for her acute interest and awareness. Yet, something as deep as her Irish roots told her it was more.

Wanting to learn more about the man who consumed her thoughts, she said, "Tell me about your home. How did the D'Arcys come to live here?"

Cormac settled himself more comfortably into the cushion of the carriage. "It's a common enough story. In the twelfth century, my ancestor Richard D'Arcy came to Ireland with the Norman invaders. He and his sons built a fortress near Wexford and lived there until the Desmonds were deposed for rebellion against the crown. One of the D'Arcys received a tract of Desmond land in payment for loyalty to the queen, and he moved his family here along the Blackwater. Since then it's been our home, though another wily D'Arcy's conversion to Protestantism was required to save our holdings from Cromwell. Even at that, the castle was burned and put to ruin before he left."

Cormac paused as the coachman executed a difficult turn in the road. "Our present home was built in 1690 with its name and the date engraved over the door. It's called Clonglas, which means 'meadow of green.'"

"What a lovely name. Do your parents live there with you? What about brothers and sisters?" More important, she wondered, did he have a wife?

"My parents are dead, but I have a half-brother, Owen, some years younger than me. He and my stepmother live with me at Clonglas. I also have a cousin, Edwina, who sometimes comes to visit."

Gwyneth's cheeks warmed as she voiced her next question. "Is there no wife?" She hoped not—prayed not. She waited for his answer, scarcely daring to breathe.

"I have no wife, and I fear no prospects of one," Cormac answered amicably.

Aware that the Irishman was amused by her high color, Gwyneth hurried to change the subject. "Does Shannonderry have an interesting history too?"

"It does," Cormac answered, "but I'm not as well versed with its history as your grandmother. I know Shannonderry has been the stronghold of the O'Briens for many centuries and that they have never looked with kindness toward the English."

Gwyneth's concern increased. She'd read enough of Irish history to know of Elizabeth's zeal to rid Munster of all who opposed the crown. The Desmonds were not the only ones to lose their holdings and have them supplanted with those loyal to the queen. "Does that mean Grandmother dislikes the English too?" she asked. "I thought that since my mother married an Englishman . . ." Her voice trailed away when she noted the way Cormac looked at her.

"Did you not know your mother's marriage didn't have your grandparents' blessing?"

Gwyneth stared at him in dismay. "No."

Aware that he'd upset her, Cormac went on in a kinder tone. "Your mother and Maurice Beddows eloped. I believe your grandmother has had difficulty forgiving them."

"I didn't know." Gwyneth's voice came thin as it always did when she was unsure of herself. She tried to gather her thoughts. "If Grandmother doesn't approve of the English . . . or my mother . . . why did she invite me to come?"

"As I said before, she needs you."

"Needs and dislikes me both?" Gwyneth shook her head. "I would never have come if I'd known how she felt."

"I didn't say she disliked you. In fact, I think she looks forward to meeting you. Even so, your coming will be a difficult adjustment."

"I still don't understand."

Not wanting to hurt Gwyneth any more than she already was, Cormac searched for the right words. "Since your grandmother is the last O'Brien at Shannonderry, she wants it left to you. You're all she has . . . but you're also English."

Gwyneth tried to adjust to the shock Cormac's words had wielded. Since she was Deirdre's daughter and Moira Donahue's only grandchild, she'd expected to be greeted with affection. Her throat ached with the need to cry. Without love, life at Shannonderry would be no better than at Hawarden.

Determined not to arrive at Shannonderry with lowered spirits, Gwyneth straightened her shoulders. Things would work out. She would see that they did.

* * *

THE RAIN HAD CEASED FALLING, and sunlight pierced the clouds by the time the carriage turned through the high arched gate to Shannonderry. Gwyneth's pulse quickened, and she peered excitedly out the carriage window. As she did Cormac called for the driver to stop.

"It will be best if you ride Toryn the rest of the way," he said.

Gwyneth waited while Mr. D'Arcy released the two horses from their leading reins and helped her mount. Although rain had washed most of the lime from Toryn's black coat, his bobbed mane and tail left him looking unfamiliar. The change was forgotten, however, as soon as she touched her heels to his side. The stallion's rippling muscles and prancing response enhanced her excitement.

The graveled approach was so narrow and heavily lined with oak and birch trees that all she could see was rain-dampened trees and heavy undergrowth. When the trees suddenly ended, Gwyneth sucked in her breath and brought Toryn to a halt. Gazing across a wide expanse of grass at the high Norman towers and turreted walls of Shannonderry, a little sigh escaped her lips.

She had often tried to picture her mother's home, but none of her imaginings had prepared her for Shannonderry's defiant facade. Situated on a rise, its ancient stone walls and turreted towers gave off an aura of strength and endurance. Gwyneth sat as if in a trance, not realizing how deeply she was moved until she felt goosebumps rise on the flesh of her arms as she looked at the old fortress through a mist of tears.

"What do you think?" Cormac's tone was gentle.

"It . . ." Her voice broke off as Toryn shied and pranced sideways. Like something from a dream, four enormous dogs bounded around the side of the castle, their appearance like silent gray ghosts.

"Dear heaven!" Gwyneth gasped when the dogs crouched and bared their teeth. Toryn gave a shrill whinny, and Gwyneth had to fight to keep him from rearing. "Easy, boy," she commanded, her eyes still on the dogs. A young boy raced from the castle, his whistle piercing the air as he called off the dogs.

"They're Shannonderry's guard dogs," Cormac said as he tried to calm his mare.

Still working to control Toryn, Gwyneth recalled that Kate had spoken of dogs.

"That's young Cluny O'Donnell," Cormac went on as the boy ordered, then followed the dogs back toward the castle. "He and his grandfather, Flynn, see to the grounds and stable while another granddaughter and Kate look after the house."

"Are they the only help?"

Determined not to speak disparagingly of the situation, Cormac kept his voice matter of fact. "Your grandmother is no longer a wealthy woman. Times have forced her to economize."

The unexpected disclosure gave Gwyneth pause. Despite Hawarden's dated furnishings, her family had always dined well, and she had never lacked for new gowns.

With the carriage following them, Gwyneth and Cormac rode along the drive as it crossed the parkland. Dressed in patched breeches and an outgrown shirt that exposed his bony wrists and hands, young Cluny watched their approach with mouth agape and fingers touching his brown forelock.

Gwyneth reined in her stallion and smiled down at him. "Good day to you, Cluny."

Eyeing the splendid stallion, Cluny seemed at a loss for words.

"This is Miss Beddows," Cormac said. "Since she has come to live at Shannonderry, the two of you will be seeing much of each other."

"Yes, sir . . . ma'am." Touching his fingers to his forelock a second time, he set off at a run for the stable.

"That's Cluny for you." Cormac chuckled. "For all his acting as if the cat's got his tongue, you'll soon discover that he abounds in decided opinions and isn't shy about expressing them. All in all, he's a good lad who shoulders far too much responsibility for one so young."

"How old is he?"

"Ten, I think . . . maybe eleven."

Gwyneth shook her head. How did a boy and an old man keep up with both the grounds and stable? Only then did she notice the signs of neglect. Instead of freshly raked gravel, the drive abounded in muddy ruts and potholes, while the shrubs and flowerbeds were tangled with overgrown greenery and a few resilient blooms. Yet, even with neglect, Shannonderry was breathtakingly beautiful.

"I'll give Toryn a rubdown and see that he's stabled," Cormac said when they halted the horses at the front entrance.

Gwyneth's mind was too filled with half-formed impressions to reply.

"Your grandmother is waiting," Cormac prompted. Dismounting, he went to help Gwyneth from the saddle. His touch and expression were gentle as he looked down at her. "All will go well," he said when he felt her nervous tremor.

It was the Irishman's nearness as much as the prospect of meeting her grandmother that made Gwyneth tremble. Aware that his hand still rested on her waist, she smiled and nodded. As she did, something flickered through his blue eyes, telling her that he was aware of her as well.

"I shall miss Cedric," he went on in a lighter tone, "although I find his replacement much to my liking. I'll join you when I've finished with Toryn." Touching his hat, he gathered the horses' reins and started for the stable.

She looked after him for a moment before turning her attention to the worn steps leading up to the nail-studded door. Her mother must often have stood in this very spot, looking up at the same towering walls, as had generations of O'Briens before her. A sense of homecoming warmed

Gwyneth's heart. Hawarden seemed but a place she'd visited, when all along the turreted facade of Shannonderry had been her home.

* * *

As she started up the stone steps, a plump woman opened the door and gathered Gwyneth into her arms. "Lass . . . me own sweet lass."

The sound of Kate's voice and the feel of her soft embrace brought moisture to Gwyneth's eyes. The faint scent of lavender touched her memory and took her back to her childhood. "Dear Kate."

She pulled away to examine the woman who'd filled so many of her memories. Kate's plump frame and the streaks of gray in her faded red hair came as a shock. In her fantasies, her nurse had been young and beautiful, but Gwyneth realized that Kate had probably never possessed much in the way of looks. Her green eyes, brimming with love, were just as she remembered, however.

"A beauty ye be," Kate declared. "And yer hair just as white and lovely as afore." She reached up and removed Gwyneth's riding hat. "'Tis so short," she exclaimed, clearly dismayed.

"I had it cut," Gwyneth answered, wanting to save the story of running away until later. "Did you know short hair is the fashion in England?"

"Is it now?" Kate's tone of voice showed that she didn't think much of the new fashion. "Come," she said, giving Gwyneth's arm an affectionate squeeze. "Yer gran be waitin' for ye in the sitting room."

As Kate led her into Shannonderry, Gwyneth caught a glimpse of a large shield hanging on the wall. Then the heavy door closed, casting the entrance hall into shadows, two arrowslits in the stone providing little illumination to the murky gloom.

Kate seemed used to the dimness and walked without pause across the hall and down an adjoining corridor. "Come along," she said, leading the way.

Some distance down the corridor, Kate paused and knocked at a door. "She be here, Mistress. Yer granddaughter be here." Not waiting for an answer, Kate opened the door, giving Gwyneth's arm another squeeze as she motioned her into the sitting room.

Gwyneth's first impression was one of austerity. None of the chairs was upholstered, and the backs, richly carved from native bog oak, gave an illusion of coldness. The room's mullioned windows were bordered with the same dark wood, as was the floor, which was partially covered with faded carpet.

Looking for her grandmother, Gwyneth stepped farther into the room. As she did, she heard a quick intake of breath. Glancing in the direction of the sound, she detected the slight figure of a woman standing in the shadows, the blackness of her clothes blending with the dark furniture.

"Mercy," a quivery voice whispered. Then in a steadier tone, "Come closer so I can better see you."

Unsure of her welcome, Gwyneth stepped into the pool of light that spilled through one of the double windows. Acutely aware of her short hair and rumpled riding habit, she lifted her chin. Though she'd joked with Cormac about her grandmother's reaction to her unkempt appearance, it was not amusing now.

When Moira Donahue stepped from the shadows, Gwyneth forgot about herself, her thoughts fully taken with the old woman's erect bearing and the flash of her vivid blue eyes. Her graying hair still showed traces of black and was surprisingly thick and luxuriant. She wore it braided and wound in a coronet around her small head, the style giving her a queenly demeanor. Although her age was evident in the lines of her face, she was still a handsome woman.

She was also proud. Gwyneth knew this even before she saw the flash of amethyst earrings and the matching brooch that held a ruff of black lace around her grandmother's thin, ropey neck. The old woman's obvious surprise and unsmiling countenance were disconcerting. Giving a nervous smile, Gwyneth dropped a deep curtsy.

Moira continued to stare. The girl was nothing like she'd imagined. And the platinum hair—Could it be? Knowing she gaped, Moira swallowed and wished she hadn't forbidden Kate to tell her the child's name. It had been foolish, and now Moira herself felt foolish. "What is your name, Granddaughter?"

The young woman looked at her oddly. "Didn't Kate tell you? It's Gwyneth."

Moira's heart gave an erratic jump. "Gwyneth . . . the white and blessed one," she whispered.

Not knowing what to think, Gwyneth attempted another smile. "Do I look like my mother? I've often wondered about her . . . about you and Ireland too. Thank you for inviting me to Shannonderry."

With her gaze fastened tightly on Gwyneth's platinum hair, Moira was too distracted to speak. Who would have thought Deirdre would name the child Gwyneth? Perhaps her daughter hadn't turned her back on Shannonderry after all. Becoming aware of Gwyneth's discomfort, Moira made an effort to speak. "Thank you for coming, child." The thawing around her heart added warmth to her voice. "I was afraid you might not want to come . . . or that your father would forbid it."

"He did . . . though, thanks to Mr. D'Arcy, I was able to get away." Gwyneth put a self-conscious hand to her hair. "I apologize for my appearance. I had to cut my hair . . . and I brought only my stallion and the clothes you see me wearing so Father wouldn't suspect I was leaving."

Moira's dark brows lifted. "Ran away, did you?" The look she gave Gwyneth was more kindly. "You've more of the O'Brien spirit than I expected."

"The Beddows have been known to exhibit spirit on occasion too." Gwyneth knew her remarks were perhaps unwise, but she wanted the woman to know the English were not without good points too.

A flicker of amusement crossed Moira's face. "So they have. It's fortunate you received a double dose, for you'll need it to make a success of Shannonderry."

Gwyneth looked around the sitting room. "It's so very old," she said in an awe-filled voice.

"It's that, all right," Moira agreed. "The great hall and solar are even older. I'll take you to see them tonight after you've had a chance to freshen yourself."

"I am a little tired," Gwyneth agreed.

"Then Biddy will show you to your room, and Kate . . ." She paused and fixed her eyes on the half-opened door where Kate still waited. "Kate will be off to the north tower where your mother's clothes are stored. Since you're without a trunk, I'm sure she'll find something for you to wear until we can have a new wardrobe made."

"That's not necessary," Gwyneth began, remembering what Cormac had said about her grandmother's circumstances.

"I think it is," Moira countered. "Ye can't be wearing naught but a riding habit over the next days." A smile softened her words. "Run along," she added. "Knowing Biddy, she's waiting with Kate, hoping to get a peek at you."

"Mistress," Kate interrupted. "Mr. D'Arcy's come."

"Good. Show him in."

Now that Cormac was here, Gwyneth was reluctant to leave.

Seeming to sense Gwyneth's disappointment, Moira stepped closer. "Again, thank you for coming, Granddaughter. We have much to learn of each other. After we've both rested, I've something I wish to show you."

Aware that Cormac had entered the room, Gwyneth dropped her grandmother another curtsy. Only then did she allow herself to look at the Irishman. "I'm much indebted to you, Mr. D'Arcy," she said in a soft voice.

"It was my pleasure."

"I doubt that." Gwyneth laughed, recalling that despite Mr. D'Arcy's threat, he'd been the one to spend each night on the pallet. She'd grown used to playing the role of Cedric and was unprepared when the Irishman took her hand and raised it to his lips.

"Miss Beddows." His blue eyes met and held hers when he raised his head. "Since we're neighbors, I look forward to seeing you in the coming days. Should you need me before that, send word with Flynn or Cluny."

His words and the warm pressure of his fingers through her riding gloves held her thoughts until Moira Donahue cleared her throat. Gwyneth hastily removed her hand, conscious of her heated cheeks and the old woman's lifted brow as she quit the room.

7

BIDDY WAS WAITING JUST AS Moira had predicted. Her smiling presence pierced the gloomy corridor like a ray of sunshine. Her red hair spilled from a white cap to frame a lovely oval face and large green eyes.

Biddy gaped openly, her lips a circle of astonishment. "Holy Mother," she whispered, crossing herself. "When Kate said—" Remembering herself, the maid dropped a curtsy. "Welcome to Shannonderry. Yer comin' will do the Mistress good. Indeed, it has a'ready. I've not seen her lookin' so well since last summer."

"I hope it remains so," Gwyneth replied. The interview with her grandmother had left her feeling unsure of how they would get on.

"'Tis certain to," Biddy said as she led the way down the corridor. "I'll show ye to yer room to freshen up. Mistress bid us ready it for ye some weeks ago."

"How could she be certain I'd be coming?"

"She couldn't," Biddy acknowledged, "but she could hope. We prayed ye'd come . . . the Mistress with bowed head and Kate and me with our beads."

At the end of the corridor, Biddy pointed to the end wall where a narrow stone staircase wound upward. "Yer room be up in the tower. 'Twas yer mam's."

The arrowslits along the thick wall provided meager light for the stairway. A rope, rather than a handrail, was Gwyneth's only support as she climbed the worn stone steps that had borne the weight of countless feet. She was reminded again of Shannonderry's age. It seemed to burrow deep into her bones along with the cold that seeped in from the dank walls. The sensation of age was so strong that Gwyneth half expected to see a knight and his lady descend the narrow stairs to greet her.

Instead, there was only Biddy leading the way, her tongue moving as quickly as her feet as she described how she and Kate had washed and scrubbed the room and its bedding in readiness for Gwyneth's arrival. They were both out of breath by the time they reached the top of the tower.

"Here 'tis," Biddy said, opening a door.

The circular room was the most unusual Gwyneth had ever seen. A polished oak floor spanned the interior, and four windows built in the crenellated battlement provided light and a sweeping view of the valley. A raised fire pit with a metal hood formed a chimney that climbed to a high, pointed ceiling. The warmth from a recently lit fire drew Gwyneth into the room where she stood with closed eyes, hoping to feel something of her mother. When nothing came, Gwyneth trailed her fingers along the length of a four-post bed with green hangings. She noted a wardrobe and desk, their construction built to conform to the circular tower.

"I hope 'twill do," Biddy said.

"Yes . . . it's lovely." Gwyneth walked to one of the windows. From its height, she felt like an eagle perched on a mountain crag. The view was magnificent, with the green of Shannonderry's fields and rich meadowland rolling toward distant, misty hills. Awe pricked her skin when she pictured her mother standing at the same window. Deirdre must have felt like a princess, though sometimes the room's isolation might have made her feel a little lonely. *Not with Kate here,* a merry voice seemed to say. *Never with Kate.*

Biddy's voice interrupted Gwyneth's thoughts. "Kate said Master . . . him what died . . . fixed this special for yer mam. When she run away—" Her voice lowered to a whisper. "Did ye know 'twas kept locked more'n twenty years?"

When Gwyneth failed to reply, Biddy joined her at the window. "'Tis lovely, ain't it . . . like the queen herself ordered it and—" Hearing singing, Biddy clapped a hand to her mouth. "'Tis Kate. She'll not like it that I be blathering so."

Gwyneth laughed. "I promise not to tell."

Before she could say more, Kate's plump figure filled the doorway, her cheerful face peering over an armful of clothes.

"There was a time when I could climb these stairs so quick ye daresn't blink. But now . . ." She paused to catch her breath.

"Why didn't ye call for help?" Biddy scolded.

Instead of answering, Kate dumped the clothes onto the bed. "Will ye be lookin' at this one? 'Twas scarce worn, as are several others." She held a pale blue gown to Gwyneth's shoulders. "I knew 'twould fit. Ye be much like yer mam."

"Tell me again what she looked like," Gwyneth prompted.

"She be . . ." Kate stopped when she saw Biddy's undisguised interest. "Mistress wants ye to fetch a tub and hot water for Miss Gwyneth's bath."

Kate refrained from saying anything more until Biddy left. "The girl be uncommon curious, and Mistress don't hold with gossipin' tongues . . . though what ye want to hear be the truth not gossip," she hastily amended. "Ye should know that yer gran frowns on any talk of Deirdre."

"She and my father seem to be of the same mind."

"Did he never tell ye of her?"

Gwyneth thought of her father's angry words. "Only that she was beautiful." She stopped, not wanting to voice the last. "He told me she betrayed him."

Kate's green eyes flashed. "'Tis a lie. And many a time I tried to tell him. The stubborn man 'ud sooner listen to gossip than trust the likes of me."

"What happened?" Gwyneth asked.

Kate looked at Gwyneth for a long moment. Many times she'd rehearsed how she'd tell the girl about her mother, but now that the time had finally arrived, she hesitated. What if she said the wrong thing or caused Gwyneth to think ill of Deirdre? "'Tis a long story," she said at last, "and one ye'll not be understandin' 'less ye know how deep Papists and Protestants hate each other."

"I know of the hatred," Gwyneth said, while inside a tiny voice warned her that she might not like what she was about to hear.

"Ye should also know that for all they said otherwise, the O'Briens remained Papists at heart, while yer granfar and the Donahues was staunch Protestants."

Gwyneth looked at Kate in surprise. "Is my grandmother Catholic then?"

"She don't count her beads or go to mass, if that be yer meanin'." Kate paused and held up one of the dresses, turning it one way then another. "Mistress used to go to the Church of Ireland regular with yer granfar, but still she was sympathetic to the Papist cause. Says the hateful penal laws come straight from the devil, she does."

"I thought the penal laws had been abolished."

"'Tis so," Kate acknowledged. "But change is slow, and was even slower in yer mam's day. 'Twasn't that yer granfar was a harsh man, but he was quick to join the Protestant Peep O'Day boys should there be a Papist uprising. He didn't hold with Papists gaining rights by force."

Gwyneth looked at Kate with interest. She hadn't expected a servant to be so well versed in Irish politics and told her so.

"How could I not," Kate asked. "What with Master and Mistress always talkin' of such? Yer mam told me how she felt too." A pleased expression crossed the servant's freckled face. "At times yer mam and me was almost like sisters. She even taught me to read and write." Kate's shoulders lifted. "Few Papist women can read and sign their name."

"I didn't know," Gwyneth said, looking up from the outdated pink dress she held. Her respect for Kate had increased, along with liking for her mother.

"I thought ye didn't. 'Tis one of the reasons I mean to tell ye the truth about Deirdre. 'Tisn't right that ye think ill of yer own mam, though I thought such would be the case when yer da forbade me to speak of her. Then when he sent me away . . ." Kate pulled Gwyneth into her plump arms. "'Tis a dream come true to see ye again."

Gwyneth returned the hug. "Just as it is for me."

Hearing Biddy on the stairs, they ceased to speak of Deirdre until the girl left to iron the blue dress Gwyneth had selected to wear that evening.

After Biddy left, Kate poured hot water into the copper tub and arranged a wooden screen around it for privacy. While Gwyneth undressed and stepped into the warm water, Kate sorted through the clothes on the bed.

The warm water felt heavenly, but Gwyneth's main desire was to hear about Deirdre. "Tell me more about Mother," she prompted from behind the screen.

"There's much I be wantin' to tell ye . . . how she loved to sing and play the harp. And horses. I doubt any besides yer gran could ride a horse like Deirdre. Talk o' the Blackwater she was, takin' a fence like 'twas no more than a bucket. Her high spirits and beauty captured many a young man's heart."

Smiling, Gwyneth pictured her mother taking a hedgerow, her face alight with happiness. *I am like her. Part of her lives in me.*

"'Twas ridin' horses and her high spirits that caused the trouble," Kate went on. "'Stead of stayin' close to Shannonderry, she took to ridin' afar. On one of her rides, Deirdre met young Rory Flanagan."

"Rory?" Gwyneth had expected to hear Maurice Beddows.

"Aye . . . and many's the day I wished it never happened. Bad news goes hand in hand with Rory and his brother Connor. If they not be burnin' the gentry's ricks of straw, they be houghin' their cattle. Angry at Catholic repression, they took to destroyin' and thievin'."

Kate paused to shake out a gown, tsking in disapproval of the Flanagans. "'Twas Rory's handsome face that caught yer mam's eye. Black Irish he was, with flashin' eyes and a smile that could get him most anythin'. 'Tween them and his glib tongue, Deirdre soon thought herself in love."

Learning that her mother had fallen in love with a thief left Gwyneth feeling empty. She absently worked the soap into a lather. "Did my grandparents find out about Rory?" she asked after a minute.

"Aye, and when they did, ye could hear Master shoutin' all the way out to stable . . . forbiddin' Deirdre to see Rory and sayin' no possible good could come of it. 'Course, Deirdre knew that, for the Flanagans was but poor croppies with barely enough coppers to rub together."

Sitting in the tiny copper tub, Gwyneth's heart twisted with pity.

"Yer mam cried for hours, but bein' headstrong, she managed to slip away and meet Rory again. When yer grandfar found out, I thought 'twould be the death of her. Livid he was . . . and so angry he had Rory and Connor carted off to Mallow and thrown into prison."

"Just because Rory loved his daughter?" Gwyneth's voice was indignant.

"'Twas more'n that. On one of their raids, Rory stole a pistol. 'Twas all the evidence the constable needed. In a week, Rory and Connor be sent to Cork and impressed into the English Navy."

Gwyneth knew the Crown used such means to man warships. Although she had no liking for Rory, a shudder ran down her spine. "How awful."

"Aye . . . awful for yer mam too. I thought her heart would break. Worse, she turned bitter against Master and Mistress. Terrible bickerin' went on, and no one spoke a civil word." Kate sighed and fell silent.

Gwyneth stared down at the now-tepid water. Although Cormac had warned her about the quarrel, hearing it firsthand cut at her heart and made her want to cry. Shivering, she stood up and asked for a towel.

Kate looped the towel over the screen. "Warm from the fire, it be."

Chilled by emotion and the cooling water, Gwyneth gratefully wrapped the warm towel around her. "How did my mother and father meet?"

"Here at Shannonderry. Mr. Beddows came on a horse-buying trip. Since he made no secret of dislikin' the Irish, no one expected him to show interest in Deirdre." Kate hung another towel over the screen for Gwyneth to dry her hair. "Beauty can make a man forget much. Though I had no likin' for Mr. Beddows, I saw straight away he had a steadyin' way with Deirdre. Master and Mistress saw it too, but neither wanted her to marry him. They sometimes differed about religion, but they both disliked the English."

Kate paused and rummaged among the clothes for a chemise and underclothes. "Here, put these on," she said as if Gwyneth were still ten years old.

With her mind solely on the story, Gwyneth did as she was told, hearing how Maurice Beddows had ridden to Cork to obtain a special license to marry.

"When he came back a fortnight later, yer mam be so pleased to see him she needed little persuadin' to elope."

Gwyneth looked around the corner of the screen at Kate. "And you went with her?"

"I did." Kate's plain face broke into a smile. "Two happier people I never seen than they was at Hawarden. 'Twas as if yer mam left all her bitterness behind her and returned to bein' her sweet self again. Mr. Beddows was happy too. Deirdre knew just how to please him."

When Gwyneth stepped from behind the screen, Kate handed her a lace-trimmed robe. Like the undergarments, the faint smell of lavender lingered in its folds. Kate had set a chair close to the fire so Gwyneth could finish drying her hair. Leaning close to the flames to dry her short hair, she continued to think of her mother. "If they were happy, why did my father think Mother betrayed him?"

Kate clicked her tongue and grimaced. "'Twas Rory Flanagan again. Somehow he and Connor managed to jump ship. When they learned Deirdre was married and livin' in Yorkshire, they followed her there."

Unease gripped Gwyneth's middle. Had Deirdre truly betrayed her father?

"Rory still cared for yer mam and hoped she felt the same. When she told him she loved Mr. Beddows and carried his child, Rory and Connor begged her to help them get to America. With them being fugitives . . . Irish fugitives at that . . . what they asked of yer mam be terrible dangerous. They be near starvin', too, and needed money for passage on a ship."

Kate sighed and began to work her fingers through Gwyneth's damp curls. "'Twas no easy task to smuggle food to them. Findin' money was even harder since Deirdre had none of her own. As ye well know, Mr. Beddows was tight with the purse strings. She ended up giving Rory the pearl necklace she wore on the day she ran away from Shannonderry."

The crackle of the peat fire settled into the silence that followed. Aware of her father's temper, Gwyneth shrank from hearing the rest of the story. "Did . . . did Rory and Connor get safely away?" she asked after a long moment.

"Aye, all would have gone well if it weren't for Parson Cranston."

Gwyneth looked up. "What did the parson have to do with it?"

"Everything, since he saw Deirdre and Rory together. 'Twas a raging storm he set loose, though he waited some months afore he told yer da." Kate picked up a comb and worked at a snarl. "Even now, I mislike rememberin'. I was in the next room, yet even with the door closed, I could hear him rage. Deirdre was already feelin' poorly, and when she got up to try to explain, she fell."

Deirdre's fear and pain seemed to reach across the years to sting Gwyneth's eyes with tears and lay like a heavy weight across her shoulders.

Kate's quavering voice slipped into the pain. "'Twas then ye was born and yer mam died."

Stillness, dark and heavy as a winter cloak, draped itself around the two women. Gwyneth's throat ached, and tears ran in a trail down her cheeks. Aware that Kate cried too, Gwyneth rose and pulled her into her arms. Gwyneth's relief in knowing Deirdre hadn't betrayed her father was as great as Kate's relief in finally being able to speak the truth.

"Thank you, Kate," Gwyneth whispered. "Ever since Father told me that she betrayed him, I've felt like I carried a terrible sickness inside of me." She gave Kate a hug. "Thank you."

"Aye." Pulling away, Kate brushed Gwyneth's tears with her fingers. "'Tis just as it used to be . . . the two of us cryin' together. I missed yer mam somethin' terrible, but even worse was watchin' yer father. He couldn't let go of thinkin' he'd been betrayed."

"Didn't you tell him?" Gwyneth asked.

"I tried. Time and time I tried, but Mr. Beddows wouldn't listen . . . said bein' Papist my tongue couldn't be trusted."

Kate took Gwyneth's hands in hers. "Yer da be wrong about yer mam betrayin' him, but he was right when he said she was beautiful . . . beautiful, and all ye could wish for as yer mother."

* * *

AFTER TELLING KATE HOW SHE'D run away from Hawarden, Gwyneth donned her mother's blue gown.

"Will I do?" Gwyneth asked as Kate finished threading a blue ribbon through her short curls.

Kate's answer was to lead her to the mirror. Although she didn't approve of short hair, Kate was more than pleased by her charge's looks. "What do ye think?"

It was Gwyneth's first opportunity to view herself since Cormac had cut her hair. She studied her reflection, noting how her eyes seemed larger and her nose more distinctive without the profusion of hair. "I was afraid I might look like a boy," she said at last.

"'Tis little chance of that." Kate chuckled. "I expect ol' Flynn will have to take out his pike to keep all the young men away." She adjusted the mirror so Gwyneth could better see the gown. The puffed fichu surrounding the low décolletage bespoke her womanly charms while the tight-fitting waist and flowing full skirt enhanced her willowy frame.

Gwyneth's inspection of her appearance was interrupted by Biddy's excited entrance, her voice breathless as she spoke. "'Ye best hurry. Mistress Donahue be waitin'." The maid's hand flew to her mouth when Gwyneth turned from the mirror. "Ye look like . . ."

"Hush," Kate scolded. "'Tis not your place to tell. 'Tis Mistress Donahue's."

"Tell what?" Gwyneth asked.

"Ye'll be findin' out soon enough. I'm certain 'tis what yer gran plans."

Biddy stared and sketched a cross with her hand. Then, giving a hasty curtsy, she led the way down the narrow stairs.

Biddy's startled reaction had piqued Gwyneth's curiosity. Who did she resemble? And why must she wait to learn the answer from her grandmother?

"Here she be," Biddy announced. Her voice squeaked with excitement.

Still dressed in the black gown and amethyst earrings, Moira studied her granddaughter. "I was right," she said. "Your resemblance to her is uncanny."

"Who?"

"You'll see soon enough." Instructing Biddy to bring the stand of candles from the dining table, she slowly led the way down the hall.

Biddy's green eyes danced with excitement, though the glance she gave Gwyneth held awe. "This way to the great hall," she whispered.

Biddy's excitement was contagious. Not knowing what to think, Gwyneth followed the maid and Moira into the adjoining room.

Age and the past settled around her, the high-timbered ceiling and worn stone floor swirling like fragments from a half-forgotten dream. Twilight pouring through the two end windows allowed Gwyneth to see a large refractory table with crouching lions carved into its massive legs. When Biddy lit stands of candles on either side of the stone fireplace, Gwyneth was able to examine the room more closely.

A magnificent set of antlers hung as a trophy on one of the rough-hewn walls, while a sword and a shield carved with the emblem of a hawk leaned in readiness by the door. For a moment, Gwyneth envisioned one of her male O'Brien ancestors conversing with his wife on the wooden settee by the fire.

Before Gwyneth could look at the room more closely, Moira led her to a portrait hanging between two windows. "Bring the candles closer," she told Biddy.

Gwyneth drew in her breath when she saw a face almost identical to her own. Vivid blue eyes and delicate features smiled down from the painting, but it was the mass of platinum hair that held her gaze. "Who . . . who is she?"

"Her name was Gwyneth . . . Gwyneth O'Brien," Moira answered. A shiver of superstition ran up Moira's frail spine. Although she'd seen the resemblance between her granddaughter and the other Gwyneth as soon as the girl stepped through the sitting room door, she hadn't realized how alike they were until she saw their faces side by side.

Striving to compose herself, Moira went on. "She lived at Shannonderry during the Desmond uprising. While the men of her family were away fighting, she held off a troop of the queen's soldiers. When the officer in charge discovered that he'd been bested by a woman and a handful of servants, he was so impressed that he returned with reinforcements and set a guard around the castle to protect it from further attack. Afterward, he petitioned the queen on Gwyneth's behalf and saved Shannonderry from being planted with English."

A thrill ran along the flesh of Gwyneth's arms. "What a brave woman."

"One with brains and spirit too. After her father and brothers fled to France with the Desmonds, the queen decreed that neither he nor his male heirs could ever inherit Shannonderry." Moira's face turned cynical. "Although Elizabeth might admire and reward another for courage, she knew our Gwyneth would someday have to marry. Since much of Munster was now planted with English, the queen assumed Gwyneth would have to marry an Englishman."

Moira paused and smiled up at the portrait. "She failed to reckon with Gwyneth's spirit. Rather than ally herself with the enemy, Gwyneth married a distant O'Brien cousin from up north to ensure that she and her children would still bear the O'Brien name."

"Gwyneth . . . the white and blessed one," Gwyneth whispered. The half-forgotten phrase came to her from across the years—words spoken by Kate and now reinforced by the tale told by her grandmother.

"Yes." Moira clasped her hands together to keep them from trembling. Taking a steadying breath, she spoke. "There is a family story . . . a legend . . . that another Gwyneth with pale skin and light hair will again save Shannonderry."

Gwyneth's pulse quickened. "Me?" she wanted to ask. She pushed the thought away, too awestruck to think clearly. "Do . . . you believe the legend?"

Moira shrugged, but as she gazed into Gwyneth's aqua eyes, a feeling of calm settled over her. O'Brien—not English—eyes met and held hers. "I don't know," she answered, "but I begin to think someone more knowing than I . . . perhaps even God Himself . . . prompted me to send for you."

* * *

THE EXCITEMENT OF THE DAY coupled with the telling of the legend had sapped Moira's meager strength. After only a few bites of the meal Kate had prepared for them, she set down her fork and called to Biddy.

"Tell Kate I need her to help me to my room." Her wrinkled hand played with the ruff of lace at her neck. Weariness edged her voice when she spoke to Gwyneth. "I'm sorry to have to leave you. Tomorrow we shall talk more."

"I'd like that." Gwyneth rose and came around the table covered by an age-yellowed cloth and set with heavy silver and patterned china. "Can I help you, Grandmother?" The name slid awkwardly from her lips. Although she was glad to be at Shannonderry, she was still uncertain how she and the old woman would get on.

Moira waved her away. "Kate knows just how to do it."

And she did, bustling from the kitchen to help Moira from her chair with movements that spoke of years of practice. "Ye've done too much," Kate scolded. "And what have ye done with yer cane?"

Moira's gray head lifted. "I do not need a cane." She shot a proud look at Gwyneth, hoping she wouldn't notice how heavily she leaned on Kate's arm as they slowly left the room.

Disappointed, Gwyneth returned to her chair and picked at her food. Tiredness and emotion had taken her appetite, and only the knowledge that Kate and Biddy had expended extra effort in preparing the food kept her at the table.

Awe seemed to have stilled Biddy's tongue. Gwyneth was glad for the quiet as she mulled over all she had seen and heard. In her mind, she pictured a long-ago time and the other Gwyneth holding off the queen's soldiers with her loyal servants. How much of the tale was fact and how much fantasy? Remembering how the Irish loved a good story, she shook her head. Didn't they believe in leprechauns and fairies? And yet . . .

When Gwyneth felt that she had eaten enough to please Kate and Biddy, she took the stand of candles from the table and made her way back to the great hall. Shadows played with the flickering light as she stood before the portrait. Her ancestor's pale features and shining hair held her mesmerized. Except for the old-fashioned style of hair and gown, she could be looking at herself. Was the legend true?

The question followed her up the narrow stairs and into her bedroom. Shivering, she sought the warmth of the fire to soothe her jumbled thoughts and nerves. How strange. The entire evening had been strange.

After she'd warmed herself, Gwyneth went to the mirror. Instead of judging her pearly hair with the accustomed prejudice, she admired its shimmer in the candlelight. The memory of her stepmother's oft-repeated words came to mind. *Such a strange color . . . not at all the thing, and your skin is as pasty as milk.* Over time Gwyneth had come to believe Sylvia. Not tonight. Tonight she felt pride and happiness.

The sound of Kate's voice carried into the room. "There ye be." She paused to catch her breath. "What did ye think on seein' the other Gwyneth?"

Gwyneth smiled. "It was a little unnerving."

"Aye," Kate agreed. "As soon as I saw ye this morn, I went to take another look. Did Mistress tell ye the legend?"

"Yes." Her eyes held Kate's. "Does my grandmother truly believe it?"

"Aye . . . leastwise now that she's seen ye."

"I'm English. I could never oppose the Crown."

"Who's askin' ye to? Our troubles don't always come from England, ye know. Perhaps yer comin' is to keep Shannonderry from being sold." Kate paused and lowered her voice. "'Tis sad times we've fallen on, Miss Gwyneth. It nearly breaks my heart to see how run down things be . . . never enough money or hands to do the work. Afore yer mam left, there was four to keep things shining and clean . . . and as many to see to the grounds and the stable. Now . . ." She shook her head. "'Tis sad. If ye could find a way to make Shannonderry prosper, the legend would prove true."

"What do I know about managing an estate?"

"Ye can learn from yer gran. 'Twould be wonderful if ye could put Shannonderry back to rights."

Gwyneth put her arms around her former nurse. "Dear Kate. What a lot you want me to do. Tonight, however, I'm too tired to think I can do anything."

"Tonight, perhaps . . . but come tomorrow, if ye be like yer mam, ye'll be thinkin' otherwise." Kate returned her hug. "I'll say an extra prayer for ye, and if I be wrong . . ." She pulled away and looked into Gwyneth's eyes. "No matter what happens, yer comin' be for a purpose."

"Why do you say that?"

"To help the Mistress get past her bitterness. She thinks Deirdre turned her back on Ireland by runnin' away to England. 'Twas naught I could do to change her mind since she forbade me to speak of it. But now . . ." A satisfied smile crossed Kate's freckled face. "Now, just by lookin' at ye, she knows her daughter's dyin' thoughts and words be of her home."

8

THE RAUCOUS CRIES OF ROOKS nesting in the oak trees near the castle awakened Gwyneth shortly after dawn. Her first thought was of Toryn. How had he settled in?

Wanting to reach the stable before Flynn and his young grandson attempted to enter Toryn's stall, Gwyneth quickly donned her rumpled riding habit and hurried down the stairs. In her haste, she forgot about the wolfhounds. When she rounded the corner of the castle, two of the dogs bounded out from the stable. Their growls and laid-back ears made her want to flee, but good sense bade her to stop. Heart pounding, she folded her arms across her waist. *What if they attack? Dear heaven, where's Cluny?*

Cluny hurried out of the stable closely followed by Mr. D'Arcy. "They'll not hurt ye."

"Are . . . are you sure?" Although she was surprised to see Mr. D'Arcy, her main concern was on the hounds because their heads came well past her waist.

"Put out yer hand," Cluny called.

Gathering courage, Gwyneth did so. One of the dogs immediately licked it.

"See," the boy chortled, "now had I set them on ye 'stead of tellin' them ye be a friend, 'twould be another story."

Reassured, Gwyneth extended her other hand, and the second dog sniffed and licked it. Gwyneth looked at the dogs with new eyes, their bristly faces reminding her of bearded old men. As large as ponies, they looked sturdy enough for a child to ride. "Have you ever ridden one?" she asked Cluny.

"Aye . . . leastwise I used to when I be small. Granfar says wolfhounds was at Shannonderry since afore his granfar's time."

"They're an ancient breed and excellent hunters," Cormac put in.

"I don't doubt it." The Irishman's appraising glance her way made Gwyneth wish she'd paid more attention to her appearance.

"In ancient times, they accompanied clan chieftains in battle, but they were mostly used to guard against wolves," Cormac went on. "They can bring down a stag as easily as a wolf, though the wolves are all gone now and the stags grow scarce. Today we use them to guard our homes. Your grandmother has four of the hounds, and I've a pair at my stable."

"Guard?" Gwyneth laughed as one of the dogs affectionately nuzzled her. "They're so gentle."

"When they're with friends," Cormac agreed. "But not all are friends. In troubled times, peasants sometimes rise up to protest their treatment. When they do, no one is safe . . . not even the O'Briens. With the dogs, Clonglas and Shannonderry cattle aren't mutilated, but we don't forget we're Protestant and that hatred between Papists and Protestants runs deep."

Realizing he'd said too much, Cormac changed the subject. "Cluny, why don't you call in the other dogs so they're familiar with Miss Beddows?"

The boy put two fingers to his lips and whistled, his pride in being able to call and control the dogs obvious.

"Are you the only one who can call them in?" Gwyneth asked.

"Granfar can. 'Twas him that trained the dogs and taught me how to call them. Granfar's been trainin' and callin' hounds since he was a boy."

"Do they always come when you whistle?"

Cluny nodded. "We don't keep dogs at Shannonderry what don't obey."

Just then another dog came into view. His loping gait as he bounded from the oak trees made Gwyneth pause in admiration. "No wonder you're no longer plagued with wolves."

"That be Fearghal," Cluny said. "He be the oldest and the leader."

A minute later, Gwyneth saw the fourth wolfhound. Gwyneth held out a hand to each of the dogs before Cluny sent them back to patrol Shannonderry. Only then did she turn her full attention on Cormac. "What brings you here, Mr. D'Arcy?"

"I came to check on your stallion."

His answer surprised her. "How is he?"

"He's settling in, but he'll bear watching." Noticing that Cluny listened, Cormac frowned. "Didn't your grandfather tell you to fetch water for the horses?"

The boy grimaced, obviously not wanting to leave.

"Then see to it." Cormac took Gwyneth's arm and led her toward the stable.

Aware of his touch, she gave Cormac a quick look. His attire in buckskin breeches and white linen shirt did nothing to diminish his attractiveness.

"You mustn't mind the boy," Cormac said, "though he'll keep you talking all day if you let him . . . Flynn, too, if you gain his good graces. You'll have to go slow with the old man, though. He considers the stable his private domain." A rueful smile lit his chiseled features. "He's let me know what he thinks of interference . . . which is good, except that he can no longer keep the stable clean."

Gwyneth looked up at the stone building; its heavy doors and slatted loft windows exuded the same sense of strength as the castle. "Doesn't Cluny help?"

"Yes, but he has a hundred other things to do and is kept running from dawn to dark." Cormac experienced sudden pity for the young woman. "You won't find things easy here, Miss Beddows. There's much to be done, and old Flynn is as proud and stubborn as your grandmother."

Cormac's pitying glance stung Gwyneth's pride. She lifted her head, wishing he didn't affect her so. "I'm not afraid of a little work. I often helped Father in the stable."

Reaching the stable door, Cormac asked, "Would you like me to introduce you to Flynn?"

Gwyneth shook her head. "I must face Flynn on my own."

Cormac frowned. Like Moira, she had spirit. "That being the case, I'll leave you. But remember . . . if you ever need me, you have only to send word."

"Thank you." Giving him a quick smile, Gwyneth entered the stable. The odor that assailed her nostrils was overwhelming. Although the outside of the stable exuded strength, the inside bespoke neglect.

"If 'tis yer stallion yer lookin' for, he be in the end stall . . . as far away from the mares as we could get him," a quivery voice informed her.

As Gwyneth's eyes adjusted to the stable's dimness, she saw the slight figure of an old man leaning on a pitchfork. "You must be Flynn."

The old man nodded and stepped closer. "And ye be Miss Deirdre's daughter." He spoke with a slight wheeze, his voice cold.

Flynn's gray hair and beard reminded Gwyneth of the dogs. Unlike the wolfhounds, though, he showed no friendliness. Instead, his hawklike features and slate gray eyes held only dislike. "Ye don't look like yer mam," he went on. "The Englishman, neither, for which ye can be glad. We at Shannonderry have no likin' for the English."

"So Mr. D'Arcy informed me."

"Mr. D'Arcy be wise, though he'd do better to keep his nose out of Shannonderry's affairs." The wheeze punctuated his words.

Instead of replying, Gwyneth's eyes traveled around the stable, taking in the clutter of tackle and the haphazard sprawl of oat sacks. "Perhaps Mr. D'Arcy believes there is room for improvement."

Flynn's light-lashed eyes narrowed. "'Tis nothin' wrong with my stable . . . and I'll thank ye to hold yer tongue if ye came to criticize."

"I came to see my stallion."

At the mention of Toryn, Flynn forgot his anger. "Aye . . . the stallion. Now he be somethin' none can criticize . . . except for his temper. I'll take ye to him."

Flynn led her to an isolated stall near the back of the stable. She heard Toryn's restless movement before she reached his stall. When she unfastened the door, she saw that two checkreins prevented him from rearing. "Easy, boy."

Hearing her voice, the stallion quieted.

"A lovely beast," Flynn proclaimed in an awe-filled voice. "'Tis the finest my eyes have seen in all my years at Shannonderry."

Flynn's voice made Toryn jerk and roll his eyes.

Gwyneth grasped the stallion's halter. "It's me, Toryn." The horse flinched when her hand touched his head, but as her soothing voice went on, he allowed her to stroke his neck, his taut muscles slowly relaxing under the familiar touch.

"Can you bring me a brush?" Gwyneth asked, unfastening the checkreins. "Toryn enjoys a good brushing."

"Toryn? Did I hear ye right?"

"Toryn is his name."

Old Flynn looked at her with suspicion. "'Tis Irish and means—"

"Chieftain," Gwyneth finished for him. "That's why I chose it."

Flynn gave a derisive snort as he went to find the brush.

Toryn responded to the brushing with his usual pleasure, his skin rippling in response to the brush as Gwyneth moved it over his body. Most of the lime had washed or worn away, but there were still areas that needed her attention. Humming, she concentrated on the patches of white mottling his black coat.

"A lovely beast," Flynn repeated. "Fine enough to be a Shannonderry stallion."

"He was bred in England," Gwyneth reminded him.

"As ye be, more's the pity. I never thought to see the day we'd harbor English at Shannonderry."

Gwyneth's resolve to make friends with Flynn was overridden by anger. "What's wrong with being English?" she demanded.

"What's wrong?" Flynn's voice came in an exasperated wheeze. "Didn't they teach ye what ye've been doin' in Ireland all these years . . . all the plunderin' and rape? Ye've bled us dry, that's what ye've done!"

"That's your side of the story."

"'Tis the only side if ye intend to live at Shannonderry."

"We'll see about that," she retorted, wanting to throw the brush at the old man.

Seeming to sense her mood, Flynn walked away.

It was well he did, as anger set her to brush Toryn's coat with new vigor. Not only did the stable need changing, the old man needed to learn respect. It wasn't until Toryn's coat was black and shining again that she stepped back to admire him. The sight of the horse's cropped mane and tail spoiled her pleasure. "I'm sorry, Toryn." She laid her head on his neck and patted him before she put him back into his stall.

As she closed the stall door, she heard Kate call to her.

"In here, Kate."

Kate's relief was apparent. "Biddy and me be lookin' everywhere for ye. Breakfast's ready and Mistress be askin' for ye." She paused and studied Gwyneth's crumpled riding habit. "Ye can't be meetin' yer grandmother lookin' like that."

"I needed to check on my stallion." Remembering how tired her grandmother had looked, she added, "Is Grandmother feeling better?"

"She still be tired, though such don't stop her from wantin' to see ye."

Hurrying to her room, Gwyneth changed into another of her mother's gowns. After she ate breakfast, she knocked on the sitting-room door.

The old woman waited in one of the dark, high-back chairs. The amethysts and black dress had been exchanged for a gray gown, and a white shawl was wrapped snuggly around her narrow shoulders.

"How are you feeling?" Gwyneth asked.

Taken aback by the sight of Gwyneth in Deirdre's gown, Moira couldn't answer. Like a breath from the past, it was Deirdre who stepped through the door, dark hair framing an excited face. The pink sarcenet gown had set off Deirdre's willowy frame just as it did Gwyneth's. For a moment, she felt the soft brush of Deirdre's lips on her cheek, heard her lilting voice as she wished her good morning. Loss and pleasure fought for position. *Deirdre*. It wasn't Deirdre who curtsied but a stranger with short platinum curls and an uncertain expression on her face.

Brought back to the present, Moira sighed. "Well enough, I suppose . . . though Kate will tell you otherwise." Striving for normalcy, she indicated that Gwyneth take a chair and said the first thing that entered her mind. "I believe short hair becomes you."

"Thank you." Gwyneth self-consciously touched her cap of curls. "Mr. D'Arcy says short hair is the fashion in London."

"So he told me." Mr. D'Arcy had told her that and a great deal more about Gwyneth. The description of her unfortunate circumstances at Hawarden had tugged at Moira's heart. "He also told me you ran away so you wouldn't have to marry someone you did not like."

"If you knew James Steane, you'd understand. He's a terrible dolt, but that's not the only reason I came to Shannonderry. Kate frequently told me about Ireland, and I often pretended that I lived here."

"Did you now?" Brought fully back to the present, Moira smiled. "Now that you're here, I hope you'll enjoy Shannonderry just as your mother did." A picture of Deirdre running in to say she and Kate had found a fairy ring filled her mind. It was a memory Moira had kept locked away for more than twenty years. The key had been inserted with the coming of this fair young woman who looked at her with Deirdre's eyes.

"There's much for you to learn," Moira said after a moment. "My health doesn't permit me to care for Shannonderry as I should, but now that you are here . . ." Her deep-set eyes held Gwyneth's in a steady gaze. Prudence cautioned her to go slowly while the scepter of her death bade her hurry. *Help me to be patient, God.* She must be patient lest her enthusiasm for Shannonderry push Gwyneth away.

"We will talk of duty another day. This morning I wish to learn more about you . . . your stallion too. Mr. D'Arcy tells me you own a fine stallion."

Since Gwyneth would sooner talk about Toryn than herself, she launched into a description with great enthusiasm, telling Moira about The Demon and how she'd begged her father to let her have the colt.

Moira's attention was completely taken as Gwyneth explained about his training and phenomenal speed. The old woman's brows lifted when she heard the stallion's name and learned of his bad temper.

"Except for Father's trainer and me . . . and now Mr. D'Arcy, no one can ride him." Gwyneth leaned forward. "Did you know Mr. D'Arcy has the touch?"

Moira nodded. "You'll find when you know him better that Mr. D'Arcy is a man of many talents. That's why I entrusted him to find you."

Gwyneth waited, hoping her grandmother would say more about Mr. D'Arcy. When Moira failed to do so, Gwyneth went on to describe the races Toryn had won. Her regret that it was Peter, not she, who rode the horse in the races was evident. "Father only allowed me to ride him at the hunt," she said. "But sometimes—"

She stopped, thinking it unwise to tell Moira about riding Toryn astride. But the need to share the excitement of being atop the great stallion when he gave his best overrode her caution. "I hope you won't think less of me if I tell you that sometimes I wore breeches and rode him astride. No one besides Peter and his son knew, and it wasn't very often . . . but, oh, Grandmother, if you could know how it was . . . his great speed and to feel like you are flying . . ."

"It's wonderful, isn't it?" Moira asked with a smile.

"It's like—" Gwyneth stopped and looked at her grandmother in astonishment. "You mean you've ridden a horse astride?"

"Many times . . . your mother too, though like you, we kept it secret."

Gwyneth laughed and her spirit lifted even more when Moira joined her. "Mr. D'Arcy said you were an accomplished rider, but I never imagined—"

"Nor did I imagine it about you."

Eyes meeting and smiles broadening, it was a moment Moira knew she would long remember. That it was with the granddaughter she'd thought she didn't want to see made it all the more astounding. With astonishing clarity, the old woman sensed that she could well come to like this young woman . . . perhaps even love her.

9

The next day Moira again sent for Gwyneth. Remembering their last conversation, Gwyneth entered the sitting room with less trepidation. Instead of sitting, the old woman stood at the window.

Gwyneth curtsied. "Good morning, Grandmother. Biddy said you wished to see me."

"I do. Since the sun is shining, I thought it a good day to show you around the estate. Though Shannonderry is not as large as it once was, there is still much for you to see." Today, instead of experiencing a sense of loss when she saw Gwyneth in Deirdre's pink gown, she took satisfaction in the direct manner with which her granddaughter met and held her gaze.

"I'd like that. Yesterday Kate showed me more of the castle, but other than the stable, I've seen nothing of the estate."

Moira grimaced at the mention of the stable. Although she hadn't ventured inside it for more than two years, she was aware of Flynn's and Cluny's limitations. Like most things at Shannonderry, the stable was not as it should be.

"Since I'm no longer able to ride horseback, I asked Cluny to ready the cart." She fixed Gwyneth with an appraising eye. "It's not as comfortable as the carriage, but it's open sides will allow you to better see Shannonderry . . . that is if you're not averse to riding in the cart."

"Not at all."

"We can also talk," Moira explained. "There's much I want to tell you."

Gwyneth learned how much Moira had to say after she joined her in the cart. Cluny, perched atop the front seat, gave Gwyneth a grin as bright as the morning sun.

Moira directed Cluny to drive the cart around Shannonderry's outer perimeter. "You'll gain a better feel for the land if you first see where Shannonderry is located." If the old woman found the old cart demeaning, she gave no sign. Her proud bearing reminded Gwyneth of a queen setting out to inspect her domain.

Gwyneth's delight in what she saw made her forget about the discomfort of the cart. Shannonderry was situated in a cove surrounded on three sides by gentle hills, with the west side lying open and rolling like a green sea until it reached the distant Kerry Mountains.

"Some say that Shannonderry gained its name from this tree," Moira said as the cart passed beneath the spreading branches of a giant oak. "Did you know Shannonderry means 'old oak' and that there have been oak trees and wolfhounds at Shannonderry for as long as there has been a castle?" Moira gave a little smile. "Of course, I know this tree couldn't possibly have lived so long, but the peasants like the tale. Some come here to pray while others tie bits of ribbon to the branches, hoping it will bring them good luck." Her expression turned wistful. "Your mother and Kate spent many hours playing under its branches when they were small."

Gwyneth looked at the tree with new eyes. Was it here her mother and Kate had looked for fairy rings?

They followed the course of the Awbeg River that morning, riding through deep woods and open meadows, past stretches of marshland where herons skimmed the rushes and the pungent smell of water peppermint filled the air. As they crossed a humped stone bridge where willow trees hung low over the water, Gwyneth caught sight of an ancient keep, its crumbling tower silhouetted against the sky.

"At one time this was all Desmond country," Moira said. "Although their reign was never easy, the remains of their castles and forts still dot the land."

"How did the O'Briens come to own Shannonderry?" Gwyneth asked.

Gwyneth's interest pleased Moira. "One of your ancestors won it on a wager . . . an O'Brien hawk against a Desmond falcon. The hawk won, and Shannonderry was part of the stakes. Our ancestor was so pleased with the bird's performance that he made the hawk his crest. You can see it painted on old shields, stamped on the silver, and engraved over the west entrance."

"It couldn't have been easy for one O'Brien to live among so many Desmonds."

"No doubt you're right. They eventually became allies. I told you how we joined the Desmonds in their rebellion against the crown and how the other Gwyneth's courage saved Shannonderry from being planted by the English."

"Is it true the O'Briens were once Catholic?"

"Catholic like all the great families of Ireland," Moira replied. "When the O'Briens were faced with losing Shannonderry, they chose to give up the old religion. It was a common practice at the time . . . turning Protestant to keep one's land. Those who didn't were either brutally butchered or driven into Connaught, a place so bleak the English didn't want it."

"Mr. D'Arcy told me some of what happened. Under the circumstances, I can understand why they converted to Protestantism."

"Yes." As Moira spoke, her expression turned pensive. "Even so, I admire those who remained faithful to their religion. Thousands of Catholics sacrificed their lives and lands for their faith."

"And their offspring still suffer."

"Who told you that?"

"No one, but since Mother was Irish, I read as much as I could about Ireland."

On impulse Moira directed Cluny to take the cart down a narrow track. "Since you've read of the plight of the Irish poor, it would be well for you to see them firsthand."

Moira soon regretted her impulse. The track was so rutted and filled with holes that conversation became impossible. She and Gwyneth had to cling to the narrow seat to maintain their balance, and low branches and thick undergrowth required that they duck or risk being scraped. Moira's concern increased when she saw two peasants walking ahead of them, one shuffling and old, the other taller and broad shouldered. Neither made an effort to step aside.

"Go carefully, Cluny," Moira instructed.

The boy nodded, but his knuckles whitened as they gripped the reins.

Fear flicked through Gwyneth's middle, making her conscious of their vulnerability. Neither she nor Cluny, and most certainly not her grandmother, could defend themselves against the men if they tried to attack.

They had almost overtaken the pair before they finally stepped aside. Deep lines etched the older man's grizzled face, and his shoulders drooped in despair. When they drew abreast, he touched his hand to his forelock. Not so with the younger. His stance was defiant, and his lean, freckled face smoldered with hatred.

The impact of his angry gaze made Gwyneth flinch. "Why does he hate us?" she asked when they were past. Before Moira could answer, a rock struck the cart, the impact so jarring that for a second Gwyneth thought she'd been struck. Her heart hammering, she looked back to see the young man's fist raised in defiance.

"Stop the cart!" Moira commanded, her voice surprisingly firm.

Cluny complied, though his eyes were large and frightened.

Turning in the cart, Moira shook a crooked finger at the younger man. "You, Sean O'Leary . . . or is it Colin? Your sainted mother would turn over in her grave if she saw you now . . . your old gran too . . . throwing rocks at women." She turned her indignation on the old man. "Shame on you for letting your son act in such a way. Did I not send for the doctor and pay his fee when your Mary was so sick . . . and you one of Emmett Weston's tenants, not mine"

There was a moment of startled silence before Sean spoke, his freckled face mottled with anger. "'Tis yer husband should be turnin' in his grave or burnin' in hell for settin' the constable on me cousins Rory and Connor. Did himself not fail to lift so much as a finger to keep me cousins from being pressed into the navy . . . and all 'cause Rory admired yer daughter?"

Pain flickered across Moira's face and her thin lips trembled. "'Tis true," she sighed, "and something my husband regretted the rest of his days. Take care that your anger doesn't lead you on a similar path of regret."

With that, Moira touched Cluny on the shoulder, telling him to drive toward the cottages of Shannonderry tenants. The boy responded by urging the donkey forward.

"Ye take care bringin' more English to Eire," Sean called. "Herself ain't welcome here."

Silence settled over the cart's occupants as it bumped along the rutted lane.

"Why do they hate me?" Gwyneth finally asked. "Flynn first . . . and now the O'Learys?"

"'Tisn't you, child, but the idea of anyone English. That will change when they come to know you."

Doubts filled Gwyneth's mind as she remembered Sean's cold blue eyes. Before she could say more, they came to a filthy hovel. The stench from human and animal refuse piled near the door made Gwyneth's hand fly to her nose, but it was the gaunt faces of ragged children that tore at her heart. She remembered the basket of food Cluny had put in the cart—food Moira said was meant for Shannonderry's tenants. Was similar poverty what she would find there as well?

Relief washed over her when Moira finally indicated that they were back on Shannonderry land. The contrast between what they had just seen and Shannonderry's neat cottages was immediately apparent. The children were better clothed and fed. She remarked on the difference.

"Our tenants don't go hungry," Moira agreed. "But they don't prosper, either. The English have placed such a high tax on our corn and grain that there's little money in farming anymore. Cattle and sheep are now a better source of money and the cause of much unrest."

"Why?"

"Landowners want the land for pasture. Many have evicted their tenants so they can turn the land to pasture. When the cottiers are evicted, they often starve."

Gwyneth began to understand why the Irish disliked English interference in their affairs. "What of Shannonderry?"

"Our tenants are loyal and hardworking," Moira said.

Gwyneth noted the fields of corn growing close to the track. "With the high tax, how can you and they prosper?"

"We don't, but if we hold on, perhaps the tax will be repealed." She pointed to the nearest cottage and instructed Cluny to turn the cart into the dooryard. "The gateposts are pointed to keep mischievous leprechauns and fairies from sitting on them," Moira went on. The contented sound of hens scratching in the dooryard greeted them as Cluny pulled the donkey to a stop.

"This is the home of Patrick and Kate O'Donnell . . . parents to Cluny and Biddy," Moira told her.

As she spoke, a sandy-haired girl of about six ran out of the cottage. "'Tis Cluny and Mistress!" she cried.

Kate O'Donnell, followed by a boy and girl, hurried from the cottage. "Mistress," she exclaimed, dropping a curtsy as she tucked a strand of red hair into her thick braid. "'Tis good to be seein' ye." She motioned to the boy. "Run an' get yer da."

Cluny jumped down from the cart to embrace his mother while his young brother set off at a run toward a field, calling as he ran. "Da . . . Matt! 'Tis Mistress and herself . . . the one Cluny and Biddy told us about."

The tale of the two Gwyneths had spread among the peasants like wildfire, the flames fanned by the eager tongues of Cluny and Biddy. Cluny had crept into the great hall to see the painting himself. The likeness had made him shiver—both ladies fair with shining hair and deep blue eyes. Was herself not come from England to save Shannonderry, and were they not part of Shannonderry too? 'Twas surely a miracle. If not that, then some wonderful magic wrought by fairies.

Moira made the introductions—first Gwyneth, then Patrick and Kate and their four children. As pleased as the O'Donnells were with the visit and food Moira brought, their interest in Gwyneth was greater. Kate's and Patrick's eyes flitted to the stranger while they answered Moira's questions about their health, and the two little girls openly stared. Maggie, the oldest, sketched a cross and furtively touched Gwyneth's pink skirt. Surely doing so would bring good luck—perhaps a doll or a litter of pigs so they could eat like kings through the long winter.

Gwyneth received the same reception from the other tenants—Mick Sullivan and his wife, Colleen, the Callihans, and the Kelleys. She closely watched what her grandmother said and did and was keenly aware of her kindness, noting that she acted as if she were visiting an extended part of her family.

Gwyneth's reception by the tenants left her strangely quiet. Instead of the hostility she'd feared, there was curiosity and wonder. Not only was she the Mistress's granddaughter, but she was also part of a legend—a position that made Gwyneth uncomfortable. When she expressed her feelings, the old woman nodded.

"I didn't expect the story of the other Gwyneth to spread so quickly, though with Cluny and Biddy, I shouldn't be surprised." She paused and gave Gwyneth a sympathetic smile. "Don't let the responsibility of measuring up to their expectations overwhelm you. You will serve them admirably by being yourself."

* * *

WITHIN A MATTER OF DAYS Gwyneth was deeply involved in life at Shannonderry. The early morning mist curled in vapory wisps as Gwyneth went to the stable each day to groom Toryn. Since the stallion wouldn't allow Flynn or Cluny near him, Gwyneth was also obliged to clean his stall.

Although Flynn grumbled at her frequent presence, Gwyneth's ability to handle the fiery stallion earned his grudging respect. It couldn't earn his affection, however, and he let her know he only tolerated her because of the stallion.

Had the circumstances been different, Gwyneth would have left the little man to his domain, but Maurice Beddows had taught her the importance of a clean stable. The deplorable state of neglect at Shannonderry wouldn't let her rest.

She knew Flynn tried, but a task that had once taken him an hour now took him two, and by afternoon he could hardly lift a fork full of hay. Since Cluny was small for his age, he was little better. More than that, he was constantly called to run errands or help with other tasks.

Gwyneth pondered the problem for several days. One morning, after a particularly frustrating encounter with Flynn, she went to the north tower in search of one of her mother's old dresses. Since Flynn and Cluny were unable to keep the stable clean, she would have to help.

A large leather trunk sat beneath one of the windows. The clasp was unwieldy and the inside smelled of age, but sprigs of lavender laid among the clothes kept them fresh and sweet smelling.

Gwyneth rummaged through several ornate gowns, all unsuitable for mucking out stalls. She was about to give up when she came to a pair of leather breeches. Folded with them were a shirt and worsted jacket. They looked to have been worn by someone her size. Her mind leaped to her grandmother's surprising revelation that both she and Deirdre had worn boy's breeches. Even so, she thought it best not to tell Moira or Kate about her plans.

The next morning Gwyneth awoke with the rooks, and she was busy cleaning one of the stalls by the time Flynn arrived.

"What's this?" he wheezed, staring at her in indignation. "Am I so old and useless yer grandmother sent a girl to show me how to keep my stable?"

"Grandmother doesn't know," Gwyneth began.

"I thought not, or ye'd not be wearin' breeches. For a moment, I thought 'twas Master Brandon come back from the dead . . . God rest him." While crossing himself, Flynn glared at her.

"Who's Master Brandon?" Gwyneth asked, hoping to divert his anger.

"Yer mam's brother who was killed in a huntin' accident. If himself was with us still, we'd not have to suffer the English livin' amongst us."

"I knew he'd died, but I didn't know his name."

"Well, ye do now, and ye should know yer not welcome in my stable dressed like that. So out with ye, girl. Out! Out! Out!"

Ignoring him, Gwyneth went to a stall and lifted a fork full of manure.

"Are ye deaf, girl?" the old man raged. "I want ye out of my stable."

It was difficult for Gwyneth to ignore him when he entered the stall, raging at her in English, then Gaelic. Although she couldn't understand much of what he said, she understood enough to know it wasn't complimentary. Turning her back, she continued to shovel straw and manure.

Uttering a guttural oath, Flynn slammed his hand against the stall and walked away.

Shaken, Gwyneth stared after him. How could Shannonderry survive with so much hatred? Couldn't Flynn see she only wanted to help? While she worked, Gwyneth carried on a silent argument with the old man. When she finished cleaning the stall, she went in search of Flynn. He was sitting on a sack of grain, his grizzled head bowed and his shoulders drooping—clearly exhausted and disheartened by the encounter.

"Can't we be friends, Flynn? I only want to help."

Flynn acted as if he hadn't heard her.

"I'm sure you had more than Cluny to help in the old days. There must have been several grooms and stable hands then."

His nod was barely perceptible.

Gaining courage, she went on. "Now there's no money for extra hands. We must work together if Shannonderry is to survive. Don't you want that?"

His grizzled head nodded.

"Try to think of me as a new stable boy. You'll still be in charge. I'll only help with things you no longer have time to do. No one will know except you and Cluny."

"'Twouldn't be right," Flynn muttered.

"Why?"

"Yerselfs a girl and Mistress's granddaughter."

"Not this early in the morning. Until breakfast, I'm the new stable boy."

Flynn fell silent. Then with his head bowed and his voice so low Gwyneth had to strain to hear, he muttered, "The bay mare's stall needs a good cleanin', and they all need fresh beddin'."

"I'll see that it's done." Gwyneth wanted to smile, but she knew better than to do so with Flynn watching. By the time she finished all he gave her to do, she was too tired to do anything more than creep back to her room.

Gwyneth was stiff and sore for the first few days, but by the end of the second week, the stable was almost clean.

Flynn was just as pleased with the improvement as she was, but, of course, he wouldn't tell her. He only spoke to Gwyneth when he gave instructions or answered questions. Even so, he couldn't entirely hide his pleasure. On several occasions Gwyneth heard him humming as he worked.

Gwyneth often sang too. One morning as she pushed the wheelbarrow out to the dung heap, she almost collided with Cormac D'Arcy. "Oh!" she cried, struggling to balance the awkward vehicle.

Before she could say more, Cormac took the barrow and wheeled it to the dung heap. "Still playing Cedric, I see." Amusement filled the Irishman's voice until he had a chance to take in her dirty boots and work-stained shirt. "You shouldn't be doing this."

Instead of replying, Gwyneth put a finger to her lips. "Flynn will be mortified if he knows you've seen me." As Cormac's gaze remained pinned on her, she silently decried the fact that he always seemed to see her at her worst. Shaking away the thought, she hurried on. "He and Cluny can't do it alone, and since there's no one else to help, I suggested—"

"Suggested?" Cormac's brow lifted. "You don't suggest anything to Flynn unless you want your head bitten off."

"It *was* bitten off, but after he calmed down, I managed to convince him we must work together."

"I see." Cormac no longer sounded amused. "What does your grandmother think of your role as stable boy?"

"She doesn't know . . . no one knows except Flynn and Cluny." Determined to guard her secret, Gwyneth held his blue eyes in an unwavering gaze. "It must stay that way, Mr. D'Arcy."

Cormac nodded. "No one shall hear of it from me." He paused before going on. "I took on an extra stable boy after his parents died. You're welcome to use him . . . in fact, you'd be doing me a favor."

Gwyneth shook her head. "Thank you, but no . . ." The close proximity of the Irishman made her giddy. More than that, it made her reluctant to let him go. Putting her mind on Flynn, she started again. "Please leave before Flynn knows you've seen me. You know his pride."

"Only Flynn's pride?" Amusement danced in his eyes, along with a look Gwyneth couldn't fathom. "I'll leave as quietly as I came." Touching his hat, he left the stable yard.

Cormac mounted his horse feeling out of sorts. "She's as stubborn as Moira," he growled. His harsh voice made his mare flatten her ears. It wasn't the first or last time that being with Miss Beddows left Cormac unsettled.

10

AT TEATIME THAT AFTERNOON, MOIRA broached the subject of a dinner party. "I'd like you to meet a few of our neighbors. We can invite the D'Arcys, and, of course, Reverend Gibbins and his wife. Perhaps the Westons too." She hesitated. Although Emmett Weston and her William had followed the hunt together, she'd never cared for the man. It would be rude not to invite him, however, especially since the widower had commenced courting Cormac's stepmother, Agatha D'Arcy. "And certainly, the Murphys," she went on. "They have a daughter about your age."

Moira began at once to prepare for the party. Invitations were written, and a message was sent to the seamstress, Mrs. Ryan, in Doneraile, asking her to come to Shannonderry to make a new gown for Gwyneth. "We'll have her remodel Deirdre's gowns into a more modish style for you as well," she concluded.

Aware of their tenuous circumstances, Gwyneth protested at the talk of a new gown. Moira brushed the protests away and would not budge from her decision. Gwyneth felt little enthusiasm for the project until she learned she could choose the fabric and style herself. Sylvia had never allowed Gwyneth any choice in the selection of her clothes. This time Gwyneth took great pleasure as she looked at fabric and fashion plates. After much discussion, she chose a bolt of rose-colored silk to be made up with a close-fitting bodice and high waistline.

As the day for the party drew near, two of Biddy's cousins came to help with the extra cleaning and baking. The dustcovers were taken off the furniture, and the carpets were unrolled to cover the bare floors.

Gwyneth was at a loss to know why so many rooms were being readied when only the dining hall would be used.

"'Tis yer gran's orders," Biddy told her. "Been years since we had guests, and she wants everythin' turned out like the old days. She's even told us to clean and freshen the great hall, for there be a seanchaí comin' to entertain with his stories after dinner."

"Shan . . . achie?" Gwyneth's tongue tripped on the strange word.

"A storyteller. Yer gran sent for Dooley O'Garvin, the most famous seanchaí in all of County Cork."

Gwyneth had read about the men who still traveled around Ireland like the bards and minstrels of old. Knowing that one was coming added to her excitement.

Not that there wasn't excitement enough already. Young Biddy flew around the house like a leaf caught in a gale, her copper curls dancing and her deft hands seeing to all that must be done before the party.

Gwyneth was pressed into service too, and she spent many hours in the large, whitewashed kitchen, stirring blackened pots hanging over a fireplace large enough to roast an ox.

When the evening of the party finally arrived, Gwyneth found herself too nervous to sit down. Cormac D'Arcy and his family were coming, and for once she looked her best.

"Ye're lovely," Kate exclaimed when she finished fastening the last of the tiny buttons on the bodice of her new gown.

Gwyneth was pleased as well. Her cheeks seemed to take on the rosy hue of the fabric, and the tiny bows edging the bodice added a touch of elegance.

"For sure ol' Flynn'll have to take out his pike tonight."

Gwyneth laughed, and her happiness grew as Kate brushed her curls until they shone like a silver halo around her face. Happiness stayed with her as she went downstairs to meet her grandmother. The old woman looked regal in a lavender velvet gown set off by the O'Brien amethysts.

"Mrs. Ryan did not fail me," Moira said after she'd inspected Gwyneth's gown. "She used to make my gowns . . . your mother's too."

Moira seldom mentioned Deirdre. Gwyneth held her breath, hoping her grandmother would say more, but Moira's thoughts were centered on her granddaughter. "Were the other Gwyneth present tonight, she would not be disappointed in her namesake."

"Thank you, and thank you for the new gown and the party. I'm excited to meet our neighbors."

Moira nodded and, taking Gwyneth's arm, started toward the great hall. "I thought we would greet the guests in here. 'Tis where the O'Briens used to entertain. We will eat here, as well, rather than in the dining room."

Baffled by the pains Moira had taken to display the O'Brien past glory, Gwyneth merely nodded. Even so, stirrings of pride flooded her heart as she stood with her grandmother to greet their guests.

Reverend Gibbins and his wife were the first to arrive. He was a tall, spare man with a long face and merry eyes. His wife looked enough like him to be his sister. Although her hair was a nondescript brown, her merry gray eyes looked Gwyneth over with undisguised interest.

"What a lovely young lady," she exclaimed to Moira. "How fortunate you must feel to have her." Turning to Gwyneth, Mrs. Gibbins hurried on. "The reverend and I have looked forward to meeting you. I hope you'll enjoy Ireland."

"Thank you."

Before Gwyneth could say more, the reverend took her hand. "I wish to invite you to attend church on Sunday. I know your grandmother is not able to attend services anymore, but don't let that prevent you. Whether one calls it the Church of England or Church of Ireland, 'tis all one and the same, you know."

"I'd like that," Gwyneth replied, realizing how much she missed the steadying influence of Parson Cranston.

They were still chatting with the reverend and his wife when Biddy announced the D'Arcy family. Gwyneth was hardly aware of those Cormac came with, her eyes taking in his white nankeen breeches and the silk frock coat that matched the deep blue of his eyes. His chiseled profile softened when his eyes met hers.

"Miss Beddows." Cormac experienced a confusion of emotions as he gazed down at the delightful creature returning his smile. Her eyes sparkled with excitement, and her generous mouth trembled slightly under his gaze. The rose gown she wore clung to the soft curves of her body and accentuated the eggshell porcelain of her skin. No one would mistake Gwyneth for a boy this night.

Gwyneth's pulse quickened when Cormac took her hand. Instead of kissing the fingers of her gloved hand, he turned it over and lightly brushed his lips across her palm.

Gwyneth's breath caught. Was he mocking her role of stable boy? When she raised her eyes, his gaze held only admiration.

"May I present my stepmother, Agatha D'Arcy?" he said.

Gwyneth tore her gaze from Cormac and extended her hand to a woman who was frankly looking her over. Although Agatha D'Arcy was not a handsome woman, her green-flecked eyes fringed with lashes that matched her brown hair were fine. Her figure, like her face, was rounded, and the excess weight strained the seams of her dark green gown.

"I'm happy to meet you," Agatha said. "Cormac has told us about you."

Wondering if Cormac had told his family of the role she'd played as his nephew, she hesitated. "I'm happy to meet you too," she finally said.

Agatha turned to the young man at her side. "This is my son, Owen."

Owen flushed and took Gwyneth's hand. His coloring was similar to his mother's, but he resembled Cormac through the nose and in his build.

Sensing Owen's embarrassment, she tried to put him at ease. "Do you raise horses like your brother?"

Owen shook his head. "I . . . I'm preparing to go up to Trinity College in Dublin . . . but I like horses and often help Cormac with his."

A dark-haired young woman no taller than Gwyneth tugged on Owen's sleeve. "You mustn't let Owen talk about horses, or he'll never stop," she warned. "Since he's forgotten his manners, I shall introduce myself. I'm Edwina D'Arcy . . . a cousin to Owen and Cormac."

Gwyneth was immediately drawn to the girl's vivacious nature and lively tongue. "How nice to meet you."

"You may soon change your mind." Edwina laughed. "I'm always saying the wrong thing. See, Aunt Agatha is frowning at me for chattering too much. I'm only visiting for a short while, but my cousin has told me about you."

"You must come to visit."

"I'd like that." Edwina leaned close. "I like your short hair. Cormac says 'tis the style in London."

Gwyneth shot an inquiring look at Cormac. Had he also mentioned he'd been the one to wield the scissors?

Cormac chuckled. "My cousin loves new clothes and will likely plague you for news of England's latest fashions."

Before more could be said, a gentleman standing nearby impatiently cleared his throat. Turning from Cormac, Gwyneth saw a tall, sturdily built man.

"Mr. Emmett Weston," Moira said.

Gwyneth was immediately aware of tension as Emmett Weston's eyes slid away from Cormac. Perhaps it was this that made her see him in an unfavorable light. His features and voice were pleasant, and his brown hair was thick and wavy, but his gray eyes seemed the abode of an inflated ego. She tried to remember what her grandmother had told her about Mr. Weston. Something about him being widowed and that he courted Cormac's stepmother. The coming of more guests prevented her from wondering more.

"This is Matthew Murphy, his wife, Elizabeth, and his daughter Anne. They live near the vicarage, but since Mr. Murphy is in business, they divide their time between Cork and here."

Gwyneth extended her hand to the thick-set man with balding hair. Unlike her husband, Elizabeth was slender and possessed a pleasant face and a head of beautifully arranged dark hair. Their daughter, Anne, was a younger version of her mother, her dark hair set off by an emerald green gown and matching hairpiece.

Anne gave Gwyneth an eager smile. "I'm most pleased that you've come to Shannonderry. Young people are in short supply along the Awbeg River."

After they'd chatted a few minutes, Moira touched Gwyneth's arm. "It's time to go in for dinner. I have asked Mr. D'Arcy to be your escort."

Cormac offered her his arm. "Do you mind?" he asked in a low voice.

"How could I?" Gwyneth teased. "Didn't you get me safely to Ireland?" Although she strove for nonchalance, she was intently aware of his muscular arm under her gloved hand, and she hoped the heightened warmth in her cheeks would be attributed to excitement.

Pride surged through Gwyneth as she walked the length of the great hall with Cormac. Tall stands of candles lit the way, and the stone floor gleamed like polished slate. The over-sized table was set in the old style, without cloth. Pewter tankards had been set to mark each place. As she looked toward the raised dais, Gwyneth half expected to hear a clarion announce their coming. "At times the O'Briens must have felt high and mighty," she whispered.

"Aye." Cormac looked around in appreciative silence. Although he hadn't been in the hall since he was a boy of twelve, his added years didn't diminish his response to the antique splendor. "We've nothing at Clonglas to match this. You've a rich heritage, Miss Beddows."

"Have you forgotten that I'm half English?"

"Bravery knows no nationality. The O'Briens were brave men."

"Their women too." Gwyneth wanted to tell him of the other Gwyneth, but their arrival at the table prohibited private conversation.

Moira, who led the way into the hall on the arm of Reverend Gibbins, showed her guests to their places. Biddy and a cousin hovered by the table in freshly laundered white caps and aprons. They were a credit to Shannonderry, as was the food, which was served in four courses.

When the last course had been cleared away from the table, Moira rose from her chair. Her stance was as regal as any queen's, and the look she bestowed on her guests was warm and gracious. "I invited you here tonight to introduce you to my granddaughter, Gwyneth Beddows. Her coming has brought me pleasure, made even greater by her resemblance to the portrait you see hanging on the wall." Moira pointed to the painting.

Involved with conversation and good food, none of the guests had paid any heed to the painting. Now they stared at it with great interest, the pale, lovely features and hair seeming to pulse with life in the flickering light of the candles. Murmurs of surprise came as they looked from the portrait to Gwyneth.

When the voices quieted, Moira went on. "This brave woman saved Shannonderry from being burned and pillaged by the English more than two hundred years ago. Although my granddaughter was born in England, it's obvious that the O'Brien heritage has been passed to her." Moira's deep-set eyes locked with her granddaughter's. "Gwyneth is now where she belongs . . . here at Shannonderry."

Silence followed Moira's words as those at the table studied the two Gwyneths. With so many eyes fastened on her, Gwyneth's cheeks colored. Her self-consciousness eased when Cormac leaned close. "It seems you're more O'Brien than you thought."

"Yes." Gwyneth wanted to tell him that in coming to Shannonderry, she felt as if she'd finally come home, but before she could do so, Moira signaled Biddy to usher in Dooley O'Garvin, the famous seanchaí. The mood was right. They were ready to listen.

Dooley O'Garvin entered the hall by a side door near the table. The seanchaí was old and frail, but he walked with his head held high, as if it didn't belong to the bowed legs and shuffling feet that carried him to the seat of honor next to Moira. After he bowed over her hand, she introduced him to Gwyneth and the guests.

Meeting the seanchaí's gaze, Gwyneth felt as if she were looking at time itself. Although the sculptured bones of his face were covered by a network of wrinkles, his eyes—coal black and sunken beneath tangled brows grizzled like the sparse wisps of hair on his shrunken skull—were much alive. His voice, like his eyes, belied his age. It came firm and strong as he took Gwyneth's fingers in his age-spotted hand.

"Mistress Gwyneth." His eyes left hers to look at the portrait of the other Gwyneth. "Yes," he said after a long moment. "Ye have the look of yer ancestor."

Returning to his place at the head of the table, the seanchaí cleared his throat and looked at the guests. "There are many tales I could tell ye tonight, but Mistress Donahue asked that I tell ye the story of Ireland itself . . . the tale of Eire."

His voice was low as he began.

"Long ago, when the mists of our gods still clung to our island, the three sons of Mileadh of Spain conquered our land from the children of the goddess Dana. 'Tis from this noble beginning that Eire's great kings and warriors began. Aye, even the O'Briens."

Gwyneth saw the seanchaí and her grandmother exchange glances before she closed her eyes and let the magic of the old storyteller's words transport her through time to places beyond Shannonderry's stone walls. His word pictures were so vivid that she felt as if she were with the Irish high kings on the sacred hill of Tara riding to take down a stag with Irish wolfhounds running at her side.

Reverence laced O'Garvin's words as he told of St. Patrick and Christianity and Ireland's Golden Age, then turned harsh and gutteral with the telling of the terrible carnage wrought by Ireland's conquerors from the Northland.

Gwyneth frowned, not liking to dwell on this dark time in Irish history and was relieved when the seanchaí spoke of Brian Baru. Through the power of his words, Gwyneth saw the red-haired giant honing his sword in preparation for battle. A shiver ran down her spine. How splendid he must have been with his mighty warriors like a wall of strength behind him.

O'Garvin paused and smiled. "We can't be forgettin' our leprechauns and fairies, Miss Gwyneth. They be part of Ireland's rich heritage too." He winked and his lined face took on a puckish air.

Just like that, Gwyneth was transported back to her childhood with tales of wee folk and tiny satin slippers and fairies, with wings shimmering in the moonlight, dancing in the meadow. Through it all, she was aware that Cormac's eyes were on her, their amusement and warmth adding to her enjoyment.

"There be dozens of tales I could tell ye," O'Garvin concluded, "but 'twould keep ye here for the rest of the night.

"Besides, my friend Conner O'Riley be waitin' to play his harp for ye. 'Twould be a shame to keep Miss Gwyneth from hearin' his wonderful music." With that, he gave a bow. "Thank ye for listening to my story. May God's peace be with ye."

The guests spoke in quiet voices while they waited for the harpist. Soon the soft strumming of the instrument filled the hall, delighting Gwyneth just as Dooley O'Garvin had said it would. As she listened, Owen leaned across the table, his voice and manner hesitant.

"Have you had opportunity to see much of our river valley?"

"Grandmother took me for a short ride around Shannonderry."

"There's a splendid view from a hill at Clonglas. I can take you there . . . that is, if you wish to go." Owen's face reddened. "We shall have an escort, of course."

"I'd be pleased to go with you." Although she smiled, Gwyneth wished it was Cormac who'd invited her, but he was in conversation with the reverend's wife and seemed not to have heard them.

Not so with Edwina. Gwyneth had scarcely accepted the invitation before Edwina asked to join them. "I can act as chaperone and get to know you better," she said.

Owen's face fell. He was all too familiar with Edwina's penchant for dominating an occasion.

"Will you be riding your stallion?" Edwina went on. "Cormac has nothing but praise for your horse, and we're anxious to see him." Edwina's hand went to her mouth. "Oh." She giggled. "I warned you not to let Owen talk about horses, and here I'm doing it. Tell me, did you truly train him yourself?"

Gwyneth couldn't resist the opportunity to talk about Toryn. Even so, she was aware when Cormac moved to speak with the seanchaí—aware, too, of the dislike in his stepmother's eyes as she watched him go. Agatha wasn't the only one to watch Cormac. Emmett Weston stared after him too.

"I wonder what your stepson finds so interesting in the seanchaí?" Mr. Weston asked, his lips lifting in a sneer.

"You know how Cormac likes to hobnob with peasants." Agatha laughed.

Mr. Weston joined in her laughter. "Considering his background, it's not surprising."

Realizing that Gwyneth had overheard, Agatha hurried on. "Such a small fault amid so many admirable qualities can easily be overlooked by a mother." She favored Gwyneth with a nod. "Did you find my stepson an excellent guide on your way to Ireland?"

"I did." Unsure of where the conversation was going, Gwyneth welcomed Owen's interruption.

"Will you be coming to church on Sunday? Should you desire a ride, you can join us in our carriage." He turned to Agatha. "Isn't that so, Mother?"

Agatha was slow to take her eyes from Cormac and Dooley O'Garvin. "Of course," she said absently. Only when her large hazel eyes looked at Gwyneth did she give her full attention to the conversation. "Your resemblance to your ancestor is truly remarkable, Miss Beddows, especially when one considers the fact that you are English."

"I'm Irish, too," Gwyneth reminded her. "And after tonight—" Her voice trailed away as she took in the shield and battle-ax leaning against the wall. "How can one sit in this hall and not feel Irish?"

"To be sure," Agatha agreed. "Your grandmother has kept Shannonderry too much to herself these past years. Perhaps now that you're here, we'll have opportunity to see it more often."

"Yes," Anne Murphy seconded. "Perhaps you could hold a ball. I do love to dance, don't you, Miss Beddows?"

"I do."

Reverend Gibbin's wife moved to join them, and the conversation became more general. Gwyneth listened with but half a mind, her heart opening to the lilting melody of the harp as she pictured the other Gwyneth enjoying a similar evening. Through it all was her awareness of Cormac D'Arcy and his dark handsome features so clearly defined in the candlelight.

As if he felt her gaze, Cormac lifted his head. His eyes held hers for a brief second, and a smile lifted the corners of his mouth. Thoughts of the other Gwyneth fled, replaced by happiness and dreams of the future.

11

MEMORIES OF THE DINNER PARTY followed Gwyneth into the stable the next morning. While she cleaned Toryn's stall, she pictured the great hall filled with music and guests, and when she looked at Flynn's weathered face, it took on the contours of the old seanchaí. It had been a delightful evening, one made even more memorable because Cormac D'Arcy had been there. She told herself not to place too much import on the way he seemed always to look at her. After all, hadn't she been the guest of honor?

Kate's praise quickly restored Gwyneth's confidence. "Everyone be talkin' about ye and how Mr. D'Arcy and his brother couldn't keep their eyes off ye," Kate confided as she helped Gwyneth dress for breakfast. "Though I worked off my feet in the kitchen, a few times, I took a peek at ye. 'Twas a wonder . . . all of it . . . just like the old days."

Moira was of a similar mind when Gwyneth joined her in the sitting room after breakfast. Instead of looking fatigued, her grandmother seemed to have gained energy from the previous evening. Her eyes were bright as she motioned Gwyneth to a chair.

"What a lovely evening. From what I observed, you seemed to enjoy yourself as well."

"I did. Thank you again, Grandmother. It was very good of you. The great hall, the seanchaí—all of it was wonderful."

Moira looked pleased. "I hoped you'd like it . . . hoped, too, that you'd make friends. Friends are important when one is young. Until last night, I'd forgotten how good it is to have them. Hannah Gibbins and I haven't had such a good talk in years. Did you know she and the reverend are cousins of a sort?" Moira paused. "Miss Murphy seems a personable young lady. What did you think of her?"

"I like her."

"Good. I don't want you to be lonely. You and Owen D'Arcy seemed to enjoy yourselves as well. He's grown into a nice-looking young man. Not as handsome as his older brother, but then few are." She nodded as if the idea pleased her. "I believe his mother has great plans for him."

But not for his older brother, Gwyneth thought, recalling Agatha's critical remarks. On impulse, she told Moira what she'd observed. "She doesn't seem over fond of Mr. D'Arcy . . . nor did Mr. Weston," she concluded.

Moira sighed. "Stepchildren and new mothers aren't noted for getting on. Agatha and Cormac are no exception, which isn't surprising under the circumstances."

"Circumstances?" Gwyneth repeated, hoping Moira would say more.

"It's a sad story, though I doubt Mr. D'Arcy will thank me for divulging it. But since you'll be neighbor to him, it's something you should know. The fact is, Cormac grew up a baptized Catholic and thought himself an O'Carroll until he was eight years old and learned who his father was."

Gwyneth stared while pieces of her conversations with Cormac tumbled through her head—*years of oppression . . . hatred between Papist and Protestant.* Now the phrases took on new import. "I never suspected."

"I thought you hadn't. Years ago the O'Carrolls were a rich family. Although that changed with Cromwell's coming and the enactment of the penal laws, they managed to acquire a few acres near Clonglas."

"Didn't the penal laws forbid Catholics to own land?"

"They did, but there were ways around the laws, especially if you had friends who'd newly converted to Protestantism. Such friends sometimes bought up leases in their name for their Catholic friends. Through this arrangement, the O'Carrolls have held on to their few acres for the past hundred years."

Gwyneth's mind hovered over the memory of the hovels she'd seen with Moira. "Are the O'Carrolls some of the poor we saw?"

"No, the O'Carrolls may be poor, but they're a proud lot and keep their place neat. When Cormac's grandmother was widowed, she somehow managed to work the holding until her son and daughter were old enough to help her . . . young Paddy with the farm and Fiona by going into service at Clonglas. Had you known Fiona, you'd understand where Cormac got his good looks."

Moira paused and looked out the window as if she were seeing another time and place. "A rare beauty, Fiona was. Some said she was the most beautiful girl in County Cork, with jet black hair, dark blue eyes, and power to charm the fairies. She certainly charmed Francis D'Arcy, who couldn't rest 'til he married her. A scandal it was—him landed and rich, she a peasant serving girl. All the way to Cork they had to go to find a Protestant minister who'd marry them. None would marry them here . . . not even a Catholic priest. It was this that caused the trouble."

Gwyneth leaned toward her grandmother, not wanting to miss a word.

"Being staunch Papist, Fiona fretted because no priest had blessed their union. By the time Cormac was born, she'd come to believe she and Francis weren't truly married and that she lived in sin."

"They *were* married," Gwyneth exclaimed.

"But not by a Catholic priest." Moira's fingers pleated the silk fabric of her gray skirt as she gathered her thoughts. "Papists are great ones for doing penance, and that's what Fiona felt she must do. As her penance, she refused Francis his rights to her as a husband."

Confused, Gwyneth shook her head. "I don't understand."

"Nor are you expected to," Moira said hastily. She'd forgotten it was Gwyneth, not Hannah Gibbins, with whom she gossiped. It had been years since she'd thought about the tragedy. Gathering breath, she went on. "Frustrated and unhappy, Francis took to the bottle. A terrible drinker he became, hosting riotous drinking parties with his hunting friends who broke the furniture and dishes. Poor Fiona huddled in her room with the door locked, fearful of what the men might do to her. This I know from Kate's mother, who worked at Clonglas at the time."

"How terrible," Gwyneth said, her heart going out to the mother and baby.

"That wasn't the worst. One night Francis's friend broke down Fiona's door and took advantage of her. Fortunately, he was drunk, and she was able to escape."

The sputtering fire was the only sound in the room. With a sigh, Moira went on, telling how the weeping woman had gathered her sleeping infant and slipped away. A winter storm raged, turning the rain to sleet that pierced and pounded the two. By the time Fiona reached the O'Carrolls', she and the babe were nigh frozen."

Near tears, Gwyneth shook her head. "And his mother died?"

"Aye . . . though not before she told her mother what had happened."

Neither spoke for a moment, the tragedy of Fiona's death seeming to throb through the room with the beat of the mantel clock.

Moira finally broke the silence. "Grief stricken and in a rage, Maureen O'Carroll refused to let Francis take the babe unless he promised before the priest that he'd stop drinking. Francis refused and fled Clonglas. No one heard of him until eight years later when he returned a reformed man and with a new wife."

Gwyneth tried to imagine how it had been for Cormac. How had a barefoot, grubby child felt when he discovered he had a wealthy father?

What were his feelings when he'd been told that instead of being Papist he was now a Protestant? The sudden change from poor to rich, Papist to Protestant, must have been overwhelming. Gwyneth glanced at Moira, who sat with a pensive expression on her face. "It must have been very difficult for Mr. D'Arcy."

"Aye, especially when he'd been taught to hate those like his father. More than that, he spoke mostly Gaelic." The old woman shook her head. "It could not have been pleasant for Francis and Agatha, either, for Cormac wasn't over clean and had little notion of manners. He also refused to eat or speak and was often defiant."

Moira fastened Gwyneth with a steady gaze. "Now do you understand why Agatha isn't overly fond of her stepson, especially when Cormac, not Owen, inherited Clonglas at Francis's death? As for Mr. Weston." She grimaced and looked away. "Fiona told her mother that Emmett Weston was the man who broke down her bedroom door."

Gwyneth looked at her grandmother in indignation. "Wasn't something done?"

"Mr. Weston vehemently denied it, and since there was only Fiona's word and she a peasant and dead at that, no charges were ever brought against him. Cormac believes Fiona told the truth, however." Moira sighed and looked glum. "Do you see why there's bad blood between them . . . especially now that Emmett courts Agatha?"

"Yes . . . but still—" Though Gwyneth understood, it didn't make her like it, nor did she care for Agatha D'Arcy. Her feelings for Mr. Weston were even less complimentary. Never one to be stingy with her opinions, she told Moira how she felt, half expecting a reprimand.

Instead, Moira nodded. "I hope you will always have your own opinions, for that is how one grows, but it would be wise to refrain from expressing those about our neighbors except when you're with me."

Having dealt with the problem, Moira smiled. "I've grown fond of our morning chats and hope we can always speak frankly with each other. 'Tis what I missed most after your mother left." The old woman's lips twitched. "Like you, Deirdre was wont to express her mind."

Gwyneth laughed. This was not the first time she'd been accused of being free with her opinions. Enjoying the new closeness with her grandmother, she was disappointed when her grandmother told her to run along. "I'm certain Kate and Biddy are anxious to talk about last night."

But Gwyneth's thoughts were on Cormac D'Arcy, not the dinner party, as she made her way down the long corridor. There was so much she wanted to know about the Irishman. Had he and his father been able to overcome the barriers between them? She contrasted the defiant boy with the polished gentleman who'd bowed over her hand at Hawarden; she remembered Cormac's competence in arranging their journey to Ireland. How had the transformation come about? However long it had taken, she knew it could not have been easy for the man, who even now might not be certain of his place in the world.

* * *

THAT AFTERNOON GWYNETH SADDLED TORYN and took him for a ride. The stallion was as eager for a brisk gallop as Gwyneth, and they traversed a good three miles before she reined him in.

"What we need is a race," she said, patting Toryn's neck. She remembered what Cormac had said about the Irish loving a steeplechase. Would he be the one she should ask about arranging one? Deep in thought, Gwyneth didn't notice the approaching horseman until he called her name.

"Miss Beddows!"

Her heart skipped a beat. Was the man in the brown coat and low-crowned hat Cormac D'Arcy? Excitement tingled her spine until she recognized Owen.

"I'm on my way to Shannonderry," Owen said when he reached her. "Edwina sent me . . ." Noting the becoming flush to Miss Beddows's cheeks, Owen lost his train of thought. "With . . . with an invitation for tea," he stammered. Embarrassed, he pulled a note from his pocket. "It's for Wednesday."

Scanning the invitation, Gwyneth felt as if a benevolent fairy had taken note of her wishes. Perhaps now she'd have a chance to see Cormac. "Tell Miss D'Arcy I'll be pleased to come on Wednesday."

Owen's attention had shifted from Gwyneth to Toryn. "I say . . ." Words failed him. "Cormac said he was a beauty . . . the fastest he's ever seen."

Such praise from an Irishman was music to her heart. "He is fast."

Owen patted his gelding. "Brutus is a great runner too . . . not as fast as your stallion . . . but I've won a race or two." He wasn't usually given to boasting, but Owen couldn't restrain himself in the lovely English girl's company. "Last month I won a purse full of guineas. If I had a horse such as yours, I'd soon be rich."

Gwyneth's interest quickened. "Is there money to be made by racing in Ireland?"

Owen nodded. "Probably not as much as in England, but there's enough . . . especially if interest is high, which it would be with your stallion." Owen's tongue tripped in his eagerness. "Did you know Cormac has won as much as a hundred pounds on a single steeplechase?"

"A hundred pounds!" Gwyneth made no effort to hide her excitement. If she entered Toryn in but a few races, Shannonderry would begin to prosper.

Carried along by Gwyneth's excitement, Owen grew bolder. "Are you interested in racing?"

"Yes, but I need a rider. Toryn only gives his best when he's ridden astride."

Toryn had been prancing restlessly throughout their conversation. Owen eyed him warily. "Will he let me ride him?"

"Only if you have your brother's touch with horses."

Owen's face fell. "Unfortunately, Cormac's the only one with the touch." Tired of always having to play second fiddle to his older brother, Owen hurried on. "I'm sure I can arrange a race for your horse. Would you like that?"

Gwyneth hesitated. It was Cormac she wanted to talk to. "Let me have time to think it over," she said. "And thank Edwina for her invitation to tea."

Giving a wave, Gwyneth urged Toryn into a canter toward Shannonderry. If she were lucky, Cormac D'Arcy would be present for tea on Wednesday.

12

GWYNETH FIRST SAW CLONGLAS THROUGH a mist of gentle rain. The house stood in a meadow surrounded by trees, the square facade and rough-hewn stone giving an impression of beauty and solidarity. Clonglas was not as large as Hawarden, but its south-facing front of limestone was enhanced by the symmetry of the multipaned windows. The house rose two stories, and the double front door topped by a fanlight was approached by a broad flight of stone steps. It was at the steps that old Flynn stopped the carriage.

Gwyneth was about to lift the knocker when Owen called to her. His boyish swagger was gone, his face solemn.

"Is something wrong?" she asked, glad for the sheltering roof of the porch.

"No," then quickly, "yes." He bit his lip, not liking to tell Gwyneth of the shambles he'd made of his visit to the Westons. "I'm in a devil of a mess. Cormac's going to skin me alive . . . You too, when you hear what I've done." Owen shook his head. "How could I have been so stupid?"

Gwyneth eyed him warily. "What have you done?"

"I challenged Percy Weston to a race with Toryn."

Gwyneth's eyes widened. "Without consulting me first?"

"I told you I was stupid. Percy's such a braggart, and he has a new mare. He and his friends were boasting that the mare couldn't be beaten, and . . ."

"So you told them about Toryn," Gwyneth finished for him.

"I know I shouldn't have, but the Westons . . ." He sighed and looked at his feet. "They think they're better than we are . . . and laugh about how Father drank and Cormac's mother was a serving girl." His cheeks flushed with mortification. "Before I knew it, I'd wagered twenty guineas that Toryn could beat Percy's mare."

Suddenly, Gwyneth didn't mind that Owen had made the bet. "Did they match you?"

"Five times over. A hundred guineas ride on the outcome. I know Toryn can win, but—" Owen's voice broke off as he met Gwyneth's eyes.

"But what?" Gwyneth prompted.

"The race is set for tomorrow morning. I was so excited I forgot you needed a rider." Owen swallowed uncomfortably. "The devil is, Cormac's gone to Mallow and won't be back until Friday. If I back out of the race, the D'Arcys will be the laughing stock of the county."

Gwyneth's hesitation about Owen's arrangement of the race fled. "We can't let that happen."

"How can we prevent it?"

Recalling what her grandmother had told her about Emmett Weston, Gwyneth lifted her head. "I'll ride Toryn."

"You can't . . . I mean . . ." Owen shook his head. He had to make Gwyneth understand. "Weston's mare is fast. His father paid a huge sum for her. And since it's a steeplechase, your stallion will have to be ridden astride."

Gwyneth stared out at the rain. Was the D'Arcy pride and a hundred guineas worth the risk of her reputation? "I can ride Toryn astride," she said after a moment of reflection. "I've done it before."

Owen gulped. "But you're a lady!"

Laughing at Owen's dumbfounded expression, Gwyneth told him how she'd disguised herself as Cormac's nephew to reach Ireland. "I can do the same for the race. Since Percy Weston and I have never met, he won't know who I am. You can say I'm Grandmother's new groom."

Owen was busy convincing himself of the plan's merits. If his brother let Miss Beddows wear breeches . . . "It might work," he conceded.

"Of course it will." Gwyneth tried to lend conviction to her words, knowing it could be disastrous if she were found out.

The thought tripped through her mind as she entered Clonglas and plagued her as she took tea with Agatha and Edwina. Afterward, Gwyneth couldn't recall one word of the conversation, nor could she wait to return to Shannonderry. There was much to do before tomorrow. Pray heaven her grandmother didn't find out.

* * *

THE SOUND OF RAIN DANCING against her window wakened Gwyneth the next morning. Her first thought was of the race. Would rain prevent it? Perhaps Percy Weston would call it off. Although Gwyneth could handle Toryn as well as any man, she'd never ridden him in a steeplechase. Spills and tumbles were common during the fast-paced event, and a wet course would add to the danger. More than that, she feared a lack of experience would put Toryn at a disadvantage.

Nerves and worry wouldn't let Gwyneth stay in bed. Donning the work-stained breeches and jacket she wore to clean Toryn's stall, she quietly ran down the stairs. She welcomed the task of grooming Toryn to keep her mind from worry. Even so, she kept a nervous eye on the stable clock. When it neared eight o'clock, her stomach tightened. It was time. Pulling her cap low over her curls, she led Toryn to the fence to mount him. With the touch of her heels, she rode away.

The rain had ceased by the time she met Owen at the agreed place. The grim set of his mouth made her wonder if something were wrong. Realizing he was as nervous as she, Gwyneth made a show of nonchalance and grinned.

"I say," Owen said, looking her over in approval. "In those clothes, no one will guess you're not your grandmother's groom."

"Thank you for the delightful compliment," she teased.

Owen blushed and stammered. "That isn't what . . ."

"I know," she laughed, "but I couldn't resist."

Owen gave a tense laugh. "I couldn't sleep a wink, I was so nervous." His face turned solemn. "Are you certain you want to go through with this?"

"I am . . . but I need you to show me the course."

Owen pointed to the spire of a church rising through the trees. "It begins at our church and covers the four miles to the church at Kilmulty then back again."

Since the most prominent landmarks were church steeples, cross-country races were frequently run from steeple to steeple, thus the name "steeplechase." The race differed from flat racing because everything along the way must be jumped.

As they rode toward the village church, Owen added bits of information. "The quickest way to the Kilmulty church is straight ahead," he said. "You'll have to skirt the woods . . . and watch out for the bog at the end of the second meadow."

Gwyneth didn't have a chance to ask any more questions before they arrived at the village church.

"What the devil!" Owen exclaimed when he saw a crowd of over fifty men and boys gathered around Percy Weston and his new mare. "Percy promised to keep it quiet. I should have known he'd spread it around."

Although the large crowd increased Gwyneth's nervousness, she wasn't sorry she'd agreed to ride Toryn. She could imagine the scorn and ridicule Owen would have encountered if he'd failed to appear.

Glancing down at her work-stained clothes, Gwyneth wished she looked more of a credit to Shannonderry. With a shrug, she straightened her shoulders. No matter what she wore, Toryn was a credit to Shannonderry.

"What's this, D'Arcy? Afraid to ride the stallion yourself?" Percy called.

"He's bad tempered and only his owner and the groom can manage him," Owen explained. As he spoke, Toryn reared and shied away from the crowd, his action sending a murmur through the spectators. "The boy's young and not skilled in the steeplechase, but if you want to call the race off . . ."

Percy eyed the fiery stallion with a twinge of misgiving. "I'm not one to go back on a bargain."

"Then let's get on with it," an older gentleman said. It was Reverend Gibbins, who, in addition to his religious calling, was an ardent lover of good horseflesh.

Gwyneth's heart jumped. Would the reverend recognize her?

He gave her no more than a glance, his attention centered on Percy. "The course is to the church in Kilmulty and back." He fixed Percy with a cold stare. "Men are posted at the church to see that you go the entire distance. The first one back wins." Motioning to the racers, Reverend Gibbins led them to an area away from the crowd.

Percy spoke out of the side of his mouth. "Your horse doesn't stand a chance against my mare."

Gwyneth ignored the jibe, her eyes on the reverend, her body primed for action as she strove to keep her prancing stallion in check.

"Ready?" Reverend Gibbins asked. At their nods, he dropped his hand and the two horses shot forward.

Gwyneth quickly realized that the race wouldn't be easy. The strawberry mare was as fleet and agile as Percy had claimed. For the first mile the horses raced neck and neck, hooves pounding over the meadow, taking each jump in unison. Percy, not the mare, was Gwyneth's primary concern. His whip was in frequent use and twice before a jump, he crowded Toryn to break his pace. Gwyneth's lack of experience showed, and she didn't know how to remedy it. If she could pull ahead, Percy couldn't crowd her.

When they reached another open stretch, Gwyneth redoubled her efforts. "On, boy . . . faster!"

Toryn responded with an added burst of speed. Gwyneth leaned low, knowing that the stallion disliked being dogged by the mare as much as she did. Little by little, they pulled ahead. Looking back, Gwyneth saw Percy flaying the mare with his whip. The mare couldn't match Toryn's magnificent stride. Toryn took the next jump as effortlessly as a bird in flight and was two paces into the next field before the mare reached the jump.

With the steeple still in sight, she glanced over the course, noting the woods and a tall hedge. She veered to the right where the way was more open but longer. She realized her mistake as soon as she came to the next hedgerow. Percy was already there, having known a way through the woods that Gwyneth couldn't see.

Toryn accepted the challenge, his legs reaching out until the horses were side by side. As they shot across a rolling meadow and made for a distant fence, Gwyneth felt as if she were riding the wind. Gauging the next jump, she paid no heed to Percy until he crowded her. She knew if she veered it would cost Toryn precious steps. "Move over!" she cried.

Percy pressed again, his leg brushing against hers. Toryn's smooth stride turned choppy and, as he gathered himself for the jump, Percy lashed out with his whip and struck the stallion on the withers. Toryn faltered and came down heavily, pitching Gwyneth over his head and into a puddle of mud.

The impact rattled her senses, and for a second she couldn't think. Wiping mud from her face, Gwyneth struggled to her feet and shouted at Percy, looking for Toryn at the same time. The big horse circled her without any sign of injury. Breathing a sigh of relief, she took his reins and, after jamming the cap back on her head, led him to a log to remount.

Then they were off again, racing toward Kilmulty's steeple with as much speed as before. They took a low wall and rounded the church without slackening speed, the faces of the men who watched no more than a blur.

Toryn's hooves continued to eat up the ground, but it wasn't until they'd almost reached the woods that she sighted Percy. "There they are!" At her cry, Toryn's great stride stretched even longer as they followed Percy through the woods.

The mare was tiring, and Percy's whip was in constant use, his savage curses accompanying his horse's labored breathing. The next hedgerow proved too much for the mare. Her front legs brushed the top, and she fell just before Gwyneth and Toryn sailed over it. Gwyneth glanced back and saw Percy remount the mare. Urging the stallion on, she saw that only a small field and a low stone wall separated them from the last meadow and the church. Toryn flew over the wall without breaking stride and set his head toward the steeple.

A loud cheer went up from the waiting crowd that had swelled in number. Toryn responded by quickening his pace. Sensing victory, Gwyneth leaned low with a cheer of her own. She and the stallion moved as one, her heart beating accompaniment to Toryn's furiously pounding hooves.

It was thus that Cormac saw them—hooves drumming, tail streaming, a small body pressed close to the horse. He stared as they raced to reach the flag at the end of the race, his eyes taking in the close-cropped hair and tiny face of Toryn's rider. Thunderation! It was Gwyneth!

13

THE RETURN TO SHANNONDERRY WAS punctuated with angry outbursts followed by periods of silence. "One would think I was dealing with two children," Cormac declared after Owen had given him the details of Percy's challenge. "I've often wondered if Owen were short on brains, but I thought better of you, Miss Beddows. Did you give thought to what this will do to your grandmother when she hears of it . . . not to mention your reputation?"

"What would have happened to the D'Arcy reputation if I hadn't?" Gwyneth countered. "Owen would have been the local laughing stock if he'd failed to show up with Toryn."

"Better that than having your name bandied around for wearing breeches."

"No one knows it was me who rode Toryn. They think it's our new groom."

"For how long? The moment you step into the church or attend a social, people will begin to suspect. Short hair may be the rage in London, but it's unusual enough here to be remarked upon. If the women don't put two and two together, their sons and husbands certainly will."

"Let them!" Clinging tightly to her anger, Gwyneth hurried on. "It would serve Percy Weston right if they do. If it's known that he was beaten by a woman, he'll be the laughing stock of the county, not Owen."

Owen's voice cut through the exchange. "If you must be angry . . . be angry at me. I was the one who asked Miss Beddows to ride . . . in case you've forgotten."

Cormac wanted to cuff Owen for his impudence. "I haven't forgotten, though *you* seem to have forgotten your manners."

"As you have yours." Owen's heart pounded at his daring while he stubbornly held his ground.

Cormac eyed him coldly. The boy had a point, but he wasn't in a mood
say so . . . at least not now. They rode in uncomfortable silence until they
reached the stand of beech trees near the castle, the overcast day and damp
grass a reflection of their mood.

Reining in his gelding, Owen reached into his pocket and took out a
leather pouch. "This is yours," he said, holding it out to Gwyneth. "The five
hundred guineas of Percy's wager."

Gwyneth looked at him in surprise. "I didn't make the wager."

"That may be, but I've already had my reward." His youthful face lit
with amusement. "Did you see the look on Percy's face when he lost the race
. . . his father's too?" He chortled with delight. "That was all the reward I
need."

Gwyneth's laughter joined his. "He was a bit upset."

"A bit! Percy was mad enough to spit rocks." Owen offered the purse
again. "Please . . . you must accept it."

When Gwyneth still hesitated, Cormac spoke. "Owen's right. You and
Toryn won the race . . . and by the look of you, it didn't come without
effort." He edged his mare closer and smiled, hoping his action would serve
as an apology for the chastisement he'd given her. Although he was still
upset that she'd risked her reputation, the need to please her was greater. "To
win after a fall took heart. I've never seen a finer finish."

Gwyneth didn't trust herself to look at the Irishman. If she did, it would
diminish her anger. "I didn't agree to race Toryn because I hoped to win
money," she said, looking straight ahead.

"I'm certain you didn't, but Shannonderry can use extra money . . .
especially when you add the purse Reverend Gibbins collected from the
older gentlemen." Cormac extracted a large purse from his pocket. "I have
no notion of the amount, but by the heft of it, I'd say you have more than
enough to feed Toryn and the mares for the rest of the year."

Gwyneth's eyes widened. "So much?" She made the mistake of looking
into Cormac's blue eyes, seeing them soften as she read his mute appeal for
forgiveness.

"It is, Miss Beddows . . . a fitting reward for a splendid performance
from you and Toryn."

Gwyneth patted the stallion's neck. "He did amazingly well, didn't he?"
She looked at her mud-spattered sleeve. She and Toryn looked a sight, the
horse lathered and splashed with mud and she not much better. She slid
a quick look at Cormac but saw only admiration in his eyes. Suddenly,
everything was all right, her anger forgotten, Owen forgotten as well, until
he handed her the purse.

"Know that I'll always be in your debt, Miss Beddows. If there is anything I can ever do to repay you . . ."

"Since I have no liking for Percy Weston, you are more than welcome. He treated his mare abominably and crowded Toryn at every hedge. I took great pleasure in beating the cad." Her voice rose in indignation as she went on to tell them how Percy had struck Toryn with his whip.

"The man shouldn't be allowed to own a horse," Cormac growled, "and his father is no better. I've long disliked Emmett Weston and have had several disagreeable encounters with him." He gave Owen a salute. "Although I'm not happy at the risk you took with Miss Beddows's reputation, I'm pleased at the race's outcome . . . pleased, too, at your tenacity at carrying out a bargain."

Owen blinked. Although he idolized his brother, they each possessed enough of their father's temper to sometimes put them at odds. "You've taught me well," was all he could think to say.

Cormac laughed. "I hope so . . . just as Da taught me. Now off with you while I accompany Miss Beddows back to Shannonderry."

Owen knew enough not to argue, and after thanking Gwyneth the second time, he set his gelding back to Clonglas.

When Owen was out of sight, Cormac dismounted and led his mare into the trees. Gwyneth did the same with Toryn, slipping his reins through her fingers as she walked. Thick-branched trees formed a canopy over their heads. Although neither spoke, Gwyneth was content to walk at his side.

Taking a deep breath, Cormac broke the silence. "Please accept my apology, Miss Beddows. A bad temper is but one of my flaws, but it doesn't excuse me for talking to you in that manner. Will you forgive me?"

"I will, though I own you made me angry." She lifted her head, intending to give him a bit of a set down, but the crooked smile on his lips made her forget everything except that they were together.

"I'm truly sorry," he said in a contrite voice. "Instead of deriding you, I should have been commending you for a beautifully run race."

Gwyneth smiled broadly and couldn't remember when she'd been happier. She and Toryn had won the race, and now she was alone with Cormac D'Arcy.

The sun had come out, and tall beech trees cast shadows over the path they followed. The lazy drone of bees accompanied the muffled sound of the horses' hooves on a thick carpet of leaves.

From time to time Cormac glanced over at her. Perhaps the race had provided a solution to Shannonderry's unkempt stable. "Since Owen gave it out that you were the new groom, perhaps it would be wise for you to hire one."

Gwyneth's light brows lifted. "You know Grandmother doesn't have the money, and if you're still worried about my reputation . . ."

"I am." Cormac's gaze was direct. "You're a newcomer . . . and English at that. Some in the area will enjoy bandying your name about."

"Because I rode Toryn astride? Surely they must be used to such from the O'Brien women. When Grandmother was young, she said she sometimes rode astride. So did Mother."

"Both had lived here all their lives, while you . . ."

Gwyneth's chin went up. "Are English," she finished for him.

Cormac saw at once that it was the wrong thing to have said. He gave a rueful smile. "I know firsthand how it rankles. It's not pleasant to be judged on birth instead of character."

"As you have been because of the O'Carrolls."

Cormac's mouth tightened. He should have known someone would tell Gwyneth his story. "Now you see what I meant about people being quick to bandy names around."

Gwyneth's voice filled with warmth. "Your name wasn't bandied but bracketed in kindest terms. My grandmother has great respect for you, Mr. D'Arcy . . . as do I."

They'd moved until they stood only a few inches apart—blind to the horses cropping the damp grass, deaf to the singing birds. The Irishman's closeness did strange things to Gwyneth's breathing, and she forgot to breathe altogether when he touched her cheek and brushed a fleck of mud from her porcelain skin. The small space between them throbbed like static air before a summer rainstorm.

Cormac suddenly stepped back and took a long, steadying breath. What had he been thinking, and what in heaven's name had they been talking about? Clearing his throat, he made a disjointed stab at conversation. "Per . . . perhaps you should mention hiring a new groom when you tell your grandmother about the race."

Certain Cormac had been about to kiss her, Gwyneth made a valiant attempt to hide her disappointment. "Yes, although . . ."

"The Westons won't take kindly to losing this morning," he hurried on, "especially with the outcome spread all over the county by nightfall." His voice gained confidence. "Emmett Weston paid a small fortune for that mare . . . brought her all the way from Kildare with the hope of bringing the steeplechase title back to County Cork. They won't waste any time trying to learn the identity of Shannonderry's new groom. When they do, they might turn nasty."

"I hadn't thought of that." The truth was, Gwyneth hadn't thought of anything but winning the race, and now she scarcely knew what to think.

"My young cousin is in need of employment," Cormac went on. "He's good with horses . . . strong, too, so he can help Flynn and Cluny keep the stable clean." He didn't tell her that since the morning he'd found her mucking out stalls, he'd tried to think of a way to get a groom for Shannonderry. Today offered the perfect solution.

"I don't know that Grandmother has the money," Gwyneth began.

"Today's winnings are more than enough to pay his salary with enough left over to buy grain for the horses." Cormac retrieved the other purse from his pocket. "All in all, you and Toryn had a very successful morning."

Gwyneth slipped the purse into her other pocket. The weight of the two bags as they banged against her hips filled her with elation. Not only had she won the race, but there was also money to give to her grandmother. She wanted to dance. Instead, she contented herself with a swagger as she led Toryn into the stable yard.

Cluny ran out to meet her, his eyes widening when he saw the mud on Gwyneth and the stallion. "Holy—!" His voice broke off. "Be ye a'right?"

"We are." Gwyneth's smile stretched wide as she instructed him to fill the water trough and bring cleaning rags.

Flynn ambled out of the stable, pitchfork in hand and an amused expression on his face. "Threw ye, did he? I knew 'twas just a matter of time. The stallion's too much for ye. Anyone with eyes can see it."

"Toryn didn't throw me," she retorted. "He's too well mannered for that." Turning her back on Flynn, she led Toryn to the trough Cluny was filling.

"Not too much," she cautioned. "Toryn was ridden hard."

"Aye." Cluny was bursting with questions. For sure, something queer had happened. "Where ye been?" he asked.

"To the church in Kilmulty and back. This morning Toryn and I won a steeplechase against Percy Weston. I took a spill, but other than that . . ."

"Ye rode the stallion?" Cluny squeaked.

"I did."

Cluny dropped his hands from the pump handle and crossed himself.

"'Tain't fittin," Flynn growled.

Cormac, who'd purposely let Gwyneth enter the stable yard ahead of him, increased his pace. "That's enough, Flynn."

The old man's mouth clamped shut, and he shot Cormac a look of dislike.

Gwyneth's eyes were bright with indignation. "The two purses I won this morning say otherwise. As you know, Shannonderry has fallen on hard times, but thanks to Toryn's great speed, we have a chance to change that."

"Still 'tain't right," Flynn wheezed.

Cormac turned on Flynn. "Like it or not, it's a fact, and one that should make you happy. For the first time in years, a Shannonderry stallion showed his rival naught but his tail."

When Cluny chortled, Toryn lifted his head from the water trough and snorted. Gwyneth quickly went to his side.

"Aye," Cormac said. "However—"

Cluny and Flynn knew enough to keep their eyes on Cormac, the boy's expression bright with pleasure, Flynn with a sour look on his grizzled face.

"It was given out at the race that Toryn's rider was Shannonderry's new groom."

Flynn made a noise in the back of his throat and scowled at Gwyneth.

"We all know this isn't true," Cormac went on, "but under the circumstances, it might be wise for your mistress to take on my cousin, Ronan O'Carroll, to help in the stable."

"No!" Flynn struck the ground with his pitchfork. "We ain't needin' help from no one."

Cormac's eyes narrowed. "I didn't say you did, but I doubt you'll like it said that those at Shannonderry are liars. Since the men at the race think you have a new groom, it will be wise to have one."

Flynn squared his bony shoulders. "I've heard naught from Mistress about a new groom."

"That's because I haven't yet told Grandmother about the race," Gwyneth said. Toryn had drunk his fill, and she started to lead him into the stable.

"'Tis ye who are to blame . . . runnin' round the countryside and—" The angry look Mr. D'Arcy shot him made Flynn catch his breath.

". . . winning money to buy oats for the mares," Gwyneth finished for him. "If Shannonderry is to prosper, we must look for ways to help instead of grumbling." She looked Flynn full in the face as she passed him with Toryn. *Smile,* she wanted to say, but the spiteful look in his rheumy eyes told her she'd said enough.

"I take me orders from the Mistress, not ye," Flynn muttered. He swung the pitchfork at an imaginary clump of straw. Now he'd have to put up with all the showin' and watchin' that went into training a new stable boy. He was too old for that, and he'd tell Mistress such when he saw her. The English woman was already bringing trouble, just like he'd known she would.

The old man watched as Gwyneth and Mr. D'Arcy prepared to unsaddle and rub down the stallion. She looked no more than a lad next to the great stallion, one who was far too full of herself. And yet—Flynn ran his tongue over the few teeth he had left—the young woman had pluck. He had to give her that. More than that, she could ride the fiery stallion. Turning so Cluny wouldn't see him smile, Flynn let his lips stretch wide. He'd like to have been there to see her beat the likes of Percy Weston. Shannonderry had a great stallion again, and for that he was glad.

14

G WYNETH HAD SCARCELY REACHED HER room when she heard her name called.

"Where've ye been?" Kate asked. Her brow furrowed when she saw Gwyneth in mud-stained breeches. "Yer grandmother will not be pleased when she sees ye. Right worried she been since ye didn't join her after breakfast. We all been worried . . . thinkin' the worst had happened . . . and by the looks of ye, 'tis not far wrong."

"I took a spill. No harm done."

They stood at the bedroom door, Gwyneth slightly out of breath from the steep stairs, Kate with eyes full of questions.

"What happened?" Kate asked, and before Gwyneth could think of an answer, she added, "What be that in yer pockets?"

Gwyneth squeezed Kate's hand. "Something exciting has happened, but Grandmother needs to hear about it first." She gave Kate's hand a second squeeze. "Could you help make me presentable for Grandmother? After I've spoken to her, I'll tell you all about it."

Kate's face showed disappointment. Something uncommon had happened, but one look at Gwyneth told her that no amount of coaxing would gain an answer. While she helped Gwyneth wash and change into a fresh gown, Kate's unasked questions snapped and cracked like wash hung to dry in a brisk wind.

"Thank you, Kate." Gwyneth said in dismissal, giving her an affectionate kiss on the cheek. "I promise to tell you later."

As soon as Kate left, Gwyneth took the purses from her jacket pockets. Their solid weight increased her excitement as she hurried down the stairs. Tiny cobwebs of worry floated through her excitement. What if Moira's reaction was like Flynn's? She paused and took a deep breath before she knocked on the sitting room door.

"Gwyneth." The gladness in Moira's voice greeted her as she entered the room. "Kate and Biddy said you were nowhere to be found. Where have you been?" Only then did Moira notice the two purses. "What have you here?"

Gwyneth crossed the room and laid the purses in her grandmother's lap. "Money, Grandmother. Look! Feel! Mr. D'Arcy says there's enough to keep our horses in grain for the rest of the year."

"Mr. D'Arcy?" Moira motioned to a chair. "I think you'd best sit down and tell me what this is all about."

"You're not going to believe it . . . and you may not like it."

Moira nodded, her bright eyes holding fast to Gwyneth's. "Tell me."

Gwyneth sat down in one of the high-backed chairs, her tongue tripping excitedly over the words as she told how she'd helped Owen in the race with Percy Weston.

Moira's gray eyebrows lifted. "You rode your stallion in a steeplechase?"

"We won the steeplechase, Grandmother!"

A smile lit the old woman's face. "Won, you say? Then why did you think I wouldn't be pleased?"

"Because . . ." Gwyneth nervously licked her lips. "Toryn doesn't give his best effort unless he's ridden astride."

Moira's eyes widened. "Oh."

Knowing nothing would be gained by trying to whitewash the affair, she launched into an explanation about the clothes she'd found in the attic. "With my short hair, Owen gave it out that I was Shannonderry's new groom," she concluded.

Moira frowned. "Everyone knows we only have Flynn and Cluny."

"I know." Gwyneth's voice was contrite. "Since you told me you sometimes rode the stallions astride . . ."

"Never in a race, child . . . though I'd have liked to." Her lips twitched as if she wished to smile.

"Grandmother." Gwyneth dropped to her knees before the old woman's chair. "I know I did wrong . . . but I hoped you'd understand. It wasn't just Owen's reputation. Toryn's and Shannonderry's good names were at stake too."

"That I understand. What I don't understand is how Mr. D'Arcy came to be part of it. I thought you said he'd gone to Mallow."

Under Moira's inquiring gaze, Gwyneth felt her cheeks warm. "He . . . he got back just in time to see the end of the race. Oh, Grandmother, I wish you could have seen it too. Toryn was magnificent. Never was there such a horse."

"Child . . . child." Despite her efforts to be stern, Moira smiled. She lifted Gwyneth's chin with an arthritic finger, tilting it to the soft light that poured through the window. "'Tis far too pretty a face to be mistaken for a groom. We must think of something."

"Mr. D'Arcy . . ." Just saying his name brought a surge of pleasure. "Mr. D'Arcy suggested that we hire a groom. He says the Westons are certain to snoop. I don't care if they do. I want Percy to know he was outridden by a woman. You should have seen the way he used his whip. He even struck Toryn."

"He struck your stallion?" Moira's voice was indignant.

"That's what caused my spill."

"Spill?" Moira's hand dropped back to her lap. "I think you had better tell me the whole of it."

Gwyneth did, her voice lifting with excitement as she described Toryn's performance and lowering indignantly when she spoke of Percy. Words like *phenomenal* and *magnificent* were used along with less flattering terms for Percy.

Moira smiled throughout the tale. "Yes!" she exclaimed several times. When Gwyneth finished, Moira took her hands in hers. "I should very much like to have been there. I'm proud of you. A true O'Brien is what you are." She looked past Gwyneth to her husband's portrait on the wall. "Your grandfather would have been proud of you as well. However—" Her expression turned pensive. "Mr. D'Arcy's suggestion about a new groom might well have merit."

She lifted the larger of the two purses. It had been years since she'd had so much ready cash. "What do you think of Mr. D'Arcy's idea, Gwyneth?"

"I agree with him." Nodding, Gwyneth hurried on. "I know it's been a long time since you've been inside the stable, but . . ." It would never do to let Moira know she helped muck the stalls. "Flynn is old, and Cluny is young. They have a difficult time keeping the stable clean. If we are to raise fine horses, we must have a clean stable," she finished in a rush.

Having noted the flush that came to Gwyneth's cheeks each time Cormac's name was mentioned, Moira hid a smile. "It's what I've wished to do for some time. Does Mr. D'Arcy have someone in mind?"

"He said his cousin, Ronan O'Carroll, is strong and good with horses. If we send word, I'm sure he could be here before evening." She shot her grandmother a quick look. "Flynn, of course, will not be happy."

"I will deal with Flynn. However, there's still the matter of your reputation." The old woman's face softened as she looked at Gwyneth. Her creamy hair and porcelain skin reminded Moira of a dazzling pearl. Like anything precious, her granddaughter must be protected.

Thoughts of taking on the Westons tripped through Moira's mind. Never one to shy away from a challenge, excitement shot through her old bones. "Yes," she said, a smile lighting her wrinkled face. "After I inform Flynn about the new groom, I will instruct him to ready the carriage for Sunday. It has been years since I've ventured out . . . too many years, truth be told." She nodded again, her smile stretching wide at the thought of the stir she and Gwyneth would create when they entered the church together. "I think it will be wise to attend church on Sunday."

* * *

THAT AFTERNOON MOIRA SENT WORD to Cormac, saying she wished to hire his cousin as the new groom. Before the young man arrived, she called Flynn into her sitting room. Gwyneth wasn't present to hear what was said, nor was she in the stable when Ronan O'Carroll arrived.

"Ye can be sure Old Flynn'll not be pleased," Kate confided later. "Cluny said there be much stompin' and mutterin' from his grandfar . . . but Cluny himself be givin' thanks now there be extra hands to clean the stable."

By then Gwyneth had given Kate a full account of the race. At first, lines of concern furrowed Kate's brow, but by the time she finished, Kate was smiling.

"Like yer mam, ye be . . . takin' chances and spills. Praise the saints it turned out right, for I'd not like ye breakin' any bones." She gave Gwyneth a quick hug. "For sure, ye've the O'Brien spirit, but then I saw signs of such when ye was young. Right free with yer opinion ye was."

Gwyneth laughed, relieved that Kate hadn't given her a scolding. All in all, the day had turned out well—her grandmother and Kate surprisingly unruffled by her actions, and a new groom hired for Shannonderry. Of course, there was still Flynn to mollify. Aware of the old man's temper, Gwyneth decided to avoid the stable for the rest of the day.

The next morning while Gwyneth was in the library looking at a map of Shannonderry, Biddy tapped on the door.

"Reverend Gibbins and two gentlemen from the village be here. Mistress wants ye to join them in the sitting room."

Unease fluttered in Gwyneth's heart. Had the reverend recognized her astride Toryn and come with gentlemen from the parish to censure her behavior? Although she didn't care two figs if Percy Weston knew, she'd hoped to keep the reverend in ignorance. More than that, she didn't want to cause Moira embarrassment. Gwyneth hastily reached for her pleated cap of white lawn and ribbons. With it fastened firmly over her short curls, she entered the sitting room.

Three men rose from chairs and bowed. Gwyneth recognized Reverend Gibbins, but the other two were strangers. Even so, she was glad that she wore her mother's pink gown. Although it was sadly out of style, it became her.

"Gentlemen," she said, making a curtsy.

As introductions were made, Gwyneth had time to study the two strangers—Mr. Berry, broad featured with graying hair, and Patrick Kilburn, a tall, lean figure with sandy hair and a liberal scattering of freckles. She thankfully noted the reverend's genial smile and how the other men showed friendly interest.

Moira turned to Gwyneth after she was seated. "Our guests have come with an interesting proposition concerning Toryn. Since the stallion belongs to you, I wanted you to be present to hear it."

Gwyneth relaxed and extended another smile to Reverend Gibbins, whose long legs were stretched out awkwardly from his chair. He returned her smile.

"Your stallion ran a splendid race, Miss Beddows. Even with your groom taking a spill, the stallion finished the race in record time. Is that not so, Sean?"

The broad-featured man pulled a watch out of his vest pocket. "Timed him myself. Never seen a horse eat up the ground like yours did. A splendid race, like Reverend said."

Praise for Toryn never failed to raise Gwyneth's spirits. "Thank you, sir."

Reverend Gibbins nodded and cleared his throat. "This brings us to the reason for our visit. Francis O'Roark from County Limerick owns a stallion that's never been beaten. O'Roark's so sure that he'll remain so that he's offered a purse of two hundred pounds sterling to any horse that can beat him. Several have tried, and one or two have come close, but the horse, Thor, remains unbeaten. That's why, Miss Beddows . . ."

"I know Toryn can win," Gwyneth broke in. "He's never been beaten either."

"So young D'Arcy told us. However—"

The clergyman fixed Gwyneth with a gaze that made her uneasy. Had he guessed the identity of Toryn's rider? Hoping to distract him, she offered him her sweetest smile. "However what, Reverend?"

"Mr. O'Roark is a wily businessman who requires an entry fee of fifty pounds from anyone wishing to race his stallion."

"Fifty pounds!" Gwyneth's voice was incredulous.

"O'Roark claims the fee is to discourage all but the most serious contenders." Reverend Gibbins glanced at his friends. "After yesterday, we don't doubt your stallion is a serious contender." His gray eyes brightened as he looked at the two women. "That's why we've taken up a collection for the entry fee . . . fifty pounds and a little more so O'Roark knows we mean business."

Mr. Berry leaned forward. "Perhaps you aren't aware that Shannonderry and County Cork are synonymous with the steeplechase. The fact that a horse from County Limerick now lays claim to the title sticks like paste in the craw."

Mr. Kilburn nodded vigorously. "'Tis time to bring the title back to Cork where it belongs, and by the looks of your stallion, he's the one for doin' it."

"Aye," Mr. Berry glanced at Moira, "I've not see a finer horse since the days of Thunder, him your late husband was fond of ridin'. Like Patrick said, 'tis time to reclaim the title."

Moira, who had remained silent during the exchange, finally spoke, her small frame erect in the high-backed chair. "Your kindness in raising money for the entry fee is commendable, gentlemen. However, since Shannonderry's stallion will be racing against Thor, Shannonderry will provide the money. I believe my granddaughter will agree with me."

Moira's show of pride struck an answering chord in Gwyneth's heart. "Yes . . . though I hope such won't prevent you gentlemen from making wagers on the outcome. Like you, I have every confidence that Toryn will win."

"Exactly." Moira's eyes held Gwyneth's in an unspoken pact. Before anyone could argue, she extended a wrinkled hand to the reverend. "Now, if you will excuse me, I find that I am tired."

It was all that the reverend could do not to give the old woman a scolding. Must her pride always rule out good sense? He longed to speak frankly as her husband had done, but the presence of others prevented him. Grimacing, he slowly got to his feet and bowed.

Gwyneth spoke as he rose from his chair. "Although Shannonderry will provide the entry fee, will you make the necessary arrangements for the race? Cormac D'Arcy will need to be contacted as well." Seeing the reverend's raised brows, she hurried on. "Our groom lacks experience to ride in such an important race. If you'll contact Mr. O'Roark, I'll speak to Mr. D'Arcy about riding Toryn."

"I'll post a letter this very day," Mr. Berry said. His satisfaction in the outcome was obvious, but like the reverend, he wondered how Moira Donahue would come up with the money. His shrewd eyes had noted the granddaughter's poise and aura of quality. Perhaps she'd brought money from England.

Gwyneth put on a bright front as she and her grandmother bade the visitors good day. Only when the door was safely closed did she speak. "How will we ever find enough money for the race, Grandmother?"

"God will provide." Conviction laced Moira's words. Hadn't prayer prompted her to send for Gwyneth? Surely now that she was here, He would continue to bless them. She nodded, knowing that if she followed a path lit by faith, answers would come.

Seeing Gwyneth's doubtful expression, she went on. "We must show faith and pray . . . Kate and Biddy too. I don't hold with the notion that only Protestant prayers reach heaven. Though Papist prayers are counted on beads, I believe God hears them the same as ours." Moira reached for Gwyneth's slender hand. "Aye. We must cultivate faith and pray."

15

Moira's words stayed with Gwyneth for the rest of the morning and followed her out to the stable when she went to groom Toryn. Gwyneth hadn't had much experience with either faith or prayer. Although her attendance at the church near Hawarden had been frequent, her attention to Parson Cranston's sermons had been more dutiful than pious. Yet, hadn't her grandmother's letter come like an answer to prayer? Cormac D'Arcy's willingness to help as well?

The sound of singing greeted Gwyneth as she entered the stable, a deep-toned voice riding clear and true on the morning air. Looking around, she saw a young man forking straw and manure into a wheelbarrow. Shaggy dark hair curled from beneath his cap, and his muscled shoulders proclaimed he was no stranger to work.

"You must be Ronan O'Carroll."

The groom's singing broke off, and his lips curved into a smile as pleasant as his voice. "Aye, 'tis such that I'm called, and glad I be to meet ye, Mistress." He touched a hand to his cap. "Mr. D'Arcy and young Owen have naught but praise for both ye and yer stallion . . . though as yet the grand beast ain't let me near."

Gwyneth caught a glimpse of Cormac in Ronan's blue eyes and full lips, but by and large the young man was cut from a mold all his own. That fact that he'd referred to Cormac as Mr. D'Arcy instead of his cousin made her suspect he was also very independent. "I'm afraid Toryn isn't of a friendly nature."

"Aye, so my cou . . . Mr. D'Arcy told me. Hopefully in time . . ." A smile lit Ronan's face. "Everyone be talkin' about his speed and the race he won yesterday. Some say he's a Shannonderry stallion come back from the grave."

Gwyneth laughed as she approached Toryn's stall. "Do you hear that? They think you're Irish instead of Yorkshire bred. What do you think of that?"

Toryn snorted and his ears flattened as he eyed the new groom. Although Ronan kept his distance, the horse was very aware of the unfamiliar groom.

"He'll be less skittish when he gets used to you," Gwyneth explained. "Isn't that so, Cluny?"

Cluny had materialized from the tack room, but as yet there was no sign of Flynn. Perhaps now that he had more help, the old man would be less vigilant.

"What's this?" a wheezy voice demanded. "Talkin' and gapin' instead of muckin' the stalls? 'Twill be no laziness in my stable . . . do ye hear that, boyo?" He glowered at Ronan and turned a face that was no less fierce on Cluny. "Back to fillin' the water trough, then see that the pail is cleaned." Only then did he glance at Gwyneth, his sour expression changing to a glower as he walked away.

Gwyneth was not of a mind to let Flynn spoil her morning. Soothing Toryn, she began to groom him, humming as she brushed his shiny black coat. Ronan commenced singing too, their music swirling through the stable and dissolving the last traces of Flynn's discordant voice.

A few minutes later Gwyneth rode the stallion away from the stable, setting him on a course past grazing Shannonderry cattle and onto the track to Clonglas. She'd been searching for a reason to see Cormac. The news of Reverend Gibbins's visit offered the perfect excuse.

Anxious to reach Clonglas, Gwyneth left the track and galloped Toryn across the countryside, jumping a wall that marked the end of Shannonderry then taking a shortcut through a copse of oak trees. As she entered the shadowy interior, Toryn shied to avoid a horse and rider barring their way. For a terrible moment, Gwyneth thought she'd be unseated. Struggling to regain her balance, she heard male laughter.

"Not so sure of yourself now that you're back to being a lady 'stead of a groom," the voice taunted. "I know who you are, and . . ."

Toryn's shrill whinny drowned out the rest. Battling with all her skill and strength to hold the big horse in check, Gwyneth recognized Percy Weston barring the way on a gelding as large and formidable as Toryn.

"How I'm dressed . . . doesn't matter," she threw at him between ragged gasps. "My horse and I can outride you any day of the week."

Percy's thin lips pulled away from his crooked teeth, his voice a sneer. "Think you're something, don't you. You'd best take care if you know what's good for you. You and your English horse aren't welcome here."

"Who says?" she flung at him, fighting to keep Toryn from rearing again.

"I do. Enter your horse in another race, and you'll wish you hadn't." Percy edged his gelding closer, gray eyes narrowed, riding whip raised.

Seeing it, Toryn reared, his neigh like a trumpet as he lunged at the gelding. Gwyneth pitched forward in the saddle, her skill and some invisible hands all that kept her from falling.

"Stop!" an angry voice shouted.

Before Gwyneth could fully regain her balance, Cormac D'Arcy entered the melee and launched himself from his mare to grab Toryn's head.

Clinging precariously to her seat atop the rearing stallion, Gwyneth feared that Toryn's flashing hooves and bared teeth would connect with the Irishman. Somehow he managed to dodge past them and grab the stallion's bridle and head. Toryn immediately stilled, the whoosh of his expelled breath meshing with Cormac's Gaelic chant.

Heart pounding, Gwyneth's own breathing came out in a rasp as Toryn shuddered and settled his hooves onto the leaf-matted path.

"There," Cormac crooned. One hand stroked Toryn's glossy neck while the other maintained its hold on his nose. "Easy, big boy. Easy."

Still stroking Toryn, Cormac spoke to Percy in a voice laced with anger. "If you speak like that again to Miss Beddows, I'll have your hide. Don't try to waylay her again, either. Now go!"

Mottled spots of color suffused Percy's face, but the sneer was back. "I'm not afraid of you . . . tryin' to act like you're one of us." Urging his gelding away from the trees, he called back over his shoulder. "Peasant! You're naught but a common peasant!"

"And glad that I am," Cormac said under his breath. Then he looked up at Gwyneth, his anger abating as he searched her face. "Are you all right?"

"Yes . . . thanks to you." She let out a long, unsteady breath. "Thank you."

"I'm glad I was close enough to help." He continued to hold her gaze, aware of the dredges of fright in her lovely eyes and that her riding hat was slightly askew. "Percy should be whipped . . . waiting to find you alone to issue his threat." He grimaced. "That's the way of the Westons."

Toryn stirred and leaned his head closer to Cormac.

"How do you calm him so quickly?" Gwyneth asked in amazement.

"Like I told you, 'tis a gift . . . one I discovered when I was no older than ten. Yours, on the other hand, is skill. Most women would have been thrown just now . . . many men as well. Your father taught you well . . . though I've a notion the O'Brien spirit has helped."

Cormac's words warmed Gwyneth's heart and melted the last of the icy fear gripping her stomach. She offered him a tentative smile. Seeing it, Cormac released his hold on Toryn's head and reached up for her. With no hesitation, she slid off the horse and into his arms. There was a moment of silence as each of them became aware of the closeness and as Cormac's hands encircled her slender waist.

Gwyneth's legs were unsteady as she met and held his searching gaze. The warm pinpoints of light in his blue eyes made her want to lay her head against his shoulder.

Cormac gently pushed a lock of fallen hair away from her cheek. The air seemed to pulse and dance around them. "You gave me a fright," he said in an unsteady voice. As he spoke, a movement from the river caused him to lift his eyes. The outline of a horse and rider was clearly silhouetted against the noon sky. "Curse Percy Weston!" Cormac growled, dropping his hand from Gwyneth's waist and stepping away.

Cormac's sudden movement cut like a knife at Gwyneth's happiness. Only then did she see Percy watching from a nearby bridge.

Cormac handed Toryn's reins to Gwyneth and walked to his mare. Anger was evident in both his voice and the taut line of his shoulders. "Blast the Westons!"

Gwyneth pulled on Toryn's reins and followed the Irishman. With the intimacy between them broken, it was better to talk of other things. "Grandmother told me what Mr. Weston tried to do to your mother," she ventured. "Was nothing ever done to him?"

Cormac shook his head. "With Mam in her grave and naught but Gran to tell the story, there was little chance the charge would stick. The Westons have lived here for over a hundred years. More than that, Emmett Weston's brother is the chief magistrate in Mallow. The family name carries much weight."

"Even more than the D'Arcys?" Gwyneth asked.

"Remember that my father had left for Dublin. Eight years later, when he came back with a new wife, he was determined to keep the past firmly behind him." Cormac glanced at Gwyneth as they led their horses into the meadow. "Although my father retrieved me from my grandmother's and took me to Clonglas, never once in all the years did he mention my mother's name. He'd bolted the door to that part of his life, and his anger when I tried to force it open was not a pretty sight . . . not for a boy of twelve or a man of twenty." A rueful smile played at the corners of Cormac's mouth. "Yet, strange as it may seem, he made me his heir."

"And you love Clonglas," Gwyneth finished for him.

His smile broadened. "That I do, Miss Beddows."

Neither spoke, the play of sunlight on the flower-strewn meadow seeming to capture their interest. Although Percy was no longer in sight, they kept a safe distance from each other.

"I was on my way to Clonglas just now," Gwyneth said.

"Were you?" The tone of his voice invited her to go on.

While Cormac listened, she told him about Reverend Gibbins's visit. "It will be an impossibility for me to ride Toryn in such an important race. Will you consent to be his rider?"

"I would consider it an honor . . . Indeed, I was on my way to Shannonderry to offer my services." Cormac gave her the lopsided smile she was coming to love. "Irish tongues are never still. I already knew that the reverend planned to visit you this morning, and since I'm well aware of your grandmother's pride, I was certain she'd reject their gift of the entry fee."

"That decision was mine as well as Grandmother's."

Cormac's smile turned tender. "Again, I am not surprised. Did I not spend nigh a week with you on our way to Ireland . . . and cross swords with you yesterday after the race?"

Gwyneth reveled in his teasing. Then her mind turned serious. "Did Percy also know about Reverend Gibbins's visit?"

"I'm certain he did. Why else would he try to frighten you? The Westons' hopes have long been pinned on bringing the title back to County Cork. For months, Emmett scoured Ireland for a horse that could beat Thor. He paid a small fortune when he thought he'd found one."

Fanning his hat at a dragonfly, Cormac chuckled. "For the mare to lose a race less than a fortnight after his purchase must rankle Emmett. I doubt either he or Percy slept well last night."

Gwyneth laughed. Although winning the race had been a dream come true, her time with Cormac afterward had been even more rewarding. She'd sensed his caring, just as she did now, his eyes filled with warmth like rays of sun on a cobalt sea. Percy's vile threat and her fright when Toryn reared were forgotten when she saw the depth of feeling on the Irishman's face.

* * *

Two days later, Flynn brought the carriage up to the front steps of Shannonderry. The ancient vehicle had been freshly polished so that the silver trim around the door glinted in the morning sun. Flynn was dressed in a dark coat and hat instead of his tattered vest and cap. Cluny jumped down from his place on the seat next to Flynn to open the door.

"Thank you, Cluny," Moira said.

Gwyneth and Cluny helped the old woman into the carriage. When they were comfortably settled, Flynn spoke to the horses, and they set off along the tree-lined lane to the road that led to the village.

Moira sighed in satisfaction. "It's been some years since I've been to church, and I'm looking forward to hearing one of Reverend Gibbins's sermons again. Although I've found much strength and comfort in reading the Bible and praying by myself, doing so is sometimes lacking." She paused and patted Gwyneth's gloved hand. "The prospect of attending church is made even more pleasant because you're with me."

Moira thought back to the dreary, lonely days that had seemed to wind in an endless circle. Gwyneth's coming had banished them like a breath of fresh air, sweeping the cobwebs of old age and self-pity out the door and replacing them with vitality. The old woman hadn't felt so alive in years.

"Have I mentioned how fetching you look this morning?" Moira went on. "That soft shade of green becomes you. Mrs. Ryan outdid herself in bringing Deirdre's gown back into fashion."

Moira's praise came like music to Gwyneth's ears. She didn't once remember her stepmother giving her a compliment, and the only words of praise she'd heard from her father had centered on her ability to ride a horse. The hope of seeing Cormac at church had already sweetened Gwyneth's morning. Moira's words topped it like a dollop of rich cream on spring-fresh strawberries. "Thank you, Grandmother. Living with you makes me happy too."

Feeling the sting of tears, Moira looked out the window and silently thanked God for the precious gift of her granddaughter. When she could trust herself to speak, the old woman reminisced about the days when she'd ridden to church with her parents. Threaded through her words were unmistakable notes of happiness.

By the time they reached the gray stone church with a tangle of ivy climbing its square tower, Sunday service had already begun. Moira was secretly pleased since she knew the sight of her and Gwyneth entering the church together would do much to further her granddaughter's acceptance.

The heavy oak door to the church was closed, the thick walls muting the sound of the organ as Cluny tugged at the door.

The two women walked up the aisle together, Moira leaning on Gwyneth's arm and the O'Brien amethysts glittering around her wrinkled neck. Gwyneth was aware of heads turning and surprised whispers. *Moira Donahue, who's been too infirm to leave home, is at church. That must be her granddaughter. Did you hear the legend about her namesake? 'Tis her who owns the stallion that outran the Westons' mare.* Gwyneth unconsciously lifted her fair head, grateful for the refurbished gown and conscious of her grandmother's regal black form beside her.

Reverend Gibbins waited at the altar for them to be seated, his black vestment making his lean body appear less spare. Soft light poured through a stained-glass window depicting Christ healing the sick—its glow reflecting off the glass onto the reverend's balding head.

Gwyneth kept her eyes on the window, the flaming colors like a beacon guiding her down the aisle to the O'Brien pew at the front of the church.

Reverend Gibbins smiled his welcome, then with a clearing of his throat, he launched into his sermon. Gwyneth stifled the impulse to look over her shoulder for Cormac. Was he a religious man, or had he remained at Clonglas to attend to estate business? There was much she didn't know about the Irishman, and she was eager to learn the secrets of his mind and heart.

Moira listened to the sermon with rapt attention, pulling the words to her heart and savoring their taste and texture. *Faith. Hope.* They were all she had to cling to in the twilight of her life. Of late, hope burned bright again, the source of its flame centered on the young woman sitting at her side.

Like Moira, Gwyneth felt warmth and a sense of homecoming gather around her as she listened to the reverend read from the Bible. After a few minutes, the sound of his voice was crowded out by feelings of the past, feelings so strong they seemed to caress the carved oak pew and draw her eyes to the plastered stone wall. Perhaps her mother had once sat in this very spot, the other Gwyneth too, listening to the swell of the old organ, beseeching God for help in their individual quests.

Her eyes strayed to two brass plaques set into the wall beside the O'Brien pew. *In loving memory of William Donahue. Born October 24, 1741. Died January 11, 1792. May he rest in peace with God and His angels.* The second plaque bore the name of Brandon Donahue, Moira's only son. He'd died just a year after his father at a mere twenty years of age. How had Moira borne it—the loss of both husband and son in the space of two years? With a flash of pain, Gwyneth realized that her mother had died just five years previous. Small wonder Moira Donahue had spoken of loneliness.

When it was time to pray, Gwyneth helped Moira kneel, the creak of her old bones and bowed gray head attesting to her advanced years. Gwyneth's heart overflowed with caring as she knelt beside her. Unseen arms seemed to gather her close—those of Deirdre, the other Gwyneth, her grandfather, and Brandon, each one bidding her welcome. Gwyneth's throat tightened and tears misted her eyes. How her life had changed in just a few short weeks.

Chords from the organ swelled as the prayer ended. Reverend Gibbins started down the aisle, nodding to Moira and Gwyneth as he passed on his way to the door. One by one, the congregation filed out after him.

Gwyneth felt the curious stares as she searched the church for Cormac. She saw him at once, standing at the end of a pew just three rows behind them. Handsomely turned out in a blue coat and white cravat, his eyes warmed as they met hers. She scarcely noticed Owen's eager expression, though she was aware that Agatha D'Arcy's face held no warmth as she offered Gwyneth a slight nod.

Moira was grateful for Gwyneth's arm as they started down the aisle. Kneeling and the long sermon had taken a toll. Before they had gone many steps, Cormac offered her his arm and asked how she was.

"Good . . . good," Moira said, gratefully accepting his help.

The aisle was wide enough to walk three abreast out of the church. Outside in the fickle Irish sunshine, people stopped to talk. Many crowded around them, anxious to speak to Moira and to be introduced to her granddaughter. Gwyneth met so many people she had difficulty remembering names and faces. Through it all, she was aware that Cormac stayed close, talking to friends, his lips lifting each time her eyes met his.

It wasn't until Flynn brought the carriage around that she noticed Percy Weston standing with a young man Moira had introduced as George Maguire. Although some distance separated them, she could feel Percy's dislike.

She turned away, grateful when Cormac took her arm to walk her to the waiting carriage. "Do you find our village to your liking?" he asked.

"I do. It reminds me of ours at Hawarden. Didn't you stay at the inn there?"

"I did . . . though that was before I met up with my nephew Cedric." His glance was teasing. "Entertaining as the young rascal was, I find his replacement a vast improvement. With the press of people, I haven't had opportunity to tell you how lovely you look today."

Heat rose to her cheeks. "Thank you." In an effort to hide her embarrassment, she hurried on in a mock whisper. "I didn't know you thought me a rascal."

"Cedric was the rascal, while you—" Cormac's fingers tightened on her arm. Aware that Owen openly listened and that Moira had turned to watch, he left the sentence unfinished. Enough was conveyed by touch to give Gwyneth hope.

That hope followed her as she and Cormac walked with Moira and Reverend Gibbins to the O'Brien carriage. When they reached it, Moira turned and fixed Cormac with an intent gaze.

"Thank you for helping in the matter of a new groom. Now that I'm feeling stronger, you and your brother must come for tea one afternoon. Your mother, too, if she'd care to join us."

Gwyneth glanced at Agatha, who was deep in conversation with Emmett Weston. Percy had left his friend and now stood with his father.

As if he were aware of her gaze, the elder Mr. Weston turned, his barrel chest rising and his face stiff with resentment. Percy's animosity matched his father's. Much too happy to let it bother her, she turned a radiant face to Cormac as he helped her into the carriage.

"Your grandmother has invited Owen and me for tea on Wednesday. I look forward with pleasure to the occasion."

"I look forward to it as well," she murmured and settled with a happy sigh onto the worn cushions of the carriage.

Although the outing had tired Moira, she was pleased at how well it had gone. She smiled as she recalled the warm reception Gwyneth had received and the gladness she'd glimpsed in old friends' faces as they'd greeted her.

"A most satisfying occasion," Moira pronounced. "Elizabeth Sheehan was much taken by you . . . though she has put on weight since I saw her last."

Moira went on to mention that Sophie McCarthy's daughter was soon to wed. Only then did she pause to favor Gwyneth with a teasing smile. "I couldn't help but note that you and Mr. D'Arcy found enjoyment in each other's company. Did I do right to invite him and his brother to tea on Wednesday?"

"You did, Grandmother." Gwyneth laughed.

"So you find him to your liking, do you?"

Aware that her cheeks were flaming, Gwyneth knew it would be useless to deny it. "Very much . . . Owen too, of course, but not . . ."

Moira's laughter cut through her reply. "You don't need to explain. Were I fifty years younger I would find excuse to admire the man as well." She patted Gwyneth's hand. "And his character is as fine as his looks."

Gwyneth nodded, clasping onto the opportunity to talk about the Irishman. "I don't believe I told you that when I went riding yesterday, I saw Mr. D'Arcy." Not wanting her grandmother to worry, she didn't mention the altercation with Percy. "He has agreed to ride Toryn in the race with Mr. O'Roark's stallion. He said it would be an honor to ride such a horse."

"Your grandfather always thought so," Moira acknowledged. "He was a skilled rider . . . as was your uncle Brandon."

"Those must have been wonderful times for you . . . the famous Shannonderry mares and stallions and winning races."

"They were." Moira's eyes grew distant. After a long moment, she turned to Gwyneth and smiled. "But my life isn't over yet. Something tells me wonderful things are about to happen again."

16

THE NEWS THAT GWYNETH'S STALLION was to challenge the horse from Limerick quickly became common knowledge. It had been one of the main topics of conversation after church on Sunday, and with Cluny and Biddy to spread the news among the cottiers, the peasants' tongues were busy too.

When Gwyneth joined her grandmother in the sitting room on Monday, Moira pointed to the neat stacks of coins on the desk. "I have twice counted the money you and Toryn won. Would you care to guess at the amount?"

A little awed, Gwyneth walked to the desk. She couldn't recall when she'd seen so much money. "It looks as if we are extremely rich."

Moira laughed. "Hardly that, but the purses did contain more than I expected . . . twenty-five pounds and twenty guineas, to be exact. Not enough to cover the entry fee, but a good beginning. With God's help, I'm confident we will soon have sufficient funds." A look of satisfaction crossed Moira's thin face. "I have asked Kate and Biddy to add our cause to their prayers as well."

Gwyneth nodded. "Kate told me at breakfast that she prays for us each time she counts her beads. Did you know she prays for Toryn too?" In a fair imitation of her former nurse, Gwyneth recited Kate's words. "For yer horse must be runnin' his best if we're to win the race. Our Biddy hung a lucky sprig of shamrock over the stable door, and Cluny fastened one on the stall next to Toryn's. With the charms and all our prayers, the grand beast be sure to win."

Moira smiled. "God has blessed me with kind and loyal servants. I don't know what I would have done without them all these years."

Gwyneth looked for the sprig of shamrock when she went to the stable. Although the leaves had begun to wilt, the bright scrap of cloth that held them bespoke confidence. "For luck," she informed Toryn.

Ronan's strong arms and enthusiasm had made a noticeable difference in the appearance and smell of the stable. For the first time since her arrival, it looked well kept. Cluny excitedly pointed out the changes, and, in an unguarded moment, Gwyneth heard Flynn's wheezy humming from the tack room.

After Toryn had been groomed, she led him to the fence to mount him. As she did, Ronan led a saddled mare out of the stable.

"You don't have to come with me. I'm used to riding Toryn alone."

Acting as if he hadn't heard, Ronan mounted the mare. "I'm but followin' orders."

"Who's orders?" she challenged.

"Mr. D'Arcy's . . . though he said ye'd object."

She stared at the young man from atop Toryn. "Mr. D'Arcy!" she echoed.

Ronan nodded. "He said I was to watch so nothin' bad happened to ye."

"It won't," she retorted, yet even as she spoke, she remembered her encounter with Percy Weston and the hate-filled look he'd thrown at her on Sunday. Though it rubbed against her pride, she saw the wisdom of having someone with her. More than that, the instructions had come from Cormac.

Holding this thought close, she set Toryn to a lope away from the stable, aware that Ronan and the brown mare weren't far behind. Toryn was aware of them too. She could feel his impatience and knew he was eager to put as much distance as possible between them. When she continued to hold him in, he skittishly pranced and tested the reins.

"You don't like it, do you? And neither do I. Shall we let them see what you can do?"

When she loosened the reins, the stallion's pace increased, his long legs seeming to effortlessly traverse the meadow. For a few minutes, Gwyneth felt as if she were flying with the wind whipping her hair and cheeks and her exuberance matching the stallion's.

A quick glance showed Ronan and the mare in hot pursuit, but it was an uneven race. Although the groom rode one of Shannonderry's mares, she couldn't keep pace with Toryn. Few could, as Percy Weston had discovered.

Smiling at the memory, Gwyneth slowed the horse. No good would come from leaving Ronan too far behind. More than that, Toryn had enjoyed a good gallop. It was time to settle him down.

Instead of chagrin, Ronan's expression was one of awe when he caught up. "What a grand horse himself is. No wonder Weston lost the race."

"Toryn has never been beaten," Gwyneth acknowledged, "though today wasn't his best effort. It can't be when I ride sidesaddle."

"So me cousin be telling me." He gave her an impish grin. "Just the same, I'm glad ye didn't leave me too far behind. Cormac has the devil of a temper and said he'd have me hide should I let ye out of my sight."

His words settled like a happy glow around Gwyneth's heart and made her think how pleasant it would be to always have the Irishman to protect her. Smiling, she set Toryn back toward Shannonderry. Clouds hung in a pearly mist over the nearby hills, and a chorus of meadow thrush filled the air with their happy song. Although it looked as if rain were imminent, the prospect didn't diminish Gwyneth's high spirits. It was enough to know that the Irishman wanted to keep her safe.

* * *

THE FOLLOWING MORNING AS GWYNETH ate her breakfast, a loud rap sounded on the kitchen door. Urgency in his voice, one of the tenants rushed inside as Biddy answered it.

"Tell Mistress there be trouble," Mick Sullivan said, his voice breathless from hurrying.

"Holy Mother!" Biddy exclaimed. "And herself not yet out of bed."

Gwyneth pushed back her chair, the bowl of oat porridge forgotten as she hurried into the kitchen. "What is it Mick?"

One look at the tenant's distraught face told her the news wasn't good. Mick hastily removed his cap. "Cattle houghed . . . four of them down. How the blighters what done it got past the hounds, I don't know. 'Twas their pitiful bellowin' sent me to the pasture." He shook his dark head. "I'm sorry to be the one to tell ye . . . and what the Mistress will say—" He shook his head again.

"For now, we won't tell her." Gwyneth's voice held purpose as she reached for Kate's green wool shawl hanging on a peg by the door. "Take me to them."

"But, Mistress—" Seeing the determination on Gwyneth's pale face, Mick stepped aside. "'Tis not a pleasant sight for ye to be seein'."

"I expect not . . . but it's something I must do."

Gwyneth followed Mick away from the dooryard, skirting the round, stone enclosure of the well, the swish of her skirt sending a chicken scurrying for cover. A misty rain was falling, and the damp grass quickly wet Gwyneth's slippers.

She had to hurry to keep pace with Mick, her skirt slapping damply against her legs while Mick muttered to himself, the brim of his cap pulled low over his furrowed brow. Questions dogged Gwyneth's steps. Who had houghed Shannonderry's cattle, and why hadn't the wolfhounds stopped them? In her mind she saw the dogs crouched, ready to spring at the horses when she'd first arrived at Shannonderry. Wouldn't they have posed the same threat last night?

Mick seemed to wrestle with similar thoughts, his brow creased as he shot a look at Gwyneth. "Who would do such a terrible thing?" he asked, his voice incredulous. "Herself a saint and ye and yer stallion come like a miracle. Yer our hope, ye know. If any good comes to ye at Shannonderry, 'twill spill over to us."

Hearing him, Gwyneth remembered Sean O'Leary and the rock he'd thrown at the cart. "Not all think well of us. One threw a rock at Grandmother and me."

"Sean O'Leary." Mick snorted. "And, aye, we heard of it. The lad has more fire than sense. Warned he be by more than one and is now kept under a tight thumb by both his far and granfar . . . the priest as well." Mick shook his head. "'Twasn't Sean."

"Then who?"

"I wish I knew."

They followed a path that led to the meadow, the way taking them through towering oak trees where the rooks nested. Their raucous cries melded with the distant bellows of the houghed cattle. Four, Mick had said. Thank heaven it hadn't been twenty.

Their pace quickened as the plaintive call from maimed cattle became more distinct. With Kate's green shawl pulled over her head and shoulders, Gwyneth was too absorbed in her thoughts to heed the drizzly rain. Even so, she shivered.

In time they reached a thick hedge that served as a fence around the meadow. Gwyneth followed Mick through a wooden gate. Her steps slowed when she saw the rain-darkened, downed cattle heaving in a futile effort to get to their feet. Bile rose in her throat, the bloody hindquarters of the struggling beasts like something from a nightmare. Gwyneth turned away. "Can nothing be done to help them?" she asked in a strangled voice.

"No'm." Mick's voice came harsh. "Cut their hamstrings, he did . . . left them to naught but a slow death. The dirty blighter," he added in an undertone.

Gwyneth turned away in an effort to avoid the blood and suffering, but she couldn't ignore the strident bellows. Only thoughts of her grandmother and the other Gwyneth kept her from covering her ears and fleeing. "Put them out of their misery," she rasped.

Her strangled words were hard for Mick to decipher. "What?" he asked.

"Put them out of their misery." Her voice was that of a stranger, harsh and brisk.

"Yes'm."

Not waiting for him to say more, Gwyneth walked away, deliberately holding herself in check instead of fleeing.

"What of the meat?" Mick called after her.

She paused. To those subsisting on potatoes and oatcakes, a side of roast beef would seem a gift from heaven. Was that why the cattle had been houghed? So the poor could have meat? Gwyneth dismissed the thought. Meat hadn't been the motivation. It was something more sinister.

"Divide the meat between the tenants and the poor of the parish. Your priest will know who needs it most."

"What of ye? Shall I bring some to the castle?"

A shudder ran through Gwyneth's slender frame. After seeing the poor cows, she knew her stomach would rebel if Kate or Biddy set a slice of beef before her. Instinct told her it would be the same with her grandmother. "No," she called. "None for us."

Gwyneth was able to hold herself to a walk until she passed through the gate. The other Gwyneth had seen worse than mutilated cattle and had maintained control. She must do the same. But doing so didn't mean she couldn't hurry away from the mournful sounds of the cows.

With the woolen shawl pulled close to ward off the rain, Gwyneth ran toward the castle. Her mind was a muddle of half-formed thoughts. Who had done this, and how would she ever tell Moira? "Poor Grandmother," she whispered between ragged gulps of air—Grandmother, who had proclaimed on Sunday that good things were about to happen.

As Gwyneth neared the castle, she saw Ronan and Cluny on their way to the stable. Pausing to peer through the misty rain, she realized Ronan carried something large and gray in his arms. Dread tightened her stomach. It was one of the wolfhounds.

Catching her breath, she hurried on. By now the shawl had fallen away from her blond hair, and the steady cadence of her feet sounded like an echo to her pounding heart. "Ronan!" she managed to get out.

The groom and Cluny stopped and turned.

"'Tis Bradach," Cluny called. "He be hurt bad."

"We must get him into the stable," Ronan added, resuming his steps.

Cluny dropped back to join Gwyneth. "Him didn't come in this mornin' when I called . . . so Ronan and I went lookin' for him." Cluny's freckled face crumpled. "'Twas awful, Miss Gwyneth . . . him hurt and bloody from a knife stuck in his belly. He tried to come but—" Sobs stopped Cluny's words.

Gwyneth pulled him close, feeling the shudder of his sobs and the pounding of his heart. "I'm sorry," she said, laying her cheek on the boy's wet head. "We must try to save him."

"Aye," Cluny said as they hurried after Ronan.

When they entered the stable, the dog was lying on a pile of straw, Ronan and Flynn kneeling beside him. The old man cursed softly as he looked down at the limp form.

"How badly is he hurt?" Gwyneth asked.

Ronan shrugged out of his wet coat and laid it over the dog. "'Tis bad . . . but he still be breathin'."

Flynn's gnarled hands gently moved the blood-stained fur away from the wound, his fingers exploring the depth of the oozing gash. "Stabbed him they did . . . as he attacked."

"Threw the knife to stop him so they could get to the cattle," Ronan added in a husky voice.

"You know about the cattle then?"

"Aye, when Mick came with the news, we wondered why one of the dogs didn't stop them. When Cluny saw one be missin', we suspected sompin' bad had happened."

"Bradach was always the first to come in," Cluny added in a tear-choked voice. He'd dropped to his knees to stroke the dog's bristly head. "Such a good dog ye be."

Gwyneth's throat tightened as she stepped away. "I'll send Biddy with rags and hot water."

"Wait, Mistress." Ronan reached into his pocket and pulled out a crumpled piece of paper. "This be stuck between two rocks next to the dog."

The writing on the paper was so crude Gwyneth had difficulty deciphering it. Suddenly the black charcoal marks merged into words that made her breath catch.

"What do it say?" Cluny asked.

Gwyneth swallowed past the tightness in her throat. "'English go home,'" she read in a quivery voice.

A tiny sound escaped Flynn's opened mouth, but his expression showed dismay rather than satisfaction. Gwyneth held his startled gaze for a long moment before she turned on her heel and hurried from the stable.

* * *

AN HOUR LATER GWYNETH SAT beside her grandmother on the sitting room sofa. Kate had stoked the peat fire to take away the damp chill, but it failed to penetrate the coldness that sat like an unyielding lump in Gwyneth's stomach. Her self-control had almost deserted her, and she wanted nothing more than to sit at Moira's knees and lay her head in the old woman's lap. Knowing she was a young woman, not a child, was all that kept her on the sofa. She'd held on to her courage as she told Moira of the morning events, and she must continue to do so. Even so, the terrible events had eaten at Gwyneth's faith. *Why, God? Why?* Not hearing an answer, she turned to her grandmother. "Why, Grandmother? Why would someone want to hurt me by doing this?"

Moira sighed and shook her gray head. "I don't know, child. Hate runs deep in Irish sod. 'Tis hard to say who picked up a piece and flung it in our faces."

"*My* face," Gwyneth corrected. Her eyes fastened on the wrinkled paper that lay on the desk like a burning accusation. "I'm the one they want to go home."

"Perhaps." Moira squeezed Gwyneth's hand, something she'd done throughout the telling of the houghed cattle and the wolfhound. The terrible news had struck deep, making Moira feel vulnerable and old. If her William were still here, he'd have taken off on one of the horses to discover who'd dared such a thing. But William was dead and she an old woman. Her vitality had fled, leaving her with the wish to climb into bed and pull the covers over her head.

But that was something Moira O'Brien Donahue couldn't do. Like other O'Brien women, she must stiffen her back and withstand the trials that blew like strong winds across Shannonderry. And so must her granddaughter.

Gwyneth got to her feet and began to pace the room. "At times like this, I wish I'd been born a man. If I had, no one would have dared do this." She swung to face Moira, her delicate chin lifted. "Do you think it was Sean O'Leary? Mick said no, that both his father and grandfather watch him closely. But who's to say that he didn't slip out after they were asleep?"

"'Twas not Sean," Kate said from her place by the fire. Though she'd pretended it needed constant stoking, her main purpose in staying was to hear what the two women said. "'Tis true what Mick said. Sean's far and granfar have put the fear of God in him . . . Father Sheehan too. No." She shook her cap-covered head. "'Tis someone else wants ye gone."

Kate's knees popped as she got to her feet. "Have ye given thought to the Flanagans? They've not forgotten 'twas yer husband what played a part in sending their sons to prison."

"That was over twenty years ago," Moira pointed out. "Did you not say Deirdre gave Rory and his brother her pearls so they could buy passage to America?" She shook her head, unwilling to place the blame for the houghed cattle on William. "No, 'tis someone else, though who—"

A knock on the sitting-room door broke through her words.

"Yes," Moira called.

Biddy opened the door. "Mr. D'Arcy to see ye . . . both of ye," she amended.

Gwyneth stopped midstride, her eyes fixed on Cormac as he came through the door. He was dressed for riding in boots and a brown tweed coat. The need to feel his strong arms around her came like a physical ache, and it was all she could do not to run to him. Now that he was here, things would work out.

Cormac's eyes were on Gwyneth, searching her face for signs of tears. Relief washed over him when he found none. A true O'Brien. Only then did he look at Moira and bow. "Ladies."

Moira nodded, and Gwyneth made a small curtsy.

"I came as soon as I heard about the cattle." The muscles in his jaw tightened. "I have spoken to Mick and Ronan. Mick is taking care of the butchering, and Ronan and Flynn are doing all they can for the hound."

Cormac refrained from mentioning that the dog was fast fading and not expected to live. He wanted to rail at those who had done it—make them pay for the wanton destruction of the wolfhound and cattle. Who they were, he couldn't say, but he intended to find out. "Ronan said a note was left beside the dog."

"Yes." Glad for something to do, Gwyneth retrieved the scrap of paper and handed it to Cormac, drawing a measure of strength just by standing next to him.

Cormac's blue eyes narrowed, and he mouthed a silent curse as he read the crude lettering. "Either they've had little schooling or they wish us to think so."

"Aye," Moira agreed. "I've come to the same conclusion. Who he . . . or they be, I have no notion. All of our tenants are well treated and loyal."

The dismay on Moira's face made Cormac's mouth tighten. On Sunday she'd exuded confidence and pleasure. Today she looked like a shaken old woman. Gwyneth looked no better, Sunday's high color and verve replaced with a grim pallor. Angry as Cormac had been when he'd heard of the outrage, it didn't compare to his boiling emotion at seeing what it had done to the two women.

He stepped closer to Gwyneth. "I have a strong suspicion that what happened has nothing to do with you being English and more to do with Toryn winning the race against the Westons."

"You mean . . ." Gwyneth began.

Cormac nodded and took her hand in his. "It is only a suspicion, but I mean to get to the bottom of it." Purpose emanated from him as he raised her hand to his lips. "I will find who did this," he promised.

With a bow, he left the room, the sound of his boots an echo to his promise.

Heartened by his words, Gwyneth's spirits lifted a trifle. Perhaps the intruders could be found. Such wouldn't compensate for the loss of the cattle, but still—Moira had explained that the cattle were insurance against taxes and unforeseen expenses. Now four were dead.

Moira's thoughts had taken a similar path. "I had thought to sell three or four of the cattle to raise the rest of the money for the race. But now—"

Moira's sigh stabbed like a dagger at Gwyneth's heart. Tears that had threatened all morning blurred her vision. Not wanting her grandmother to see them, Gwyneth dropped a quick kiss on her wrinkled cheek and hurried to the door. "I must see how Bradach is doing."

Kate followed her into the corridor, her quick steps an echo to Gwyneth's as they walked the length of the corridor and climbed the stairs. Kate's breathing was labored by the time she reached the top, but she refrained from speaking until they reached Gwyneth's room.

"Are ye all right, darlin' lass?"

The use of the pet name was Gwyneth's undoing. It sent her back to her childhood and a time when she needed comfort and reassurance. "Oh, Kate."

Kate gathered Gwyneth into her plump arms, patting and soothing her. "There, there," she crooned. "'Tis not all lost. Is not the Holy Father watching over us just as He's always done? 'Twill soon be a'right again."

"How can that be with cattle houghed and Bradach dying?" Gwyneth swallowed a sob, aware that her tears had wet Kate's shoulder. "And the note—Go home! They want me gone."

"They be but dolts who don't know their front from their backside. Fair gavel-hammered they be."

Gwyneth wiped at her tears with her fingers. "Did I do wrong to come to Ireland?" she asked in a quavering voice. "None of this would have happened if I'd stayed in England."

"Perhaps not." The tone of Kate's voice made it sound as if houghed cattle were a regular occurrence. "Neither would ye know and love yer old gran and her ye." A knowing smile lit Kate's plain face. "Aye . . . one would have to be blind not to see it . . . and herself happier than she be in years." She shook her head and touched Gwyneth's damp cheek. "Don't ye be blamin' yerself and sayin' ye shouldn't have come. Mistress's not the only one thankin' the Holy Father and the fairies for bringin' ye. Meself gives thanks every day . . . Biddy too." Kate's face worked, and her gray eyes moistened. "'Tis like a part of me was stolen and then brought back again."

"Oh . . . Kate."

"No more tears," Kate warned with a final pat. "Did I not tell ye things will be a'right again?" With that, she went to the wardrobe. "Will ye be ridin' Toryn this mornin'?"

Gwyneth's shoulders lifted as she followed Kate to the wardrobe. A brisk ride would be the very thing to raise her spirits.

17

Gwyneth's optimism faltered as soon as she entered the stable. Instead of Ronan's singing, Cluny's sniffles greeted her. He and Old Flynn sat with the dog, the wolfhound's grizzled head pillowed on Cluny's bony lap.

Her first thought was that Bradach had died, but when she stepped closer, she saw the dog's labored breathing. She bent and stroked him. "How is he?"

"Bad." Cluny's voice was a ragged whisper. "Granfar says he be dyin'."

Gwyneth glanced at Flynn, saw him nod, and read the accusation in his rheumy eyes. *'Tis yer fault. If ye'd stayed in England, the cattle and Bradach would be alive. Naught but harm will come to Shannonderry if ye stay.*

"I'm not going back to England," she said. "Shannonderry is my home now." Anger lifted Gwyneth's head and put a bite to her voice, the words echoing through the stable to collide with Flynn's unspoken accusation.

Turning on her heel, she stalked back to Toryn's stall. Despite her turbulent emotions, she spoke softly to the stallion as she hurriedly led him to the snubbing post and saddled him. Quick as she was, Ronan was faster, and when she led Toryn to the fence to mount, Ronan was already waiting on one of the mares. She gave him a scowl. He and the mare would be hard put to keep up with her this day.

Gwyneth set the stallion down the lane, avoiding the meadow where Mick and the tenants butchered the beef. She'd had enough of unpleasantness and wanted only to feel the exhilaration that came when she rode Toryn. The horse took the first hedge without breaking stride and sailed as effortlessly as a leaf over the second. On they raced, past the stream that bordered Shannonderry and on to the tenants' cultivated fields, but the sweet elixir that always came from riding Toryn didn't come. Like a dog refusing to give up the chase, the ugly words on the paper followed her,

eating at her pleasure and striking blows to her confidence. For Moira's sake
. . . Shannonderry's too . . . perhaps she should leave.

"No!" The word bit the morning air and stiffened her spine. O'Briens
were not cowards, and neither was she. She must stay and show them she
wasn't afraid. Upset . . . aye, upset . . . but not frightened.

On impulse Gwyneth turned Toryn down the lane Cluny had taken
them in the cart, the one leading to Emmett Weston's tenants. Although she
never used a whip on Toryn, Gwyneth always carried one. It was as much a
part of her riding apparel as her hat. Her mood was such that she hoped to
meet Sean O'Leary and other of the Weston tenants . . . even Percy Weston
himself. They'd soon see she didn't fear them. Let them come. Let them see!

With her face set and her whip raised, Gwyneth slowed Toryn and
scanned the lane. A man carrying a hoe was its only occupant. When he
heard Toryn, he quickly moved aside to let Gwyneth pass, touching a finger
to his worn cap as he did. Pity warred with anger in Gwyneth's heart when
she saw his face and ragged clothes. Instead of hatred, she saw only despair.
Her pity increased when she passed a hovel where a dirty, half-naked child
played with a piece of rope and stared at her with listless eyes.

Gwyneth regretted the impulse that had sent her on that course. She
regretted it more when she rounded a curve in the hedge-lined lane and
found two young peasants in her way. Surprise and resentment registered on
their faces as they jumped back against the hedge to avoid Toryn's prancing
hooves.

Gwyneth met their dislike with a challenge, chin lifted, her gaze direct
and cold. She couldn't know that to them she appeared like a pale avenging
angel with whip lifted to impart retribution. Holding Toryn in check, her
gaze raked one man's scraggly brown hair and the other's freckles. Though
no one spoke, she was certain they knew about the houghed cattle.

The brown-haired youth raised fingers to his cap, and the freckled one
attempted a weak smile. "Good day to ye, Mistress."

"Good day." Giving a nod, she set Toryn down the track, aware that
Ronan was close behind as he called a greeting to the young men. Then,
as if they had crossed a line dug into the earth, the lane opened to a vista
of cultivated fields and a distant cottage. Gwyneth slowed Toryn to a trot,
her eyes noting fields of potatoes and barley and cows grazing in a stone-
enclosed meadow. Peace seemed to emanate from the scene, an isle of
contentment in a sea of discord and poverty.

Ronan and the mare had almost caught up with her. As they neared
the cottage, a girl spreading wash on a bush to dry set down her basket and
stared.

"'Tis Ronan, Mam. Ronan and the young miss from Shannonderry."

Gwyneth looked back at the groom. "It seems you are known."

"Aye . . . 'tis me home and herself hangin' out wash me sister Gracie." Pride ran through Ronan's words. Love too. It shone on his face as he looked at the thatched cottage with smoke curling from the chimney and a brown rooster perched on a gatepost.

Realizing this was where Cormac had spent his early years and where his mother, Fiona, had taken refuge from the advances of Emmett Weston, Gwyneth reined in Toryn. For a long moment, she looked at the cottage, taking note of the gray stone exterior and ropes that held the thatched roof in place against the wind.

The door to the cottage opened, and a woman stepped outside, pulling a dark shawl over her shoulders as she did. "Ronan . . . are ye a'right? We heard of trouble at Shannonderry. I been worried."

"I be fine, Mam. Fit as a fiddler on the meadow, as ye can see."

Relief flooded his mother's face. Although the woman's words had been addressed to her son, her gaze was pinned on Gwyneth, her pale eyes bright with interest. In her middle years, the woman's features were still pretty, though her waist had thickened and her abundant chestnut hair worn in a thick plait showed streaks of gray.

"Are you not going to introduce us?" Gwyneth asked.

Gwyneth's words took Ronan by surprise. "Aye . . . a'course," he stammered, his cheeks reddening. He'd thought only to wave and call a greeting.

"'Tis Mistress Beddows from Shannonderry and this, a'course, the stallion what beat Percy Weston's mare." Taking a deep breath, Ronan hurried on. "This be me mam, Bridget O'Carroll, and herself with the basket me sister, Gracie."

At Gwyneth's nod and smile, mother and daughter each dropped a curtsy. "Your son has wrought wonders on our stable," she ventured.

"Aye. Like his da, he be—hard workers the both of them."

No one seemed to know what to say, and an uneasy silence settled over them.

"Will ye not come inside and share a pot of tea?" Bridget suddenly blurted. Her color was high, and she twisted one end of the shawl with her fingers.

Knowing that tea was dear among the cottiers, Gwyneth threw a quick glace at Ronan and saw his nod and the look of pleasure on his face. "Thank you. A bit of tea would be refreshing after our ride."

By the time Gwyneth had dismounted and made her way to the dooryard, a girl of about eight had joined Gracie, her excitement at seeing a lady about to enter their cottage clearly evident.

"This be young Maureen, named after our gran," Ronan said. He pulled at one of his sister's dark braids. "Spoiled she be, what with bein' the baby. Smart too and a'ready learnin' her sums and letters."

"Aye," Bridget put in with pride. "She goes regular to the hedge school. Gracie, too, as did Ronan and Seamus when they was young."

"You have another son?" Gwyneth asked as she followed Bridget past a rose bush that bloomed under a small window.

"Aye, he and me husband, Paddy, be gone to dig and bring in a load of peat." Bridget turned to usher them into the cottage. "In ye come now."

The smell of a peat fire greeted Gwyneth as she went inside. In the dim light from the door and small window, she made out an old woman sitting on a chair by the fire. She knew at once that the frail figure was Cormac's grandmother, the fiery Maureen O'Carroll who'd kept her small acreage solvent until Paddy was old enough to take over the farm.

Age had stripped Maureen of most of her fire, but her deep-set blue eyes were bright with interest. When Bridget introduced Gwyneth, they brightened even more. "I heard of ye and yer stallion. They say ye be like yer gran with horses . . . takin' the fences witho' fear." She paused and blinked rapidly. "Come close so I can see ye better."

A network of wrinkles crisscrossed the aged face, and wisps of white hair strayed from the coiled braid atop her head. Despite the wrinkles, her delicate bone structure proclaimed that Maureen O'Carroll had once been a beauty like her daughter Fiona. A worn but clean black dress completed the picture, her lap filled with knitting needles and a partially knitted gray stocking.

"Aye," Maureen said after a long moment. "A beauty . . . just like me grandson Cormac said."

Gwyneth's heart warmed with pleasure.

"Did ye know Cormac spent his first years here . . . meself like his mam and Paddy his da, though he not be married to our Bridget yet? That come later . . . after Mr. Francis D'Arcy took Cormac away."

A long sigh escaped the woman's narrow lips. "'Twas a terrible time with the boy cryin' and wantin' to stay and us not able to help. He ran away to us more times than I can count, but by and by he settled down." A smile lightened her features. "He never forgot his old gran, though. Comes by every week, he do, to chat and see how we be. A regular—"

The door suddenly burst opened, the thud as it hit the wall making Gwyneth jump. She turned, half expecting to see an angry peasant but instead finding Cormac D'Arcy standing in the opening, his tall frame silhouetted against the pale light, his expression one of consternation.

"What—?" Gwyneth was so surprised she could only stare.

"Cormac . . ." Bridget stammered. "'Tis a surprise ye be—though the morn's been full of surprises."

"It has." Cormac's eyes remained fastened on Gwyneth, his worry and puzzlement clearly evident. "I saw Toryn outside."

"Mistress Beddows and me went for a ride," Ronan put in.

"And I invited them in for a bit of tea," Bridget finished. The look she threw Cormac was uneasy, as if she feared she'd erred in issuing the invitation.

"Oh." The word left Cormac's lips in a sigh of relief. Although Bridget had explained Gwyneth's presence, it didn't entirely diminish his concern. What had possessed her to ride so far from home? Didn't she realize her actions courted danger? Aware of the curious eyes fixed on him, Cormac swallowed his questions and replaced them with a smile. "I see that you have met my gran."

"I have . . . Bridget and the two girls as well." Color flushed Gwyneth's cheeks when she recalled the compliment his grandmother had shared with her. A beauty, he'd called her.

"Will ye be wantin' to join us for tea?" Bridget asked.

Cormac hesitated. His heart wanted to stay with Gwyneth, but he'd come to enlist his uncle's help in discovering who'd houghed the cattle. "I'd like to, but . . ." He shook his head. "Where's Paddy? I didn't see him in the fields."

"Gone to fetch peat . . . Seamus too, though they should be back soon."

"They be here now," young Maureen said, pointing out the door to a man leading a donkey loaded with baskets of peat. Excited, she hurried to tell him of their visitors.

"They'll be wantin' to warm themselves," Bridget said. She set a kettle on the hob and blew on the coals. "Sure and I'll make tea for the lot of us." Glancing at Cormac, she added, "Ye can talk to Paddy over tea."

Gwyneth watched the two men as they came inside—Paddy, tall with slightly stooped shoulders and the O'Carroll dark hair and blue eyes— Seamus, a younger version of his father, his expression curious as Cormac made the introductions. Paddy removed his cap with a peat-grimed hand and nodded, his eyes seeming to take a measure of her before he smiled. Seamus followed his father's example, nodding as he removed his cap.

In a short time, the O'Carrolls and their guest were settled, Gwyneth and Maureen on chairs by the fire, the rest sitting on benches at the scrubbed table.

Gracie brought Gwyneth a cup of scalding tea, and young Maureen carried a plate with a slice of oatcake liberally spread with butter. The younger girl gave a shy smile, her eyes busy taking in Gwyneth's riding habit and the matching hat set on her short curls. After she'd handed the oatcake to Gwyneth, she surreptitiously fingered the rich aquamarine fabric, looking at it as if it were fit for a queen.

While Gwyneth sipped her tea and made polite conversation, she took note of the cobbled floor that was partially covered by a faded rag rug and the cupboard filled with oddments of crockery and cooking utensils. A door opened off the main room to a tiny bedroom, and a ladder led to a loft where the children slept.

Remembering the ornate furnishings at Clonglas, Gwyneth wondered why Cormac hadn't done something to make the O'Carroll home more comfortable. A quick look at Paddy's proud gaze told her the reason. Everything about him shouted that though he was poor, he was better off than his neighbors. Didn't the cottage boast two rooms? And were they not able to afford the luxury of tea? As long as Paddy O'Carroll could provide for his family, he would do so without anyone's help.

Through it all, Gwyneth was acutely aware of Cormac—aware, too, of the young girls' adoring expressions as they giggled with him. She was not the only one who found the Irishman appealing. As if conscious of her scrutiny, Cormac's eyes met hers, their warmth making her want to laugh with happiness. His pleasure in seeing her with his family was as obvious as Paddy's pride.

The others were aware of it too, the most obvious Maureen O'Carroll. Despite her failing eyesight, she saw enough to know that her grandson was clearly smitten with the young miss from Shannonderry and that Gwyneth was not immune to his charms. More than that, Miss Beddows didn't take on airs, nor had she shown any sign of distaste at taking tea in their humble cottage. Maureen nodded to herself. It was past time for her grandson to take a wife, and if Mistress Donahue's granddaughter were the one to catch his heart, she'd not say a word to discourage it.

After Cormac had exchanged a few quiet words with Paddy, he turned his attention back to Gwyneth. "Will ye not share the story of yer race with Percy Weston?" he asked, his voice taking on a more pronounced Irish lilt.

Wanting to impress Cormac's family, Gwyneth launched into the tale. The room stilled except for her voice and the crackle of the peat fire as everyone listened in rapt attention.

"Can we have a look at him?" Gracie asked when Gwyneth finished.

Seamus added his request, and even Paddy seemed eager for a closer look.

Cormac helped his grandmother from her chair, her thin body leaning heavily on his arm. "Stay back," he warned the children. "The fire that makes Toryn a great racer also burns as temper. Isn't that so, Ronan?"

"Aye, himself only lets Miss Gwyneth and Cormac near him . . . though of late he doesn't try to knock down the stall when he sees me."

"Ronan is good with the mares," Gwyneth said to Paddy, "and our stable hasn't been so clean in years."

Ronan's ears reddened, and Paddy's expression showed pleasure. "When is the grand race to take place with the horse from Limerick?" he asked.

"Soon, I hope. Reverend Gibbins is making the arrangements."

Paddy nodded. "Though all be anxious for yer stallion to win, ye must take care . . . Ronan too. If men be bold enough to hough Shannonderry cattle, they might try to harm yer stallion as well."

"Aye," he said when he noted Gwyneth's concern. "Ye'd be wise to keep the great beast close to home, and take care to set someone besides yer dogs to keep watch at night. A'course, 'tis but Paddy O'Carroll talkin', but I lived here all me life and know that some men's feelin's run deep."

His unflinching gaze made Gwyneth swallow. "Who do you think did it?"

"That I don't know, but we plan to keep our eyes and ears opened." He shot a glance at Cormac. "Was that not why ye came?"

Cormac nodded. "You know the temper of the people better than I."

"Aye." The two men exchanged a significant look. "After ye've seen the young miss on her way home, ye can give me a hand stackin' peat." Mischief twinkled in his eyes. "Much can be said a'tween two men stackin' peat."

"Ye must come again," Maureen said in a quivery voice as Gwyneth prepared to leave. "Not on yer fine stallion, a'course . . . for me son be speakin' wise. 'Tis me guess there be other horses at Shannonderry, though."

Pleased at the invitation, Gwyneth nodded. "I'd like that." As she spoke, she took Cormac's offered arm and walked to the tree where she'd tethered Toryn.

"Let me repeat my uncle's warning," Cormac said. "I want you and Toryn safe. Had I any idea you'd take him for a ride, I'd have cautioned you sooner."

"I want those who did it to know that I'm not afraid."

"I understand. Just the same . . ." Cormac covered Gwyneth's fingers on his arm with his free hand. "If anything happened to you, I'd be devastated." He paused and looked deeply into her eyes. "Please, will you take care?"

Happiness swirled past Gwyneth's concern and made her voice soft. "Yes . . . and thank you." Young Maureen's giggle reminded her they were not alone. It took effort to force her mind back to Paddy's warning. "If everyone wants Toryn to win the race, why would they try to hurt him?"

"Perhaps not everyone wants him to win."

"You mean the Westons?"

"Perhaps. No one will be overlooked."

His words hovered in the air as Cormac released Gwyneth's hand and went to untie Toryn. After speaking to the horse and stroking his neck, the Irishman helped Gwyneth mount, his hand lingering on her waist as he did. When she'd settled her right leg around the saddle's pommel, he smiled up at her. "It pleases me that you've met the rest of my family. They are good people . . . all of them."

"And they love you."

"Aye, and I them. That's why I know I can depend on them to help us."

Us. He'd said it as if he'd already joined his life with hers. Happiness filled Gwyneth once more. Waving and calling good-bye to the O'Carrolls, Gwyneth started Toryn away from the cottage.

"Don't let her out of your sight," Cormac instructed Ronan.

"Aye."

"I'll be sendin' Seamus to help ye keep watch tonight at the stable," Paddy called after them.

His words pushed worry more firmly to the back of Gwyneth's mind. Not only did she have Cormac to help, but she also had the O'Carrolls.

18

ON FRIDAY THE D'ARCYS CAME for tea. Aware of the toll the houghed cattle had taken on her grandmother, Gwyneth had suggested that perhaps the event should be postponed.

Moira shook her head. "Company is the very thing to take my mind from our troubles. And unless I miss my guess, Mr. D'Arcy will be a tonic to lift your worries as well. Even a woman as old as I can see you two continue to draw closer day by day."

"Grandmother." Pleasure and color leaped to Gwyneth's face.

"Aye, child . . . completely taken and you just as smitten." She smiled up at Gwyneth from her favorite chair. "Fetch Kate so we can plan what to serve for tea, and ask Biddy to freshen one of your gowns. The pink one makes you look especially fetching."

Laughing, Gwyneth dropped a kiss on the old woman's wrinkled cheek. "Thank you, Grandmother."

That afternoon, Biddy showed the D'Arcys into the sitting room where Moira and Gwyneth waited. Gwyneth wore the pink gown with a high waist and a swath of lace at the bodice, and Moira was regal in dove gray, which, though sadly out of style, didn't diminish her aristocratic appearance.

Gwyneth's thoughts and attention centered on Cormac as soon as he stepped through the door. She was at once aware of how his muscular build filled the shoulders of his blue coat and that his dark-fringed eyes immediately sought hers. Her pleasure abated a trifle when she noted Owen's adoring gaze, and it came to a full stop when she saw that Agatha accompanied them.

The woman was splendidly turned out in a gown of lavender silk and a hat with an enormous feather. Although Gwyneth made a show of cordiality, her heart wasn't in it. Memory of how Agatha had dominated the conversation at the dinner party told her there would be little opportunity to talk to Cormac.

In this she was not mistaken. Not only did Agatha seem bent on rehashing all that had happened with the cattle, but she also lost little time in letting them know whom she blamed.

"I know it's not something you wish to acknowledge, but have you realized that those who benefited most from this terrible thing are your own tenants?" Agatha raised a plump hand when Moira opened her mouth to protest. "Are their bellies not bulging from the extra meat they've been eating . . . most likely their pockets as well? I have it on good authority that some have sold the surplus meat in the village."

"Who told you that?" Moira demanded, the pleasure she'd hoped to derive from the D'Arcys clearly gone.

"When Mr. Weston called on me yesterday, he said he'd not be surprised if such were the case. You know how sneaky peasants can be . . . yes, even those at Shannonderry."

"That is only Mr. Weston's opinion," Moira countered in a firm voice. "I know my tenants far better than he does. What's more, I trust them."

"You are free to believe what you wish," Agatha said. "But experience has shown me that peasants cannot be trusted." She smiled as she spoke, her hazel eyes fastening on Cormac.

Cormac had borne Agatha's barbs about peasants so often that they no longer had the power to upset him. Acting as if he hadn't heard her, he turned to Gwyneth. "Has there been a reply from Mr. O'Roark about the race?"

Gwyneth gave Cormac a grateful look. "Not yet, but Reverend Gibbins promised to bring word as soon as it comes."

"The race is the talk of the county," Owen put in. His desire to be noticed by Gwyneth was as palpable as the beat of his heart. He hurried on, his ears coloring at Gwyneth's smile. "Your stallion is magnificent, Miss Beddows."

Before Gwyneth could thank him, Agatha cut in. "Although I bow to your superior knowledge of horses, son, I think perhaps you overrate Miss Beddows's stallion." She gave Gwyneth an apologetic smile. "I mean you no offense, and from what Owen tells me, I'm sure the horse is a magnificent beast, but . . ." Her voice trailed away, and when she resumed speaking her tone was hushed as if she were imparting a secret. "I am told that Percy's loss was a fluke . . . that the mare suffered from a touch of colic and was not running her best."

Cormac's low chuckle filled the room. "Is that what the Westons claim? That the mare suffered from colic?"

"It's the truth," Agatha retorted, her nose lifting. "Emmett told me so himself."

"And you believe him?"

"I do. What's more, I do not like it that you question my judgment."

"My apology, madam." Laughter edged his words, and he made no attempt to hide his smile.

Moira's lips twitched as well, but her voice was smooth as the cream she poured into her tea when she spoke to Agatha. "I heard that you spent a week in Cork. Is your lovely gown one you purchased while you were there?"

"It is." Without further encouragement, Agatha launched into a description of her week in the city and the shops she had visited.

With Agatha occupied, Gwyneth was able to turn her attention back to Cormac, but any hope for private conversation was thwarted by Owen, who openly listened to all they said and added his opinion at every opportunity.

Cormac was able to see the humor in the situation and leaned back in his chair, crossing his legs. From the look on Gwyneth's face he knew that Owen wasn't making any progress. While his young brother held sway, Cormac watched the play of emotions on Gwyneth's delicate features and noted how light pouring through the window seemed to make her eyes bluer. In the past he'd avoided the empty trappings of teas and socials, but since bringing Gwyneth to Shannonderry, he openly vied for the chance to be in her company. No one had been more surprised than he when he found himself entranced with this woman who'd ridden into his life and captured his heart. *Admit it. You've tumbled hard.*

With a shy smile, Gwyneth glanced at Cormac. The room and the others seemed to fade, leaving only the two of them—Cormac's cobalt eyes holding hers, Gwyneth's lips slightly trembling. The caring she saw on his face crashed in pleasurable waves against her heart, building until she thought she would burst with happiness. Threads of longing stretched between them, the gossamer strands gilded with pleasure while neither of them remembered to breathe.

Agatha's harrumph jerked Gwyneth back to the present. As she tore her gaze from Cormac, she realized that Owen and his mother were staring at her. "I'm sorry," she stammered, her color heightening. "Did you say something?"

"No," Owen muttered, but his expression told her he'd glimpsed what had passed between her and Cormac.

"I asked if you would show me more of Shannonderry," Agatha contradicted. "What I saw the night of the dinner party was most impressive." She glanced at Moira. "I've heard much about the tower room you built years ago for your daughter. I wouldn't presume to ask you to climb the stairs, but perhaps your granddaughter could." She smiled at Gwyneth.

Gwyneth didn't want to leave Cormac. More than that, she didn't relish being alone with Agatha. Not seeing any way out of the uncomfortable situation, she nodded. "If you wish."

"I wish it very much. Even my friends in Cork have heard of Shannonderry." Getting to her feet, Agatha looked at Moira. "I hope you don't mind being left with only the D'Arcy men for company."

"Not at all. Although Mr. D'Arcy and I are already good friends, this will give me opportunity to become better acquainted with Owen."

When Gwyneth's eyes sought Cormac's, his smile lifted her spirits. Even so, the unease that attached itself to her as she left the room was much like the tenacity of a rook clinging to a tree branch in a windstorm.

Agatha kept up a stream of conversation as Gwyneth led her along the corridor and up the stone stairs, commenting on the shield in the entryway and the antiquity of the old dwelling. Shortness of breath gradually slowed her progress, and she seemed glad to stop and rest when they reached Gwyneth's room.

"A most unusual place," Agatha said as her eyes swept over the room and its furnishings. The curl of her lip implied that everything was sadly lacking. The crystal dish holding Gwyneth's few ribbons was examined and quickly dismissed, and the worn fabric of the green bed covering elicited a tsk as she ran her fingers over its surface. It was all Gwyneth could do not to fly at her.

"Most unusual," Agatha repeated. "Much too rustic for my taste, but I suppose to some it might hold charm." She walked over to the window. "You do have a lovely view," she conceded.

"I find it to my liking." Unexpected emotion tightened Gwyneth's throat. To her, the room's dark wood and stone walls exuded permanence. Like the O'Briens and Ireland, it was solid and dependable.

"Do you not miss your home in England?" Agatha asked.

Remembering the angry words her father had hurled at her before he left for the race in Doncaster, Gwyneth shook her head. "Shannonderry is my home now."

"Interesting." Agatha's voice came soft as if she mused to herself. "I also find it curious that it was Cormac who brought you to Ireland." Agatha turned from the window with an amused smile. "Did you know that my stepson and Mr. Weston have long been rivals?"

"I heard such," Gwyneth replied, her unease rising.

"And that each was determined to find and own a horse fleet enough to bring the steeplechase crown back to County Cork?"

Gwyneth shook her head, uncertain of the game the older woman played, for a game it was—of that she was certain.

"I thought as much," Agatha went on. "Few knew of it. Since Cormac is my stepson and Mr. Weston my close friend, I am privy to the information. Emmett left in April to look for a horse in Ireland, and Cormac departed a fortnight later on a horse-buying trip to England. Do you not think it peculiar that he returned with both you and your stallion?"

Something deep inside Gwyneth twisted, but she made a show of nonchalance. "I'm afraid I don't, especially since Mr. D'Arcy came to Hawarden to bring Grandmother's letter. As for Toryn—" Gwyneth lifted her chin and met Agatha's hazel eyes. "I know you are acquainted with the circumstances that led me to run away from home. The fact that I brought my stallion shouldn't seem strange. He and I have been together from the day he was foaled. Even if Toryn weren't an incredible racer, I would still have brought him with me."

Agatha's lips lifted. "Exactly. You and your stallion go together . . . a fact of which I'm certain Cormac was well aware." She paused and her smile widened. "I should think an intelligent young woman like you would find that a trifle odd."

Gwyneth knew she would lose the battle if she bandied words with Agatha. The woman was accomplished at twisting facts and sowing discord. Despite the shock twisting her insides, Gwyneth forced herself to be calm. "I do not." She lifted her head, grateful for the years she'd practiced nonchalance with her stepmother. Not for anything would she let Mrs. D'Arcy have the satisfaction of knowing that the information about Cormac and Mr. Weston had struck at her very core, making her bones feel watery and unsubstantial. Taking a deep breath, she went on, her bearing, had she been aware of it, very like Moira's. "That being said, I think we should rejoin Grandmother and the men in the sitting room."

Agatha gave a short laugh. Although the English chit had remained surprisingly calm, she was confident her arrow had struck home. A smug smile remained on Agatha's face as she went down the steep steps from the tower room.

Dismay clutched Gwyneth's middle as she followed her. Cormac cared for her. She knew he did. Even as the comforting thought found a home, doubt reminded her of the exorbitant price Cormac had offered her father for Toryn. In her mind she relived the night when Cormac had dined with them at Hawarden. His words came to her as clearly as if he'd just spoken. "Your secret it safe with me," he'd whispered. Then, raising his voice so all could hear, "I wish to buy your stallion, Miss Beddows."

A feeling of sickness joined her dismay. Had that been Cormac's purpose from the moment he set eyes on Toryn—to woo and win her so he could have the stallion?

No! The thought shot through her as if she'd spoken it aloud. Cormac D'Arcy wasn't the kind to purposely set out to deceive her. She knew he wasn't, and yet—She tried to push the thought away, but it persisted, clamoring and pounding at the door like an unwanted guest. Had she been duped? Had her feelings for the Irishman so blinded her that she'd been taken in by his charm, believing his smile held tenderness when it had only been a ploy to gain Toryn?

Anger cut through her dismay. How could she have been so stupid— Gwyneth Beddows, who prided herself on her intelligence? She wanted to rush past Agatha and confront Cormac. Never had the corridor seemed so long, the interfering woman such an annoying encumbrance.

Gwyneth glared at Agatha's back, the woman's smug satisfaction as evident as her widening hips. Sudden revelation came. *This is what Agatha wants. This is why she came to tea—so she could fill my mind with poisoned thoughts and make me doubt. But why?*

Not knowing the answer, Gwyneth slipped past Agatha to open the sitting-room door, taking care to wipe all expression from her face as she did. She saw the three people in the room as if from a great distance, their faces no more than a blur. Fearing she might discover that Agatha was right, Gwyneth kept her eyes on her grandmother. What she said and did, she couldn't recall, nor could she bring herself to meet Cormac's eyes. If she did, she might read what she could not bear to see, and her heart would shatter into a hundred tiny pieces.

* * *

A HALF HOUR LATER, GWYNETH hurried outside to the stable. Kate's love and her grandmother's tact had prevented either from pelting her with questions. Instead, their faces filled with concern, they'd let her leave the sitting room.

Changing into her riding habit had taken longer than usual, but at last the task was done, with the jacket properly buttoned and the hat pinned to her curls. A quiet moment on her knees had helped quell the worst of her turmoil, but the uncertainty wouldn't leave. Who should she believe? Agatha or her own heart? If only she could blot out the memory of how badly Cormac had wanted to buy Toryn and replace it with his numerous kindnesses. If only . . .

The thought skidded to a halt when Gwyneth entered the stable and saw Cormac talking with Ronan and Cluny. His low voice stopped midsentence, his expression mixed with pleasure and concern.

"Miss Beddows." Unspoken questions trailed after her name.

Gwyneth gave a stiff nod on her way to Toryn's stall, purposely keeping her eyes averted. Even so, she was aware that the Irishman followed her, his long legs matching her quick strides, his nearness hammering at her emotions. She wanted to shout at him even as she wished he'd take her into his arms and tell her Agatha's implications were untrue.

"May I saddle Toryn for you and accompany you on your ride?" he asked.

Gwyneth wanted to tell him she was capable of doing it herself, but the sight of Flynn peering at them from the tack room made her bite her tongue. Not only that, but she also knew her words would sound childish. "Thank you."

Cormac opened Toryn's stall and spoke in a low croon as he stroked the big horse. Toryn immediately stilled. Under the spell of the Irishman's magic, Toryn acted as if they communicated in a secret language.

Gwyneth's anger increased. It had taken her months—years—to obtain such a relationship with Toryn, but Cormac had accomplished it in minutes. She wasn't the only one to notice. Cluny and Ronan watched in awe, and Flynn left the tack room to get a better look. Toryn followed Cormac from his stall like a docile lamb, his black coat quivering with pleasure each time Cormac touched it or spoke to him.

Continuing to ignore Gwyneth's stiffness, Cormac saddled Toryn and helped her mount. He was so close that she caught the tangy scent of his shaving soap, and his touch seemed to pulse with life through the fabric of her riding jacket. She had known since that first night at the inn that Cormac was a man she could trust. Why did she doubt him now? Silence stretched long, and a quick look revealed Cormac's dark brows lifted in question. "What?" she asked.

"Nothing . . . except you looked about to ask a question and—" Conscious of three pairs of watching eyes and listening ears, Cormac shrugged and handed Toryn's reins to her. A moment later they left the stable yard, Cormac's mare abreast with Toryn as Cluny waved from the door.

They rode toward the copse of oak trees, neither speaking, the subdued light of the overcast day playing on their solemn faces. The muscles in Cormac's jaw were knotted with tension, and Gwyneth looked everywhere but at him.

Even with the tension, Gwyneth felt bittersweet pleasure in riding next to Cormac. Thoughts of happier times filled her mind—the breeze blowing through his thick dark hair, his eyes alight with laughter as he teased her.

Aware that what lay between them couldn't be solved by smiling or jesting, Cormac was silent as they entered the oak trees. The rooks fluttered and squawked at the disturbance, and old leaves crunched under the horses' hooves. The copse soon gave way to a meadow where a breeze carried the sound of a stream and the distant lowing of cattle. Silence and tension followed them into a larger copse of trees. Here the way was less distinct, the heavy undergrowth impeding their progress into the shadowy interior.

Cormac swung from his saddle and lifted his arms to help Gwyneth dismount. "Let's walk," he said, standing next to her.

When Gwyneth stole a quick glance at Cormac's face, she had to quell the urge to trace its outline with her fingertips. She felt Cormac's breath on her cheek, his hand on her waist, while his awareness of her pulsed to make her shiver.

"Are you all right?" he asked in a soft voice.

She nodded and stepped away, her legs as unsteady as her heartbeat. In an effort to gain control of her emotions, Gwyneth concentrated on the thick tree trunks and dewy ferns while Cormac tethered the horses.

When he finished, Cormac touched her arm and led her farther into the grove of trees. "Now . . . tell me what's wrong. What went on between you and my stepmother this afternoon?"

"She . . . I . . ." Gwyneth's throat closed around the words. How could she explain Agatha's implication when Cormac had never said he cared for or loved her? Not wanting to sound like a presumptuous goose, she shrugged. "It was nothing."

Cormac stopped and looked down at her. "How can you say it's nothing when you refuse to speak or look at me?"

Gwyneth kept her gaze averted. Not only did she not know how to word what had passed between Agatha and her, she was afraid that if she looked at Cormac she might learn that his stepmother was correct. The moment stretched long, with only the restless buzz of insects to break the uncomfortable silence.

"Just tell me what she said," Cormac prompted in a softer voice. "I'm helpless to fix what's wrong if you won't tell me what it is."

Gwyneth's gaze fastened on a place above Cormac's shoulder. *Help me know what to say without looking a fool.* Somehow she found the courage to look at him and saw softness and concern play across his handsome features. "She said—" Her voice stalled.

Cormac sighed, but when he spoke his voice was gentle. "This is only a guess, but knowing my stepmother, she told you something unpleasant about me . . . perhaps that I drink too much, which I don't. I'm not stupid enough to take to liquor like my father did." When Gwyneth made no reply, he went on. "Did she say I have a vile temper? That, unfortunately, is true, as well you know after my display the day you and Toryn beat Percy in the race. Or perhaps . . ."

Cormac's voice broke off, and he lifted Gwyneth's chin with a finger, his face alight with sudden comprehension. "Did she tell you the only reason I'm wooing you is so I can get my hands on Toryn? That's it, isn't it."

When Gwyneth nodded, he laughed. "The woman actually told a truth. I am wooing you, though not to have Toryn. I want to have you . . . to hold you and love you and . . ." He brought her cupped face close to his ". . . kiss you," he finished.

Cormac's lips found hers, soft and tender and full of questions, as if he needed to know she loved and wanted him too.

Gwyneth's lips responded to his as an unimaginable happiness coursed through her, her arms encircling his neck as he pulled her into his embrace. The feel of his warmth and closeness was sweeter than anything she'd ever experienced, as if something lost had been found, as if something empty had been filled.

"Gwyneth . . . my darlin' girl." Cormac's voice shook as his lips made a slow trail across her cheek and over her closed eyes. "Everything I've done these past weeks was prompted by love . . . even my temper the day of the race. I didn't want you hurt by gossiping tongues, yet I was bursting with pride because you won."

Cormac laughed and pulled her closer, the pressure of his arms like a welcome bulwark against her uncertainty. "Who would have supposed a mere slip of a woman could beat the Westons at their own game . . . for a game it was since I'd had a hand in bringing Toryn to Shannonderry."

Gwyneth lifted her head from the hollow of his shoulder. "Agatha told me about the rivalry . . . how you each wanted to buy a horse fast enough to beat O'Roark's stallion."

Cormac's face turned solemn. "It's something I badly wanted. When I saw you and Toryn take the hedgerow at Hawarden, I knew I'd found the horse to do it. But somehow my desire to own the stallion got lost in the tangle of wanting to win you." He touched Gwyneth's cheek with the back of his hand. "I understand why it would be easy to believe my stepmother. What she told you is true. I've long disliked Weston, and I'd like nothing better than to thwart him and his son, but my love for you is greater. I know how it looks . . . how it might seem . . ."

"Shhh . . . it doesn't matter." Gwyneth ran her fingertip along his jaw line, her lips wanting to follow its course. After he kissed her the second time, she pulled away. "I believe your first words to me were that you wished to buy my stallion," she teased.

"Going that way are you? Well, if you are, then the price I offered your father stacks the evidence more firmly against me. Don't forget, though, that I gave you your grandmother's letter." He paused and placed his hands on Gwyneth's slender shoulders, looking deeply into her eyes. "If my only purpose was to own Toryn, I could have kept Moira's letter in my pocket and returned to Ireland with the horse instead of you."

"What would you have told Grandmother?"

"That I couldn't find you . . . or, heaven forbid, that you were happily married and not interested in her offer." Cormac continued to hold her gaze. "Had I not been a man of my word, I might have toyed with the idea of deceit. Honor and my belief in God wouldn't allow me, nor would it let me refuse your pleas for help."

"I'm very glad you didn't. I would have been terribly lonely if you'd left me behind."

"Only lonely?" A ghost of a smile crossed his features. "By then, I'd taken my measure of you and knew you were exactly what Moira needed. Your O'Brien spirit was much in evidence . . . and, just like that, I was half in love."

"I wasn't far behind you," she replied. "And before I knew it, I was in all the way." Having him look at her in such tender fashion made it difficult to breathe. "I love you." Tears misted her eyes at the wonder and joy of it. Held close, she felt the happy dance of her heart and his like the drum setting the rhythm.

Cormac smiled against her cheek. "If Toryn were the slowest plow horse in Yorkshire, I'd still have fallen in love with you." He paused and lifted his head, his smile like sun touching the tips of greening trees after a long winter. "I love you, my darlin' Gwyneth . . . love you totally and completely."

* * *

EVENING WAS COMING ON BY the time Gwyneth and Cormac made their way back to Shannonderry. They walked together, Cormac's arm encircling her waist, the horses following behind.

When they reached the oak trees, Cormac pulled her close and tucked a short curl beneath the brim of her hat. "By rights I should speak to your grandmother before I ask you to marry me, but it's your answer I want to hear, not hers." Cormac dropped the mare's reins and lifted Gwyneth's chin. "I want to be with you always . . . to love you and have you as my wife. Please say yes."

"Yes . . . gladly." The pressure of Cormac's mouth on hers made Gwyneth forget everything except that he loved and wanted her for his wife.

"Thank you." When he'd finished kissing her again, Cormac gave a little chuckle. "For an afternoon that started badly, I couldn't ask for a nicer ending . . . you in my arms as well as your promise to be my wife."

Arm in arm, they resumed their walk toward the stable. One of the wolfhounds raced to meet them, his tail waging in recognition. The dog's coming penetrated their happiness and made Cormac grimace and stop. "Your safety has long been first in my mind, but now—" His features turned fierce as he looked toward the meadow where the cattle had been houghed. "I mean to find who did it. You have my promise as well as my love."

After a moment, the fierce look died. "I've a notion Cluny and Ronan have counted the minutes since we left . . . Old Flynn too, or I miss my guess." He adjusted Gwyneth's hat, smiling as he did. "When we reach the stable, I must revert to being Mr. D'Arcy and you Miss Beddows . . . that is until I speak with your grandmother."

Offering Gwyneth his arm, they entered the stable yard as sedately as a couple strolling along a London street. Had Old Flynn looked closely, he would have known by the radiance of Gwyneth's face that, like Cormac, she had found the afternoon most satisfactory.

19

THE FOLLOWING MORNING AS CORMAC made his way to his stable, he heard someone call his name. A moment later, Seamus O'Carroll stepped from the trees that skirted Clonglas. Cormac's first thought was of trouble, for Seamus now spent his nights at Shannonderry helping guard Toryn. "Is something wrong?"

Seamus shook his head. "I've brought someone with a message for ye." He motioned to a boy waiting in the trees. "This be young Collin Haggarty from over Macroom way."

"A message, you say?"

"Aye, sir." The boy, who looked no more than seven or eight, held out a grimy hand clutching a piece of paper, his eyes large with nervousness and excitement. "A man what I never saw afore gave it to me. Said I could have a copper if I'd take it to Mr. D'Arcy at Clonglas."

Cormac took the paper and unfolded a crudely written note: *If ye want to know them what houghed cattle, come to the old church tonight after the bonfire.*

A grim smile lifted Cormac's mouth. With luck, by midnight he'd know the names of those who'd maimed Shannonderry's cattle. He studied the boy for a moment. "What did the man look like?"

Young Collin frowned. "Funny like . . . with his cap pulled low so's I couldn't see his face. His voice sounded funny too, but I be right sure I never saw him afore."

"Probably a disguise," Cormac mused. Even so, he was pleased as he reached into his pocket and took out a coin. "You've more than earned your copper, Collin. Thank you."

Collin's grin showed a missing tooth. "Thank ye, sir." With that, he scampered back through the trees.

Cormac gazed after him, his mind going over the information. "You know where the ruins of the old church are, don't you?" he asked Seamus.

His cousin nodded. "In the woods close by Shannonderry. Me and Ronan used to play there . . . pretend we was soldiers and the church a castle."

"Will you be at the bonfire tonight?"

"Wouldn't miss it."

"I thought as much. Though I don't expect trouble, I'd feel better if you and your da came to the old church after the bonfire. Even if the informer's disguised, one of you might recognize him."

Seamus grinned, pleased at being a part of the intrigue. "I'll be for tellin' Da. Ye can be sure we'll be there."

"Not a word to anyone else. We don't want to scare them away."

Seamus's face turned solemn. "I'll only tell Da." He set off through the woods for his home.

* * *

GWYNETH WOKE WITH THE SUN, her mind immediately closing around thoughts of Cormac. He loved her! She wanted to shout the news to the morning breeze, dance down the stairs, sing. She settled on singing, her voice an extension of her happiness as she went to join her grandmother in the sitting room after breakfast. When Moira showed her a note from Mr. D'Arcy asking to speak with her the following afternoon, Gwyneth's smile widened.

"I wonder what Mr. D'Arcy can want?" Moira teased, the twinkle in her eye as bright as her smile. One look at Gwyneth's face when she'd returned from her ride with Cormac the day before had told Moira all she needed to know. The happy glow on her granddaughter's face this morning served as further confirmation. A marriage proposal was imminent.

Gwyneth's excitement meshed with that of Kate's and Biddy's, but theirs was from a different source. Talk of the bonfire was paramount in their conversation, and they were not alone. All the peasantry looked forward to the evening. Was it not St. John's Eve and the longest day of the summer?

Biddy had talked of little else the entire week, and with the day finally come, she flitted about like a skittish colt. Kate was not immune to the excitement either. She brushed Gwyneth's short curls with vigor, her hands quick as she chattered of the coming event.

"I wish ye could be goin' with us, for there'll be music and dancing in the meadow. All will be there . . . even the seanchaí. 'Twill be a grand night."

"Some will even jump over the bonfire," Biddy put in. "Lads to show how brave and strong they be, and lasses to see if they be wed afore the year be out."

Gwyneth's brows lifted.

"'Tis true," Biddy affirmed. "Did not Mary Sullivan jump over the bonfire last St. John's Eve, and was she not wed by Christmas?"

"If St. John's magic is so strong, you must take care not to jump over the fire," Gwyneth teased. "You're much too young to be thinking of marriage."

Biddy giggled. "I'm not that daft . . . though I'd not protest if Dan Sullivan claimed me for the dancin'. What of ye, Miss Gwyneth? Do ye not wish ye could know if ye'll be wed afore the year be out?"

Gwyneth flushed, but much as she longed to tell them her secret, she wanted to wait until Cormac spoke to her grandmother. "Why do you think I'd want to know such a thing?" she asked innocently.

"Anyone with two eyes can see how Mr. D'Arcy looks at ye . . . and ye—" A sharp look from Kate closed Biddy's lips, but it didn't dampen her enthusiasm. She lifted her skirt and broke into a little jig. "Tonight I'll be wearin' my green dress . . . green ribbons too. What of ye, Kate?"

"'Twill not matter. 'Tis enough just to be goin'."

Gwyneth's thoughts flew to Cormac. Would he be at the celebration too? "Can I not go with you?"

Kate looked askance. "Mercy, no. 'Twouldn't be fittin' or safe, especially after the note Ronan and Cluny found . . . not to mention there'll be drinkin' aplenty along with music and dancin'. Such be a powerful mixture for some of the lads." She offered Gwyneth an apologetic smile. "'Twill not be safe for ye."

That evening after Gwyneth had seen Kate and Biddy off to the bonfire, she slowly climbed the stairs to her room. Restlessness made her sanctuary seem dull. She attempted to read, but when her mind kept flitting to Cormac and the bonfire, she gave up and went to the window. Sighing, she opened the sash.

Moist air, heavy with the scent of summer flowers, flowed around her while a symphony of crickets and katydids filled the night. The dark shadow of the castle lay in silhouette across the grass, the grounds pearly in the luminous light of a half moon. In the distance, past the woods, she saw the glow of the bonfire.

Listening, she heard distant laughter and the scrape of a fiddle, quick and lively, as if for a jig. When a chorus of pipes joined the fiddle, the music called to her with a restless urgency and made her forget Kate's warning.

Impulse sent her from her room and down the stairs. Her slippers made little noise, nor did the front door, which opened easily at her touch. She waited in the deep shadows of the castle to get her bearings, knowing she took a risk in trying to find Kate and Biddy. The glow of the bonfire and the song of the pipes and fiddle called with greater impatience. Her feet responded, running across the parkland, not stopping until she reached the giant old oak.

Gwyneth rested a hand on the oak's broad trunk as she looked up through its wide, spreading branches at the pale sky. What scenes had the old tree witnessed over the years? Had other O'Briens touched it when it was no more than a sapling, taking courage from its sturdiness as she found herself doing now? Courage was what she needed if she meant to press on in the darkness to reach the bonfire.

She left the old oak and hurried on across the parkland to the copse of trees where the rooks roosted. They moved restlessly in the high branches when she paused to listen to the music, which was closer now, accompanied by voices and bursts of laughter. The knowledge that the rough voices weren't those of gentlemen and perhaps belonged to the ones who'd knifed Bradach and maimed the cattle gave Gwyneth further pause. Her steps were more cautious as she went on. It was well that they were, for the heavy undergrowth snagged her skirt and made walking difficult.

When she emerged from the woods, a shadowy figure bounded out of the darkness. Gwyneth's scream died on her lips when she recognized one of the wolfhounds. "It's Gwyneth," she said in an unsteady voice. The dog halted and sniffed the night air then slowly trotted away.

Unease bade Gwyneth turn back, but the music urged her across the small meadow and into another wood that smelled of moist earth and peppermint. Was it here Cormac had kissed her and declared his love? The music and celebration were forgotten while she relived her time in Cormac's arms. Only when she realized he might be at the bonfire did she go on. Tangled branches obscured her view, and she was forced to rely on the sound of the soaring pipes to lead her. Finally, she caught a glimpse of firelight, and a moment later she stepped from the trees.

Gwyneth's breath caught at the sight of the leaping flames and joyful figures dancing in the meadow. For a second, she felt as if she'd stumbled onto a gathering of fairies, the graceful movements of hands and feet an extension of the glorious night and music. Her own feet unconsciously responded as she enviously looked at the animated faces. Watching their nimble feet, she wondered how, after working all day, they could dance and twirl with such abandonment.

Entranced with the scene, it was some moments before Gwyneth remembered to look for Cormac. Hard as she tried, she couldn't find him, though she saw Biddy twirling with the dancers. There was no mistaking her pretty face and russet curls that shone like the flaming bonfire.

Looking more closely, she saw Flynn standing near Dooley O'Garvin, the seanchaí.

From her place in the shadows, Gwyneth continued to search the crowd. There were Paddy and Bridget O'Carroll—Seamus too, but still no sign of Cormac. Just then the fiddle came to a scraping halt, and the dancers threw themselves to the ground in happy exhaustion. All grew silent as a man she recognized as one of her grandmother's tenants stepped forward and began to speak in Gaelic. Although she understood little of what he said, the peasants listened intently. After a moment, he stopped and bowed to Dooley O'Garvin.

The old seanchaí stepped forward, his gray head and craggy features illuminated by the bonfire. The audience leaned close. It was a great honor to have the famous seanchaí in their midst. The magic of the music was transformed into the rich resonance of his voice. The bonfire leaped and crackled with a pulsing rhythm of its own, its flames painting the crowd's glowing faces with shifting light and shadows. Gwyneth shivered when the peasants chanted a response to Dooley's words, their voices coming like the litany to an ancient moonlit mass, which perhaps it was—for was it not St. John's Eve?

Mesmerized, Gwyneth stepped closer. Had her mother joined Kate at a similar celebration when they were young, the two of them jumping over the coals of the dying fire with the hope of being wed before the year was out? Engrossed in the moon-bathed night, she forgot herself until one of the cottiers turned and looked toward the trees. Gwyneth's heart leaped in alarm. Had she been seen?

Fear propelled her back through the woods, her arms outstretched to avoid the trees, her steps awkward and stumbling as she ran. In her hurry, she tripped and fell, the force as she struck the leaf-littered ground driving the air from her lungs. Stunned, she lay still and listened for any signs of pursuit, but all that came was the rasp of her breathing and the distant voice of the seanchaí.

Rubbing a bruised knee, Gwyneth slowly got to her feet. Her flight had robbed her of all sense of direction. More than that, the thick trees hid the moon so that everything was draped in inky blackness. She stumbled on, tripping on the undergrowth. Twice she stopped to get her bearings, but each time she only became more disoriented in the maze of vines and trees.

After what seemed an eternity, her fingers brushed against a stone structure. She felt along it, hoping it was a fence that would lead her back to Shannonderry. After a few steps, she realized that instead of a fence, it was the remains of an old building camouflaged by a mass of vines and shrubbery, its roof collapsed from the ravages of time.

The feel of the rough stone restored Gwyneth's courage and gave dimension to the shadowy maze that held her prisoner. If she could but climb up onto the wall, she could get her bearings. She tested the branch of a tree and, after an awkward scramble, was able to reach the top of the wall. Moonlight shone bright from the height to disclose that the wall was part of an old church, complete with nave and transept. From this height, she was also able to see Shannonderry. Relief fell around her like a comforting cloak in the cool night air. The contented chirp of crickets added to her sense of safety. Instead of immediately climbing down, Gwyneth sat down on the wall and leaned back against a sturdy tree branch. The memory of the mesmerizing scene at the bonfire played through her mind. What she had witnessed was another facet of Ireland—the dancers and the seanchaí's tale calling like a piper's voice, a talisman from her past.

The crunch of stealthy footsteps pierced her reverie. Suddenly alert, Gwyneth strained to listen while half-formed, anxious thoughts tumbled through her mind. Had someone seen and followed her? The footsteps paused, and after a long, tense moment a dark figure cautiously stepped inside the ruins of the church.

Gwyneth shrank back into the branches, hardly daring to breathe, the rough surface of the wall and tree scarcely noticed now. Seconds slipped by, their passage marked by the steady drum of her heart against her ribs. The stranger's stillness seemed to cry with a voice of its own, his tightly coiled muscles crouched and ready to spring as his eyes made a slow circuit of the trees and wall.

When a twig snapped, the man started, his head lifting like an animal testing the wind. In a rush, Gwyneth realized that the burly man was as fearful of discovery as she was. When the stealthy sound came again, he noiselessly slipped out of the ruins and into the trees.

Had he left the woods, or was he still hiding? Afraid to move, Gwyneth waited, her senses tuned for any sound or movement. After what seemed like hours, she carefully shifted position and peered down at the area outside the church. Night masked the trees and undergrowth in shadows. Even the breeze carrying the sound of the pipes and fiddle had ceased. Was it safe to climb down?

Nerves taut, Gwyneth carefully rose, her legs tingling from her cramped wait, her senses sharpened. Holding her breath, she listened. When she heard no sound, Gwyneth lifted her skirt and began a careful descent from the tree.

Halfway down, a sudden noise stopped her. She balanced on a branch, her hands gripping the tree as she peered down through its leaves. A man stepped around the corner of the ruins, his height and bearing such that she knew it wasn't the heavy-set person she'd seen inside the ruins. Something in his stance chimed like a familiar chord, making her draw in her breath. Cormac! It was Cormac D'Arcy!

Before she could open her mouth and call to him, the burly man leaped from the trees and wrestled Cormac to the ground. The Irishman fought fiercely, but his heavier, muscled attacker had the advantage of surprise. Caught in a vice of fear, Gwyneth stared down at the grappling men, their arms and legs a melee of frenzied thrashing, the sound of their harsh breathing filling the night.

Too frozen to think or move, Gwyneth stifled a gasp when the attacker's fingers fastened in a strangle hold around Cormac's throat. As Cormac's efforts slowed, his assailant straddled him and pulled a pistol from his pocket.

"No!" Gwyneth leaped from the tree, branches scraping her flesh, the sensation of falling meshing with anger and fear as she collided with the burly figure. Pain from the impact forced a cry from her lips as she and the man struck the ground and the pistol flew from his hand.

For a second, neither moved, the man's body inert under hers. Cursing, he flung Gwyneth aside and lunged to his feet. Before Gwyneth could blink, he aimed a kick at Cormac, his boot striking hard at Cormac's ribs.

"No!" Gwyneth's protest and Cormac's groan collided with a shout and crash in the undergrowth.

"Get him, Seamus!"

The burly attacker grabbed his fallen gun and fired into the woods. Not waiting to see if his aim was true, he dashed around the ruins and disappeared into the darkness.

Jarred and hurting, Gwyneth crawled over to Cormac, her skirt tangling around her legs to impede her progress. "Cormac." Her voice was a sob.

Hearing it, Cormac moved, his eyes flickering open in the murky moonlight as he struggled to sit up. "Where is he? What . . . ?"

"Gone. Someone chased him away."

"Paddy . . . and Seamus." Only then did his eyes seem to take her in. "Gwyneth . . . why are you here?"

"I went to the bonfire and . . ." Gwyneth took Cormac's hand and pressed it to her lips, her brain a muddle of emotion that made her laugh and cry. "He tried to kill you. When I saw him . . ." Tears blocked her throat. "Oh . . . Cormac."

"Hush . . . it's all right." Cormac pulled her close as they knelt on the leaf-matted ground. "It's all right," he repeated.

"What happened?"

"A boy brought me a note telling me to come here . . . that someone would give me the names of those who houghed your cattle. It was a trap. I see that now. But why?" He paused and shook his head. "Thank heaven you're safe . . . and that you were here."

"Yes." Trying not to think of what could have happened, she buried her face against his shoulder. He was safe! Thank God he was safe, but fear remained coiled like a snake inside her. "What if the man comes back? He has a gun!"

"Paddy and Seamus will take care of him."

"Shouldn't they have caught him by now?"

"Not if he hid somewhere."

Cormac got to his feet and helped Gwyneth to hers, his arm keeping her close. "The first thing is to get you safely back to Shannonderry."

Unlike Gwyneth, Cormac knew exactly where to go, pushing a path through the trees and undergrowth, his hand holding hers. Confident as he seemed, Gwyneth could tell he still wasn't entirely himself. The choking and kick to his ribs must still be causing him pain.

Hearing voices, Cormac tensed and pulled Gwyneth behind a large tree. "Who is it?" Gwyneth whispered.

"I don't know."

Ears straining, they heard a giggle followed by a guffaw. "Ye'd best watch where yer goin' else ye'll lead us off the path and we'll be lost for sure," a boyish voice said.

"Not me," a female voice retorted. "I know these woods like the back of me hand. 'Tis ye who'll be for gettin' us lost."

Gwyneth let out a breath of relief. "It's Biddy and Cluny," she whispered.

"Go with them," Cormac said. He lifted her chin with his hand. "Don't tell them you've been with me. You understand why, don't you?" Seeing her nod, he brushed his fingers across her cheek. "I love you, darlin' girl."

Gwyneth covered his hand with hers. "Please take care . . . and remember I love you too."

"I'll not be forgetting that." Cormac chuckled. His lips found hers, warm and filled with love. Then with a gentle push, he sent her away.

Taking a deep breath, Gwyneth called to the servants. "Is that you, Biddy?"

Her question was met with silence. "Who . . . who be there?" a shaky voice asked.

"Miss Beddows."

"Gwyneth?" Kate's voice held surprise and censure. "What are ye doin' here?"

Before Gwyneth could think of a plausible answer, Kate and Biddy came through the trees with Cluny and Flynn but a step behind.

"Thank the sweet Virgin," Kate said, pulling Gwyneth in a hug. "Like to scared me to death, ye did. Whatever made you leave the castle? Didn't I say 'twasn't safe?"

"You did, but I wanted to see the bonfire . . . then somehow I got lost."

"Yer lucky gettin' lost was all that happened," Kate scolded.

"Aye," Cluny agreed. "If fairies catch ye, they can change ye into a donkey." He shot a quick look over his shoulder and reached for his grandfather's arm.

"Cluny," Biddy chided, noticing how her mistress kept looking back through the trees. It wouldn't do to frighten her more. "Come," she said, leading the way. "We'll have ye home and in bed afore ye can say a Hail Mary."

"Aye," Kate agreed, "though 'twill be wise to keep what ye've done from yer gran."

Old Flynn snorted and shook his head The young miss was nothin' but trouble and had hardly a speck of gumption, but like Kate, he didn't want his mistress to be upset either.

A half hour later, Gwyneth was tucked into bed with a fire burning to fend off the late-night chill. Despite the comfort and warmth, her mind wouldn't let sleep come. Half-formed pictures of Cormac struggling with his attacker as she leaped from the tree tumbled through her mind. She rubbed a bruised arm, her stomach tightening as she remembered the terror of dropping down through the branches. Had she waited but a few seconds longer, Cormac's windpipe would have been crushed by the man's strong fingers. She shuddered at the thought. So much could have gone wrong—the pistol going off and she or Cormac killed—Paddy and Seamus coming too late to scare Cormac's attacker.

"Thank you, God," she whispered into the darkness. Had it been God who'd sent her to the bonfire instead of the pipes and fiddle? Was that how God worked?

She rolled onto her side and looked out at the pale stars shining through the window. Questions pricked her mind like the sharp points of the stars. Why had someone lured Cormac with the promise of names and then tried to kill him? Since the houghed cattle and note had been aimed at her, why had Cormac been attacked? Nothing made sense. Unless . . .

"It's me!" Her whisper punctuated the stillness. "They're trying to get to me through Cormac." Gwyneth tried to push the thought away, not wanting to believe that she'd put Cormac in danger by staying in Ireland.

"No!" The fierceness in her voice hissed like spitting coals in the peat fire. But the thought continued to grow, swelling like a bubble before it bursts, the pressure an actual pain. If she didn't leave Shannonderry, Cormac's life would remain in danger.

"No . . . please, no." The whispered words were like a prayer. How could she leave Cormac when their love had just begun to flourish? Never to see him again? Never to feel his strong arms around her and to savor his tender kisses?

Gwyneth rolled out of bed and knelt on the floor to pour out her heart to the one who'd always listened in the past. "Please tell me what to do, Father," she prayed. "Must I leave Cormac to keep him safe? Is that the only way?"

She closed her eyes and waited. If the answer said she must leave Ireland, would she have the strength to obey? Gwyneth shivered, the thought pressing on her chest like an icy blanket. To leave Cormac would snuff out the light that filled and gladdened her existence, smothering its warmth and leaving nothing but burnt, lifeless ashes.

Cormac. Her mind curled like soft fingers around his name, remembering his face just inches from hers and how she'd wanted to trace the line of his jaw before she'd whispered good-bye.

"I love him, Father. Is leaving him what I must do to keep him safe?"

Gwyneth waited, her senses straining to know the answer, afraid of what she might hear. Time seemed to halt, holding its breath in expectation like Gwyneth. But hard as she listened, no answer came.

20

SUNLIGHT STREAMING THROUGH THE WINDOW wakened Gwyneth the next morning. She lay for a moment trying to understand why she felt as if something were terribly wrong. Then memory crashed through, bringing images of Cormac grappling with his attacker. Had it not been for her torn, grass-stained dress draped on the bedpost, Gwyneth might have thought she'd dreamt it. The ache of her bruised muscles when she moved clearly proved it true.

Another pain hovered close. She skirted around it, not ready to face the fact that her presence at Shannonderry endangered Cormac. Small wonder that she felt as if a black, ugly specter waited to pounce and dash her dreams to pieces. *Not yet. Let me bask in Cormac's love for a few more minutes, remember the gladness that springs to his face each time he looks at me, the warmth of his kisses.*

Reality refused to be shut out, its harshness rubbing like a rough stone in the toe of her slipper. Someone wanted her and Toryn gone. To drive the point home, they'd attacked Cormac.

Too upset to stay in bed, Gwyneth put on her wrapper and went to the window. Sunlight bathed the grass with rays of shimmering gold, and a chorus of wrens sang from the oak tree. For a moment, the beauty of sun-dappled trees and the scent of roses erased the memory of the night before. Yet, lurking like a riptide just under the surface of shining water was the knowledge that she must leave Shannonderry.

Wanting to intercept Cormac before he spoke to Moira, Gwyneth hurried downstairs to the library and stationed herself by a window. She paced the room, her slipper-clad feet measuring the shabby rug that covered the floor. She paused to look at the map on the wall then returned to the window, her mind rehearsing the words she must say.

After what seemed an eternity, she heard Cluny call off the wolfhounds and saw Cormac canter his mare into the stable yard. Her senses drank in the sight of his lithe body as he dismounted, heard the rich timbre of his low voice as he spoke to Cluny. In two short months, she'd come to love him more deeply than she'd thought possible, memorizing the way he held his head and how an untidy lock of black hair often fell onto his forehead.

It was all she could do not to run outside and throw herself into his arms. She needed his closeness, his strength, but if she selfishly clung to Cormac, she would put him in further danger. The thought stiffened her faltering resolve. Willing herself to be strong, Gwyneth hurried to intercept him, the false smile pasted on her face painful in its stiffness, urgency of what she must do pushing her forward.

Cormac stopped as soon as he heard her voice. The gladness on his face almost undid her. How could she lie to him when she was suffused in his love, douse its flame with the sound of her words?

"What a pleasant surprise." Happiness tinged his voice.

"Can we talk?" she asked, using directness to bolster her courage.

Sensing that something was wrong, Cormac's expression turned wary. "Of course."

Cormac took Gwyneth's arm and led her past the herb garden to a small arbor overgrown with climbing foliage. It was Kate's favorite spot to sit for an evening with her knitting, the wooden bench half hidden by tangled leaves and blooms, a quiet sanctuary away from Biddy's chattering tongue.

As soon as they entered the leafy bower, Cormac pulled her into his arms and kissed her, his love and gladness as evident as the pulse of his heart. Unable to resist his warmth, her mouth melted under his as her arms encircled his neck. She wanted to stay there forever, to love him forever. Reality crashed around her, making her stiffen.

"What's wrong?" Cormac asked.

"I . . ." With him standing so close, it was difficult for Gwyneth to think. Where were the words she'd so carefully rehearsed? "I've changed my mind. I can't marry you," she blurted. Willing herself to meet his gaze, she saw puzzlement cloud his face.

"Changed your mind?"

She forced the word from her mouth, her voice cracking with the effort. "Yes."

"I'm afraid I don't understand."

She moistened her lips, her mouth and throat so taut with pent-up emotion it was difficult to speak. "I . . . I no longer wish to marry you," she managed to get out.

"This from a woman who risked her life to save mine?" Incredulity filled Cormac's voice.

Gwyneth turned away, knowing that if she continued to look at him, her resolve would melt. "Anyone would have done it."

"No . . . only someone with indomitable courage . . . someone who loved me, which I know you do." Cormac took her by the shoulders and turned her to face him. "Now start over, and this time tell me the real reason you've changed your mind." In the stillness that followed, he lifted her chin with his finger. "You love me just as I love you."

Knowing she couldn't lie any longer, Gwyneth met his gaze, her voice unsteady as she spoke. "I . . . must leave. My being here has put you in danger."

"Danger!" Cormac's chuckle robbed the word of importance. "What a courageous goose you are. How could—" With a happy laugh, Cormac pulled her tight in his arms, his voice a murmur of love as he kissed her cheek and forehead. "It's Toryn they want gone, not you. Even though Paddy and Seamus weren't able to catch the man who ambushed me, I'm certain his trail will lead to the Westons."

"The Westons." Gwyneth breathed the name against Cormac's shoulder, his nearness robbing her of any desire to move.

"Paddy and I have suspected them from the start. It's true the houghed cattle and note were intended to make you and Toryn go back to England. When that failed and they heard I would be riding him in the steeplechase, I became next on their list. With me dead or hurt too badly to ride, the race would have to be called off."

Enlightenment filled her. "The Westons. Of course." Gwyneth's relief was so strong it made her giddy. She pulled Cormac closer, willing him to kiss her once again.

Cormac quickly complied, making a thorough work of it. "Did I not say I knew you loved me?" he whispered against her cheek.

"You did, though my love was never in question . . . only what I must do to keep you safe. I was afraid they would continue to try to hurt you."

"As you can see, I'm very much alive," Cormac assured her. "More than that, Paddy and his friends are looking for the man who attacked me while others keep watch on the Westons. It won't be long before someone makes a mistake. When they do, we'll have them."

Cormac paused as the stable clock struck eleven. "It won't do to keep your grandmother waiting. I mean to ask for her permission to marry you."

"I'll not protest at that."

"And claim you as my wife as soon as possible."

"That meets with my approval as well."

After another kiss, Gwyneth watched Cormac walk toward the house. Happy tears misted her eyes as she thought of the wonderful turn the morning had taken. Cormac—How she loved him! "Hurry," she whispered to the morning sky. Her fears had melted along with her dread of the days ahead. With Cormac and Paddy keeping watch, surely all would turn out well.

* * *

ALTHOUGH GWYNETH WASN'T PRESENT TO hear what was said between Cormac and her grandmother, she was not long in being apprised of the outcome. Cormac had scarcely ridden from the stable yard when Moira sent Biddy to fetch her.

Gwyneth felt like a girl of sixteen instead of a woman of two and twenty when she entered the sitting room. "You wish to see me, Grandmother?"

"I do." Seeing that Biddy lingered at the door, Moira said, "That will be all, Biddy." And to Gwyneth, "Please, close the door."

Gwyneth pulled the door shut, her lips lifting into a smile when she noted the twinkle in the old woman's blue eyes.

"I have had a most interesting conversation with Mr. D'Arcy. It seems he wishes to marry you." She made a significant pause. "By the look on your face, I believe you are not opposed to the proposal."

"No . . . indeed, I welcome it."

Moira made a show of solemnity, but her eyes snapped with pleasure. "You are certain, my dear? Remember, marriage is not something one should rush into."

"I am certain, Grandmother . . . more than certain."

Moira gave up her pretext and laughed. "Good. I think it a splendid idea as well. Indeed, I have wished it since the night of our dinner party." Seeing Gwyneth's lifted brows, she hurried on. "I can tell he's smitten. It was written on Mr. D'Arcy's face that night and hasn't left it since."

Gwyneth looked askance of her grandmother.

"It's true, and I couldn't be more pleased. Mr. D'Arcy has been a loyal and trusted friend these past years, and I don't doubt he'll make you an excellent husband. The fact that he loves you is an added bonus."

"I love him too."

"Yes, even a fool can see that." A smile creased the wrinkles on Moira's face. "Come and sit with me. We have much to discuss, for Mr. D'Arcy wishes to see you his wife before the summer is gone."

Gwyneth kissed Moira's cheek as she joined her on the sofa. "You've made me very happy."

"I've a notion it's Mr. D'Arcy who makes you happy, but if I can claim part of the credit, I am pleased to do so." Moira took Gwyneth's hand.

"Would you mind if instead of being married in the church, we hold your wedding in the great hall? It's where I was wed and my mother and grandmother before me. I had hoped for Deirdre to marry there as well, but when she eloped—" A flicker of regret weakened Moira's smile.

As of yet, Gwyneth hadn't given any thought about the wedding. To start her married life surrounded by the ancient walls and trappings of the O'Briens would add pleasure to the occasion. She squeezed Moira's hand. "What a wonderful idea."

"You're not just humoring an old woman?"

"How could you think that?"

Before Gwyneth could say more, someone tapped on the door. Moira grimaced. "It's likely Biddy. I swear the girl has three pair of ears and an extra nose for sniffing out excitement."

At Moira's call, Biddy popped her pert head around the door. "Company for ye, Mistress. 'Tis Mr. Berry from the village."

"Show him in." Moira glanced at Gwyneth. "It's not often we have company at Shannonderry. To have it twice in the same day is almost unheard of. Small wonder Biddy is all agog."

Gwyneth's first thought was of the steeplechase. Had a letter arrived from Mr. O'Roark? One look at the man's face told her it had. Mr. Berry held himself as if he were bursting with good news, his round, freckled face pink with pleasure.

"How good to see you again," Moira said.

Mr. Berry crossed the room and bowed, taking Moira's outstretched hand, then Gwyneth's. "My pleasure, ma'am." His words were automatic, the bulk of his attention taken with Moira's granddaughter. He still had difficulty reconciling the lithe, boyish figure he'd mistaken as a young man racing against Percy Weston with the fetching young woman who smiled at him from the sofa. What a smashing good rider, but when she turned those magnificent eyes on him, he couldn't imagine how he'd mistaken her for anything other than a lovely young woman. Small wonder that village gossip claimed both of the D'Arcys were smitten with her.

Moira's invitation to be seated jolted Mr. Berry back to the purpose for his visit. He settled himself in the chair closest to the sofa and extracted the long-awaited letter from his jacket pocket. "I have heard from Mr. O'Roark," he announced. "Not only has he agreed to a race, but he has set the date and place."

Gwyneth's heart gave a thump of pleasure. "Where? When?"

"Twentieth of July at the Killiwreathe churchyard." Mr. Berry handed Gwyneth the letter. "Here, you may read it for yourself."

Gwyneth hastily perused the bold handwriting, her mind snagging hold of the date and place while she searched for the amount O'Roark had asked to race his stallion. Fifty pounds sterling, just as the reverend had said. The words leaped off the page and landed with a thud in the pit of her stomach. Would they be able to find money for the rest of the fee in so short a time?

"Excellent," Moira exclaimed when Gwyneth stated the amount. "I have always thought July the perfect time for a race." Neither Moira's voice nor her expression conveyed concern about having enough money for the fee.

Taking her cue from Moira, Gwyneth nodded. "Tell Mr. O'Roark we shall be there with my stallion."

Mr. Berry cleared his throat. "And the fifty pounds?"

"It will be there with my granddaughter's stallion," Moira stated.

The proud tilt to the old woman's head and the direct manner with which she challenged him made Mr. Berry feel like a gauche adolescent.

"Only one month," Moira went on in a lilting voice that seemed to brim with anticipation.

"Aye," their visitor agreed. "Plenty of time to get the word out. Half the county will be there, or I'll miss my guess." He returned the letter to his pocket. "'Tis a winner ye have, Miss Beddows, and all of County Cork will be cheering him on." Mr. Berry rubbed his hands in happy anticipation and got to his feet. "If you'll excuse me, I'll be off to write a reply to Mr. O'Roark's letter. We don't want him to say he didn't have time to prepare his horse for the race."

Gwyneth arose and followed him to the door where Biddy waited to show him out. Not until the door was closed and she heard retreating footsteps down the corridor did she look at her grandmother. "How are we to raise the rest of the fee in so short a time?"

Moira returned Gwyneth's gaze, her face as calm as if they were discussing what to have for tea. "It won't be easy, but I'm confident we'll succeed."

Before Gwyneth could voice her concerns, Moira went on. "For some weeks I have prayed that love would grow between you and Mr. D'Arcy. I don't mean to imply that my prayers made it happen, but I like to think that they played a part." She nodded and smiled. "I firmly believe that a loving God likes to help His children the same as parents do, and that if we have faith and do our part, He'll do what He can to make it happen."

Gwyneth crossed the room and took Moira's hand. "I wish I had your faith."

"When I was your age, mine was small too, but life has taught me that it's more pleasant to believe than to doubt. We must do our part, of course . . . search for answers, just as I'm doing now."

"You seem so certain the money will come," Gwyneth said.

"I am." Moira's voice was firm. "I also have an idea or two of how to bring it about." She squeezed Gwyneth's hand. "But such can wait, for I'd much rather talk about your wedding. Kate and Biddy will be ecstatic when they hear the news." She lowered her voice. "I wouldn't be surprised if you opened the door and found Biddy waiting. See if I'm not right."

Gwyneth moved toward the door. "Biddy," she called. Before she could reach the door, it opened.

"Ye called, Miss Gwyneth?"

"I did. Please find Kate. I've some news I wish to share with you."

Biddy's face broke into a smile. "Me and Kate thought as much. She be waitin' in the hall same as me."

"Kate."

The older woman's cheeks were flushed when she entered the room, but she was much too happy to try to hide the fact that she'd been waiting by the door. "Yes?" she answered, her eyes on Gwyneth.

"I thought I had a surprise to share with you, but I see by your faces that my secret has been found out. Just the same, I want the pleasure of saying it aloud." She paused and cleared her throat like a preacher about to begin his sermon. "Mr. D'Arcy has asked me to be his wife."

Kate's eyes filled with happy tears. "'Tis what I prayed for this past month and more." Casting aside her role of servant, she gathered Gwyneth into her arms. "I been lovin' ye like ye was me own daughter all these years. Since yer mam's not here, I'll speak for her. I'm certain she be burstin' with happiness . . . same as me and yer gran and yes . . . Biddy too."

Remembering all the times Kate had held her on her lap and loved her brought tears to Gwyneth's eyes. Kate had been her bulwark against her father's rejection and a warm refuge from the storms that had assailed her. "I love you, Kate."

"I know." Wiping her tears, Kate pulled away. "'Tis a happy day," she exclaimed. "Ye could not a found a better man to marry had ye searched the whole of Ireland. Am I not right, Biddy?"

Biddy giggled. "Half the girls in the county be in love with him, but I knew 'twas ye he had his eyes on since the night of the dinner party." She dropped a quick curtsy. "My best wishes, Miss Gwyneth."

"Thank you, Biddy."

Moira cleared her throat. "Did I not tell you they'd be ecstatic?" Like Kate and Gwyneth, happy tears glistened on her wrinkled cheeks. "All in all, I could not have asked for a better day."

"Have ye set a date for the wedding?" Kate asked.

"Later this summer." Gwyneth glanced at her grandmother. "With the race set for the end of July, we have much to prepare for."

"Race?" Biddy asked.

Kate nodded. "Did I not tell ye as much? 'Tis the only thing that would bring Mr. Berry all the way from the village without the reverend."

Biddy went on as if Kate hadn't spoken. "There be hundreds of wonderful things to plan . . . the weddin' and all the food and, of course, a new gown. Have ye decided what ye'll wear?"

"Not yet."

Moira's quiet voice slipped into the conversation. "I had a lovely gown for my wedding, one with yards of satin and trimmed with finest Irish lace. My father shook his head when the bill from the seamstress arrived, but he said it was worth every guinea when he saw me in it." Moira's eyes grew distant. "Such a lovely gown, and William so handsome I could scarce take my eyes off him."

Gwyneth looked at the portrait of her grandfather. In his middle years, William Donahue had nonetheless been a handsome man. A white wig hid the true color of his hair, and the wide collar of his coat clearly spoke of another time. "I think you were just as beautiful as he was handsome," she said.

"I suppose I was," Moira mused, "for I had my pick of suitors." Her face broke into a smile. "That day, especially, I was beautiful. Anyone would appear so in such a lovely gown."

Gwyneth's interest was piqued. "Do you have it still?"

Moira nodded, the faraway look still on her face. "It's packed in a trunk in the north tower. Deirdre liked to look at it when she was young." A tiny sigh escaped her lips. "We planned that she would wear it on her wedding day, but that was before Maurice Beddows stole her away."

Kate grimaced at the mention of the Englishman, but before she could express her opinion, Gwyneth spoke.

"Would you mind if I wore your gown for my wedding?"

"Mind?" Moira laughed, clearly pleased. "I can't think of anything I'd like better. You are much the size I was, though even if it doesn't fit, I'm sure Mrs. Ryan can remedy it." She looked at Gwyneth with fond eyes. What a lovely creature she was with her cap of platinum curls and shining aqua eyes. "You know where it's stored don't you, Kate?"

Kate nodded. "I know the very trunk. Would ye like me to fetch it for ye?" At Moira's nod, she beckoned to Biddy. "I'll need ye to help me carry it. Ye'll not believe how beautiful it be."

Left alone, Gwyneth and Moira filled the time with talk of the wedding. As they did, a loud pounding sounded on the front door.

"Now, who can that be?" Moira asked. "First Mr. D'Arcy, then Mr. Berry, and now this."

Remembering that Kate and Biddy were up in the tower where they likely couldn't hear the door, Gwyneth glanced at Moira. "Would you like me to answer it?"

The pounding came again, louder and more insistent. "I suppose you must, though only the most boorish would carry on in such a manner."

Wondering whom it might be, Gwyneth hurried down the corridor. "Coming," she called when the pounding came the third time. Whoever it was certainly wasn't given to patience. Slightly out of breath, she pulled back the lock and opened the heavy oak door. Shock froze her to the spot, and for a second she forgot to breathe. Surely not, but the red, angry face of the man on the doorstep couldn't be mistaken. It was her father!

21

"FATHER!" GWYNETH GASPED.

Maurice Beddows's angry voice cut through hers. "So you are here. I might have known. Running off and stealing my stallion."

"I didn't steal your stallion. Toryn's mine!" Gwyneth's voice shook with emotion, as did her legs, which felt as if they'd suddenly turned to butter. "Toryn is mine," she repeated in a firmer voice.

"Show me his papers . . . which you can't, as well you know."

"Just as you know that you promised Toryn to me if I could train him to the saddle . . . which I did." Anger put iron to her words and sent strength to her quivering bones.

"What about your promise to marry James?"

"I never promised to marry James. It was your idea to sell me off with no regard for my feelings." Gwyneth paused and took a breath, her flushed face just inches from his. "You can't make me marry James, nor can you take Toryn."

Maurice's eyes narrowed, and he raised his hand. A menacing growl jerked his gaze to the steps where Cluny struggled to keep one of the wolfhounds in check. "The blasted dog tried to bite me and scared my gelding!" Maurice shouted. "Keep him back; you hear me, boy?" His scowl deepened as he caught a glimpse of the hound's flashing teeth. "Get him away!"

"He's only doin' what he be trained for," Cluny retorted.

"I don't care what he's trained for. Keep him away from me and my horses." Maurice's eyes shifted back to Gwyneth. "I mean to take Toryn back to England with me." He went on just as if there had been no interruption. "Peter's already with him in the stable."

"Peter . . . you brought Peter with you?"

"I did. Don't think you can wheedle him into doing your bidding either. Peter's hard under my thumb."

Gwyneth was no longer listening. Peter had come. He'd help her. Vaguely aware that Kate and Biddy had come to the door, she hurried past her father and around the house to the stable yard. *Dear Peter.* What a good friend he'd been, his wife too, baking plum cake for her and their son John to eat in their cheery kitchen. Peter had taken Gwyneth's part when it had come to training Toryn, too, and he was the only one besides Gwyneth the stallion had allowed on his back.

Gwyneth recognized her father's horses as soon as she entered the stable yard, but there was no sign of Peter or Flynn and Ronan. The low murmur of male voices when she entered the stable told her they were with Toryn.

"Peter." Gladness filled Gwyneth's voice and a like pleasure emanated from her father's trainer when he turned from Toryn to greet her.

"Miss Gwyneth." Peter touched a finger to his cap, the same battered gray one he'd worn for as long as she could remember. As her eyes took in his ruddy face and the blue eyes that crinkled at the corners when he smiled, she thought of how much she'd missed him. "'Tis good to see ye," he added. Despite his words, she sensed a wariness that hadn't been there before.

Hoping to put him at ease, she asked about his wife and family.

"John be fine. Ellen too, but Grace . . ." Peter's voice trembled over his wife's name. "Grace ain't doin' so well. She had a spell right after ye left. Doctor said 'twas her heart. Now just walkin' cross the room tires her." He shook his head. "Grace ain't doin well, Miss Gwyneth."

Hearing such news about the cheery woman squeezed Gwyneth's middle. "I'm sorry to hear that. She was my special friend."

"She thinks the same of ye. Always talkin' of ye, she is."

Before either could say more, Flynn broke into the conversation. "'Tisn't true, is it?" he demanded. "That devil . . . Mr. Beddows says Toryn don't belong to ye. And he . . ." Flynn pointed a gnarled finger at Peter. "He said they came to take the stallion back to England."

"Toryn is mine and has been since the day he was foaled," Gwyneth stated in a firm voice. Aware that Cluny had crept into the stable to join them, she went on. "My father knows this and so does Peter." She met Peter's blue eyes and saw him look away. "Tell them what Father promised that day in the stable . . . and what he repeated over the years."

Peter moistened his lips. "He said the stallion be yers if ye could train him to be ridden."

"Didn't I succeed? Didn't you and I train him to the saddle?"

"We did, though 'twas mostly ye what done it." Peter's gaze flicked to Flynn, his face taking on animation. "Ye should a' seen her . . . a fair wonder she be with the stallion. Her da be pure amazed." Peter paused and looked down at the toes of his worn boots. "The only trouble be, he never put Miss Beddows's name on the stallion's papers."

"He said he'd do it when Toryn entered his first big race," Gwyneth said.

"Which never happened." The trainer kept his eyes carefully fixed on Flynn and Ronan. "Mr. Beddows says he means to file charges against ye if ye don't behave . . . said ye not only stole the stallion but broke a bigger law by takin' him out of England." Only then did Peter's eyes meet hers. "I wish it weren't true, Miss Gwyneth, but yer da explained it to me three times or more . . . his agent, too. The law's clearly on his side."

Although Peter's words poured without let up and left Gwyneth's insides feeling like mashed turnips, her voice was filled with scorn when she spoke. "And you mean to help him? Without you to control and ride Toryn there's no way Father can take him back to England."

"I don't want to," Peter rasped. "I told yer da I wanted no part of it, but when he said he'd turn us out . . . that we'd not have a place to live and that he'd make it so no one else would hire me—" Peter's mouth worked as he strove for control. "I couldn't do that to Grace," he said softly. "She's too sick to be put out of our cottage." The trainer shook his head, moisture showing in his eyes. "Though I wanted to in the worst way, I couldn't tell him no, Miss Gwyneth. I couldn't do that to my Grace."

Gwyneth spoke past the ache in her throat. "Of course you couldn't." As she patted her friend's arm and looked into his moist eyes, she said, "I understand, Peter." She fought to control her tears. "There's nothing else you could do."

"I'm sorry," Peter whispered.

"I know."

Unspoken grief permeated the air of the stable, causing Ronan and Cluny to shuffle their feet and making Flynn's face look even glummer. Deep as the grief was, a flood of anger burned through Gwyneth's insides, its hotness so fierce it dried her tears. In the past, she'd sometimes questioned whether her father possessed a heart. Today she no longer wondered.

* * *

GWYNETH'S MIND, LIKE HER LEGS, jerked unnaturally as she hurried back to the house. Scrambled thoughts urging her to flee with Toryn pounded like the hasty rhythm of her heart. Where could she go? How could she escape her father and Peter? *Think*, a part of her brain urged. *You've outwitted him before. With careful planning, you can do it again.*

When Gwyneth reached the house, she paused and leaned her head against the peeling paint on the back door, drawing in a deep breath, willing herself to calmness. Experience had taught her that Maurice Beddows responded more favorably to a soft voice than one filled with anger. Hadn't such tones and demeanor gained her Toryn when he was first foaled?

"Please, God," she whispered. "Show me what to do."

Her shoulders straight, she walked into the deserted kitchen where the smell of roasting chicken permeated the air. Although she would show a pleasant face, her father would know she was a woman to be reckoned with.

She made her way toward the sitting room, certain her father would be there with Moira. When she reached the connecting corridor, she saw Biddy carrying bed linens and a pillow.

"Have ye ever heard such a thing . . . yer da comin' all the way from England, and Mistress tellin' him he must stay the night even though he means to take yer stallion?" Biddy paused for breath, her face pleading for reassurance. "Surely he can't do such a thing . . . take yer stallion, can he?"

"He cannot." Despite her best effort, Gwyneth was aware that her voice was not entirely steady.

Biddy smiled in relief. "I thought not, 'specially now that the race be arranged with the man from Limerick and Mr. D'Arcy plannin' to marry ye." She clicked her tongue. "What a pucker for Kate and me, with a special meal to fix, a room to ready, and all done within the hour."

Although Gwyneth didn't care two figs whether her father passed a comfortable night and indeed in her present mood hoped he slept badly, she didn't want him to know how understaffed they were at Shannonderry. "Let me help."

"Would ye? I know 'taint fittin', but if ye can give me a hand with the bed, 'twill free me sooner to help Kate in the kitchen."

The young maid kept up a steady stream of chatter while they made up the room. Concentrating on ways to outwit her father, Gwyneth had no idea what Biddy said. Somehow she must get herself and Toryn to Clonglas. Once there, Cormac would know what to do. It was how to get the stallion away from the stable that eluded her.

Realizing her father would be staying for dinner, Gwyneth decided to go to her room to collect her thoughts and decide what to do.

An hour later, Gwyneth descended the tower stairs dressed and ready to dine. Unfortunately, her plans to get Toryn away from Shannonderry were not as ready. Since she knew her father would instruct Peter to spend the night in the stable, she must either try to persuade her father to change his mind or find a way to outsmart him. But how?

Recalling how God had answered her prayers in the past, she paused at the bottom of the stairs and bowed her head. Someone far wiser than she would show her what to do. She hoped her grandmother would be inspired too. Gwyneth hurried to the sitting room and softly knocked on the door.

Instead of finding Moira drooping with fatigue, Gwyneth saw anger banked like hot coals simmering in her blue eyes and heard harsh determination in her voice. "Twenty-four years ago Maurice Beddows outwitted me and eloped with Deirdre. I will not let him win a second time. We must think, Gwyneth . . . think and win."

Gwyneth nodded as she joined Moira on the sofa. "I plan to take Toryn away as soon as Father is asleep."

"It's the very thing I'd have done had I been fifty years younger. That's why I insisted your father spend the night. It will give us more time." Her bony finger tapped Gwyneth's wrist. "You must take care, though, for there's not much that gets past that man. Kate says he told his trainer to keep a sharp watch during the night." The old woman paused and looked thoughtful. "If we could persuade him to change his mind—" Moira nodded, pleased at the thought. "Men such as your father are more apt to be persuaded when they're flattered by seemingly compliant women."

Certain that Moira had overheard the angry words she'd exchanged with her father, Gwyneth flushed. "I know I made a mistake by flying at him, but he . . ."

"I don't fault your outburst," Moira interrupted. "In fact, I applaud it. The man deserves a lashing . . . if not with a whip, then most certainly with the tongue."

Moira's praise brought a grim smile to Gwyneth's face. "I must confess it felt good to meet him toe to toe. Even so, I realized that doing so only made him more stubborn. I will take pains to be more gracious at dinner."

"If we both take pains, perhaps we can persuade Maurice to change his mind," Moira agreed. "But if we fail—"

"I will go ahead with my plan." Gwyneth stared past her grandmother and frowned. "If it weren't for Peter, it would be simple to take Toryn out of the stable, but Father has a hold over him so he can't help me."

"I know. Cluny was quick to tell Biddy what was said, and she passed it on to me. Even so . . ." Moira paused and held Gwyneth's eyes. "I'm certain we can think of something."

The two women sat in silence, the encroachment of dusk filling the room with shadows and the ticking clock marking the passing minutes.

"Yes!" Moira whispered, her gaze on the Queen Anne desk that sat against the opposite wall. "Fetch me the bottle from the middle drawer of the desk."

Gwyneth crossed the room and removed a small brown vial from the drawer. "This?" she asked, bringing it to her grandmother.

The old woman nodded. "Laudanum. The doctor gave it to me to ease the pain in my joints. It does wonders for my rheumatism, but since it makes me want to sleep all day, I seldom take it. I have another bottle in my bedroom that I sometimes take on a bad night. If it will make me sleep soundly . . ."

". . . it will do the same for Father and Peter," Gwyneth finished with a laugh. "You are wicked, Grandmother. Brilliant too. Now all we need to do is find a way to slip it into their drinks." In her mind she saw Kate lacing Maurice's dinner wine with a few drops of laudanum and Ronan doing the same with the bottle of Irish whisky she knew Flynn kept hidden in the tack room. Suddenly there was a solution to a situation that had seemed fraught with failure.

"Should we fail to win your father over at dinner, I will invite Maurice to join me here for a nightcap. I'll have Biddy ready a tray with two glasses and a bottle of port . . . one with a few drops of laudanum in the bottom."

Their excitement grew as they planned how Kate would carry the vial to the stable and instruct Ronan and Flynn in the role they would play.

"What if Flynn refuses?" Gwyneth asked. "You know how he dislikes me."

"Not as much as he detests Maurice." Moira patted Gwyneth's hand. "I think you misjudge Flynn's animosity. He's always been one to growl and complain, but under his tough hide is a loyal heart for those at Shannonderry."

They sat in companionable silence, the bond forged by conspiracy as thick as their O'Brien blood.

"Have you thought of where you and Toryn will hide?" Moira asked.

"No, but if I can get to Clonglas and waken Cormac, he's sure to know some place safe."

Moira nodded, her mind busy with all they had discussed. "It will not do to keep your father waiting for his dinner. First, however, you must find Kate and Biddy and let them know of our plans. When you've finished, come back for me. I would like us to enter the dining room together."

Optimism quickened Gwyneth's steps on the way to the kitchen. Both Kate and Biddy quickly grasped what they were to do and met the plan with excitement.

Gwyneth's smile faded when she returned to the sitting room and saw her grandmother sitting with her eyes closed. "Are you all right, Grandmother?"

Moira's eyes flew opened, and she nodded.

"Kate and Biddy know what to do. They're anxious to be a part of it."

"I knew they would be . . . just as you shall play your part at dinner."

"And what is that?"

"That of Maurice Beddows's beautiful and gracious daughter. Though you may not believe it, you can be most persuasive when you put your mind to it. Did you not charm your way into both of the D'Arcys' hearts?"

"That was purely unintentional." Gwyneth laughed.

Moira's eyes crinkled with amusement. "Was it?" Seeing Gwyneth blush, she went on. "If you fail at dinner . . . if we both fail . . . we still have the other plan." She set the medicine bottle onto the table next to the sofa. "There."

"Bless you, Grandmother."

Moira beamed and, after pushing herself up from the sofa, took Gwyneth's elbow with a thin, blue-veined hand. Neither spoke as they made their way into the dining room where sconces of candles lit the table and Maurice Beddows waited.

He came forward to greet them, bowing to Moira, then to Gwyneth, his gray eyes not quite meeting hers. *He does have a conscience,* Gwyneth thought, the idea bringing her hope. Perhaps she and Moira would be successful without using the laudanum.

With just three for dinner, Biddy had set only one end of the long table, its oak surface covered by a carefully mended linen cloth, the best china and silver gleaming in the glow of the candles.

After Maurice had helped Moira into her chair, he turned to Gwyneth, pulling out her chair with his customary flourish. Despite their quarrel, she sensed that, like her, he had determined to follow a more prudent path.

"I believe I neglected to tell you earlier that you are looking well," Maurice said after he'd taken his seat. "Though I'm not in favor of short hair for women, I own it becomes you. I think your stepmother would concur."

"Thank you, Father." Gwyneth unfolded her napkin and laid it across the lap of her gown. To compliment her father on his looks would be an untruth. Not only was his brown coat rumpled and boots mud stained, but his wig also badly needed a brushing. That he had ridden hard was much in evidence. "How are Mrs. Beddows and the boys?" she asked instead.

"Fine. All are fine."

Gwyneth tensed herself to introduce the subject of Toryn. But before she could, Maurice began to regale them with a story of his latest trip to York. From there he went on to tell of a man he'd met on the ship as he'd crossed the Irish Sea. Gwyneth's frustration grew as Biddy served hot soup followed by roast chicken and tiny buttered potatoes, their flavor and texture scarcely noticed. Would her father never stop for breath? It didn't seem that he would, for when dessert was being served, Maurice began a discourse on the state of affairs at Hawarden.

Moira's voice slipped into his narrative. "I am puzzled to know how you learned that Gwyneth was at Shannonderry."

A smile flitted over Maurice's face. "Strangely enough, I received communication from Ireland saying that my daughter and a black stallion had taken up residence at Shannonderry near the village of Macroom in County Cork."

Gwyneth choked on a bite of fruit. "Communication?"

"Aye." Maurice's expression was smug. "Most strange, don't you think, especially when no name except that of 'friend' was used by the one who sent it."

Moira's eyes widened, and her mouth tightened with surprise and sudden comprehension. Other than Cormac and Owen, Agatha D'Arcy was the only person who knew Maurice Beddows's name and place of residence.

"Agatha," Moira said.

"Yes," Gwyneth agreed.

"Who, pray tell, is my friend Agatha?" Maurice interjected.

"Cormac D'Arcy's stepmother."

Maurice's heavy brows lifted as he looked at Gwyneth. "Your grandmother told me earlier that you are engaged to marry Mr. D'Arcy."

"I am."

Her father's amusement became more evident. "So, daughter, am I to believe that you have found a man more to your liking than James?"

"I have. Someone who loves me as well."

"You are certain of this?"

"I am."

His lips lifted in a smirk. "So certain that you have failed to realize that like James, Mr. D'Arcy only wishes to marry you for your stallion?"

His words stung like a slap to the face although the smart faded quickly. Gwyneth knew how deeply Cormac's love ran, and knowing it, she didn't care what her father thought or said.

"Such a remark is unbecoming and unworthy of you, Mr. Beddows." The clatter as Kate dropped a piece of silver vibrated through the anger in Moira's voice. The old woman struggled to her feet, her dessert forgotten. "After you have apologized to Gwyneth, you will join me in the sitting room."

"And if I . . ." Maurice's lips clamped down on his refusal. Slowly rising from his chair, he nodded to Gwyneth, his voice barely audible. "You have my apology." Pausing, he took a deep breath, his eyes meeting Gwyneth's for the first time that evening. "Not only was it unworthy of me but mean-spirited as well. Forgive me, daughter."

Gwyneth had also arisen, her eyes firmly on her father. "Your apology is accepted. Before you join Grandmother, however, I have something I wish to say to you. All of my life I've known that you didn't love me as a father should . . . that your wife and sons and horses came first. Despite this, I've always taken pride in the fact that you were my father. Your name is known throughout Yorkshire as a breeder of the finest horses. More than that, you are known as a man who can be trusted . . . one who, if he gives his word, will never break it."

Gwyneth paused, aware of Maurice's wavering gaze and the nervous working of his mouth. "You gave me your word, Father. You said Toryn was mine if I could train him to a rider. I have kept my part of the bargain. Not only can Toryn be ridden, but he has won races." Afraid that her trembling emotions would win out, Gwyneth willed her eyes to dryness, her voice to firmness. "But what of Maurice Beddows of Hawarden? Is his word not a bond to his own daughter? You promised Toryn to me. By all you stand for, Toryn is mine."

With that, Gwyneth left the dining room, her steps quick and measured on the wooden floor, her stance reflecting the regal grace of the O'Briens, though she did not know it. She only knew she'd said what needed to be said without crying, had met her father head on without giving in to anger. Toryn was hers, and she would ensure that he remained so. Yet, as she left the room, she felt a glimmer of hope, for she'd seen regret and the shimmer of tears in her father's eyes.

22

GWYNETH PACED HER BEDROOM FLOOR as she waited for Kate to finish in the kitchen and put Moira to bed.

"What a day," Kate said when she finally came through the door. "I never imagined Mr. Beddows would follow ye to Ireland." Kate's face showed bitterness. "I never liked the man afore, and after what he said to ye at dinner—" Angry tears brightened Kate's gray eyes. "'Tis unnatural for a father to talk such to his own daughter. I've a mind . . ."

"It doesn't matter, Kate." Gwyneth gathered the servant into her arms, needing her closeness as badly as Kate did hers. "I know Cormac loves me for myself, not Toryn, so none of what Father said is important. What's important is that Father doesn't take Toryn."

Kate sniffed and patted Gwyneth's shoulder. "Aye, and I mean to help all I can. I took the medicine to the stable meself. Ronan and Flynn and Cluny know what they must do to keep Peter from stoppin' ye."

"What would I do without all of you? And Grandmother—" Gwyneth searched Kate's round, freckled face. "How is she?"

"Tired but anxious that ye be off with the stallion. She thought Mr. Beddows would change his mind, but in the end, he said he meant to take Toryn."

"She gave him the laudanum then?"

"Aye, I listened at the guest-room door, and he be snoring fit to wake the dead."

Gwyneth gave her a grim smile and turned so Kate could unfasten the buttons on her gown and help her into the leather breeches and jacket laid out on the bed. At last she was ready. "Wish me luck," Gwyneth whispered.

"Luck, and extra prayers to the Virgin," Kate said. "Be careful."

"I will." Gwyneth's feet were quick on the stairs and just as quick as she skirted the well on her way to the stable. Clouds covered a full moon, and the stable loomed like a stony fortress out of the shadows. *Pray to heaven the ruse with the laudanum and whisky had been successful with Peter as well.*

She paused at the stable door and listened, her senses alert for any sound. Silence and the distant hoot of an owl was all she heard. Carefully easing the heavy door open, she listened again, the rasp of the hinges seeming unnaturally loud in the quiet of the night. She took a cautious step into the dark interior. Was Peter awake and listening? A rustling made her jump.

"This way, Mistress. 'Tis a'right," Ronan whispered.

Sighing in relief, Gwyneth moved toward the sound of Ronan's voice. As her eyes adjusted to the blackness, she was able to discern the outline of sacks and the door to the tack room. Looking toward the stalls, she heard the strike of flint against stone as Cluny lit the lantern.

"There," he whispered, the glint of his smile caught in the lantern's yellow glow. "And himself sleepin' like a babe," he added, pointing to Peter lying on a blanket close to Toryn's stall.

"Hurry," a quavering voice rasped. "Take the horse and be gone."

Looking over her shoulder, Gwyneth saw Flynn in the doorway of the tack room with the whisky bottle in his hand. For once his rheumy eyes didn't glare at her, though he pointed impatiently at Toryn's stall. "Hurry afore the Englishman wakes and we have the devil on our hands."

Stepping around Peter's prone form, she approached Toryn's stall, aware of the stallion's restless movement as she did. She spoke reassuringly as she opened the door. The stallion's tossing head and flattened ears warned her that he'd picked up on the tension and might try to bolt.

"Easy," Gwyneth crooned. Toryn's taut muscles rippled under her fingers as she ran them along his neck. "It's all right, big boy."

"What . . . ?" a muddled voice began.

Gwyneth's throat tightened when she saw Peter struggle to sit up. Before she could think what to do, Flynn swung the whisky bottle down onto Peter's head. A muffled groan followed the resounding smack.

"Pesky English," Flynn growled. "That'll teach ye to barge into my stable and try to steal Shannonderry's stallion." A smile of satisfaction split the crevices of the old man's face, his grin widening when he noted Gwyneth's startled expression. Touching a finger to his cap, he nodded. "That should do the trick." Without further ado, Flynn turned and walked back into the tack room.

Toryn snorted and tossed his head, and it took all of Gwyneth's strength to hang on to the big horse. Through it all, she was vaguely aware of Cluny bending over Peter's unconscious form.

"Is he all right?"

"He be fine," Cluny assured her.

Ronan came with a saddle. After it was secured, Gwyneth led Toryn to the fence and mounted him. Toryn pranced in a circle as she held him in. "Thank you," she called in a soft voice. "I couldn't ask for more loyal servants and friends."

When Gwyneth touched her heels to his side, Toryn set off through the shadowy night. Tension and excitement tingled around them as they passed the far pasture where one of the wolfhounds patrolled the demesne, head lifted, his gray fur shining silver in the light of the full moon as it emerged from the scattered clouds. Glad for the moonlight, Gwyneth set Toryn to a faster pace, leaning forward as they took the wall at the edge of Shannonderry, the stallion an ebony Pegasus and she a lithe silhouette astride his back. Although they had succeeded in getting away, she still worried that her father or Peter might rouse.

"Hurry!" she called, looking over her shoulder. The word meshed with the steady cadence of Toryn's hooves as they crossed the meadow and skirted the copse of trees that separated Shannonderry from Clonglas. Ahead she saw the house, its walls dark against the moonlight. Cormac was there. He would help her.

Gwyneth slowed Toryn when they reached the circular approach to the house. After tethering the horse in the trees, she cautiously approached on foot. Thick shadows from a stand of yews offered cover when she crossed an open patch of grass. As she moved around to the back of the house, Gwyneth was grateful for the tour of Clonglas Agatha had given her the month before and that she'd taken special note of the location of Cormac's room.

Looking up at the exterior of the rambling stone structure, she was almost certain Cormac's window was the first to look out on the back lawn. Stooping to pick up some pebbles, she offered a silent prayer and threw one of them at the upstairs window. The stone hit the wall with a tiny thud, but the second flew true, the ping of glass sounding loud to her ears. Gwyneth sucked in her breath and watched for movement at the window. Nothing.

She threw another pebble, and it, too, hit the glass. Shivering, Gwyneth waited, counting the seconds and watching. Finally, the curtain moved, and the silhouette of a man appeared, the white outline of his nightshirt sharp against the darkness.

Gwyneth stepped from the shadows and waved, her heart lifting when she saw Cormac nod and step away from the window. She paced in a nervous circle around the yew tree, aware of its spicy odor and the croak of frogs. At last a dark figure detached itself from the shadows of the house and hurried toward her. Gwyneth ran to meet him. "Cormac."

Cormac pulled her into his arms and moved under the tree. "What's wrong? Are you all right?"

"It's Father . . . he's come to Shannonderry to take Toryn."

Cormac pulled away to stare down at her. "Maurice Beddows is in Ireland?"

In disjointed sentences Gwyneth told him of her father's arrival and how, when she and Moira couldn't dissuade him from his purpose, they'd resorted to laudanum. "I must hide Toryn. It's the only way . . . but I don't know where. Please . . . will you help me?"

"You know I will." Cormac rested his chin on her head. He must think of somewhere safe for Gwyneth and Toryn. It was a moment before he spoke. "I know the very place."

"Where?"

"An abandoned mill. It's not far. I went there as a boy . . . a runaway, more precisely . . . when I couldn't deal with Father and Agatha. Few know of it, and most certainly not your father."

"He's sure to post a reward when he discovers we're gone."

"Let him." Cormac touched her cheek with his finger. "Don't worry. I'll deal with your father." He bent his head and kissed her, his lips soft and reassuring. "My sweet, brave Gwyneth." Then he kissed her in earnest, his closeness driving away her worry, his muscled arms enclosing her in a safe cocoon.

Gwyneth heard his amused chuckle. "Even dressed as a boy, I find you alluring." As he pulled her closer, Toryn whinnied. Cormac tensed. "Go to him," he whispered. "I'll come as soon as I've saddled my mare."

Cormac left her, his steps as silent as ghosts' as he melded into the shadows. Gwyneth hurried in the opposite direction, keeping close to the yews as she ran lightly across the grass. Toryn was openly agitated when she reached him, pawing at the ground as he nickered the second time.

"Easy, Toryn." The stallion jerked his head so hard she feared he'd break his tether. "Easy, boy. Easy."

When her voice failed to calm him, she laid her head against his neck and stroked his long nose. "Toryn," she crooned, making an effort to slow her breathing and hoping the stallion would do the same. By the time Cormac led his mare to the trees, Toryn had begun to quiet.

"He knows something is afoot," she said.

"Horses are quick that way. The fact that one of my mares is in heat doesn't help. The sooner we get him away from Clonglas, the better it will be."

Despite the need to be gone, Cormac grasped the stallion's nostrils and spoke to him. Toryn immediately quieted, seeming to blow away the last of his nervousness with a loud release of breath.

"We'll need to lead the horses until we're farther away. Agatha is a light sleeper, and I don't entirely trust her."

"When you learn what she's done, you'll trust her even less," Gwyneth said. While they retreated through the trees, she told Cormac about the letter.

Shaking his head, Cormac digested the information in silence. "There's no longer any doubt she's firmly in the Westons' camp," he finally said. "We mustn't waste any time." He helped Gwyneth mount Toryn, and after springing into the saddle, Cormac set his mare to a trot along the road away from Clonglas.

The night was bathed in moonlight, the road a gray ribbon between the darker hedgerow and trees. It was a world robbed of color. Although Cormac's presence lessened Gwyneth's nervousness, her eyes continued to search the trees for any sign of her father or Peter.

"How much farther?" she asked when they'd ridden a ways.

"Just past the river." Cormac pointed to the outline of the stone bridge over the Awbeg River. When they crossed it, the horses' hooves sounded loud above the rushing water. Once on the other side, Cormac urged his mare through a narrow opening in the trees and onto an overgrown path along the rushing stream.

They hadn't gone far before the heavy undergrowth made it necessary to dismount and lead the horses. "The way is difficult even in the daylight. At night—" He shook his head, deciding not to tell Gwyneth that before the Awbeg reached the bigger Blackwater River, the swift water had hollowed out a rocky channel between steep cliffs. The power of the water as it exploded through the narrow chasm had awed Cormac as a youth. Even in the darkness, it had the power to intimidate. "I think it will be better if I lead Toryn." He handed the mare's reins to Gwyneth and laced his fingers through Toryn's, speaking to the stallion as he led them along the narrow track.

Aware that his voice reassured both Gwyneth and the stallion, he continued to talk. "You'll know by the roar of water why the mill was built here. It prospered for more than a hundred years, and why it was abandoned, no one seems to know." He looked back at Gwyneth and grinned. "Maybe the miller's wife grew tired of the noisy water."

Gwyneth was glad for the sound of Cormac's voice as she followed his dark form along the narrow path—glad, too, that she wore breeches and boots to protect her legs from the undergrowth and to give her firm footing on the uneven terrain. A night creature suddenly took flight, startling Gwyneth and making the mare and Toryn prance skittishly.

Trees grew close and tall along the river, their branches shutting out the moonlight. The roaring of water increased, the crash so loud that speech became difficult. Stumbling along the narrow path, Gwyneth felt as if she were enveloped in a world of crashing sound and darkness with she and Cormac and the horses as its only inhabitants. Placing one foot carefully in front of the other, she wondered how much farther they had to go.

As if he'd read her thoughts, Cormac dropped back and tethered his mare to a tree. "How are you doing?" he asked, his mouth close to her ear. At her nod, he gave her a quick squeeze. "It's only a little ways now."

With his arm around her waist and leading Toryn, Cormac ducked under the trailing branches of a willow. Ahead was the dark outline of the old mill. Like everything along the Awbeg, it was almost lost in the dense growth of trees. Cormac had to urge Toryn to follow them through the overgrown barricade, but at last they came to the walls of the massive structure.

The roof had fallen in years before, but the walls were mostly intact. A gaping hole marked the place where once a door had hung. Moonlight forged a path through the opening to highlight the crumbling interior.

"Just as I remembered," Cormac said. "It's not much for comfort, but it should do to hide from your father."

Gwyneth took a tentative step around a pile of debris and looked up at a stone stairway that climbed along one wall to the empty shell of a loft where wheat and flour had once been stored. Inside, the noise of the tumbling water was less deafening. "I could never have found such a place."

Toryn's skittishness made him uneasy, and the idea of leaving Gwyneth in such a rustic place wasn't to his liking. Unfortunately, it would have to do until he could persuade Maurice Beddows to change his mind. First, he must tether Toryn and try to make Gwyneth as comfortable as possible.

While Cormac tied Toryn to a tree branch growing through the opening of a long-ago window, Gwyneth wandered around the inside of the mill. At first she only saw debris and pieces of crumbling stone, but back in a corner, she came upon a pile of rushes and leaves. "Look," she called. "The very thing to make a little sofa."

When Cormac joined her, he pushed at the pile of rushes with the toe of his boot, half expecting a rodent to scurry away. When nothing stirred, he nodded his approval. "The bed was probably left by someone else seeking shelter."

Images of furtive outlaws or desperate Irish defenders leaped to Gwyneth's mind. She laughed nervously. "This old place must hold many secrets."

"Aye," he agreed, thinking it unwise to tell her that the old mill had once housed a band of thieves who'd preyed on the local gentry. Instead, he took flint and stone from his jacket pocket. "A fire will make it more cozy. Are you cold?"

The damp coldness had begun to seep through the fabric of Gwyneth's jacket. "A little."

"Try to find some sticks," Cormac said, though he would far rather have gathered Gwyneth into his arms to warm her. Instead, he concentrated on building a fire, using dry leaves for tinder and showing Gwyneth how to lay the sticks.

Gwyneth was intently aware of Cormac's deft fingers as he struck flint on stone and of the strong angle of his jaw as he blew softly on the sparks. Soon a fire burned brightly, its red flames licking hungrily at the sticks. "How did you become so proficient at building fires?"

Cormac's mouth lifted as he looked at her. "There's much you don't yet know about me, much I want to share." His teeth showed white in the firelight, and his eyes held hers across the flames. "One day when we are both old, perhaps you will decide you know too much about me."

"Never," she said, her voice soft and tremulous.

"I hope not, but to answer your question, as a boy I sought adventure. For a time staying out late at night and building a fire passed for adventure." He shifted position, his eyes still holding hers. "I also learned to catch trout. One night after we're married, we'll steal away, and I'll build another fire and bake fresh trout in the hot coals." His eyes were luminous in the firelight, and his voice grew husky. "After we've eaten our fill, we will curl up in a quilt and look up at the stars and—"

The intensity of Cormac's eyes made it difficult for Gwyneth to breathe. "And what?" she whispered, picturing them by the fire, their arms entwined.

"That, darlin' Gwyneth, is for us to experience when you are my wife, but tonight I will make a bed for you by the fire and watch while you sleep." He moved around the fire and kissed her, his lips warm but brief on her mouth. "I told your grandmother I wish to marry you as soon as possible. I hope you don't mind," he said against her cheek.

"No . . . in fact, I'll do all I can to expedite the matter."

"Expedite," he teased. "I rather think I like that."

Still chuckling, he helped her plump up the leaves and ferns. When he finished, he glanced up at a moon that was already beginning its descent. "I must leave, you know."

"Why?" The word slipped out before Gwyneth could think.

"If your father knows I played a part in helping you hide, he'll refuse to see or talk to me . . . for see and talk to him I will, and if diplomacy and a fat purse don't change his mind, then I shall persuade him in a more forceful manner."

Cormac moved away to collect more wood for the fire. When he returned, he took off his jacket and spread it over the pile of leaves.

"Now you will be cold," she protested.

"I'll be warm enough." Cormac added more wood to the fire and pointed to the improvised bed. "See if it meets with your approval."

Gwyneth found the bed surprisingly soft. Better than that, the warmth and familiar scent of Cormac lingered in the folds of his jacket. She lay back with a sigh. She hadn't realized how weary she was—on a day that had begun with worry, she had already passed through a gamut of emotions and excitement. Her mind jerked to a halt when she recalled the moment she'd opened the door and seen her father's angry face. What a day it had been, and here she lay under a waning moon and a sky filled with jeweled stars with the man she loved sitting beside her. Who would believe such a thing? Not Gwyneth of Hawarden. Gwyneth of Shannonderry believed it all. Wasn't Eire a land of leprechauns and fairies, where wishes were made on rainbows and blown with puffed cheeks into the Irish sky?

Gwyneth had expected to drowse and talk to Cormac until he left, but the warmth of the flickering flames were as much a sedative as the laudanum they'd given her father and Peter. They numbed her brain and made her eyelids heavy. Reluctantly, she gave in to the feeling, her thoughts growing smaller until there was only the black silhouette of Toryn against the wall and Cormac, vigilant and beloved, sitting cross-legged by the fire.

23

CORMAC RETURNED TO CLONGLAS AS darkness still mingled with mist along the river, he and his mare carefully picking their way along the narrow path in the starlight. Only the need to make it appear that he'd spent the night in his bed had the power to take him away from Gwyneth. It wouldn't do for Maurice Beddows to know he'd helped hide his daughter, and now that Cormac knew Agatha was hand in glove with the Westons, he had to be doubly cautious.

So it was that he descended the stairs for breakfast with Owen and Agatha at his usual time. The fact that he said little wasn't noticed, for he was never one to say much at meals. It didn't prevent him from observing Agatha's smug expression, however. Her pleased look made him wonder if perhaps his stepmother knew that her letter had brought Maurice Beddows to Ireland.

Anxious to resolve the problem with Gwyneth's father, Cormac spent little time over his breakfast. His steps were quick as he made his way out to the stable. Men such as Maurice liked to exert their will over women, but after their talk, the Englishman would know he couldn't ride roughshod over Cormac. Instead, he'd face a man eager to cross swords with him.

His mind filled with the upcoming confrontation, Cormac didn't notice his uncle until he stepped out of the shadows. "Paddy . . . what brings you here?"

Instead of answering, Paddy took Cormac's arm and led him back into the trees. "I think we've found the man we be lookin' for . . . or at least Father Sheehan has. He sent word at first light that he's nursin' a man what's been hurt bad . . . one who twice mentioned yer name."

"At last," Cormac breathed, his mouth lifting.

"Aye, but the boy said to hurry, for the man be fadin' fast." Paddy paused and fixed Cormac with a steady gaze. "If ye'll lend me a horse, I'll be for goin' with ye."

A few minutes later the two men were riding to the Catholic church in Macroom. Although Cormac regretted having to postpone his visit with Maurice Beddows, the urgency of Paddy's news couldn't be ignored. Pray heaven they wouldn't be too late.

The Catholic church sat on the edge of the village, the edifice weathered and small like Father Sheehan. The horses' hooves clattered on the paved stone that separated the church and Father Sheehan's cottage. Mrs. Haggarty, the housekeeper, opened the door as soon as they'd dismounted.

"This way," she said, leading them through the kitchen to a bedroom off the priest's study. Father Sheehan sat beside the bed, a pair of gold spectacles perched on his nose as he read his Bible.

The priest removed his spectacles and pointed them to the man lying in the bed, mouth agape in a broad face, his breathing loud and raspy. "I found him when I went to lock the church last night," Father Sheehan said without greeting. "At first I thought him dead, but when I heard him moan, I called for Mrs. Haggarty to help me get him into the house. Never have I been so glad for such a brawny woman. Even at that 'twas a struggle, what with him being so large."

Cormac looked down on the man's battered face and saw his cut lip and swollen eye. As he did, he recalled the hard pressure of the large hands as they'd pressed down on his throat. This was the one, all right. From the glimpse he'd caught of him as they'd grappled in the darkness, Cormac recognized his build and the crooked nose.

"He's been badly beaten . . . probably left for dead," the priest went on, his sharp features wearing a mournful expression.

Before he could say more, a loud knock sounded on the door. "Dear heaven," Mrs. Haggarty exclaimed from the kitchen. "Who be comin' now?"

Cormac turned in time to see Constable Downey enter the cottage. "I came as soon as I got yer message," the balding man said, his florid face and quick breathing evidence of his hurry. "The boy said ye'd found a man in yer church."

Father Sheehan nodded. "Bad hurt he be and talkin' out of his head. Kept beggin' me to forgive him for trying to kill Mr. D'Arcy."

The constable gave Cormac a quick glance as he crowded into the tiny bedroom. "Ye don't appear to have suffered any great harm, Mr. D'Arcy."

"It wasn't from his lack of trying." Cormac loosened the cravat that hid the bruises on his neck.

"I say," the constable said, catching his breath. His gaze shifted to the unconscious man. "Any idea who he is or why he wanted to kill ye?"

Cormac shook his head. "I was set upon in the woods after I was given a note telling me to go there."

"Why would ye be doing such?"

"The note promised that I'd be told who'd houghed the Shannonderry cattle."

"And why . . . ?" The constable paused and cleared his throat. "Ah, yes . . . yer sweet on the English girl."

Cormac made an effort to control his impatience. "We plan to marry." Glancing at the little priest, he asked, "Did he mention any other names or why he was sent to kill me?"

"Not that I could make out."

"What makes ye think the man was sent?" Constable Downey interrupted. "Maybe 'twas he who houghed the cattle."

"Why wouldn't he just lie low? No . . . this runs deeper than houghed cattle."

"Ye seem mighty certain."

Rather than answer, Cormac looked down on the man in the narrow bed, watched the slow rise and fall of his burly chest, and willed him to speak. When he didn't, Cormac leaned close. "Who did this to you? And who sent you to kill Cormac D'Arcy?"

The man's brown eyes flew open, fear and confusion flitting through them. "Where . . ." he asked between ragged gasps for air.

"Who hurt you?" Cormac repeated.

The injured fellow's eyes shifted to the crucifix on Father Sheehan's bedroom wall. His parched lips moved. "Forgive . . ." he whispered.

Cormac wanted to roar his frustration. Instead, he repeated the question.

His attacker's gaze shifted to Cormac as his lips moved. "We . . ."

Cormac's heart leaped. "Do you mean Emmett Weston?"

The man weakly shook his head.

Cormac stared in disbelief. Surely the man wouldn't lie after begging for forgiveness.

"Then who?" Paddy questioned, his voice harsh.

The man's battered head jerked, and his eyes rolled back as if seeking escape from Paddy's rough voice. "The . . . son," he whispered, his voice so soft Cormac had difficulty hearing it.

"The son? Do you mean his son Percy?"

A long shuddering breath escaped the injured man's lungs, and his head lolled to one side.

Father Sheehan hastily picked up a bundle lying on the table. "Leave," he instructed. "He's dying, and I must administer the last rites."

The priest spoke with such authority that no one dared oppose him. Cormac wanted to. He was so close to having the information. All he needed was another minute or two. The clergyman was already closing the door, the wooden structure and his body pushing the three men out of the room.

"Thunderation!" Cormac growled. "We all but had his confession."

"No buts about it," Paddy said. "Did he not say 'twas Percy?"

"He did not," the constable answered. "All the blighter said was 'the son.'"

"'Tis one and the same."

"'Tisn't at all. The poor creature might a' been talkin' of the Father, Son, and Holy Ghost. Ye know how Papists are always crossin' themselves and mutterin' such things."

Paddy glared at the constable. "Ye'd best watch what ye say about Papists."

"I be but sayin' what's true."

Mrs. Haggarty's fingers fussed with the hem of her apron. She didn't like having so many in her small kitchen, especially men who said such about Papists.

Cormac's voice interrupted the tense silence, his tone hard and his blue eyes narrowed. "I hope you don't intend to turn a blind eye to what you heard in the other room."

"'Tis me practice to keep both me eyes and ears open," the constable replied, his eyes as narrow as Cormac's.

"Good."

"However," Constable Downey interrupted, "I don't like to see anyone jumpin' to hasty conclusions. What makes you and yer uncle so certain 'tis the Westons involved?"

Tight control was all that kept Cormac's voice hard and even. "All know that Emmett was upset when Miss Beddows's stallion beat his new mare. As constable, you should be aware of the houghed cattle and the threatening note left near the wolfhound."

"I know of the note, but as to it bein' threatening, I—"

Cormac banged his fist on the kitchen table. "Blast it, man! Must you quibble at everything?"

Constable Downey's balding head lifted, and his broad chin jutted out. "You may not be aware that I must sometimes testify in court. I see how clever solicitors twist words and ask questions, while you, Mr. D'Arcy . . ."

"Am convinced that Emmett Weston is behind the attacks on both me and the man in the bedroom," Cormac finished for him. "Weston doesn't like it that Miss Beddows asked me to ride her stallion in the steeplechase against the horse from Limerick. I'll concede that my attacker may only have been instructed to harm me enough that I couldn't ride, but I will not let go of my certainty that Weston's son hired him to do it."

"'Tis a bold accusation ye make," the constable countered.

Cormac stepped closer. "And one I mean to bring to light. What of you, Constable? What do you intend to do about the matter?"

Downey scowled at a spot above Cormac's left shoulder. Then, lifting his shoulders, he met Cormac's steely eyes. "I mean to keep both my eyes and mind open."

Cormac nodded, his gaze never leaving the constable's face. "See that you do."

Before either man could say more, Father Sheehan quietly opened the bedroom door.

"Is he—?" Paddy began.

"Alive . . . but just barely. I wish the doctor would come. With his skill and our prayers, perhaps the poor fellow can still be saved."

Mrs. Haggarty paused as she took a dish from the cupboard. "Deliverin' babies takes time."

"Did he say anything more?" Cormac asked.

The priest gave a sad shake of his head. "Not a word. And I have no clue as to who he might be. After the doctor comes, I plan to ride to the next parish and talk to Father Walsh. Maybe he'll know who he is."

"I'll see what I can find out as well," the constable said. "Someone is sure to have seen or heard of him." He scowled at Cormac. "And, yes, I'll call on Emmett Weston."

The two men measured each other, each aware of the fact that Emmett Weston's assault of Cormac's long-dead mother had been quietly swept under the rug. Despite Weston's close ties with the county magistrate, Cormac was determined Emmett would not go unpunished this time.

"If you don't call on him, I will," Cormac said in a voice taut with determination. Glancing at the priest, he said, "Please let me know if there's any change in the stranger's condition." Cormac left the little kitchen and mounted his mare, Paddy but a step behind him. There was still much to be done and little time to do it.

* * *

WHILE CORMAC WAS AT THE church, Owen was preparing to ride to the village. As he descended the stairs with a fresh cravat intricately tied around his neck, Owen caught a glimpse of Emmett Weston being shown into his mother's parlor. Owen's dislike of Percy ran high, and what he felt for the father was almost as consuming. The fact that his mother and the elder Weston had of late become friends rankled him, and to see the man calling on his mother at such an early hour stopped Owen on the stairs. What in the devil was Emmett Weston up to? No good if past experience could be relied upon. How he detested the man!

Owen quietly approached the parlor, curiosity and his dislike of the caller making him pause at the door. Mr. Weston's booming voice was clearly audible.

"Your idea to send Maurice Beddows a letter was a stroke of genius, my dear. Not only has it brought him and his trainer post haste to Ireland, but, if rumor can be believed, he intends to take both daughter and stallion back to England."

Stunned, Owen stepped closer to the door, his mind reeling as he heard his mother's high-pitched laugh.

"Excellent, Mr. Weston. Did I not tell you a letter would be just the thing?"

"Unfortunately, there is a problem." Emmett's voice held a note of frustration. "Sometime during the night Miss Beddows took the stallion from the stable. Now both she and her horse are gone."

"Disappeared," Agatha exclaimed. "Then you must find them. Dear heaven, where could they have gone?"

"'Tis what I intend to find out and why I rode to Clonglas. Miss Beddows will need help to hide, and who better to assist her than your son?"

"Cormac," Agatha said, her voice so low Owen had difficulty hearing it. He'd known since taking tea at Shannonderry that Gwyneth preferred Cormac to him, but to hear that his mother had come to the same conclusion stung like salt on a fresh wound.

"Exactly," Mr. Weston agreed. "And now that they are engaged to marry—"

"Marry?" Agatha's voice cut through his. "Where did you hear such nonsense?"

"One of Shannonderry's maids is sweet on my groom. Yesterday she told him that Miss Beddows accepted your son's proposal of marriage."

The words hit like a blow to Owen's stomach. There was no hope for him with Gwyneth. No hope at all. His mother's distraught voice came like an echo to his bruised emotions.

"Do you know where Cormac is?" Weston asked.

"I think he's ridden out on estate business . . . but then that's what I thought yesterday, and all the time he was courting that English girl." Anger replaced the shock in Agatha's voice. "How could he? And she? I was certain I'd blunted her interest in Cormac so that Owen could have a chance."

Owen swallowed and stared at the ornate molding on the door without seeing it. Did his mother think him so incompetent that she had to woo Miss Beddows for him?

"What about last night?" Emmett persisted. "That's when Miss Beddows would have come. Did you see anything suspicious . . . hear anything?"

"No . . ." Agatha's answer was slow, as if she were thinking. "Wait. Something did cause me to rouse . . . a sound like an object striking the window."

"It was Miss Beddows! I'd stake my life on it. Cormac helped hide her and the stallion, and I mean to find them. Is there somewhere he could have taken them?"

"I . . . I don't know." Agatha sounded as rattled as Owen felt. "You must give me a moment to collect myself."

"Take your time," Emmett said in a soothing voice. "You've been so helpful. I'm certain you won't fail me now. Who knows Cormac better than you, dear lady, and who knows hiding places better than he?"

Owen bit his lip as he listened to his mother pace around the room. Agatha's eager voice jumped into the silence. "I think I know the place he's taken her. When Cormac was young, he often ran away." Agatha clapped her hands with excitement, the noise making Owen start. "He's taken her to his old hiding place . . . a deserted mill along the Awbeg River."

"Yes." Pleasure sounded in Emmett's voice. "I know the very spot. It's so remote and overgrown no one would find them."

There was a little pause, one that made Owen suspect that Weston had taken Agatha's hand and raised it to his lips. The thought made his stomach turn.

"Dear lady, I knew I could depend upon your brilliance to save the day. What a treasure you are, and what a treasure will be ours when I appear at Shannonderry with Miss Beddows and that blasted stallion. I'm certain her father will offer a reward for their return, and I mean to be the one to collect it."

"You must take care," Agatha interjected. "If Cormac is with them, he won't let you near them without a fight."

"Cormac." Emmett's voice was derisive. "He'll not be as fortunate as he was on St. John's Eve. Besides, I'll take Percy and George with me."

Owen didn't wait to hear what else was said. His only thought was to get away from the two people in the parlor. He'd long disliked Emmett Weston, but to hear him plotting and planning with his mother was past bearing. He clenched his hand, wishing he could slam it into the man's smug face. As for his mother—

Owen growled a curse as he flung open the back door and stalked outside. How could his mother let herself be used in this fashion? He'd recognized for some years that she was self-centered and sometimes foolish, but to do this!

Owen was halfway to the stable yard before he let himself think of Cormac and Gwyneth. Jealousy iced through the heat of his anger. Why must his older brother always get the best? A handsome face and strong physique. Clonglas. And now Miss Beddows. It wasn't fair, and Owen was tired of playing second fiddle.

While the groom saddled the gelding, Owen paced the stable, his angry face and stiff walk making the groom eye him warily. As Owen mounted and prepared to ride away, the groom called to him.

"Should ye be lookin' for Mr. D'Arcy, he and his uncle left an hour ago for the Catholic church in the village."

Ignoring the groom, Owen galloped his horse away from Clonglas. Fast as the gelding ran, it couldn't outdistance Owen's thoughts and anger. It would serve Cormac right if the Westons outwitted him.

Resentment pounded Owen like the gelding's drumming hooves as he urged the galloping horse over a wall. The jolt of the awkward landing almost pitched him over the horse's head. What a donkey he'd been to take the jump at such a pace. Cormac had taught him better. He'd taught him dozens of better ways—how to properly bait a hook and catch a fish, not to mention the proper way to hold his fists to parry Percy's bullying taunts and blows. The memories diluted Owen's anger. Hadn't he and Cormac always stood together against Percy and his father? Were they not D'Arcys?

Owen reined in his horse and stared without thinking at the green fields and hedges before him. Thoughts of Gwyneth seeped into his mind—her radiance on the night of the dinner party, her mud-spattered face when she'd ridden Toryn past the finish line ahead of Percy. Then a terrible realization hit him. With Cormac in the village, Gwyneth would be alone and unprotected at the mill. The thought made him flinch. Percy Weston's reputation with women was as unsavory as his father's, and although the elder Weston had learned a little prudence, his son would savor the opportunity to make sport with a defenseless woman.

Gritting his teeth, Owen turned the gelding and dug the heels of his boots into its side. With luck he'd be able to intercept Cormac and Paddy on their way back from the village. The horse's galloping hooves ate up the distance, the beauty of the summer morning unnoticed as he leaned over the gelding's neck to call encouragement. Blast the Westons and his mother for helping them!

24

GWYNETH SLEPT LATE INTO THE morning, the hypnotic cadence of rushing water like an opiate to her fatigued body. Toryn's whinny finally wakened her, piercing the warm darkness of sleep to pull her up with a start. For a second, she didn't know where she was, the rumble of falling water and the sight of crumbling stone walls like remnants of a dream. With a rush the memory of her father's arrival and the midnight ride on Toryn returned, along with thoughts of Cormac, competent and steady, leading them through the darkness to the abandoned mill.

Stretching, Gwyneth looked up at the leafy canopy of tree branches and wished Cormac were still with her. All that remained of him was the coat that had pillowed her bed while she slept and the blackened remains of the fire he'd built. She knew Cormac would return, just as she'd known he would lead her to safety. She only had to be patient and wait.

Gwyneth shivered as she got to her feet, the damp chill coming off the water penetrating her limbs like the touch of icy fingers. She picked up Cormac's coat and pulled it around her shoulders, savoring the faint scent of him that lingered in its creases. Although she was anxious to explore her hiding place, Toryn's impatient nicker reminded her that she must tend to him first.

"Impatient, are you?" The stallion's reply was another whinny. The indignity of being tethered to a tree was clearly not to his liking. Neither were the churning water and the absence of his morning oats. Gwyneth reached up to stroke and comfort him. "What a complainer you are. I'm hungry too, but we must try to make the best of it. There's grass, I'm sure, and obviously plenty of water."

Moisture from the river saturated the air. Beaded drops glistened on the walls and dampened the feathery sprigs of moss growing between the crevices. Although the sight was lovely, its wildness made Gwyneth shiver.

She kept up a steady string of conversation to the horse as she slipped her arms into Cormac's over-large coat. Unfettering the stallion, she led him out of the mill.

The sight brought her to a halt. Sucking in her breath, she stared at the narrow channel carved by the river, the tumble of rushing water like a wild, untamed beast. Water leaped and beat against the stone, flinging spray high into the air to form fragile prisms of color against the morning sun.

"Oh," Gwyneth breathed. Before she could say more, Toryn jerked his head and tried to pull away. "Easy," she said, understanding the horse's fear. She must find a quieter place for him . . . for her . . . one well away from the churning, violent water.

Leading Toryn around the crumbling mill, she pushed her way through the dense trees and undergrowth until she found a little clearing. Lush grass was strewn with wild flowers, and a tiny stream meandered down to the river. Here, the trees muted the sound of the river, and for the first time that morning, Gwyneth was able to hear the cheerful song of birds.

Toryn quickly snatched a mouthful of grass while Gwyneth looked for a place to tether him. Once he was securely fastened, she found a sunny spot on a rock where she could bask in the warmth and listen to the birds.

As she watched the horse graze, she felt hunger pangs. What she'd give for a plate of eggs and one of Kate's scones spread with jam and freshly churned butter. Instead, she turned her mind to Cormac. Had he ridden to Shannonderry yet to confront her father? She could imagine her father's anger when he found her and Toryn gone. Peter's too. She didn't like to think of the rage that would follow, directed at her grandmother instead of herself. Gwyneth winced.

"Poor Grandmother," she whispered. Needing reassurance that she'd done the right thing, Gwyneth closed her eyes and prayed for Moira. "It will be all right," she told herself. But would it, or had she taken a wrong turn when she'd stolen Toryn from the stable?

* * *

A loud pounding on the bedroom door wakened Maurice Beddows that morning. He pushed his way up through a fog of confusion, his thoughts muddled and disjoined, his eyes unfocused. What in the devil was going on? Didn't people know he was trying to sleep?

The pounding continued and was joined by a strident voice, one that sounded like Peter's. "The stallion's gone and so is your daughter . . . gone who knows where . . . and no one will say how or why!"

Understanding penetrated Maurice's foggy brain as anger and the need for action seared through his middle. Toryn was gone . . . Gwyneth too! Blast the girl and blast him for being taken in. He should have left Shannonderry with the stallion as soon as he'd arrived. It had been a plot—a clever plot devised by the old woman and Gwyneth. Most likely the servants were involved as well.

Calling for Peter to saddle his horse, Maurice pulled on his mud-splattered boots and left the bedroom.

"Yer horse already be saddled and ready," Peter said, joining him as he strode to the stable. "I've scoured the neighborhood . . . looked everywhere."

"You let them get away!" Maurice accused. "For two guineas, I'd thrash you. Didn't I warn you to keep a close watch on the stallion?"

"Ye did, sir, and I did . . . at least fer awhile, but then the old man offered me a nip of his Irish whisky, and I . . ." Ashamed, Peter looked away.

"Whisky!" Maurice exploded. "You should have known better." As he spoke, Maurice remembered the glass of port Moira had given him and the slightly bitter taste it had left in his mouth. Shock made his steps waver. He and Peter had been drugged! He'd stake his life on it.

Fury sent Maurice into the stable a good three steps ahead of his trainer. Tricked. Drugged! His anger at being taken in by two women was greater than what he felt for Peter. He should have suspected. Blast!

Maurice rode from the stable at a gallop, determined to find Gwyneth and the stallion. Although Peter was secretly relieved that Gwyneth had gotten away, his concern for his wife and his future kept him at his master's side. The attempt to locate their quarry was as unsuccessful as Peter's had been. The few peasants they saw met their questions with a shake of the head. "No, sir. I ain't seen either the lady or her horse."

Maurice's offer of a reward brought a glitter of interest to the eyes of some but failed to elicit anything more than vague suggestions. They met with the same when they rode to Clonglas. Mr. D'Arcy and his brother were not at home.

It was afternoon when Maurice rode back to Shannonderry, his temper frayed and his horse winded. His determination to find his daughter and the stallion had not lessened one whit. In fact, if anything, it had grown stronger. Although the morning efforts had come to naught, he hadn't yet confronted Moira Donahue. His steps were quick as he entered the house and strode with rapid purpose to the sitting room. The old woman was likely gloating at her success, but by heaven, she wouldn't gloat for long.

Maurice threw open the sitting room door with a bang, expecting to see a face filled with surprise. Instead, the expression Moira turned on him was one of calmness.

"I believe you forgot to knock."

"I did not forget, nor do I intend to apologize. I want answers, and I intend to get them if I have to remain here the rest of the day."

"You shall certainly have your answers," Moira replied in the same maddeningly calm voice, "but I doubt you will like them any better than you will like my questions."

"Questions?" Maurice's voice was a shout. "Egad, woman, what blasted questions can you possibly have for me?"

"There are several, but this conversation will not go any further until you remember your manners and sit down. Do I make myself clear?"

His eyes scoured the frail woman sitting as regal as a queen in her chair. Who did she think she was to tell Maurice Beddows what to do? Glaring, the Englishman swallowed an oath and took a chair. Granted, he'd shown bad manners, but didn't she know what a frustrating morning he'd had?

"That's much better," Moira said, her voice still disconcertingly calm. The coldness of her blue eyes reminded him of a day many years before when, as an unruly schoolboy, he'd been taken to the head master.

"Sit," the head master had ordered, and young Maurice had sat, but he hadn't liked it anymore than he liked being pinned under Moira Donahue's unflinching gaze. Although her face might sag from the ravages of time, the sound of determination clearly rang through her steely voice.

"Now," Moira went on. "I'd like to hear your explanation of why you came to Shannonderry, and—" She paused and wagged an arthritic finger at him. "I don't want to hear that Gwyneth stole your horse, for we both know she didn't. What is the real reason you came all this way to Ireland, Maurice?"

The Englishman stared at his mother-in-law, his brain a muddle of confusion. "I don't know what you're talking about," he sputtered.

"I think you do and that you refuse to admit it." Moira's chin lifted as her voice rose. "Isn't the real reason you came and why you've been less than a father to Gwyneth because you believed Deirdre betrayed you and that Gwyneth isn't your child?"

Maurice felt as if he'd had the breath knocked out of him. It took great effort to make his voice forceful. "What a thing to say!"

"I'm saying it just the same," Moira retorted. "You're angry at Gwyneth because you think Deirdre betrayed you."

"Ha," he managed to get out. "You admit your daughter betrayed me."

"Don't be foolish. Deirdre loved you. Didn't she leave her family and all she held dear to go with you? It's an affront to her memory and the loyal, courageous woman she was to say or think such things."

"Parson Cranston saw her with another man . . . not once, but twice," Maurice shouted. "Deirdre betrayed me with another man!"

Moira struck the floor with her cane. "I'll thank you to remember that this is my home, Maurice." She struck the floor again for emphasis. "I will not have you speak ill of my daughter."

"I'll say what . . ." The fire in the old woman's eyes scorched the rest of what he'd intended to say.

Moira was as surprised by her outburst as he was. This was not the way to make the Englishman admit his mistake. Sighing, she spoke in a softer voice. "I know that what happened wasn't easy for you. Being made to look the fool is never easy, but—" She paused and pursed her narrow lips. "The parson truly did see Deirdre with another man, but have you ever thought that the meeting might have been entirely innocent?"

"Yes . . . at least I wanted to believe it, but when I asked Deirdre, she became upset . . . and then the baby started to come, and then—" Maurice's throat closed so that he wasn't able to go on. It had been a terrible mistake to come to Ireland. Being at Shannonderry where he'd first seen and fallen in love with Deirdre had brought back painful memories, ones he hadn't been prepared to face. He'd loved the Irish miss—loved her completely. Unbidden moisture gathered in his eyes. "She died," he finished in a whisper.

"Yes," Moira agreed sadly. "You were devastated. We were both devastated." Emotion made it difficult to go on. "Deirdre was too young to die . . . so very young . . . but she left you the wonderful gift of a daughter."

"One who may not be mine," Maurice rasped.

Moira's voice firmed. "Gwyneth is yours. If you'd but asked Kate all those years ago, she would have told you the true circumstances of Deirdre's meeting with Rory Flanagan."

Maurice's head jerked. "You knew the blighter then?"

"I did, as did Deirdre and Kate." Moira met his accusing gaze across the space that separated them and strove for calmness. So much depended on the next few moments. "I'd like you to listen to what Kate has to say about those meetings."

"Kate!" Maurice's voice dripped with scorn. "Do you expect me to take the word of a Papist servant above that of Parson Cranston?"

Moira's mouth tightened. "To question Kate's integrity is an insult to a God-fearing woman. More than that, she accompanied Deirdre each time she met with Rory." Not wanting to listen to any more of Maurice's arguments, she tapped on the floor with her cane. "Kate," she called. "Will you come here for a moment?"

Kate opened the door as soon as Moira spoke. "Ye called?" she asked in a respectful tone, but the look she shot Maurice lacked that quality.

"I would like you to tell Mr. Beddows all that happened when Deirdre met with Rory Flanagan."

"Yes'm." Kate nervously cleared her throat and edged closer to Moira. "I . . . I tried more'n once to tell ye that despite what ye heard, Miss Deirdre didn't betray ye. In fact, ye should be praisin' yer wife's name for resisting Rory, for he put great pressure on her to go away with him. I know, for I was there both times she was with him."

Maurice heard her in silence. Although he'd regarded Kate as no more than a lowly servant and a Papist one at that, her voice and demeanor in Moira's sitting room could not be so easily dismissed. She spoke like a woman bent on telling a truth that battered at the old barricades he'd erected against it.

Kate nervously fussed with the edge of her apron and took a deep breath before going on. Hadn't she waited more than twenty years to tell Mr. Beddows the truth about Miss Deirdre? "First ye should know that Rory and Miss Deirdre had long been friends. For a time she thought she might even be in love with him." Kate hurried on when she saw Maurice's mouth tighten. "That all changed when Rory and his brother was pressed into the English navy for bearing arms and houghin' cattle. Then when ye came—"

Kate paused for breath, the only sound in the room the steady ticking of the ormolu clock on the mantel. "Once Miss Deirdre set eyes on ye, there weren't no room for thoughts of anyone else. Completely taken with ye she was and remained so till the day she died."

"Then why did she sneak out to meet this . . . this Rory?" Maurice demanded.

"'Cause he and his brother jumped ship. Desperate they was and needin' help gettin' to America." Kate's voice rang with purpose. "'Twas no one more loyal to her friends than Miss Deirdre, but she made it clear from the start 'twas ye she loved, not him."

The look she shot Maurice made him think she questioned her mistress's sanity. The maid wasn't finished speaking, however. Her arms, which had been tightly folded across the waist of her white apron, dropped to her side.

"The only reason Miss Deirdre agreed to see Rory again was so she could give him money to buy passage on a boat to America."

"Money?" Maurice exploded.

"Aye . . . of course, she knew she couldn't ask ye for it. 'Twas then she came up with the idea of givin' him her pearls." Mr. Beddows's mouth dropped open. "Ye know how much she loved them. They came from her old gran."

"Her pearls," Maurice whispered. He remembered a long-ago afternoon when he'd found his wife crying because she claimed she'd lost the pearls while out riding. Knowing how precious the necklace was to Deirdre, Maurice and two of the grooms had mounted a search. When he'd failed to find them, he'd bought another beautiful strand of creamy jewels to surprise Deirdre after the birth of their baby. Although his wife's death had ended his plan, he'd been unable to part with the necklace. For twenty-two years the velvet box containing the rope of pearls had remained locked in the drawer of his desk.

Kate's voice cut into Maurice's thoughts. "That's the truth, Mr. Beddows. Whether ye believe it or not, God and His holy angels know I speak the truth. Miss Deirdre loved ye. Ye be her life . . . ye and the comin' babe."

"If that's true, why did Deirdre tell you . . . not me . . . to take care of the babe?" Maurice asked in an anguished voice. "Why?"

Moira's voice penetrated the emotion-fraught room. "Deirdre wanted her daughter to feel a woman's love during the early months. Since she knew she wouldn't be there herself—" Moira's voice broke.

Aware of his quivering emotion, Maurice girded himself for a final question. "If the child was mine, why did Deirdre insist she be named Gwyneth? Why didn't she consult me about the name?"

"Gwyneth is yours. She's always been yours."

It was Kate who spoke, not Moira, for the old woman's attention was focused on attempting to rise from the sofa. With a final push, Moira got to her feet. Taking her cane, she crossed the room to her son-in-law. "If you'll allow me the use of your arm, Maurice, I'll show you why."

The Englishman absently offered Moira his arm, his mind in such a muddle he no longer knew what to think. Could it be true? Could he have been mistaken?

Maurice was dimly aware of Moira instructing Kate to light the candles in the great hall and of the red-haired maid who hurried ahead with Kate. Although he had no notion what Moira intended to show him, he suspected it would leave a mark.

Impatient to find out, Maurice forced himself to slow his steps to match the slower gait of the old woman. The pull of her frail hand on his arm was like everything he'd heard in the sitting room—tugging at things he'd kept hidden and nudging the knowledge that he'd been wrong more forcefully into his mind.

Moira's quivery voice intruded into his thoughts. "What Kate told you is true." The tap of her cane on the stone floor punctuated her words.

"Perhaps." Pride wouldn't let him say more. *Why? Why do you hold on to your anger and pride with such stubbornness?* Maurice blinked the question away. He wasn't ready to admit he'd been wrong. Instead, he quickened his pace.

When they entered the great hall, the two servants were lighting candles in the sconces on the far wall. The ancient hall had made a deep impression on Maurice when Deirdre had shown it to him all those years before. Her pride in her O'Brien heritage had been as palpable as the huge refractory table and the red and gold shields on the wall.

"This way," Moira said, pointing with her cane at the lighted area where Kate and Biddy waited. "This is what I want you to see."

A portrait of a woman dressed in a blue gown hung between the sconces. The flickering flames from the candles cast light over platinum hair and pearly skin. The hair on the back of Maurice's neck rose when he took in the woman's delicate features and turquoise eyes. "Gwyneth," he said in awe.

"Aye," Moira replied, "though her name is Gwyneth O'Brien, not Gwyneth Beddows. My ancestor was a woman of great courage who kept Shannonderry from falling into enemy hands. I was raised on her story, as was Deirdre. This is why she chose the name Gwyneth for her daughter . . . your daughter. Not because Deirdre's thoughts were on another man but because of the babe's white hair. That's what the name Gwyneth means, you know . . . the white and blessed one."

Maurice continued to stare at the portrait. The resemblance between Deirdre's ancestor and Gwyneth was uncanny. It was as if an artist had dressed his daughter's hair and body in the trappings of a long-ago era. "Who would believe it?" he asked in an unsteady voice.

"Yes," Moira agreed. "I thought the ghost of Gwyneth O'Brien had stepped into my sitting room when my granddaughter first arrived. Now do you understand why I wanted you to see the portrait?"

Maurice nodded, his eyes going over each detail of the painting. It was true then. Gwyneth was his . . . at least if he were to believe Kate, and he saw no reason not to. Painful emotion laced with regret made it difficult for him to swallow, but exaltation hemmed the edges. Deirdre had loved him as deeply as he'd loved her. Fearing his overwrought emotions would change to tears, he turned away.

Seeing Maurice's trembling mouth, Moira reached out and patted his arm. "Dear boy, Deirdre truly loved you."

Pride and too many years of repressed emotion clogged Maurice Beddows's throat and sent him away from the portrait. It was too much for him to bear. Tears blurred his vision when he turned and looked back at the three women and the portrait. "Thank you," he rasped. With a bow he left the room.

25

THE SUN HAD REACHED ITS zenith when impatience and boredom drove Gwyneth back inside the old mill. Perhaps by now Cormac had spoken with her father and persuaded him to reason. When this was done, she knew Cormac would waste little time in coming for her.

After she tethered Toryn to the tree branch growing through the wall, she made a slow circuit of the mill's interior, looking into the shadowy crevice under the crumbling stairs where moss grew thick and ivy twined the wall. Usually Gwyneth was comfortable with her own company, but today she wished she had someone to take her mind off of her worry and tell her things would work out.

Tired of fidgeting, Gwyneth returned to the pile of leaves and lay down on Cormac's jacket. If she couldn't have him in person, she would find comfort in what she had. She lay there for several minutes, her mind flitting from thought to thought while the hypnotic cadence of the water soothed her. Gradually, her vision blurred and her eyelids closed, shutting out everything but the rushing river.

Toryn's whinny and the strike of boots on stone jerked Gwyneth awake. Her eyes flew open to see a man step through the opening to the mill. Shock closed her throat as she recognized Emmett Weston, closely followed by Percy and the young man formerly introduced as George. Instinct cried at her to run, but the three men blocked the only exit. Gwyneth cautiously got to her feet, hoping the noisy water and shadow-shrouded corner would conceal her.

"There's the horse," Emmett exclaimed, the triumph in his voice audible. "If the stallion's here, Miss Beddows can't be far away."

"Unless she hid the horse and left," Percy interjected.

"She wouldn't do that. Not with a horse as valuable as this one."

Agitated by the strangers, Toryn whinnied again and tossed his head.

"What a beauty," Percy's friend said. "I've never seen such a horse."

Emmett suddenly pointed at the corner. "Look. There's Miss Beddows!"

Gwyneth dashed toward Toryn, hoping to mount him and force her way past the men. Her booted feet scrabbled across the stone floor as George threw himself into her path and Percy leaped at her. Gwyneth flew forward, slamming into George as Percy wrestled her to the floor. The jarring impact stunned her.

Breathing hard, Percy scrambled to his feet and roughly pulled Gwyneth to hers, panting from exertion. "There . . . not so high and mighty now, are you?"

Infuriated, Gwyneth fought to break his grasp. Percy's fingers bit deep into her flesh, and his arms tightened around her middle. "If you try to get away, you'll wish you hadn't," he growled. To make his point, he squeezed her so hard she thought her ribs would break. "Understand?" he hissed.

Refusing to speak, Gwyneth glared up at him. Her stomach tightened when she saw the anger glinting in his yellow-flecked eyes. She hadn't realized how much Percy hated her. Losing the race had been a bitter blow to his pride. Even worse, he'd been forced to endure snide remarks about being beaten by a woman. *I'll make you pay for this,* his narrowed eyes seemed to say.

Reading their silent message, Gwyneth's mouth tightened and her chin lifted. She wouldn't let him know she was afraid.

But her fear increased at Percy's next words. "Even dressed like a boy, she makes a toothsome morsel. Don't you agree, George?"

Rubbing his elbow, George got to his feet. "More than toothsome," he agreed, grinning. "I've been wanting a taste of those red lips since I saw her at church." He stepped closer and lifted Gwyneth's chin for a better look.

Revulsion washed through her when George thrust his pudgy face close to hers. The moisture beaded on his splotchy skin as he licked his lips made her recoil. "No!" she cried, twisting to avoid him.

"Quiet!" Emmett commanded. "Every time I try to get close to the stallion, one of you opens your mouth and scares him."

Gwyneth had momentarily forgotten Toryn. Backed against the wall, his ears flattened and head tossing, his shrill neigh trumpeted through the ruins. The sound was one of challenge rather than fear, and Emmett Weston was smart enough to jump back.

"Why are you trying to take the stallion?" Percy asked. "Let the girl's father come for him. The reward's for his whereabouts, not his return. Besides—"

Emmett's voice cut through his son's. "There's no guarantee what Beddows will do with him, but if I destroy the stallion . . . run him off the ledge and into the river, neither D'Arcy or his woman can plague me with him again."

Enraged, Gwyneth twisted her head and bit Percy's hand.

Yelping, Percy grabbed Gwyneth's short hair and forced her face up until it almost touched his chin. His voice came out in a snarl. "Don't ever do that again!"

Gwyneth was past reason. She had to get to Toryn before Weston unfastened the rope and drove him off the ledge. Hands flailing as she gave a savage thrust, she tried to break Percy's hold, but his arms tightened even more as his breathing rasped in her ear.

"Watch what my father's going to do to your stallion," Percy said as Emmett shrugged out of his coat and waved it at Toryn.

"No!" Gwyneth screamed.

Cormac D'Arcy's harsh voice came like an echo to her scream. "Hold it, Emmett. You too, Percy."

Gwyneth's heart leaped when she saw Cormac in the doorway with a raised pistol in his hand.

"I have a pistol too," Owen called, his voice unsteady as he joined Cormac.

The sight of Gwyneth pinioned against Percy's chest made Cormac's blood turn cold. "Let her go, Percy. I'll shoot if you don't."

Before Gwyneth could blink, Percy pulled a knife from his boot and held it against her throat. Fear coursed in icy rivulets through her body, numbing her mind and making it impossible to swallow.

Using Gwyneth as a shield, Percy turned to face the two men in the doorway. "You're not going to shoot me," he taunted. Exalting in his hold over the D'Arcys, Percy brought his open mouth down onto Gwyneth's lips.

Enraged, Cormac thrust the pistol at Paddy. Turning, he pushed his way through the trees and undergrowth outside the mill toward a window opening in the wall not far from Gwyneth. If he could get there in time—

Anger and revulsion drove Gwyneth past her fear. With strength she hadn't thought possible, she brought the heel of her boot down onto Percy's foot. Percy swore and pressed the knife harder against her throat. "Dear God," she prayed. "Please help!"

A shrill neighing sliced through the air. In a daze, she watched Emmett rush at Toryn, saw the flash of hooves as the stallion reared and knocked him to the floor. Weston's scream meshed with Toryn's trumpeting neigh. Rearing again, Toryn brought his hooves down onto the fallen man.

Into the chaos, Cormac leaped from the crumbling window ledge, using a tree limb he'd found to strike Percy's head as he wrestled him to the floor.

Caught in the melee, Gwyneth was only vaguely aware that Percy's knife had fallen to the floor and that his hold on her had broken as he fought to fend off his attacker.

As Gwyneth scrambled away from the thrashing hands and feet, a pistol cracked. George screamed as a bullet from Owen's pistol plowed into his leg. His cry and another thud from Cormac's cudgel on Percy's skull came simultaneously. Percy groaned and went limp, unaware that Cormac stood over him.

Satisfied that Percy was no longer a threat, Cormac reached for Gwyneth's hand. "Are you all right?"

At her nod, Cormac ran and pulled Emmett away from the frenzied stallion's hooves. Straightening, he spoke to the horse. "Easy, Toryn." His voice had no affect on the big horse, whose wild thrashing shook the tree branch. Dodging past the lethal hooves, Cormac grasped Toryn's reins and reached for his nose. A mighty shudder ran along the stallion's frame, and his attempt to throw off Cormac slackened. With a long sigh, Toryn stilled.

Gwyneth wanted to run and throw herself into Cormac's strong arms. Instead, she gave Paddy, who'd run to stand over Percy, a weak smile. "Thank you," she managed in an unsteady voice.

Paddy grinned. "Aye, though ye put up quite a fight yerself. I'd not like to be in yer way should ye be in a temper."

Paddy's try at humor released some of the tightness in Gwyneth's middle, as did the sight of Owen standing by George with pistol in hand and a fierce expression on his face.

"Don't move so much as an inch or I'll shoot again," Owen warned. "You're lucky I only aimed to wing you."

George stared in horror at the wound in his leg, his face paling as he watched blood ooze between his fingers. "I'm going to bleed to death. Do something!" he begged.

"Ye won't bleed to death, though ye deserve to," Paddy said in an unsympathetic voice. Even so, he unfastened George's crumpled cravat and tied it around the young man's leg to stanch the blood. When he finished with George, he used Percy's cravat to tie the unconscious man's hands securely behind his back. "That should hold him."

"Gwyneth." Though Cormac's voice came low, she heard it at once. "I need your help with Toryn."

Walking on legs that seemed as soggy as porridge, she had to concentrate on each step.

"Toryn's quiet enough that you can hold him," Cormac went on softly. "Keep him calm while I see to Weston." When she reached him, Cormac reached with an arm and briefly pulled her close. "Thank God you're safe."

Gwyneth gratefully sank into Cormac's embrace. She wished she could stay there, but Toryn's tossing head reminded her of the stallion's uncertain temper.

"Have you got him?" Cormac asked. At her nod, he slowly released his hold on her and the horse. "Don't look at Weston," he warned in the same quiet voice. "What Toryn did to him isn't pleasant."

Cormac's warning was enough to keep Gwyneth's full attention on Toryn. The stallion's shudders and nervous movement spoke of his agitation. Running her fingers along his neck, she began her familiar croon.

Gwyneth heard Weston's pitiful whimper when Cormac moved him. "My legs," he moaned. "I can't move them."

"You're lucky to be alive," Cormac growled. "You don't know how close I came to letting the stallion finish you off. It's what you deserve." The thought of what the men would have done to Gwyneth had he not arrived in time clogged his throat.

Straightening, he glanced at Owen and Paddy, giving a grim smile when he saw Owen's vigilant stance over George. "How are they?"

"Mine's out like a snuffed candle, and him—" Paddy began.

"George won't be doing much with his leg for awhile," Owen finished. "My aim was good."

Satisfied that Paddy and Owen had the situation in hand, Cormac carefully moved back to Gwyneth. Circling her slender waist with his arms, he laid his chin on her head. "My darlin' girl," was all that came out, the horror of what had almost happened still too fresh to make ordinary speech possible. He pulled her more closely against him while his lips made a trail over the silken cap of her hair. "I was afraid we'd be too late." Cormac trembled, the soft look in his eyes mirroring the depth of his feelings. "Thank God you're safe."

In her mind, Gwyneth seconded the sentiment. God had certainly answered her prayer. Savoring his closeness, Gwyneth slipped her arms around Cormac's neck and buried her head in the hollow of his shoulder. She didn't care that Paddy and the others watched or that Toryn fidgeted. Cormac had come, and she was safe again.

* * *

AN HOUR LATER GWYNETH AND Cormac rode their horses out of the copse of trees separating Clonglas from Shannonderry. Dr. Moore and two servants were on their way to the old mill to bring Emmett Weston back to his home. Even if he survived his injuries, Cormac doubted the man would ever walk without the aid of a cane. Percy and George were being held in Clonglas's stable with Paddy and Owen serving as guards until the constable arrived. Percy nursed a pounding head, and George's leg would take some time to heal. Although the man Father Sheehan had found in his church still hadn't regained consciousness, he was still alive, and Cormac was optimistic that the truth about the Westons was about to come out.

He wished he could be as confident about their meeting with Gwyneth's father. Maurice Beddows was a man who didn't like to back down, but Cormac was determined to make him do so. Despite his reassuring words to Gwyneth, Cormac feared they would feel the backlash of Beddows's tongue.

Cormac's chest constricted with love when he glanced at Gwyneth. Her mussed hair and rumpled boy's clothes as she sat atop the big stallion endeared her to him even more. He nodded, more determined than ever to guard her against Maurice Beddows's anger.

Gwyneth saw his nod. "What are you thinking about?"

"I want you to stay in the stable with Toryn until I've spoken to your father." Cormac's voice and look were firm.

"No." Her voice was as firm as his. "He's my father, and we will speak to him together." A smile played at the corners of her lips. "In light of what transpired with the Westons, a confrontation with Father will seem like a Sunday stroll. More than that, you'll be with me."

"That I will, but I still think it would be better for you to stay in the stable."

Gwyneth shook her head. "I know my father. A united front is best."

They said no more as they crossed the meadow. Although the sun hid itself in the clouds, the rolling green hills interspersed with darker hedgerows were still a lovely sight. When they reached the stable yard, Cluny and one of the wolfhounds hurried to meet them.

"Miss Beddows," Cluny called, wanting to warn her of Maurice Beddows's presence in the stable. Before he could do so, the Englishman stepped outside with Peter and Ronan following.

Gwyneth reined in Toryn, half expecting her father to order Peter to take the stallion's bridle. Instead, he placed his hands on his hips, his bushy eyebrows raised and an unreadable expression on his face.

"So, daughter, you've come back."

Gwyneth patted the skittish stallion's neck. She hadn't expected her father's calm greeting. His change of tactics made her uneasy. "I have," she replied.

Maurice nodded at Cormac. "Brought reinforcements with you, I see."

Cormac held the Englishman's gaze. "My intent in coming is to persuade you to take a more reasonable course. If not, I intend to—"

"Reasonable," Maurice cut in. "That's all I've heard from the girl's grandmother this past hour or more . . . the maid too, both of them yammering without let up." Maurice threw up his hands in disgust. "Get down . . . get down. I'm not going to take your stallion."

Gwyneth shot Peter a quick look. When she saw him grin and nod, she sighed with relief. Noting Peter's grin, Cormac slowly dismounted and went to help Gwyneth from the saddle.

"What the devil?" he whispered.

Gwyneth shook her head and kept a wary eye on Maurice.

"He's a beauty, all right," Maurice went on, acting as if they'd come to ask his advice about horses. "He looks a trifle out of sorts, though."

"It's Toryn's way," Gwyneth hedged, not thinking it wise to tell him what had happened at the mill. Keeping her hold on the stallion's reins, she continued to eye her father. "What made you change your mind about taking Toryn?"

"All the yammering . . . though what you said last night—" He looked uncomfortable. "My word has always been my bond." Aware that Flynn had joined Ronan and Cluny, he scowled at the three, well aware that they'd been part of the duping. More than that, he didn't like talking in front of servants. "Shall we go inside to discuss this?" Not waiting for an answer, Maurice started for the house.

"What happened?" Gwyneth asked Peter when he came to take Toryn.

Peter shook his head. "I be as surprised as ye when he announced we wouldn't be takin' the stallion back to England."

Cormac took Gwyneth's arm to follow her father. "Do you trust him?"

Gwyneth shrugged, not daring to get her hopes up until they heard what her father had to say. Even so, she skirted the herb garden with a lighter step. Hadn't he said his word was his bond?

Maurice waited at the back door, his expression impatient. "Hurry," he instructed, ushering them into the house as if it were his. "What I mean to say should rightfully be for Gwyneth's ears only," he said as they made their way through the kitchen and on to the sitting room, his boots loud on the stone floor. "Your grandmother has an interest in this, however . . . you too, Mr. D'Arcy." He shot Cormac a quick look. "Especially since I've been informed that you wish to marry my daughter."

"I do." Cormac's reply was stiff. He hadn't liked Maurice Beddows's high-handed manner when he'd met him at Hawarden, and he liked it even less now.

Gwyneth hurried ahead, her slender form encased in borrowed breeches and jacket, giving her the look of a youth. There was a dignity in her stride that hadn't been there when she'd lived in England, one that had fallen like a cloak around her shoulders when she'd looked up at the portrait of the other Gwyneth.

"You won't gain my permission to marry my daughter until I ascertain that your motive isn't tinged by the wish to own her stallion," Maurice said.

Cormac swung to face the Englishman, his anger pounding like a hammer against an anvil as he spoke in clipped, forceful tones. "With all due respect, sir . . . what you say is an insult to the love I bear Miss Beddows. I would wish to marry her even if she owned no horse."

Seeing the icy fury in Cormac's eyes, Maurice attempted a smile. "As her father, it is my duty to ask your intentions."

"My intentions are honorable." Several seconds elapsed before Cormac resumed walking.

Blimey, Maurice thought, reminding himself not to cross swords with D'Arcy in the future. Even so, the Irishman's reaction pleased him. He certainly wouldn't have to worry about Cormac not looking after Gwyneth's interests.

Moira called for them to come in as soon as Gwyneth knocked on the sitting-room door. Her expression was expectant, for Biddy had wasted no time in letting her know that Miss Gwyneth and Mr. D'Arcy had returned with the stallion.

Wanting the comfort of Cormac by her side, Gwyneth waited until the men caught up with her before she opened the door. "Grandmother," she said in greeting. She dropped an affectionate kiss on the old woman's cheek instead of attempting to curtsy in breeches.

"You are back," Moira breathed, not knowing whether to smile or worry, for Cormac looked ready to exchange blows with Maurice, and the Englishman had an unsettled expression on his face.

"Yes," Gwyneth replied as she sat down next to Moira on the sofa.

Moira nodded at the men, indicating with her hand that they sit down. "There's no need to stand on ceremony and kiss my hand. Are we not all friends and family?" Her blue eyes locked with Maurice's.

"We are," Maurice agreed, though he made no move to sit down. "It's for that very reason I wish to speak to you . . . all of you." His gaze made a circle of the room's occupants, but it was to Gwyneth he directed his words. "I am not a man who likes to dillydally, so I'll come at once to my point." He paused and lifted his shoulders. "I promised Toryn to you, and I wish to make good on that promise."

Gwyneth waited nervously while her father reached a hand into his jacket pocket and extracted a paper. The only sound in the sitting room was the paper's rustle as he unfolded it.

"This gives you sole ownership of Toryn. He is now legally yours, daughter." Crossing the room, Maurice handed the paper to Gwyneth.

"Thank you," she murmured, too stunned to say more. Her eyes scanned the bold strokes of the pen, reading the words that said Toryn belonged to Gwyneth Beddows. Her gaze lingered on the familiar swirl of her father's signature. With the scratch of ink and pen, he'd made Toryn legally hers. "Thank you," she repeated, not knowing whether to laugh or cry.

Maurice nodded and, like a man girding himself for an ordeal, took a deep breath. "There is something else I wish to say . . . and since I don't wish to have to say it more than once, I have asked your grandmother and Mr. D'Arcy to be present."

Gwyneth's gaze flew to Cormac, who watched her father intently.

Acting as if he'd forgotten his purpose, Maurice's gaze roved the sitting room, taking in the dark, heavy furniture and carved mantel over the fireplace. Taking another deep breath, he looked down at the toes of his boots.

"I haven't always shown you the affection a daughter deserves from her father," he began, shrugging his shoulders like an awkward schoolboy reciting his lesson. "Perhaps it was because I wasn't ready for fatherhood, or perhaps—" Maurice shook his head. "No, that's an excuse, not a reason. The reason . . ." Maurice paused again, and Gwyneth saw perspiration bead his broad forehead. "I feared your mother had betrayed me with another man . . . that you weren't my daughter," he said in a rush. "In my anger I determined to punish you for what I mistakenly thought your mother had done."

Disbelief and emotion tightened Gwyneth's throat, making it difficult to breathe or swallow. In all her dreaming, she'd never expected to hear words such as these from her father.

In the stillness, Moira took Gwyneth's hand and gave it a comforting squeeze.

Keeping his eyes on his boots, Maurice swallowed, the sound audible to those in the room. "Today Kate told me I was wrong . . . that your mother was true to me in every way, and that . . ." His voice dropped so low Gwyneth had to strain to hear. "And that Deirdre loved me as I loved her."

Gwyneth watched her father's lips tremble and his eyes moisten. Her own eyes filled as she realized the great effort it had taken him to swallow his pride and confess his mistake.

"Thank you, Father." An unseen force seemed to push her to her feet. Heart pounding, Gwyneth stood on tiptoe and, for the first time in her life, kissed her father's cheek.

Maurice blinked, as surprised by the impulsive gesture as Gwyneth. "I say," he sputtered, embarrassment flushing his face.

For a moment, Gwyneth thought he'd wipe the kiss away. Instead, a slow smile spread across his features. "I say," he repeated, his tone pleased. Seeming to remember that Cormac and Moira were present, he cleared his throat. "I have said what I planned. That being the case, I will take my leave."

Maurice reached the door in three quick strides. Opening it, he turned to face them, his voice unsteady as he spoke. "Since there is soon to be a wedding, I am thinking to delay my return to England so I can give the bride away." His eyes searched Gwyneth's face, their appeal like that of a child who had been banished to his room. "That is, if you would like your father to do so."

The tension around Gwyneth's middle melted and sent her across the room to take her father's hands in hers. "I would like it very much."

Maurice nodded and gave her hands a squeeze. "Good . . . good. That's what I had hoped." With that, Maurice Beddows turned and left the room.

26

THE FOLLOWING DAYS PASSED IN a blur of happiness for Gwyneth. At times she felt as if she'd been knocked slightly off balance, what with her father taking up residence in Shannonderry's guest room and Cormac pressing for a speedy wedding. Although the latter was her dearest wish, it left only a fortnight to complete the plans for their marriage.

One morning as Gwyneth and her grandmother were in the sitting room writing invitations, Moira gave an amused laugh. "Your father—" The old woman shook her head in amusement. "Seeing him try to walk a humble path does my heart good . . . though I still see him battling with his pride a bit."

Gwyneth smiled. "I feel a little sorry for him, especially when I see how hard he tries. As unbelievable as it seems, part of me misses his bluster."

"Aye . . . though I'm secretly pleased that he spends most of his time out in the stable. All of his talk and enthusiasm can sometimes be daunting."

Before Gwyneth could agree, Kate and Biddy came through the door with Moira's wedding dress. "Here 'tis," Kate announced. "Is it not the loveliest thing ye've ever set eyes on?" She held up the gown of pink silk overlaid with white lace while Biddy fluffed out the wide skirt. Age had faded the fabric to the palest pink, but it hadn't diminished the richness. The silk skirt shimmered in the sunlight streaming through the window, and the lace's delicate fretwork looked like something fairies had woven.

Gwyneth fingered the lace that cascaded over the silk. "It's lovely."

Moira nodded with pride. "Irish lace. There's nothing quite so exquisite . . . or costly, as my father was quick to point out." She looked from the gown to Gwyneth. "It should come very close to fitting you. Go to my bedroom, and try it on."

Gwyneth and Kate carried the heavy gown between them into the bedroom while Biddy followed with Moira, the tapping of the old woman's cane a happy accompaniment to the morning's adventure.

Like the sitting room, the dark, heavy furniture in Moira's bedroom came from a much earlier time. A green coverlet spread over the bed, and faded draperies hung at the two windows. Kate led Gwyneth to a flowered tapestry that screened Moira's copper bathing tub.

"A bit of privacy for ye," Kate whispered, helping Gwyneth out of her blue muslin gown.

Standing in her chemise, Gwyneth waited while Kate fastened the heavy underskirt around her waist. The rustle and coolness of the silk against her skin added to her excitement. Except for the length, the underskirt fit as if it had been made for her, as did the lacy bodice and overskirt.

"Yes," Kate breathed, arranging the cuffs of the long sleeves so that the points of lace came exactly over Gwyneth's wrists.

Gwyneth looked down at the skirt. "It's a little long."

"Slippers will fix that. First, let yer gran and Biddy have a look."

Lifting the skirt, Gwyneth stepped from behind the screen, her smile tentative.

"Is she not grand?" Kate asked.

Biddy's hands flew to her mouth. "Like a fairy queen!" she squeaked.

Moira's lips lifted. "Lovely. Both you and it are lovely. Go to the mirror and see if you don't agree."

Biddy stepped across the room to remove the silk shawl draped over the mirror.

"I keep the mirror covered so it doesn't remind me that I'm a wrinkled old woman," Moira explained.

Age mottled the corners of the rectangular glass, but the center reflected the image of a young woman dressed in a pink shimmer of silk and lace.

"Am I not right?" Moira asked.

"It is lovely," Gwyneth replied, too modest to admit that the gown became her. In her mind she saw Cormac looking at her on their wedding day, his blue eyes alight with pleasure.

"Now for the shoes," Moira said. "You did bring the shoes, didn't you?"

"We did." Kate unwrapped a pair of slippers from a packet that had been stored with the gown. "Sit down, and I'll help ye put them on."

The shoes, fashioned with pointed toes and little heels, were also made of silk, the sheen of mellow pink exactly matching that of the gown. Gwyneth giggled as she extended a foot. "I hope the slipper fits."

"It will." Moira stated with certainty.

The slipper glided over Gwyneth's toes and instep as easily as if it had been made from a pattern of her foot. When Kate slipped on the second shoe, Gwyneth rose and pirouetted around the room, dropping a low curtsy before Moira as she finished. "How can I ever repay you, Grandmother?"

Moira laughed, as pleased with the morning as Gwyneth. "I wouldn't object if you were to give me a kiss on the cheek."

"Gladly." As Gwyneth pulled the old woman close, she felt the outline of her bones through the gray silk of her gown, bones so fragile Gwyneth feared they might break if she held her too tightly. "I love you, Grandmother."

Emotion tightened Gwyneth's throat then washed over her like the warming rays of sun when she heard Moira's whisper. "I love you too, Granddaughter."

* * *

THE NEXT DAY CORMAC RODE over from Clonglas to join them for tea. He entered the sitting room with a spring to his step, nodding to Maurice and kissing Moira's proffered hand. It was on Gwyneth's face that his gaze lingered, as did his lips when he raised her hand and kissed it. The sight of her always gave him pleasure, but today, in a simple green gown that set off her fair skin and hair, he thought her ravishing.

"I hope I find you well, Miss Beddows."

"You do, Mr. D'Arcy." Gwyneth's eyes drank in the sight of his muscular legs encased in dun-colored breeches and leather boots, his broad shoulders nicely set off by a tweed riding coat. "Indeed, I don't recall when I have felt more alive."

Cormac laughed and squeezed her hand. "That's exactly how I feel."

Looking at his daughter's radiant face, Maurice couldn't doubt her happiness. Although he'd always considered his daughter comely enough, today she was beautiful. More than that, Cormac D'Arcy seemed as besotted as she. Rather like he and Deirdre had been when they were first wed.

"I've a piece of good news," Cormac announced as he took a chair next to Maurice. "The man who attacked me on St. John's Eve regained consciousness and has named Percy Weston as the man who hired him to make the attack."

Maurice's head shot up. "A man attacked you? Why? I don't understand."

Not wanting to mention Gwyneth's name, the account Cormac gave was an abbreviation of the facts. He grew more descriptive, however, as he told how Father Sheehan had found his attacker. "Today, the man roused enough to name Percy Weston. Luckily, the constable was also present. The peasant said that when he went to collect his money, Percy refused to pay him since I appeared to be unhurt."

Cormac pursed his lips. "I can well imagine the scene—the man demanding to be paid and Percy laughing. The poor fellow made the mistake of threatening to tell the constable. Before he could do so, Percy and George beat him senseless. That he was able to drag himself to the church is a miracle, and that he is alive and able to speak is an even greater one."

"I'm surprised the rascals didn't threaten to harm his wife and children," Maurice interjected.

"Apparently he has neither. No home or steady work, either. Perhaps that's why Percy hired him. If a man is desperate enough, sometimes he'll stoop to doing almost anything."

Gwyneth felt a wave of pity for the peasant until she recalled his hands closing around Cormac's windpipe and his vicious kick afterward. Thank heaven for Paddy's shout and the reckless shot the man had taken at them instead of at Cormac. Otherwise . . . Gwyneth pulled her mind away from the thought and looked at Cormac. "Will charges be made against Percy?"

"They will if the man recovers and can testify. Unfortunately, he slipped back into unconsciousness, but Dr. Moore is hopeful of his recovery."

The arrival of tea prevented Gwyneth from asking about Emmett Weston's condition. While Gwyneth poured cups of tea and Biddy passed around cucumber sandwiches made fresh from the kitchen garden, they talked of generalities.

As soon as Biddy left, Maurice turned to Cormac. "The stable boy told me that Gwyneth and Toryn won a race against someone named Percy. Is he the same chap who hired this fellow to attack you?"

"The very one. The loss of the race rankled him, and when Percy learned that I'm to ride Toryn in the steeplechase against the Limerick stallion, he plotted the attack on me."

Maurice set down his cup and leaned forward. "The boy was full of the steeplechase, too, though it doesn't take much to set his tongue wagging."

Hoping Cluny hadn't divulged all of Shannonderry's secrets, Gwyneth took a nervous bite from her sandwich. It would be a blow to her grandmother's pride for Maurice to know how badly they had to scratch for money.

Maurice wasn't a man to be easily put off. "Why is this race so important?"

Gwyneth glanced at Moira. The race was less than a month away, and they still lacked part of the money for the fee. She listened with but half a mind as Cormac told her father about the long-standing rivalry between County Cork and County Limerick. Would they be able to find the money in time?

Moira's calm gray eyes met Gwyneth's. Faith, she had said. Remember faith.

"The man demands an exorbitant fee to race his stallion," Maurice stated. "Is it always so high in Ireland?" Gwyneth grimaced, realizing Cluny must have said something.

Cormac shook his head. "O'Rourk wants to keep the crown in Limerick. To try to do so, he's asking twice the usual amount."

"I see." Maurice frowned. "Who's responsible for providing the fee?"

"I am," Gwyneth answered. "Since Toryn is mine, I must raise the fee."

Her father's brows lifted. "Where, pray tell, did you find such a large sum?"

"I . . . Grandmother." Taking a quick breath, Gwyneth began again. "What I won in the race against Percy makes almost half the amount, and Grandmother is hoping—"

Maurice cut in. "In other words, you don't have the price."

For a second, Gwyneth felt as if she were a child called into her father's study; then just as quickly she was herself again. "No, but I'm confident we'll have it in time for the race."

"I plan—" Cormac began.

"No, Mr. D'Arcy. Since Toryn was foaled by my best brood mare, I have a vested interest in the stallion." Maurice's face softened as he looked at Gwyneth. "If you will allow me, daughter, I should like to provide the rest of the fee."

"Father . . ." Gwyneth's voice cracked. "You don't have to."

"I want to. Please . . . I would very much like to be part of the race."

Despite the brusqueness in her father's voice, she read pleading in his eyes. "Yes . . . of course. Thank you, Father."

"Very good." Maurice loudly cleared his throat. "When is the date for the steeplechase?"

A smile wreathed Moira's wrinkled face. She'd never doubted that with sufficient faith and prayer the good Lord would provide a way, but who would have thought Maurice Beddows would be God's answer?

"July twenty-first," Moira answered.

"The week after my wedding," Gwyneth added.

"That being the case, I must write a letter to my agent and instruct him to send me the necessary funds." Maurice rose and bowed to Moira and Gwyneth. "If you will excuse me, ladies." A nod to Cormac. "Mr. D'Arcy."

Startled silence settled over the sitting room as the door closed. Cormac was the first to speak. "I planned to provide what was needed for the fee . . ."

"And we would have been most grateful," Moira finished. "It seems, Mr. D'Arcy, that you have been replaced by Gwyneth's father. Although I own I'm vastly surprised, I'm also pleased. It's past time for the man to play the part of an indulgent father. More than that, I'm convinced it's what the good Lord intended." She smiled over at Gwyneth. "Your future wife and I have been praying for a small miracle, and today it has occurred."

Cormac shook his head in bemusement. "It has. Considering Maurice Beddows's high-handed manner when he arrived here, it's certainly not something I expected."

No one spoke as they tried to assimilate the surprising turn of events.

"What of Emmett Weston?" Gwyneth asked after a moment. "Have you heard of his condition?"

Cormac frowned. "He is expected to live, but his leg is so badly crushed the doctor fears he will have difficulty walking again."

"Such a shame," Moira sighed. "But in light of all he tried to do, I can't help but feel he deserved it . . . Percy too. Now, more than ever, I understand why my William never cared for the Westons."

Gwyneth pulled her mind away from the picture in her mind of Emmett's broken body. The man's effort to force Toryn into the raging river had reversed itself in a terrible way. "What of your stepmother?" she asked. "How has she taken all of this?"

Recalling the angry words Agatha had hurled at him when she'd learned about Emmett, Cormac's expression turned grim. "She has taken to her room and refuses to speak to anyone except her personal maid." Past experience told Cormac she would soon tire of her self-imposed exile. When Agatha did, she would find her status at Clonglas greatly changed. Shaking his head, Cormac got to his feet.

"If you'll excuse me, there are things I must see to," he said to Moira. His mouth softened as he looked at Gwyneth. "Would you care to see me off?"

Eager for them to have a moment alone, Gwyneth nodded, confident that Cormac would find a spot well away from prying eyes to say his farewell.

Cormac led her into the arbor by the kitchen garden as soon as they left the house. He pulled her to him, his lips eager and warm on her mouth. The sensation made Gwyneth's knees grow weak and her heart quicken.

"This is why I came," he said against her cheek. "Not for tea and small talk."

Gwyneth laughed. "You must admit some of that small talk was surprising, but like you, I prefer this."

Cormac lifted her chin and looked deeply into her aqua eyes. "Sweet Gwyneth. And in less than a fortnight, you will be my wife."

27

Dawn came early on Gwyneth's wedding day, setting the peaks of the Galtee afire with color that shot down the valley in slender fingers of light. She wakened as the first rays of the sun touched the window, and she climbed out of bed to welcome the morning. Her eyes drank in a world filled with sunshine, though the morning mist still hugged the distant hills. How quickly she had settled into this land of leprechauns and fairies. The familiar sight of oak trees and the chattering of rooks had been absorbed through her skin and into her bones as completely as if she'd been born there.

Like the dew-damp world outside the window, it seemed Deirdre's spirit had been roused this day as well. The sensation of her mother's presence, as light as gossamer, pulsed with love like sun rays reflected in delicate prisms. Once, Gwyneth would have attributed such thoughts to fantasy, but at Shannonderry they came as naturally as breathing. Hadn't Deirdre once looked out on this very scene and felt the moist, soft Irish air and love's warmth and happiness just as Gwyneth did now?

Hearing a tap at the door, Gwyneth turned from the window. Kate, followed by Biddy, entered with fresh towels in her arms, while Biddy carried pails of steaming water.

"For yer bath," Kate said, moving the screen aside so Biddy could begin to fill the copper tub. "Here's rose attar too, fresh-pressed by Maggie Haggarty and sent over this morn by her Mary. Washing yer hair with it will make ye smell like roses and bring ye good luck."

"Aye," Biddy agreed. "Roses are for luck on yer weddin' day. There be a tub of them sittin' on the back step . . . some for yer bouquet and the rest for petals to throw at ye and Mr. D'Arcy when ye leave the hall." Biddy clapped a hand over her mouth. "Throwin' petals was to be a surprise, so please forget I said such. 'Tis just that I've never been part of such a grand weddin' afore. Did ye know the cottier children got up at first light to pick roses from the hedgerows?" Keeping a safe distance from Kate, who'd frowned at Biddy's slip of the tongue, the maid hurried from the room to fetch more water.

"That girl." Kate shook her head, but her excitement was too great to let Biddy's rattling tongue spoil her happiness. It was a dream come true to see her charge so obviously in love with a man that fair worshipped her. Kate had counted her rosary beads on Gwyneth's behalf more times than she could remember. Was not today an answer to all those prayers?

That afternoon, wearing a robe and silk slippers, Gwyneth knocked on her grandmother's bedroom door. At Moira's invitation, she entered with Kate and Biddy. The old woman sat on a chair, her small body erect in a lavender silk gown accented by the amethyst necklace glowing around her thin neck. One look at Moira's white hair wound in intricate fashion around a matching amethyst comb told Gwyneth that Kate and her grandmother had been up since dawn.

"You look like a queen," Gwyneth said in greeting.

"An old queen," Moira amended. "Since all eyes will be on you, I'm not concerned about my looks." She pointed to the rippling folds of the wedding gown on the bed. "Time grows short. I've heard some of the guests arriving."

Gwyneth's heart tripped in happy anticipation as she stepped behind the tapestry screen and removed her robe. After carefully slipping the silk and lace gown over Gwyneth's freshly brushed curls, Kate began to fasten the tiny buttons while Biddy arranged the folds to flow in a circle around Gwyneth's slender form. The touch of the pale pink silk caressed her like the cool whisper of a summer breeze against her skin. When the final button was fastened, she stepped from behind the screen for Moira's final inspection.

"Yes," Moira breathed. "If only William and Deirdre could see you. Like me, they would say there was never a more lovely bride and—" A rap on the door interrupted her. "Who is it?" she called, annoyance edging her words.

"Maurice Beddows. I have a gift for my daughter on her wedding day."

Gwyneth and Moira exchanged surprised glances.

Maurice entered with an apology on his lips, but it slid to nothing when he saw Gwyneth. "I say," was all that came out, but his admiring smile said much. The sight of this dazzling woman who was also his daughter made Maurice's heart swell in a manner he hadn't expected. His wife, Sylvia, wouldn't believe him when he told her how changed Gwyneth was. Then maybe she would. Maybe, unlike him, she'd seen his daughter's beauty all along and had tried to cover it with a steady monologue of criticism.

"I . . . I'm sorry to disturb you, but what I have can't wait . . . not if you're to wear them for the wedding." Pausing, Maurice reached into the pocket of his black coat and drew out a strand of creamy white pearls. Sudden constraint prevented Maurice from looking his daughter fully in the face, but he managed to get out the carefully rehearsed words. "Before you were born, your mother told me she'd lost a pearl necklace her grandmother had given to her. Seeing her tears and wanting to please her, I bought these . . ."

Gwyneth's gaze went from the pearls to her father's face. A surge of love tightened her throat when she saw the emotion that made his mouth quiver. The sight of his vulnerability made her eyes mist.

". . . intending to surprise Deirdre with them after your birth," the Englishman went on. "But when she died—" Too overwrought to speak, Maurice thrust the pearls at Gwyneth, begging her with his eyes to take them, the glitter of moisture in their gray depths clearly visible.

"Wear them . . . keep them," he said as Gwyneth took the delicate strand. "Your mother would want it." Not pausing to bow, Maurice hurried from the room.

Gwyneth stared through tears at the cluster of white jewels in her hand. They were beautiful, the creamy texture like nothing she'd ever seen or held. That her father had bought them to give to her mother made them all the more precious.

"What a lovely gift for a father to give his daughter on her wedding day," Moira said in an unsteady voice.

Kate made a noise in the back of her throat. "About time he started actin' like yer father. When I think of the times he acted as if ye wasn't there—" She shook her head. "That be enough of complainin'. 'Tis yer weddin' day, and the necklace be the very thing to set off yer gown." Kate gently touched the pearls. "Would ye like for me to put them on for ye?"

"Would you?" Feeling as if her father's gift were part of a lovely dream, Gwyneth handed the rope of pearls to Kate.

When the necklace was securely fastened around Gwyneth's neck, Kate turned her to face the mirror. "Are they not grand?"

Biddy stepped close for a better look. "Like somethin' for a princess."

Gwyneth's breath caught as she took in the regal figure in the mirror. Everything was lovely, even herself. She could hardly wait for Cormac to see her.

"Now the veil," Moira instructed from the chair.

Kate lifted the sheer fabric and fastened it with a comb to Gwyneth's platinum curls. "There," she whispered, stepping back to view her handiwork.

"Don't forget the shamrocks," Biddy reminded, handing Kate a sprig of green to fasten with the veil. "Shamrocks bring good luck too," the girl said.

Moira smiled. "I wore shamrocks in my hair on my wedding day."

When the shamrocks were securely fastened, Kate handed Gwyneth a bouquet of roses. "Roses for love and happiness," she said. "The children brought them for that very reason, though anyone lookin' at ye and Mr. D'Arcy will know ye already have such aplenty."

The mention of Cormac sent a shiver of excitement down Gwyneth's spine. Soon she would be Mrs. D'Arcy. Three months ago the thought of marriage to the Irishman would have given her pause, but this day it seemed like something she'd longed for all of her life.

Holding the thought close to her heart, she walked with Moira to the great hall, Kate and Biddy following, the tap of her grandmother's cane a happy echo to the beat of her heart. Gwyneth's father waited by the door dressed in a black frock coat that had been sent from Hawarden along with the necklace. His wig was freshly brushed, and a satisfied smile lifted his lips as his eyes took in his daughter. Although she bore little resemblance to Deirdre, she was a beautiful young woman.

Owen waited with Maurice to escort Moira to her place of honor in the hall. After the old woman had been seated and Kate and Biddy had slipped into the kitchen where they could watch from the door, her father offered Gwyneth his arm.

"Shall we, daughter?"

At her nod, they entered the great hall. Although it was late afternoon, sconces of candles lit the room, bringing out the warmth of the ancient beamed ceiling and playing over the richly colored tapestries hanging on the walls. Instead of the deep chords of an organ, the high notes of an Irish pipe filled the old hall. Clad in a green coat, the lone piper stood to one side of the raised dais, the strains of the hymn he played reminding the guests that although they were not assembled in a church, it was nonetheless a religious occasion. The presence of Reverend Gibbins standing spare and tall in his black vestment added emphasis to the piper and the strains of the hymn.

The faces of the guests sitting below the dais were no more than a blur as Gwyneth walked the length of the great hall with her father. For the pulse of a heartbeat, she felt as if long-dead O'Briens followed her—the ancestor who'd won Shannonderry on a wager, the other Gwyneth, her mother, and great-grandmother. All seemed to accompany her as she went to meet Cormac.

Then there was only the man she loved, standing tall and handsome in a coat of superfine blue fabric edged with silver, his waistcoat and breeches embroidered with the same silver thread. Her eyes remained on his face as her father escorted her onto the dais, where she saw his love flowing toward her like the shining light of the candles. When the final notes of the pipe faded away, Reverend Gibbins stepped forward.

Cormac's reply to the clergyman's question was resonant and firm, her own a soft murmur but no less fervent. Gwyneth's hand trembled when Cormac took it to slip an etched gold ring onto her slender finger. His touch sent currents of happiness through her, ones that sparked and pulsed when he lifted the lace of the veil and kissed her, not on the cheek as she'd expected, but on the mouth, the warmth of his lips reaffirming his love.

Murmurs from the guests mingled with the notes of the pipe as Gwyneth left the hall on Cormac's arm, her face radiant and Cormac's happiness evident in his proud smile.

Kate and Biddy had gathered with the villagers and tenants to curtsy and greet them with a shower of rose petals and happy shouts.

"Best wishes to ye, Mr. D'Arcy, Mrs. D'Arcy," one of them called. "'Tis a happy day for us all.

Cormac grinned and pulled Gwyneth to his side. "My wife," he said.

* * *

THAT EVENING GWYNETH STOOD WITH Cormac on the front steps of Shannonderry, bidding the last of the wedding guests good night. Happiness surrounded them, its light as suffusive as the glowing torches' that lit the tall double doorway. Gwyneth's curls gleamed like polished silver, and in the torchlight her pink gown shimmered as it fell from her slender waist in yards of silk and lace.

She stole a glance at Cormac, his handsome features highlighted by the flames. Feeling her gaze, Cormac smiled down at her. "Happy?" he asked.

"Yes," she answered, waving to the last of the carriages as it pulled away. They lingered on the doorstep. A thousand stars were strewn across the hollow of the darkened sky, and the moon hung so low it appeared to be caught in the branches of the trees. It seemed that nature had conspired with Kate and Biddy to create the perfect setting for their wedding.

Cormac's arm tightened on her waist. "Shall we go inside?"

The low murmur of voices in the dining hall told them that the hired help from the village was still clearing away the remains of the feast.

"I'll see to locking up if you'd like to go upstairs," Cormac suggested.

Nodding, Gwyneth lifted her heavy skirts and began to climb the stairs. Kate was waiting when she reached her bedroom.

"I came to help ye out of yer gown."

Thinking of all Kate had done that day, Gwyneth gave her a hug. "I'm glad you did. Thank you."

"I wouldn't a missed it for anythin'. I've not seen the likes o' this in all my days . . . nor anyone more happy than ye and Mr. D'Arcy." She put her hands on Gwyneth's shoulders. "'Twas worth every minute of it."

Gwyneth touched Kate's freckled face. "Thank you, Kate . . . for today . . . for the years in England . . . for everything." She pulled Kate close—her servant and dear friend.

"I've been paid a thousand times over," Kate said in an unsteady voice. She sniffed and set herself to the task of unfastening the clasp on the pearl necklace, then to undoing the tiny buttons down the back of the bodice. After Kate had helped Gwyneth out of the gown, she hung it on a hook in the wardrobe. Kate was just lifting a ribbon-trimmed nightgown over Gwyneth's head when they heard Cormac's step on the stairs.

"I'll see to puttin' yer gown away proper in the morning." Kate whispered, giving her a quick peck on the cheek. "May the blessed Virgin watch over ye."

Cormac waited for Kate to leave the room before he slowly closed the door.

"Gwyneth." The yearning in his voice and eyes made Gwyneth catch her breath. Then his mouth was on hers, sweet and incredibly tender. When she stood on tiptoe and slipped her arms around his neck, his lips became more demanding, and she felt his heart quicken. Then, as if Shannonderry and generations of O'Briens had never existed, they meshed into a silhouette of one against the old castle's moonlit window.

28

A WEEK LATER GWYNETH AND Cormac approached the meadow next to the church where the steeplechase was to be held, she on one of Shannonderry's mares and Cormac riding Toryn. Owen accompanied them while Maurice and Moira followed in the carriage, Flynn driving the team and Cluny perched on the high seat beside him. Crowds of men interspersed with a few women thronged the meadow while pennants and brightly colored strips of cloth and ribbon fluttered from the trees. The colorful sight and happy voices reminded Gwyneth of fair days in Yorkshire. It was evident from the size of the crowd that everyone in the countryside considered it a holiday.

Gwyneth glanced at Cormac and Toryn. She couldn't recall when the stallion had looked more sleek and fit, his freshly brushed coat a black sheen under an overcast sky. Cormac sat atop him like an Irish warrior, head erect, his lithe, muscled body displaying the green and white jacket Moira had asked him to wear.

"Shannonderry's colors," she'd told Cormac as she handed him the silk jacket and cap. "William wore them when he raced . . . said they brought him luck. Since Toryn is now a Shannonderry stallion, it's only fitting that you wear our colors."

Cormac had been deeply touched by the gesture. As Gwyneth saw pointing fingers and nodding heads, she knew many remembered the days when William Donahue had raced and won the crown wearing the same colors.

As they neared the starting point, O'Rourk approached on his stallion. An appreciative murmur rippled through the onlookers as they made a path for horse and rider. The horse's dappled gray coat and broad chest proclaimed his Arabian ancestry, but it was the length of his legs that caused Gwyneth's stomach to tighten. What would they do if Toryn lost? Gwyneth saw similar concern on Owen's face, but Cormac looked the stallion over with no change of expression. Like Cormac, O'Rourk wore a silk jacket and cap, his red and white attire a splash of color against the gray stallion.

Suddenly aware of her husband's gaze, Gwyneth turned and was immediately immersed in the glow of his love. A long look passed between them, then with a little salute, Cormac urged Toryn away.

Calls of encouragement followed the two stallions as they approached the starting point, their skittish prancing showing their eagerness to be off. The officials, one from Limerick and the other from Cork, stood a little apart from the crowd. When one raised a hand for silence, the people quieted, their ears straining to hear the instruction.

Gwyneth and Owen joined the men on horseback who planned to ride after the racers for a better view. Gwyneth was the only woman among them, but none looked askance. Was she not the black stallion's owner, and hadn't she ridden him and won the race against Percy Weston?

The Westons were conspicuously absent from the festivities—Emmett convalescing from the trampling and Percy, with his friend George, in prison and awaiting trial for houghing Shannonderry's cattle and beating a peasant.

Agatha also wasn't present, nor had she attended the wedding. Although she gave it out that she had tired of country living and had decided to move to the city, she had been told to pack her bags and leave.

"One of the conditions of my father's will is that I must provide for you until your death," Cormac had told his stepmother. "My solicitor assures me, however, that it does not say I must provide for your living at Clonglas. That being the case, I have leased a residence for you in Cork. It is not so fine as Clonglas, but it's adequate for a woman of your station. If you practice prudence, you should be able to live comfortably on the allowance my father left you."

Agatha had flung down her napkin, her breakfast untouched and two angry spots of color on her cheeks. "You think to pack me off like a piece of unwanted furniture, do you? Well, let me tell you—"

"You will tell me nothing, madam, and if you don't wish to have the true nature of your duplicity with Emmett Weston made public, you will pack your things and take yourself off quietly to your new home."

"Mr. Weston will have something to say—" Agatha began.

"Weston is extremely fortunate not to be under arrest like his son," Cormac countered. The hardness in his blue eyes made Agatha look away. "You played the traitor, and now, madam, you must pay the price."

What else passed between them, Cormac had not said, but knowing Agatha, Gwyneth was certain it hadn't been pleasant. Nor had it been pleasant for Owen. Although he knew Agatha was a conniving woman, she was still his mother, and he had seen her off to Cork with some regret.

Turning her attention back to the race, Gwyneth heard an excited murmur when an official raised a pistol. Overwrought, Toryn snorted and pawed the ground. Cormac struggled to hold him in check. The pistol cracked and the crowd roared. Startled, Toryn reared and got off to a bad start that gave the gray the lead.

The two horses charged across the open stretch of grass with O'Rourk clearly in the lead. Several spectators exchanged coins, while others surged after the stallion to vie for places to witness the race. Watching, Gwyneth saw Owen and the gentlemen on horseback urge their mounts after the racing stallions.

Gwyneth nervously tightened her hold on the mare's reins as the galloping racers approached the first hedge, the gray clearing it before Toryn arrived. "Go, my boy!" she whispered, the words like the chant of a prayer.

Once the hedge was cleared, Gwyneth was no longer able to see the racing horses. Sighing, she edged the mare past milling onlookers to make her way to the knoll where Kate and Shannonderry's tenants had saved a place for Moira and the carriage. "He'll win. I know he'll win," she told herself.

Those on the knoll were saying the same, assuring themselves with talk as they anxiously watched the two stallions thunder across another open stretch, the red and green capped heads of their riders bent low over their mounts as they urged the horses on. Gwyneth's emotions faltered when she saw that O'Rourk still led.

"Go, you blasted beast," Maurice called. "Show the Irish what an English-bred horse can do!" He'd gotten out of the carriage to pace, stopping from time to time to watch or call encouragement. Flynn still sat on the driver's seat, his eyes fastened on the distant riders. Gwyneth doubted he could see them, but his voice was as loud and enthusiastic as Ronan's.

"Where's Cluny?" Gwyneth asked when Ronan came to help her dismount.

Ronan pointed to a boy perched high in the branches of a tree. "Said he'd watch and let us know how the race goes."

As if he'd heard, Cluny called down to them. "Toryn's gainin' . . . and there's a wall comin' up. There they go . . . but the gray's still ahead."

Gwyneth joined her father in his nervous pacing beside the carriage, her aqua riding skirt swishing just inches from Maurice's boots.

"Go, blast you!" Maurice called. He glanced at Gwyneth. "You should have let Peter ride Toryn. He knows racing better than Mr. D'Arcy."

It was an opinion Maurice had frequently voiced, but Gwyneth had remained firm in her resolve to have Cormac ride the big horse. She was confident that his magic touch would more than make up for his lack of racing experience. "Cormac will do fine," she countered, "and so will Toryn." Gwyneth spoke as much for herself as for Moira. The old woman watched from the open door of the carriage, her expression intent, as if willing Toryn to a faster pace.

"Where they be?" Flynn asked. "I don't see nothin' but trees."

"On the other side," Cluny called.

For a few minutes they could do nothing but wait, the time spent in nervous pacing or staring over the valley at the distant spire of the neighboring church. The tenants had grown silent too, and Gwyneth noted that Kate and Mrs. Haggarty were counting their beads.

"There they be!" Cluny shouted. "Comin' back!"

"Who's ahead?"

"The . . . no, maybe the gray's still ahead!"

Maurice's low curse mingled with Flynn's protest. "Don't the beast know he be a Shannonderry stallion?"

Unable to bear the tension any longer, Gwyneth hurried to the tree and called up to Cluny. "Can you see them?"

"Aye . . . they be runnin' neck on neck." The boy paused and after a moment gave a squeak of excitement. "He's ahead, Miss Gwyneth. Our horse be ahead!"

Cheers greeted the news, Gwyneth's voice joining the tenants. "Go, Toryn! On Chieftain!"

Unable to contain her excitement, Gwyneth ran back to the carriage and climbed inside to lean out the open carriage door.

"Can you see them?" Moira asked.

"No . . . Wait. There they come. Toryn's ahead!"

Following Gwyneth's example, Maurice scrambled up to join Flynn on the driver's seat. "Yes," he called. "Our stallion's clearly ahead!"

Gwyneth could tell by Toryn's long confident stride that he couldn't be stopped now. "He's done it," she cried.

"Are you sure?"

"Yes . . . he's running beautifully. He can't be stopped now."

"She be right, Mistress," Old Flynn called to Moira. "Ye don't have to worry no more."

"Who said I was worried?" Moira retorted, but the relief on her face was as evident as the pennant Cluny had snatched from the tree.

All eyes were on the finish line, the excited crowd egging Toryn on to a faster pace. He flew past the officials a good three lengths ahead of the gray, his thundering hooves drumming above the noise and cheers.

"Toryn! Shannonderry! Cork!" The excited chant caught hold like a rollicking youth set free from school. Elation cracked like thunder. Their stallion had won! The title and honor had returned to County Cork.

For a second, Gwyneth wished she could be part of the excited throng milling around Toryn and Cormac, but a glance at the glowing faces of Moira and those from Shannonderry made her glad she'd decided to watch from the knoll.

"What a glorious win!" she exclaimed to Moira and anyone else who would listen, though most were so busy cheering they paid her little heed. They waited expectantly as Cormac turned Toryn away from the crowd and rode toward the knoll, the stallion prancing and tossing his head.

Lifting her skirts, Gwyneth jumped down from the carriage and ran to meet them, her heart quickening when she saw Cormac grin and wave. Cormac slipped from the saddle and handed Toryn's reins to Peter. Spreading his arms wide, he caught Gwyneth and twirled her around.

"You were magnificent!" she cried.

Laughing, Cormac set her down and kissed her. "Toryn . . ." He shook his head in amazement. "I've never had such a ride. At the end I felt like I was flying!"

They turned to admire the stallion who was being led in a circle by Peter to cool him down. Flecks of foam splattered the big horse's shoulders, and his black coat glistened with sweat.

Those on the knoll gave the skittish stallion wide berth as they came to congratulate Cormac. Maurice reached them first and clasped Cormac's hand in a warm handshake.

"An excellent race, D'Arcy. I doubt Peter could have done better."

"I had little to do with the win." Cormac laughed. "It's Toryn you should congratulate. All I had to do was keep my seat and hang on."

Looking at Toryn, a look of regret crossed the Englishman's face. "The stallion is one in a million, and why I was too blind to see it when he was foaled is something I'll always regret. But Gwyneth—" Maurice paused and gave his daughter an affectionate smile. "She recognized a winner when she first saw him . . . and it appears she did the same when she saw you. I . . ." Maurice paused to clear his throat.

Before he could go on, others pressed close to offer praise and take Cormac's hand, Cluny's voice high with excitement, Ronan's filled with pride. Was not Cormac his cousin, and did he himself not have the privilege of filling the stallion's feed bag with oats each morning?

"'Tis a grand day for Shannonderry," Flynn chortled, his face wearing a grin instead of a frown. Similar words came from the tenants. They would have much to talk about in their cottages for weeks to come.

Breaking away from the cottiers, Cormac and Gwyneth made their way to the carriage where Moira waited.

"Weren't they wonderful, Grandmother?" Gwyneth asked.

"They were, indeed. My William would have enjoyed such a rousing race. He always took great pride in Shannonderry's stallions." She extended her frail hand to Cormac. "An outstanding race, Grandson."

Cormac bowed over the old woman's hand, his pleasure at being addressed as "Grandson" evident in his flushed cheeks. "I was riding an outstanding horse . . . and lest Toryn think me ungrateful, I must tell him so."

Elation swirled around the happy couple as they made their way to Toryn. The horse lifted his head, ears pricked and his tail swishing. Even covered with sweat, the stallion's sleek form was a stirring sight.

Several tenants watched with hope-filled smiles. A grand stallion was once again installed in Shannonderry's stable, while a young O'Brien inhabited the old castle.

* * *

A merry group gathered in Shannonderry's dining room that night for dinner. Owen had been invited to join them, his excitement in being part of the race an extension of their own. Kate and Biddy paused to listen as they served the meal, smiling and nodding as if they were guests as well.

Since Agatha's departure, Cormac and Gwyneth had taken pains to include Owen in their activities. Although Cormac hadn't yet decided whether to combine the management of Clonglas and Shannonderry or keep them separate, he and Gwyneth wanted Owen to be part of it. Since he was but twenty, the young man still had his studies at Trinity College to complete. After that, Cormac would let Owen decide what his role would be.

That evening Owen seemed to think his role was that of making conversation. His tongue rivaled Biddy's as he recounted the praise he'd heard of Toryn. "Half the county wants to have him sire one of their foals," he concluded.

Owen's enthusiasm was repeated as toasts were raised to the newlyweds and to Toryn. Gwyneth smiled up at Cormac, her excitement as palpable as Owen's. Everyone had something to say, and even after Kate and Biddy had cleared away their plates, they lingered at the table to talk.

"The income from stud fees will do much to put Shannonderry back on its feet," Moira stated. Setting down her goblet, she went on. "Before we retire, there's something I wish to say. If one of you gentlemen will help, I would like for us to go to the great hall." She glanced at Kate as Maurice helped her to her feet. "Has Biddy done as I requested?"

"Aye, Mistress. The candles are lit."

The younger people followed Maurice and Moira to the hall, Moira leaning heavily on the Englishman's arm.

Candles were lighted on either side of the door to the big room, their flames creating a shadowy path to the portrait of Gwyneth O'Brien. For dinner, Gwyneth had donned the blue gown that had once belonged to her mother. With both in blue, the resemblance between the two Gwyneth's was so powerful that Maurice sucked in his breath.

A familiar tingle scurried up Gwyneth's spine as she looked up at her namesake. No one spoke until Moira stretched out a hand and touched her granddaughter's arm.

"Do you remember the legend I told you when you first saw this portrait?"

Gwyneth nodded, the words her grandmother had spoken clearly remembered. Yet when she spoke, her voice was hesitant. "That someday . . . another Gwyneth would come to save Shannonderry again."

"Aye," Moira breathed, the sound making the hair on Gwyneth's arms rise.

"She . . . you . . . have come. Today Shannonderry was saved a second time."

Moira's words poured through Gwyneth. She recalled her skepticism when she'd first heard the legend. How could she save Shannonderry? And yet, she had . . . she and Cormac and Toryn. Feeling Cormac's arm tighten around her waist, she leaned into him as her grandmother's voice went on.

"Two hundred years ago an old seanchaí predicted that another Gwyneth would come. The O'Briens have watched and waited, and . . ." Moira's voice faltered. Swallowing, she went on. "That I should live to see it happen has long been my heart's desire." The old woman touched Gwyneth's cheek. "Had there been no legend, I would still have loved and welcomed you to Shannonderry, but to be privileged to see the legend's fulfillment—" Tears moistened Moira's eyes. "Thank you, Granddaughter."

Unable to answer, Gwyneth gathered Moira into her arms. She breathed in the faint aroma of rosewater, savoring the knowledge that Moira had indirectly given her life. "Thank *you*, Grandmother."

Pulling away, Moira patted Gwyneth's cheek. With a sigh, she tugged on Maurice's arm. "Today's excitement has left me a little tired. Would you be kind enough to help me back to my room?"

Maurice was slow to respond, his eyes going from the portrait to his daughter, not knowing whether to believe the legend or not. With a start, he realized that his animosity toward Moira Donahue had dissipated and that he hoped she'd live out the rest of her days in happiness. More than that, he wanted Shannonderry to prosper. Perhaps there was magic in Ireland after all. Something unexplainable had certainly happened to him.

Maurice experienced a pang of regret as he witnessed the love that flowed between Moira and Gwyneth. What a pompous fool he'd been. But perhaps it wasn't too late. There was nothing to prevent him from visiting Shannonderry from time to time. Maybe Gwyneth and D'Arcy could even be persuaded to visit Hawarden. There would be grandchildren. He was certain of it. He would take pains to see that pride didn't deprive him of them.

The Englishman patted the old woman's hand as she positioned herself to walk away, while Owen hurried ahead to open the door. A myriad of thoughts filled Maurice's mind as they walked the length of the room. A man would have to be blind not to notice that hard times had fallen on Shannonderry, but that was certain to change now.

Aware of the pull of Moira's hand on his arm, Maurice slowed his steps. Like Gwyneth and Deirdre, the old woman had pluck. She had faith too. He'd felt it when she'd looked up at the portrait, heard it when she'd spoken with conviction about the legend. Perhaps the legend truly had been fulfilled, and Maurice was just too blind to see it. But he wasn't too blind to believe that Moira's faith in God had played a part in it as well.

When he and Moira paused by the wide double door to look back at Gwyneth and Cormac, Maurice read the love on their faces. For a second, it was as if fairies had lifted a curtain to allow him a glimpse of how it had been with him and Deirdre. His heart constricted as he watched Cormac tenderly lift Gwyneth's chin and kiss her.

Had he been closer, Maurice would have heard Cormac's, "I love you, darlin' Gwyneth," and her soft reply. A silent wind seemed to sweep through the great hall to make the candles dance and flicker around the two lovers and the portrait. It is said that the past can sometimes merge with the present to touch us like the brush of butterfly wings and whisper that love and things of the heart never end.

About the Author

Books have always been an important part of Carol Warburton's life. In addition to writing several novels, she worked thirteen years for the Salt Lake County Library. Her novels have been set in the United States, Mexico, Australia, and now Ireland. She is currently busy writing another historical romance adventure set in the Smoky Mountains of Tennessee at the end of the Civil War.